THE Raven AND THE Hart

IAN BURDON

GOLDSPINK

ISBN 978-1-7398247-6-1
Ebook 978-1-7398247-7-8

Cover design & typesetting by Raspberry Creative Type

Websites: https://www.ianburdonwriter.com
https://www.cosmicsurfer.co.uk

Also by Ian Burdon *Coyote in the Corner*

for Mum

Quhan Iefuis twin in Ynde gangand
And hailly gofpel proclamand
He Iofephis gyfte giftit awa
Til Egipt þyns til Scottis fchoir
Quhair Lanwethis twynne fchall tak na fleip
Quhyle Iofephis gifte in gombraich keip
Fals Noftradam and Hercyldoun
Fra hie renoun be nacht cafte doun
Til fic daye he maun dree his weird
Betuixt Elfame and Middil-ʒeird

From dittay of Jonet Wilkie,
tried for sorcery, witchcraft and incantation,
Edinburgh, 8 November 1605

CHAPTER 1

I barely noticed my calling disappear. The toll was cumulative, the little daily failures, the constant feeling that I was wasting my time, the endless meetings and petty feuds amongst the clergy. Venny was right to warn me all those years ago, and I lost her too.

The only person I told the truth to was Betty Boards. She said my break in the Highlands was like a band heading to the country to get their heads together but without the acid and the groupies. She was right. It was my chance to find my identity again and make peace with myself before it was too late, in case the next health scare wasn't a false alarm. I wanted my name back, to not have it prefaced by 'Reverend' with all the baggage that brings.

I'd planned this trip for months but kept putting it off. Did duty stop me? A feeling of obligation to people who relied on me for succour and comfort? Maybe, but mostly it was fear of what I might find out about myself. In the parish magazine I said it was a sabbatical after the cancer tests, but I had a suspicion it might be permanent when the collar from the tunnel neck of my clerical shirt hit the back of the wardrobe.

Mrs Mackay's cottage was rented for seven months. The first thing I did when I got there, tired, shoulders tight, was to flop on a settee and gaze out of the picture window at the squally dressage of white horses on Loch Eriboll. Later, after dark and torchlit, I breathed the sharp, clean air, and paddled in the freezing water, my ankles too cold and sore to be numb.

I had the best night's sleep I'd had in years, but Highland air can't cure everything: my greying hair and the lines around my eyes and mouth were still there in the morning. When I was about ten and Mam nearly forty, she said life is short, and I thought that was a ridiculous thing to say. I don't think so now. Who wants to live to be hundred? Anyone who's ninety-nine.

I made a pot of tea with two teabags, one Scottish Breakfast, one Earl Grey, polished my glasses, and looked over the sea loch from the small patio outside the back door. The susurrating water on sand and shingle and the crash of distant breakers were interrupted by an unseen cockerel and the cries of gulls. Black darts of cormorants and shags skimmed the lace crests in the bay.

I shivered, and Granny said in my ear, clear as you like, *someone just walked ower your grave.*

I did nothing at all except nap that first full day, but set off the next morning, dodging tourists in their campervans, all in blind pursuit of that mythic, shortbread-tin Scotland where the winters are mild and the rain is soft. But myths are as slippery as wet tarmac, and the landscape up there is harsh. North of Ullapool the peat is a fragile skin stretched taut over old bone and sinew.

The ancient road from Hope was rudimentary, rutted and cracked. Weeds, fingers of wilderness, reached up to grasp my boot-tread through crumbling tarmac. I reckoned three and a half hours' walking should see me to Dun Dornaigil; I wasn't in any hurry. My tent and sleeping bag were good for the single night I planned to be away. I had enough food and water, plus a survival bag and extra food and clothing, in case the weather turned.

It all seemed a good idea when I planned it in the vicarage all those miles away, an adventurous interlude in my conventional life, but my body complained about the weight of my gear almost as soon as I set off, and I'd forgotten how short the days are that far north in November. I was the perfect casualty, the perfect headline: English vicar lost in Highland winter.

In the parish, every once in a while, I'd kick back and let go with a single malt and *Tales from Topographic Oceans* or Bruckner's *Mass in D Minor* and hope the phone wouldn't ring. Here, I had the birds and the sounds of branches and grasses creaking and whispering in the morning air. Hooded crows, in their grubby Dominican habits and tunics, tilled the grass running down to the loch. Old birch woods rose to meet the slopes of Ben Hope. Early accounts of this area say the woods were never the same after wolves were eradicated four hundred years ago, leaving deer and goats to overgraze the young shoots of new trees.

A pair of deer, black-eyed, mocked me from the treeline before melting into the undergrowth. A stag watched my progress from the ridgeline it commanded. Something moved ahead of me on the road, on the edge of sight. Another walker?

Please let it be an illusion. Let me have this for myself.

My shoulders ached and I shifted the rucksack with a shrug, hunched tight, holding myself in and the world out. I struck out again, walking through memory as much as landscape.

Where did my calling to ministry come from? I've no idea. I don't even know what a calling is, really; the old explanations ring false. No Damascene moment of revelation for me, no sudden presentiment of the Divine, just a slow-growing certainty over several months. I changed my academic plans at school from sciences to languages and applied to study theology at university.

Friends and family were astonished, found it ridiculous even. No one tried to talk me out of changing subjects, though, except Venny. She made her feelings plain, said if I wanted to press on with it, that was my lookout. That was her way, to let you know what she thought then leave you to work it out for yourself. She was more than my best friend, she was my confidante and companion, my first fumbling lover, and I hers. All through my flirtations with fundamentalism, with speaking in tongues and chorus songs and laying-on of hands, she was my anchor to reality. Teenage me thought it was love, and maybe it was. God knows I hadn't found anything like it, or her, since.

But, of course, I knew best and wouldn't take any advice, even from her, so I ignored her, we had a blazing row and that was that.

A lazy keening overhead signalled a pair of buzzards riding air currents, wheeling and drifting into a hazy distance, caressing contours only they could see.

Where was Venny now? Did she find someone and settle down? Was I just a half-remembered face in a school photo whose name cropped up in the pub with old friends: *do any of you remember Canty? The strange one?*

I could have found out at any time over the decades, tracked her down, called her up and asked, but I hadn't, even when a passing face in the street or the scent on a stranger reminded me of her, or when a voice on the radio spoke in my carefully discarded Derby accent. I'd seen it before, when a parishioner contacted an old crush online and before you knew it there were lawyers, recriminations and regrets.

I lost her to my certainty, yet, looking back over my life, what I remember most is doubt. I doubted all the time but told myself it was just a test of my faith, that all would come good and God would deliver on the promise I thought She'd made. And God knows it was hard enough when they first allowed women to be priests, all the petty resentments and misogyny from men who venerate Mary but can't cope with her gender.

Then one day I was pushing sixty, single, in holy orders I didn't deserve or even want any more, too late to make another life, preaching sermons I didn't believe. I recited the words in the lectionaries, sang the hymns at full volume while the congregation muttered along, trying to keep up with tunes pitched for trained choirs rather than introverted laity, embarrassed by Victorian and Edwardian words and rhymes or, worse, their modern equivalents. I spent my time searching for hints of immanence and meaning, but here I was on sabbatical trying to remember my name.

The hooded crows had kept pace with me, always slightly ahead, patrolling the lochside for scraps and whatever the loch washed to shore. Ben Hope loomed, clouds draped across its summit. Dun Dornaigil was beyond it, past where the loch became the Strathmore River, fed by the runoff from the surrounding hills.

Heavy drizzle called for my waterproof jacket, rolled inside my rucksack, which meant stopping to unpack it. I looked about, and wasn't where I expected to be. The road runs more or less due south to the broch before meandering east to Altnaharra, and I hadn't passed the broch yet. I hadn't walked for long enough, and it isn't something you can miss. Loch Hope was where it ought to be, but instead of Ben Hope, dense forest rose into what I took to be low cloud until I wiped my glasses and looked again. It was like an out of focus photograph, as if the mountain couldn't decide what form to take. The road was gone, replaced by a faint path of compressed dirt, almost an animal track.

Too much wandering in my thoughts to watch where I was going: the story of my life.

I retraced my steps fifty metres or so, but it made no difference. Where Ben Hope ought to be there was only a dark blur.

The drizzle thickened without warning into a downpour. I stumbled through shifting, sheeting rain, my glasses too wet to see through. A rough wooden structure, a dilapidated boathouse, was down at the lochside across an expanse of wet grass. I might at least find sanctuary there until the weather cleared, then decide whether or not to admit defeat and call it a day.

I was halfway across the grass when the wolves howled, distant, out beyond the grey nothingness that was only feet away, masking any chance of working out where the sound came from. All the noises of the day were lost in the sizzle of the rain and the croaking of crows and the lapping of the wavelets at the lochside.

The howls were louder, closer. A visceral response kicked in: I ran as best I could through the sodden grass, my boots heavy, rucksack bouncing, to where the boathouse should be, but wasn't.

Why the hell are there wolves?

I guessed a direction and kept running, into a hidden drainage ditch, and fell headlong, drenched, winded. A brackish puddle claimed me, my head missing a boulder by inches. Filthy water filled my mouth and nose. On my feet again, rucksack discarded, the panting breath of a beast, maybe two, maybe more, was nearly on me. Over left shoulder, over right, run, faster, cough and snort, catch my feet. Down, head shielded by my arms, too late: tree trunk, consciousness fading. Triumphant slavering as they rush to claim their prey.

Calm saturated my body, and I waited for the rending teeth and claws.

Well, that's that then.

And from somewhere, a chuckle of satisfaction, and voices:

Sweet seer sister
Singer of circumstance
Lark in the heather,
How fares the light of our Lord?
    The Lord's light fa's fu'-faint on Ynys Pridain.
    Haily blood bled on bloody banners
    His body lies broken, in bondage biding
    'Til light that fades White Spectre lights.

Dim light. Old-fashioned bed linen. Smells of heather and polish and cooking. Singing, humming, from another room, a familiar tune I couldn't put a name to: Irish maybe. I was in my underwear, vaguely embarrassed I wasn't wearing a newer bra. My head stung, sensitive to touch, beneath a bandage. Movement hurt my face and forehead. No saline drips, no machines monitoring and bleeping, no bustle of nurses, no smell of hospital antiseptic.

Light stole into the room like a burglar, between drawn curtains, teasing my dark-accustomed eyes with hints and outlines of uncertain forms until furniture took substance in the shadows. The voice, a fine contralto, sang to the rhythm of chopping and slicing, like a waulking song. My stomach grumbled to the smell of roasting chicken and fresh bread.

'Hello,' I called. Then again, louder.

She came and sat on the edge of the bed, and felt my forehead below the bandage for signs of fever. I winced, but her fingers were warm and her touch gentle.

'That was quite a crack you took. How does it feel?'

Accented: Gaelic perhaps, but not Highland. Who is this?

'It hurts when I move. I've got a headache, like I slept too long. My mouth tastes funny.'

'Close your eyes and I'll open the curtains a little. Let's see how that goes.'

The curtains parted slowly until they were half-drawn. Slanted sunbeams picked out dust in the air. The furniture was old wood, hand-crafted by a master by the look of it: a chest of drawers, a dresser, an armchair. There was only one window. A table stood in front of it, with a vase of fresh-picked wild flowers on a lace doily. The walls were whitewashed stone. There was no ceiling, just open wood beams under a cavity with thatch above, as if I were in a folk-life display. Candles were everywhere, unlit, in holders and sconces, with oil lamps – museum pieces but functional.

'Where am I?'

'In my spare room. I'm Rowan. I found you.'

She was straight and slender. Her hair was like Maureen O'Hara's in *The Quiet Man*, straight from the book of Celtic clichés, and she carried herself with an easy presence.

'There was a ditch and a tree in the rain. I didn't know where I was.'

'Well, you can tell me about it later.'

'Do you have my glasses?'

'They were broken. Ingrid is trying to repair them. Are they your only ones?'

Who's Ingrid?

'I have prescription suns in my jacket pocket: I can use those if I need to.'

'Of course.'

Did she understand what I just said?

14

'I'll bring soup and bread if you feel up to it,' she said and went to fetch it.

Her soup was very, very good – a simple stock with meat and herbs and a freshness and vitality. The bread was a wheat field in sunshine. I'd never eaten anything so satisfying.

Clean clothes were on the dressing table. They were old, and curiously unisex: linen top and tweed trews, topped off with a fine, Shetland-style cardigan, all handmade. The sort of things you might admire on a stall at a craft fair but not feel even the slightest inclination to buy. I put them on and felt like the first arrival at a fancy-dress party, but I didn't know what I'd come as.

I ventured out of the room carrying the tray and empty soup bowl; the door opened onto the kitchen, where Rowan sat at a wooden table. She wore linen too, white, and good quality: a brave choice in a rustic setting, but it looked good on her.

'There you are. You look much better now I must say: more colour about you. I made you this.'

The stoneware mug was full of a steaming herbal tea. She led me through to a sitting room where ancient stuffed chairs and a settee sat in front of a fireplace, a peat fire burning in the grate. The floors were stone-flagged, worn and grooved by centuries of feet. She tended the young fire with practised and precise movements, letting it draw long enough to get well established before she sat opposite me.

'Let's have another look at you. You had a nasty split in your forehead when I found you, and there's a fine show of colours on your face.'

How long was I out?

With the gentlest of hands, she unwrapped the long linen strip of bandage and inspected my wounds. She dipped two

15

long fingers into a jar of ointment and massaged the lotion into my forehead, taking extra care when I sucked my teeth at the sting. I asked for a mirror. She was right, my forehead was a wild mix of yellows, browns and blues, with the line of a clean split in the skin running across my temple just above my hairline. The cut was scabbing, but there was no redness of infection.

'It's healing nicely. It's clean, but there might be permanent discolouration: there's a trace of bark in it.' She reached for a fresh dressing. 'And now I think the tea will have done its work and you'll be ready to sleep again.'

Whether it was the bump on my head or the tea, I slept very well. When I woke and lifted my head from the pillow there was no pain. I couldn't remember going back to bed.

Rowan made another infusion that, unlike anything I'd ever bought in a supermarket, actually tasted of fresh herbs, wild mint dominating over camomile. We sat together either side of her kitchen table in easy silence for a while. Through the single window I could see trees and the tops of hills beyond. The day was bright and sunny under high clouds. The kitchen, with its farmhouse table and benches, was homely but disconcerting: it was far too big for a croft house, and there were too many rooms leading off it. We went back to the settee in front of the fire.

'Well now, you'll want to know where you are.' She gazed into the fire with a look I'd seen before, on the face of the doctor who sent me for the cancer tests, a false alarm as it turned out. I couldn't imagine what Rowan thought I couldn't take if she told me straight out. I didn't feel dead, but how would I know?

'I've been here for a very long time,' she said. 'I came from Ireland. This is my refuge, my Sanctuary.'

'From the Troubles?'

She smiled.

'In a manner of speaking.' She sighed and looked into the unseeable. 'But that was just a Post Office. I've known many troubles.'

'Post Office? The Easter Rising, you mean? No, sorry, that's silly of me, that was a century ago.'

'Was it? Well, there's the thing. You might find this hard to believe.'

'You'd be surprised. I'm told a lot of strange things. I've learned not to judge on first hearing.'

'Wise of you. What do you do?'

'I'm a priest.'

'Oh! I didn't expect that. Maybe …' She drifted off, leaving her words dangling. 'This place, my Sanctuary, my *termonn,* my *chomraich*, isn't what it seems. We are, you might say, in a pocket of somewhere else alongside Scotland, in a manner of speaking.'

'Come again?'

'Alongside, sort of. It's the best way I can describe it.'

Oh my Lord: she thinks we're in Narnia.

I put on my professional face, attentive, interested, and considered how long would be polite to wait before I made my excuses and went back to Mrs Mackay's cottage.

'When I found this place, I wrapped my borders around me and left your world outside,' she said.

'That doesn't make any sense.'

'No, I don't suppose it does, not at first, but there we are. The thing is, I made myself very difficult to find. Not many know I'm here, and those who do can't get in, though not for want of trying. But you ran right in, and I'd like to know how you did it.'

I told her all I could remember of my walk.

'Well, well, well: wolves. How unusual.'

'I know, it sounds daft. I mean, wolves running wild in Scotland!' I picked at an imaginary loose thread on my cardigan.

'No, I mean they don't usually go down that far.'

'But there aren't any – they were hunted to extinction, and all the rewilding proposals have been blocked.'

'Yet you heard them, even though wolves hunt in silence. If they really had been after you, you wouldn't have known about it until too late.'

I'm quite used to humouring people, keeping them talking. The Church is a haven for many who won't find a welcome anywhere else, or it should be anyway. All the same, I wasn't sure what to say. She was plainly sincere and trying her best to explain something to me. I'd seen it before when my evangelical brethren tried to explain something inherently absurd.

'There was something else: a voice talking in rhyme. What was that?'

She busied herself by the range, mixing up another infusion. 'A complication,' she said after a lengthy silence, but offered no further explanation.

'I don't see things the way you do,' she said, bringing two fresh drinks. 'Think of a length of cloth that looks flat, but when you get closer you see it's pleated. We're inside the pleat.'

'I think I understand that.'

'Really?'

'Yes. If you only know the cloth as a single layer, you can't see the folds or behind the weave.'

'Just like that. This is part of the world too, just a part you haven't noticed before.'

'Right: not Narnia then.'

'Narnia?'

'A place in children's stories. You get to it through a door in the back of a magical wardrobe.'

'Oh, what a charming notion! But no, not like that.'

No, I should think not.

'How big is this place?'

'The house or Sanctuary?'

'Um, well both. The house reminds me of something in another children's story: bigger on the inside than on the outside.'

'They're as big as they need to be once you're inside. On the outside, Sanctuary exists for six miles in all directions from this house. There are boundary markers, but they're only visible if you have eyes to see. That's by design. Which brings us back to you.'

'Me?'

'I don't understand how you got here without an invitation. Now that you *are* here you're very welcome to stay as long as you like, but I have to warn you it can be confusing to go back if you stay too long. People lose track of time here.'

Maybe that's why my bruise appeared so quickly?

'Like Rip Van Winkle?'

'Who's that?'

'Yet another story: Rip Van Winkle helps some strange men on a mountainside, has a drink with them and falls asleep. When he wakes up, twenty years have gone by.'

She clapped her hands with delight.

'Exactly like that. There, that wasn't as hard as I expected. You're remarkably accepting of all this.'

'To be honest, I don't know if I am, but what can I do? I'm in no position to argue.'

'Would you argue, usually?'

'When I was at university, someone asked if I'd be interested in starting a group to explore spirituality. I asked her how she defined "spirituality". She took that as a no.'

Rowan laughed.

'I think you'd fit in here very well if you wanted to. Some of the neighbours are keen to meet you, by the way. You're a curiosity to be inspected. I'm giving you fair warning.'

'You have neighbours?'

'Oh yes, there are several others here for various reasons. Most keep to themselves, even from me, and you won't meet them. One or two are sociable.'

'People you invited?'

'Yes. I like the company. They stay a while and leave when they're ready. It takes some longer to move on than others. It depends what they were running from. What were you running from, I wonder? Don't tell me if you don't want to.'

'I wasn't aware I was running from anything.'

I knew it for a lie the moment I said it. Rowan made no comment. It would be rude to ask what she was running from.

'Tell me, are you a good priest?'

Gah! How do I even begin to answer that?

'The relentlessness, the endless useless meetings about nothing at all, ground me down like so much coffee in a mill,' I said. It was true, but the whole truth was more brutal.

My ministry kicked off with the usual overload of incense and innocence, heavy with grand notions of bringing the light of Christ to a grateful world. I really did hope I could be a vessel through which God flowed, that I might somehow make a difference. I tried sometimes to connect to that young me, the motivated me, but never could, not after thirty-odd years of baptising ungrateful brats and marrying couples who hadn't troubled the doors of a church since their own christenings, if ever. Three decades of perfunctory winter funerals for corpses I never knew, for whom no one came to weep.

I couldn't even go to the pub for a Sunday lunch without setting tongues wagging behind the weekend supplements. Heaven forbid a vicar might be human in a parish where, despite high-status gadgets and luxury vehicles outside overpriced and undersized executive villas, the weekly collection plate barely covered the cost of the church flowers, and charity never began at home except as a tax deduction.

Rowan's gaze was neutral. I was uncomfortably aware of pressure behind my eyes, a welling-up of all the things I'd so carefully not articulated before, even to myself.

She said, 'There used to be more to priesthood than that. I remember when priests were set apart, not quite human, not quite sane, doorkeepers to somewhere else, the voices of the beyond, more likely to gut you for a sacrifice than to heal you, maintaining the rhythms of the seasons.'

'How long ago was that?'

'When I was young. It's an interesting thing, time. I've come to think that "how long" has no meaning – that all of history is equally distant. All that matters is that it is not now. Anyway, that's by the by: you don't look like the sacrificing type. I see why you were running. No, don't bristle. It's in your voice and the way you sit, the way you keep your body closed. I thought perhaps you fled your status as a priest, but I think you flee from something else. I don't think you know what it is to be a priest.'

'Did the sacrifices work?'

'What sacrifices?'

'To maintain the rhythm of the seasons.'

'Well now, that depends what you mean by work.'

'Were the gods propitiated? Did they bend to the priests' will?'

'The rains fell and the sun shone and the harvests were gathered.'

'And has that ever not happened since the sacrifices stopped? You're right, I struggle with what it means to be a priest, but I know it isn't that.'

'And now you're angry with God for wasting your life?'

But that wasn't it at all. I wasn't angry with God. I was angry with myself.

CHAPTER 2

The range was lit. A kettle sat on a trivet across a hot plate. There was nothing I recognised, only unlabelled jars of herbs and dried leaves. I poured a mug of hot water, which did me well enough. A new loaf and a pat of butter were in the centre of the kitchen table, with a jar of honey and a bowl of fresh bilberries.

Rowan wasn't there.

I waited, but hunger overcame politeness. After eating, I looked for a sink to rinse my dishes, but couldn't see a tap. The utter lack of what I accepted as modernity was disconcerting. I'd seen no pictures on the walls, no paintings, no fading samplers. There were utensils and pots of stone and iron but, apart from a miniature pine tree in a pot, no personal items were displayed at all. A collection of hazel staffs, fashioned into walking sticks, leaned against the wall by the door. Leaving the plate and mug on the table, I chose a staff that felt the right size for me, opened the door and stepped outside, ducking to avoid the stone lintel.

The cottage was built on the side of a hill, far enough above the stream that tumbled through the glen below not to be concerned by spring spates or winter floods. I presumed Rowan drew her water there.

Something about the sun niggled me: judging by its height I was looking south, with a view of several hills running east to west. The whole vista was pristine, with no sign of other habitation or use. Everywhere was thick, natural woodland rather than the heathered moorland I'd expected.

I walked along the front of the cottage, in which only two windows were set, one for the kitchen and one for another room beyond. I couldn't see into that room. The only door was the one I'd walked through, and there was no byre. At the gable-end was a rough enclosure fenced by woven strands of willow patched with hazel. A large coop butted against the wall and ten chickens and a cockerel pecked around in the scrubby grass. The taste of the chicken soup was strong, and I avoided their clucking and their accusing eyes. Beyond the enclosure, a line of wild rowan trees formed a natural boundary, after which the woodland had heavy ground cover. A pair of blackbirds gorged themselves on shining red berries.

I looked back at the cottage from the tree line. Despite the apparent size inside, the outside looked like neither more nor less than a traditional black house, albeit one well maintained and freshly whitewashed. Peat and logs were stacked in its lee. The thatch looked new.

A rough path led beyond the rowans and uphill, keeping to the banks of the stream, though rarely less than six feet above it. The sky was unfeasibly blue and the heather down to the burn an unlikely purple, the colours so saturated that they appeared false, like an old colourised postcard. The clean air and quicksilver light encouraged long fringes of lichen to drape from branches. I felt well, but was pleased I'd brought the staff, stopping from time to time to lean on it while I caught my breath.

Eventually, I reached a series of narrows where the water squeezed between and over rocks and boulders. Above them, a large pool was fed by a waterfall. The poolside was nearly inaccessible on foot, and I kept to the steep path as it rose to the top of the natural stone bowl in which the pool swirled.

The water was clean and clear, and much deeper than it appeared from its outlet, scoured by the torrents of countless Highland winters and springs. The waterfall was beautiful and benign, but I imagined it would be energetic and powerful when winter snows melted.

I carried on for the forty or fifty metres to the lip of the waterfall itself. Beyond it, the trees thinned somewhat and the terrain was bleaker. A dipper flittered around the water sixty or seventy metres below me. A single standing stone rose from the grass. One face was cloaked with moss and lichen, but the obverse was incised with whirls and whorls and strange sigils, unmarked by time. They reminded me of those on Pictish stones, but seemed more ancient somehow.

The trees up here were mostly Scots pines, twisted but sturdy. A track ran through them. Just visible further on was a dead tree, its bleached bones reaching up to the sky like a charismatic calling on the Holy Spirit for the gift of tongues.

I sat on a log to rest and think about all the things I'd let build up. Rowan's question about priesthood reverberated around my head as I walked. She was right: I'd bristled, outraged at her suggestion that I didn't understand priesthood, all the more so because she was correct.

Every Sunday, the congregation all stood there, staring into space, mouthing the words, while I chasséd the old soft-shoe shuffle at the altar. I read the words and waved my hands about with occult choreography: *Strictly Come Liturgy*. I instructed them to stand up, sit down, stand up, kneel, sing, pray, and they all complied, obedient to their instructions, abasement hardwired into muscle memory, waiting for the workaday magic of death and resurrection in a silver chalice.

Do this in remembrance of Me.

The words came and went, an oblation here, a touch of anamnesis there, and I barely noticed when, somewhere along the way, probably while I was thinking about lunch, the sliver of ersatz 'bread' and the cheap communion wine became the body and dripping blood of the poor sod nailed up on His cross.

Every Sunday, after the wizardry and the handshakes and the platitudes at the door, the flock wandered off to listen to *The Archers Omnibus* and get pissed on the surprisingly good Chianti they'd found in the supermarket, discounted for a case of twelve, while I retired to the cold vestry that smelled of damp and cheap polish. I'd fold my robes and put away the chasuble and leave the linen for the laundry. I'd check the silverware was locked away in the safe with the counted and bagged money from the collection plate, and walk out to the rhythm of rain plopping softly into yellow plastic buckets on the chancel floor beneath holes in the roof.

It's not as though I could jack it in and find something else. All I was good for was a nifty funeral, some fancy footwork and the weekly miracle. I hadn't put much aside to supplement the meagre pension I might one day draw if the Church's dodgy investments came good, so early retirement wasn't a great option either.

What was there for me to cling onto despite it all? Sculptors like to say they get a piece of stone and chip away all the bits that aren't statue, exposing the form latent in the raw material. What would be revealed if I cut away all the bits of religion and Church from myself? What would be left of me?

God knows, but She and I hadn't been speaking so much, and She wasn't letting me in on the secret.

A mountain hare, white in its winter coat, sat unmoving at the base of the standing stone. I shivered, though it wasn't especially cold, and made my way back down to the cottage. I met Rowan walking along another path that led behind the house and down the hill into the valley beyond.

'Oh, you're up! I thought I might find you still lying abed. Did you eat the food I left out?'

'Thank you, yes, and had a walk to stretch my legs, up to the waterfall back there.' I gestured with the staff, her staff, though she could hardly not know where I meant.

'Yes, I like it up there too.'

We walked to the cottage together. The burn, now on my right, tumbled down to a confluence of several run-offs from the hills. It was beautiful. A notch in the hill beyond was familiar, and I knew where I was.

My rucksack – retrieved by Rowan – my gear and phone, were all anachronisms. The phone battery was low, and there was no signal, but I slipped the phone into a pocket in the trews out of habit. I took my journal and pen from the bottom of the rucksack to the desk. Funny, I hadn't noticed it or the hand-carved captain's chair before.

Leaning over the broad sill of my bedroom window, I put my head out and looked around. There was only one window to my right, and no sign of the kitchen door at all. In front of me the river tumbled downhill to what I knew was the east, so I was looking south. But according to the layout of the cottage that I'd formed in my head, my view ought to be north, onto the hill rising behind the cottage. Leaving the window open, I went back to the desk, pursued by the gossiping chatter of the water.

The beauty of the walk had made me forget that I had no idea at all where I was or what the hell was happening to me. I opened the notebook and jotted my memories and Rowan's tale down before the details muddied, setting it all down without comment.

Rowan knocked and entered as I was finishing up.

'You're a writer too?'

'An occasional diary, notes for sermons, memory jogs, that kind of thing. I was just noting what happened in case I need to refresh my memory later.'

'Does anyone else read it?'

'I don't expect anyone will see this until I'm dead and gone and they're throwing out my stuff.'

'Is it about me?'

'What I remember of how I got here, what you said, yes.'

'I'd rather you hadn't. I don't want knowledge of me or my whereabouts getting out.'

I tore the pages out and took them to the living room, where the peat fire burned. We watched as the paper was consumed. I had the oddest impression that the flames took only the paper, not the words, which rose into the chimney on hot smoke as individual letters.

'Thank you. You didn't have to be quite so thorough, but I appreciate it. It will save a lot of awkwardness later.'

'No problem. I should have thought. Can I ask you something?'

She looked wary. 'Did I touch a nerve, with the priesthood thing?' she said.

'No, not that, it's about the window in the spare room. If I've got it right, I should be looking north onto a hillside, but I'm not. And there are only two windows on the south side, and this isn't one of them. Look.'

I went back to the bedroom, opened the window and

moved the vase of flowers from the table to the windowsill, then we went outside through the kitchen door.

I pointed to bare stone where my window should be at the east end of the front wall. Rowan walked to the other end, towards the chickens and the second window. She reached in and took out the vase, sniffing the flowers.

'Pleats within pleats.'

An infinite regression of Sanctuaries receded from me in a never-ending splintering of fractal dimensions. I staggered, toppled by vertigo, and reached to the wall for support.

Rowan was by me in a moment and helped me back to my room, where I lay down. She brought me a beaker of fresh water.

'What happened?'

'When you said *pleats within pleats* the strangest thing happened, like there was an impossible number of worlds within worlds, all existing at the same time, all connected in ways I couldn't understand, and I was right in the middle of them, unable to tell what was real.'

Rowan put the vase back on the table, straightening the doily beneath it, closing the window.

'Remarkable. No one else has seen that before.'

Something clicked in my mind.

'The sun.'

'What about it?'

'It's too high in the sky for November, and it stays light too long.'

'Really? I wouldn't worry, I dare say things are just a bit out of kilter here compared to what you're used to.'

Her gaze landed on the pile of things I'd taken out of my rucksack.

'Is that a guidebook? I haven't seen one for years. May I look?'

'Please, you can have it. It's the least I can do.'

'Oh, thank you. I'll read it now! I have some old books you're welcome to browse. You should look in the library and see if anything interests you. It's through here.'

Library? Where can she keep a library?

She led me through the kitchen and the sitting room, which already seemed big enough to take up all the available space in the house, even without my guest room and wherever Rowan slept.

'Remember, as big as it needs to be: pleats within pleats.'

The four walls of the library were lined with shelves up to where the stonework stopped and thatch started. The books were all antiquarian, but pristine, with a surprising quantity of manuscripts and scrolls. In the centre of the room stood a lectern, polished by innumerable years of use. Next to it were a chair and a writing desk on which sat an angled board.

'This is from a scriptorium,' I said, recognising the style.

'Yes, from Beannchar originally. You'd call it Bangor.'

'Wales?'

'Ireland. It's from Comgall's time, but came over with Máel Rubha when he set up at Apur Crossan.'

I'd read about that in the guidebook.

'Didn't Máel Rubha die in the early eighth century? Viking raid or something? How did it end up here?'

'I told you. I've been here a long time. I used to go visiting, when the world was quieter, seeing what tide and time brought to me. He died peacefully, by the way; he was eighty-one after all.'

'Isn't Applecross called Chomraich too?'

'A' Chomraich, yes. Similar idea, but more recent.'

I am no expert on manuscripts, but the look and feel and smell of the collection hinted it was something special. I'd seen ancient material as a student, but only from a distance, watching medievalists examine it with great care. This collection seemed newly written and bound: the paper smelled fresh and the spines were complete and unbroken. Where there were titles on the spines, they were either Latin or classical Irish Gaelic. None were later than mid-seventeenth century. I opened some at random to find notes written on the front or back plates of several. Some had marginal annotations in Secretary Hand or earlier scripts that I didn't recognise.

One alcove contained several collections of documents kept loose in leather wrappers. They were written in several hands and well beyond my ability to decipher.

'Are these recipes?' I asked, identifying parts of the texts as lists of ingredients.

'After a fashion. They're old collections of herbal remedies that I'm looking after, though I don't suppose there's anyone left who remembers they're here.'

I'd sometimes handled eighteenth- and nineteenth-century volumes in the university stacks, and more often than not come away with an itchiness in the back of my hands, a feeling of mites in the disintegrating leather swarming under my unbound skin, but not with Rowan's books.

'See anything that particularly interests you?'

'I'm sure it all would, but I'm no linguist.'

I noticed a volume sitting alone, low down in the corner. The text, handwritten in a fluent, confident cursive script, ran along lightly inscribed lines. The sheets were folded, bound by chain-stitching through holes, wrapped in a soft leather cover stiffened with scrap material of some kind.

'This, for instance. I don't even know what this is. Is it Greek?'

'No, but you're close: it's a mix of Greek and Egyptian symbols, written by a Coptic monk. Interesting you should pick that one – Antonios is the only other person to have found me here without an invitation.'

'Can you read it?'

'It tells how he left Egypt and travelled through Ireland before coming here. He wrote it in my kitchen.'

I admired the pages for their own sake as pieces of art, the single column of text neatly spaced and ordered, the black letters glistening as if only recently set down.

'What did you use for ink?'

'Oak gall, cherry sap, some ancient iron pieces and water. He might have added some pine bark too. It wasn't perfect, a little too corrosive. Some of the text is already fragile. I brought him goose feathers for quills, but he preferred to use reeds from the loch.'

'This isn't papyrus though.'

'I'm sorry?'

'Papyrus, you know, Egypt.'

'Well of course not: where would he get papyrus in Scotland? That was a frustration for him, now I come to remember it. No, I stretched some goatskins and prepared the surface, then he put the volume together in the way he was taught. He did that chain-stitching himself with hemp and grass and some leather to reinforce it.'

'There's a lot of sheets.'

'We had a lot of goats.'

'He lived here?'

'He built himself a place from stones and rocks out on that path you walked up, beyond the waterfall. I thought it would be too rough up there in winter, but he stuffed the cracks with moss and heather and insisted he was quite comfortable. I rather enjoyed having him living up there, close enough to chat but not so close that we got in each other's way. And then one day he said he was of a mind to go back to sea in a rudderless boat and let the currents take him. It was the fashionable thing to do. It's how he fetched up here in the first place.'

'When was that?'

'Oh, let me see: the Romans were gone but ...' She trailed off. 'I think some time in the four hundreds as you'd count it. Maybe a bit later.' My face must have shown something. 'You don't believe me?'

'Well, that would be fifteen hundred years ago.'

'Fancy that. Anyway, the text begins: *IN THE PEACE OF GOD! May His holy blessing and the blessing of all the saints come upon us and may we all be saved. AMEN.*

'Then he tells his story. Didn't you learn ancient languages when you were training?'

'Greek, but it was a long time ago. I scraped a pass on a resit.'

'There's the pity, you'd find it interesting, I think.'

'Maybe someone could translate it for me.'

'It can't leave here. There'd be too many questions asked. He left it with me for safekeeping.'

'Who from?'

'Not like that. He wanted to leave something of himself here where it would be safe and I could look at it and remember him, rather like those herbals. That's all he left, apart from his plant.'

'Plant?'

'The miniature tree in the kitchen. He said he got the idea from some silk merchants he met in India. I've kept it alive for him all this time. Fifteen hundred years, you say? Imagine. Anyway, I'll leave you to look around; I'm going to read your guidebook. I haven't caught up with the world beyond for a while.'

I turned my attention back to the shelves so Rowan couldn't see my face. I hadn't completely ruled out that I was lying in Raigmore Hospital in a coma, my brain working hard to make sense of random images and sensations. It was just too bizarre, too irrational to be true, to be in a fold in the world with an ancient woman who remembered the Romans leaving and said wolves hadn't been hunted to extinction.

I often visited the elderly, and not so elderly, living with dementia. Conversations with them had something of the same quality as talking with Rowan, an obliqueness to the world. I sometimes wonder what it's like – if you know what's happening and are powerless to free yourself, or whether everything makes perfect sense within your understanding. When I was newly ordained, the medical policy was to try and bring dementia patients back to the 'real world'. But what if they were happy where they were? Sanctuary felt real to me, but how could I tell?

Rowan reached into a pouch in her apron.

'I almost forgot: Ingrid returned these.' She handed me my glasses. The bridge had been replaced with three strands of what looked like silver wire, twisted together and fixed to the old mountings. I hadn't even noticed I'd been walking around without them, right up to the edge of a waterfall. I shuddered at the thought and put them on, but my eyes rebelled and I took them off again.

'Thank you.'

'I've also cleaned and pressed your clothes. I liked those trews you wore, all those pockets. Very practical, but aren't they incongruous? Fashions change, but they're not what I remember clergy wearing.'

'They're made for walking in the wild, but I learned a long time ago that if you are in a position of privilege you can wear whatever you want. The worst that happens is people think you're eccentric. Once you have that reputation, you get a free pass to do what you like. Thank for sorting out my clothes: I really don't want to be a burden.'

'You're not. It's difficult, isn't it, to accept what I've said? Don't worry, I'm not offended. It's hard for everyone at first.'

'I'm a priest. I'm expected to believe things that sound irrational.'

'But you don't anymore, do you? Believe them?'

She waited for me to say something else, to implicate myself in my own moral cowardice.

'It's something I think about a lot; it's what I was thinking about just before I found myself here, actually. I can't string it together rationally yet. I wouldn't make much sense, even to myself. That's why I came away in the first place, to get time and space to work it out.'

'Well, rational is all well and good, like distinguishing the practice of sacrifice from the passage of the seasons, but not everything is so neat.'

'What about Antonios? Did he doubt?'

'Ah, now. Doubt is it? Doubt is good. Doubt is important. I don't trust anyone who doesn't doubt. I've seen too many people kill, or die, because they had no doubts. As for Antonios, well, he was of a different time and place. He wouldn't have called it doubt, but he was thoughtful and reflective, which often amounts to the same thing. It's a shame you can't read him, but there we are. What do you doubt?'

'Pretty much everything.'

'Excellent! That's promising, once you're ready to find a way to resolve it. Now, a cup of something hot, I think.'

I wandered round the shelves for a while, hoping for something interesting in readable English, but Antonios's manuscript drew me back, even though I couldn't read it.

Unless I wanted to photograph the manuscript for later study. Were I a student I'd have found a photocopier. No chance of that, of course, but my phone had a perfectly good camera, more than good enough for this, even on a low charge.

After I'd slipped the phone back into my pocket and put the manuscript in its place on the shelf, I told myself I hadn't breached Rowan's rules by copying it, and, after all, she would never think to ask about technology she didn't know anything about. My unhelpful brain flashed back to a Moral Philosophy lecture in my first year at university, and discussion of whether it is possible in logic to deceive oneself, since knowledge of the lie negates the possibility that you are deceived by it. I ignored the memory.

Rowan had nursed the embers of the peat fire in the sitting room back to life and settled down to read my guidebook.

'Is this true?' Rowan called. 'Five and a half million people live in Scotland? And only sixty thousand have the Gaelic?'

'That sounds about right. Probably more in Ireland, and there's Welsh too.'

'And priests don't learn Greek. Changed days. You still learn Latin though?'

'I did at school, and a bit as a refresher at university, but I've forgotten most of it.'

'Hmmm. And these illustrations are really photographs? This is what Perth and Edinburgh look like now? They've changed so much.'

'You know them?'

'I used to visit, until the burnings.'

I went back to my room and wrote an edited account of my travels up to the point where I found myself lost. I drew the curtains, making sure I did not look out of the window, and settled down to nap.

What did she mean by the burnings?

A long howl echoed from out of the borders of sleep, but I was too tired to think any more of it.

I dreamed I was with Venny, who looked just as she had on our last day together, though I knew we were in the present. In the dream there was a link between us, sometimes strong, sometimes stretched, always present, binding us together though we were separated by distances I couldn't measure. *All of history is equally distant, and so 'how long' has no meaning*, Rowan had said. Comforted, I settled into a deeper sleep.

I stepped outside to take the air and found a place to sit on a rock overlooking the tumbling burn. I unfolded my Ordnance Survey map and tried to fit the vista into the map, orientating it by eye to match the summits of surrounding hills. I was used to a bare landscape of heathers and grasses with managed plantations of conifers. Everywhere was wooded here: the space around the cottage was cleared, but, as far as I could see, everything else was natural.

I was right about where we were. The peaks and tops matched the map. Ben Hee was, as near as makes no difference, due south of where I sat. The high ground running west would be Carn Dearg round to Meall a Chuirn and, out of sight, Foinaven. The long valley running south-east away from me through the gap I'd recognised earlier went to Altnaharra and Strath Naver, where mapmaker Timothy Pont had written of wolves.

I was in Gleann na Goille – Glen Golly – about six miles from where I had run into the tree. The name means the glen of the trees, and it made more sense here than in the world I knew. The river below me was Amhainn Gleann na Goille, and the hill rising behind Rowan's house, the one my room didn't look onto, must be Foinne bheinn Mhor.

Glen Golly and the river were not as the map showed them. They were wilder, and time had found different routes for the water, but I was certain it was the same place.

Rowan's voice made me jump.

'That's a good map. The lines and colours mark the height? Very clever. May I?'

She studied it intently for a while and gave it back.

'Names change while staying almost the same, like Ben Hee for Bheinn Shith over there. When you decide about whether or not to leave, I'd appreciate it if you didn't mark anything on the map.'

'You have my word – in fact, you can have the map – but can I ask why not? You said people would look for you: who would still want to find you?'

'Who's to say when a story is finished, or who the players are? Or your role in it.'

'Me? What have I to do with it?'

'You followed in Antonios's footsteps, though you didn't know it. It really is a pity you can't read his story. Then again, if you are part of the story, you'll find a way. Then we'll know.'

'And if I leave?'

'Then it will stay a mystery until you come back, if you can.'

'Rowan, the burnings you mentioned, when was that?'

Her face fell into stillness. Pain flitted across it.

'They burned the women I talked to, who obtained things for me.'

'The witch trials?'

The indefatigable, placid air about her that I'd known since I first woke in her house evaporated in an instant. Her body stiffened, her face hardened, her voice became a growl on the wind.

'Do not speak that word in my presence.'

I hadn't felt so small, so utterly crushed, since the day Granny had checked me for some long-forgotten slight. Rowan stood up and stalked off towards the trees beyond the gable end, scattering chickens as a toddler scatters leaves in the autumn.

When she came back, she spoke as though nothing had happened, brushing her hands down the front of her apron.

'We should get ready. We're expected at Yrreddell in an hour, and it doesn't do to keep Ingrid waiting.'

'Isn't Yrreddell the old name of the River Strathmore, that flows down to Hope and the sea?'

'Old? To you maybe. It's the river and the tower.'

'The broch? At Dun Dornaigil? That's where I was walking to. I was there once, years ago, when I was little. I remember the ruin as mysterious, haunting in its isolation.'

'Ruin? Well, you should find this evening interesting.'

'What are they like, the others?'

'You can make your own judgements. Only one or two will turn up.'

'How long have they been here?'

'William is the most recent of the ones you'll meet. He came just after – let me think – when Elizabeth died and James went to London. When was that?'

'Four hundred years ago.'

'Really? It doesn't seem that long.'

'How long have I been in Sanctuary – measured outside, I mean?'

She thought for a while.

'You're fine, I think. You haven't committed to living here and that makes a difference. Incidentally, do you know any good stories? Ingrid likes a good story.'

'What kind of story?'

'She was a warrior once, so blood and honour, or weird. She likes weird.'

'Warrior?'

'Dane. You'll like her.'

CHAPTER 3

I've always hated middle-class dinner parties. Goodness knows why I was ever invited. They would all shuffle in their seats when I was asked to say a grace that would go down like an incantation in a horror film. Then there were the fake regrets when I apologised for having to leave early. I sometimes wonder what wealthy people think Jesus was talking about. Do they really think it somehow doesn't apply to them? Do they really think there is a fine calculus of giving that tips the balance in favour of the giver, that ethics is, in the end, a form of double-entry bookkeeping, the balances netting off to leave Virtue carried forward as a promissory note to be redeemed by the heavenly treasurer when it falls due?

But a function in a broch hosted by a Danish warrior called Ingrid was a new one, even for an Anglican. At least I wouldn't be expected to feign admiration for a new car and fend off questions about why I stuck with my old Volkswagen Estate, or give a tolerant smile at a roguish joke told a bit close to the bone by old Peter, who'd had one too many glasses of absurdly powerful New World wine. I wouldn't have to indicate approval for token efforts at charity, or respond to passive-aggressive, or just plain aggressive, antagonists who'd skim-read Richard Dawkins and thought they were advancing reasoned approaches for atheism to put me on the spot. And that was before the ever-so-politely disguised racism.

The closely-fitted, unmortared walls of Yrreddell rose forty feet or so, tapering inwards at a gentle angle, then tending to near-vertical towards the top. A thin ribbon of smoke rose from an unseen opening in the unseen roof and up into the evening sky. The entrance, with its massive triangular lintel, was almost at ground level at the Dun Dornaigil I knew, but head-height at Yrreddell, as I found out when I cracked my forehead.

'That's a bad habit you have,' said Rowan.

'I'll duck next time.'

'No need: the door knows you now.'

A fresh bruise. I'd been surprised earlier to see in the mirror that my previous injuries had disappeared. The cut on my temple was just a thin line, invisible if you didn't know it was there. That was too fast. I tried to count how long I'd been in Sanctuary, but couldn't reckon it as more than two days.

'This is Ingrid,' said Rowan.

I'd imagined a Scandinavian with flaxen hair, as in a fantasy novel or a fairy tale. I'm never quite sure what 'flaxen' means, but I didn't think her hair, long, dark and interwoven, the weave threaded through with coloured braids, was it. She carried her height well in a creamy-white soft linen garment beneath a bright red woollen gown with shoulder straps fastened by ornate silver buckles. It reminded me of the cassock alb I wore in church, but her sleeves were chased with red embroidered dragonheads of the fabled longships, highlighted with gold thread. Around her neck was a silk scarf of what looked like Byzantine design.

She wore very little jewellery: no rings, no earrings, only a fine gold brooch in the shape of a double-headed ship with matching dragonheads at stem and stern, the eyes picked out with garnets. Its simplicity had a compelling beauty, and I guessed she'd crafted it herself. A leather belt around her waist bore a silver buckle matching those at her shoulder straps. A tooled leather sheath hung from the belt, from which a carved horn handle with silver pommel emerged.

I was distinctly underdressed.

'A pleasure. Please excuse my embarrassing entrance.'

'I have made worse and survived.' She smiled. 'Welcome. The hospitality of my hall and hearth is yours to enjoy. I find a perfect cure for a sore head, and for many other ailments, is mead, and I make the best mead in the *grið*.'

'*Grið*?'

'Sanctuary, home, safety.'

'Do many people make mead here?'

'No, only me – that's why mine is the best.' She found this uproarious, and it seemed rude not to laugh with her.

I'd barely touched alcohol since my brush with cancer. A lot of my student life was spent in pubs, drinking too much, being stupid. In my first parish, I became much more aware of how booze washes through society, the destruction it leaves behind. Most people can drink with nothing more than the occasional hangover to show for it, but I met too many of those who couldn't. And I knew the dangers to clergy of taking refuge in a bottle.

'I've nothing to offer in return.'

'Your gift can be to tell me what's become of the world, and of how you came to be here. The bees tell me stories of a raven snaring a hart. Does that mean anything to you?'

'I'm sorry, no.' I took a tentative sip. 'Your mead has something about it, a spiciness, and it's dry, not sweet.'

'The recipe requires birch sap and heather, and herbs found in the birch woods and on the mountain sides if one knows what to look for.'

'And pine? There's a hint of resin.' She clapped my shoulder with unexpected force.

I knew a broch was a circular structure with double walls, and stairs ascending from the ground-floor chamber to others above. This was nothing like that. I was in a great hall, more or less rectangular, though the walls bulged a little in the middle, with massive wooden pillars supporting a panelled roof. Zoomorphic carvings scampered up the pillars into and around the rafters. The light of an open fire burnished gold leaf, highlighting faces and scurrying creatures.

The panelled walls were lined with shields and weapons arranged around three gleaming swords, functional and deadly with cut-throat edges, themselves framing a mighty, ornamental war sword, its blade etched with runes, the guard and pommel in gold, decorated with interlined beasts with rubies and emeralds for eyes. It wouldn't be practical in battle, but it was never meant to be: it was a statement of status.

A spit threaded a substantial haunch of meat near, though not over, the flames, fat and blood dripping into large metal pans in which vegetables cooked, sizzling and spitting.

Rowan stood by me.

'This hall,' I said.

'Yes. Isn't it magnificent?'

'It is, but it's not a broch.'

'It's what it needs to be.'

'You said before *as big as it needs to be*; this is something else.'

'Often it's a long house, other times it's a broch. Once it was the deck of a longship with a sail for a ceiling. Today there are guests, so here it is.'

'I don't understand.'

'It's best to just accept it for what it is. Watch out for that mead, by the way, and try not to talk about the passage of time *outside*.'

'Ingrid's already asked me about that – and what was that about talking to bees?'

'Her people say the bees fly between the worlds to drink the sap of Yggdrasil. Sometimes they carry messages.'

'Right. Is there anything else I should know? Any more surprises?'

'Oh I'm sure, but nothing to bother you with today.'

A young man stood to one side so as not to interrupt us. Rowan touched his elbow and encouraged him closer.

'This is Cathal. He came here with Ingrid.'

'You're her partner?'

He looked quizzical.

'Partner? I don't understand how you use the word. Oh! No. No, I was her slave; now it's complicated.'

Rowan patted him on the back and left us alone.

'I'm sorry, I didn't mean to embarrass you. I wasn't told anything about you all.'

'No, Rowan's like that: she lets people find things out for themselves.'

Like Venny used to.

'You came here with Ingrid as her slave?'

He didn't answer straightaway and I thought I'd made some dreadful faux pas. He replied as if he were reading his own story from a book that only he could see.

'I was born in a grand place, with plentiful food, where orange and red sunsets lit the sky behind purple-silhouetted mountains and willows trailed idle fingers in clean rivers. In the frosty, clear nights of winter we watched shooting stars flash between the constellations. Grandfather taught me their names: the trout, the bear, the hunter. Grandmother told our fortunes.

'I remember my mother's smile, and the back of her hand, as I did my chores while Father hunted or fished or tended our land and animals. And I remember the worried looks on Mother and Father's faces, their whispered conversations, the honing of the swords and axes, the stringing of bows and fletching of arrows.

'It made no difference. They came in daylight, no skulking around at twilight or dawn for them. They knew exactly what they wanted – our lives and our goods. Father lifted his axe, but was stopped by a single arrow to the throat before a sharp sword opened him up.'

His voice changed, slipping without effort from speech to verse, declaiming with confidence, without any sing-song tone.

> Bold man of the morning,
> Plough blade in the song fields,
> Proud giver not taker,
> A deep well of stories.
> Blue head of an elm reed
> Bit. Sharp battle-serpent,
> Its tongue tipped with darkness,
> Brought blood feast for ravens.

Cathal paused and looked far away. His voice softened. 'I watched him die, my eyes stinging, my breeches filling. The fight left Mother when he fell. They burned her alive in the house with my brother and sisters. Ingrid was their leader. I thought she was my death, but she took me as her property. There came a day when we sailed to Port-na-coulter. The first band forayed inland under moonless skies. Ingrid's crew were the second wave, their task to mop up stragglers and finish off the wounded. I was there to do as I was told and not get killed.

'They knew we were coming. We heard the battle and went to support our comrades, but ran into the middle of the slaughter. The night was full of swords and death. The cry went up to retreat, but we were chased and picked off

46

as we ran. Ingrid's hands and armour were slick with the blood of many foes. Her sharp sword sent two score to the soil to sleep the long sleep, but in the end even she tired. I had my chance to flee, but knew I'd be treated as just another Dane and killed with the rest.

'A huge warrior was about to deliver his deathblow to Ingrid. Without thinking, I took a spear from a dead man's hands and ran him through from behind.'

He shifted into verse again.

A feeder of eagles,
Cold eyes of a death cloud,
Pitiless war viper,
Blood dripping, life-stealing,
By holly shaft vanquished.
Pierced prey of the she-wolf,
The prize of the raider
His mistress redeeming.

'That mighty fighter, felled by a frightened slave. Imagine that. I preferred enslavement to death, but our ships were already on the open water, and we were abandoned on the shore. Ingrid's beloved *Skarfr* was a pale whisper on the waves. And then Rowan was with us, and Ingrid assured me we were dead and were granted a place in the afterlife.'

'And you're no longer a slave?'

'Ingrid freed me for saving her, and Rowan doesn't hold with slavery.'

'And you remain with her.'

'What else can I do? And at least here we won't be run through with swords or spears, or burned alive in our homes, or drowned in the icy sea. I heard you found your own way here?'

I told the story of the wolves again, and his response

was quick and certain: 'Some other force was at work. You are here for a reason.'

'I can't think what. I'm just an ordinary priest.'

'Ah, now: not everyone here has reason to think kindly of the Church.'

'Don't assume I think kindly of it myself.'

'So, you're escaping something too. You've nearly finished your mead and you can't have an empty horn – Ingrid will be affronted.'

'Are there any soft drinks? And thank you for your story.' He inclined his head.

'I think that might be the first time I've told it. And my verse needs work: the alliteration is wayward. Soft drink?'

'Without alcohol.'

'Water?'

'Water would be lovely, thank you.'

'What's this!' Ingrid strode across. 'Water? My guests will have better than water. You don't like the mead after all? You were being polite? I have ale—'

'The mead is wonderful, but I have taken to cracking my head, it seems. The spirit, indeed, is willing, but the flesh is weak.'

'The Gospel of Matthew, at chapter 26 and verse 41. Well said there, well said. And yet one may question whether *willing* is the best translation for πρόθυμον; perhaps *ready* or *prepared* might be the better reading?'

The speaker was a rotund yet compact man, in a black doublet and breeches with hose gartered at the knee. On his head was a neat blue bonnet of wool. His breeches were puffed out in the way I'd seen in early seventeenth-century portraits.

'I have a distant memory that πρόθυμον is also translated as either *eager* or *ready* in Romans 1.15,' I said. 'The phrase has become so much a part of everyday speech that the battle for precision is lost.'

'Part of everyday speech? May I ask when that became so?'

'Since the King James version of the Bible in the early seventeenth century.'

A chasm opened beneath me as the words left my mouth.

'And may I enquire how long ago that was for you?'

Shit! I couldn't answer without breaking the only bit of advice Rowan had given me. I looked over his shoulder to see if Rowan was on hand to rescue me. She wasn't.

'Perhaps we should talk about the weather or the fishing, or you can instruct me in Greek.'

Too late: he was on the spot and couldn't back down.

'Thank you, but now the question is asked I would have the answer, lest it torment my mind for all time coming.'

'How long do you think it's been?'

'Ah now, there's the rub: sometimes I feel I have been here my whole life. Other times that it's a matter of months.'

'Then I have to tell you that, for me, it is four hundred years, more or less.'

He looked into the darkness of the roof cavity, his face unreadable. When he looked at me again, his eyes glinted.

'Forgive me. I should have talked of fishing and Greek as you suggested. I should be grateful were you to excuse me.'

He picked up a horn filled with mead and walked away.

'Who was that?' I asked Cathal.

'William.'

'The most recent arrival, Rowan said.'

'Yes. A pleasant man, but distant. There is great tragedy in his life. He never talks about it. He isn't the most reclusive, but not the most sociable either.'

'Who is the most reclusive?'

'Lallig. I think he's been here almost as long as Rowan herself. I've only seen him a handful of times. He usually wanders the forests of the far south, muttering to himself in verse. Ingrid says he's quite mad. Rowan doesn't discuss him. I suspect William had some encounter with him of which he will not speak. We only know of each other what we tell of ourselves. We don't ask why people come here.'

And with that my faux pas was laid bare. I closed my eyes and sighed.

'I'm sorry, no one told me, and I asked you that very thing.'

'Sure and I'm not bothered, I was happy to remember, and I asked how you came here too. But best not ask the others.'

'You look like you're ready to eat,' said Ingrid, joining us.

A table was set with seven places, Ingrid, Cathal, Rowan and me, William should he return, and two others: the unexpected guest, Ingrid said, and absent friends. We sat two on either side with Ingrid at the head, the space between us filled with a massive haunch of roast meat and ashets overflowing with roast vegetables. A large platter held a complete salmon which had been baked in a hot oven, crackled skin curling away from pink meat, accusatory white eyes glaring. Fresh-baked brown bread was in baskets, and at each place-setting was a pat of fresh butter in a bowl. There were several flagons of mead and, thankfully, a pitcher of fresh water.

'What happened with William?' Rowan said.

'I couldn't get out of saying how long he has been here as measured in the real world.'

'*The real world*? An interesting expression. Is the *griđ* not real? Are we in some netherworld of the gods, do you think? Or a fantasy world of the imagination?' Ingrid's face was expressionless as she carved, but I know a loaded question when I hear it.

'Honestly? I don't know. One minute I'm walking along a road and the next I wake up here. I don't know if I'm alive or dead or dreaming. I don't think I'm dead because I'm talking to you and drinking your mead and the food smells wonderful. Beyond that I haven't the first idea. I spoke loosely, but this isn't the world I'm used to.'

'The world you ran from?' asked Cathal.

'No. If I ran from anything it was what my life has become.'

'How do you understand the children's story you mentioned?' said Rowan. 'Not the wardrobe one, the other one, Rip Van Winkle.'

'I do not know that story,' said Ingrid, so I told it.

'Ah, I *do* know it,' said Cathal. 'Father spoke of fairy mounds and the Tuatha Dé Danann, and of unwary travellers entranced by music who didn't notice the years pass as they listened. And is the mountain to the south not Bheinn Shith?' I noticed a watchful look on Rowan's face.

'We had those tales too,' said William, approaching the table. He bowed to us all and looked at Ingrid for permission. 'The Kirk is keen to paint them as tricks of the Devil, naturally, and thus doth a lie become their truth and the innocent are punished for it. Did not King Herla spend but three days at a wedding feast only to find three hundred years had passed? It is, I believe, the same as the story told by Diogenes of Epimenides.'

'Forgive me my earlier weakness,' he said as he sat beside me. 'My rudeness was intolerable.'

'I was thoughtless.'

'Thank you, but you warned me. The fault is mine.'

'We'll have no talk of fault,' said Ingrid. 'Let's talk of food and drink and companionship and not embarrass our guest.'

I had been careful with the mead, but underestimated its potency. Through a thickening head and slurred speech, I put up a barricade of small talk to fend off questions about my life *outside*. At last, despite the excellent food and the free-flowing mead, weariness got the better of me and I asked to be excused, pointing to the bruised bump on my temple. And that was a genuine reason, but William's mention of King Herla had struck home: three days becoming three hundred years. Assuming I wasn't in a coma, I'd been in Sanctuary for two days.

Ingrid wrapped me in a great hug.

'I enjoyed tonight very much. I don't often entertain visitors with a discriminating palate. Your presence did me honour and I give you this as a token of friendship between us.' She pressed the silk scarf she had worn into my hand, and I felt a hard weight wrapped inside. 'No, don't open it now. Wait until morning and think of me then. It may serve you in time of need. And if we meet again, you can tell me all the things you so cleverly evaded tonight. And perhaps then we can consider the raven and the hart and the nature of the real world. And you must tell me a story – I am starved of them here.'

'Then remind me to tell you my favourite saga.'

'I'll treat that as a promise.'

I remembered to duck at the door, but the bottom of the lintel was now a clear five or six inches above my head. Further along the path, which was a lot shorter than it ought to be, I looked back at the black shape of a broch silhouetted against the hills. In the perfect sky, with no trace of light pollution, the glittering silk scarf of the Milky Way wrapped around the stars of the northern sky. The hanging greens and reds of the Northern Lights shimmered.

Dead or alive, for a fleeting moment I glimpsed heaven.

That night I dreamed of longships skimming the tops of the waves, and wolves running in the wilderness, rejoicing in the living air, unhindered by the snares and deceits of men.

CHAPTER 4

Raging thirst forced me to get up. I shuffled into the kitchen like an extra in a zombie movie. Mead on top of two cracks on the head will do that. Rowan was already up and cooking. I couldn't face the idea of eating, or so I thought, but made short work of a mug of herbal tea and a plate of leftover venison and vegetables with toast and fried eggs.

'Was I really drunk last night?'

She laughed.

'Not as bad as you might have been. You did well to avoid answering subtle questions. You had quite an impact on Cathal and William too.'

'Get away with you.'

'Cathal is more reflective this morning than I've ever known him, and Ingrid likes anyone who appreciates her mead.'

'You've seen them already?'

'Not everyone was in bed so long. Life goes on.'

'And William?'

'Hard to say. He doesn't give much away.'

'I found him hard to read.'

'His wife and daughters were strangled at a stake and their bodies burned together on the Castlehill in Edinburgh. William was made liable for the executioner's costs.'

Holy crap!

'He said it sometimes feels like he's only been here a few months. You didn't tell me it's taboo to ask people why they came here.'

'Was it a problem?'

'Just embarrassing. Cathal told me the story of his early life.'

'Then you already know more of his past than I've found out in a thousand of your years. That explains his mood this morning.'

'How does that work? That Cathal is still alive? That all of you are still alive? It sounded like he and Ingrid came here on the point of death.'

'I told you, it's a sanctuary.'

'But immortality ...'

'Oh no, don't get that idea. No one is immortal, not even me. Everything dies. That's how the universe works: you can't change it. Does that frighten you?'

'Dying? I don't think frighten is the right word somehow. I don't like the inevitability of awareness just stopping without a me being there anymore to know it has stopped. And there are things I'd like to do, people I'd like to see again, even if only to say a proper goodbye.'

'So if you could delay death?'

'I'd be a fool to say no, but I'd want to know the price.'

'Why should there be a price?'

'There's always a price.'

Rowan's face became very even, her eyes distant.

What price did you pay, Rowan? There was a twinge where my lump had been. Yes, it had turned out to be benign, but there's nothing like the prospect of personal extinction to alert your mind to every random signifier of mortality.

'Have you decided whether you'll stay?'

The change of subject threw me, but I already knew my

answer. Sanctuary, whatever it was, felt real, and I wanted to know it better, to get to know people. But I'd told my truth already: there *were* things I'd like to do and people I'd like to see. Venny, for one.

'I don't want to force a decision on you, but the longer you stay the more the issue of time here and on the outside becomes an issue,' she said.

'By my count, this is my third morning here.'

'We're not yet like King Herla. I think it might be different for you because I didn't bring you here.'

'Could I ever come back?'

'Well, you got here without my help, so I think you could if you wanted.'

She cleared the dishes and busied herself with chores, refusing my offer of help. I excused myself, saying I needed to clear my head.

The air chilled my lungs as I strolled, head clear, bruising and stiffness gone. The green of the hills and the tumbling clatter of the river worked their own enchantment, distracting me from the effort of the walk up to the waterfall.

The dipper down below was in and out of the pool. *Look at the birds*, Jesus is reported to have said, *they don't sow or reap or store, but they are fed*. I'd written sermons about that, and hadn't thought about it much. But the thing is, it isn't true: there's a lot to be said for sowing and reaping and storing up against hard times. Sometimes the birds don't get fed, and they freeze or starve to death as a result.

I sat on dry ground, my back against the mass of the standing stone, losing myself in the rumble of the rolling water below, hypnotised by the torrent over the lip of the fall, unchanged, never the same. Who wouldn't want to sit here every day and become part of it? It was beautiful and alluring, but it was not for me. It was the myth of Eden – the allure of the pure. Retreat to Sanctuary would be as much a trap as my office and title and discarded collar.

Nothing is immortal, Rowan had said, and I couldn't live out my remaining years in a lie, even though I had no idea what I would do with myself. If I was running from anything it was fear – not of a decision but of its consequences. Staying would not resolve anything and would not bring me peace.

The mountain hare, its white winter fur now flecked with brown, gave me side-eye for sitting in its spot. The standing stone vibrated against my back to the rhythm of the falls, as if charged by the water's energy. The whorls and sigils carved into it had a weird look, a faint glow: a trick of the light, no doubt.

Rowan came up to join me, guessed my decision, or read it on my face. Or maybe she'd known what it would be all along.

'So be it. It's best not to linger,' she said.

'I felt something last night, Rowan, just for a moment, under the stars, something I've wanted for a long time. And being here has brought a kind of clarity. But I have to go home and work it out there. And there are people I need to say a proper goodbye to if I can, to bring my life full circle while I'm alive and have that chance. I could be happy here, but not yet. I can't just run here to escape the truth.'

Something flickered behind her eyes. Understanding? Regret? Both, I thought.

'If I'd died and this were an afterlife of some kind, I'd have left so much behind unfinished, because that's what death does to everyone. Going back is a chance to fix things while I can. It's a gift, really.'

The hare bounded over to the stone when Rowan and I left, her arm through mine.

'I've just thought of something,' I said, as the chickens scattered by the gable of the cottage.

'What's that?'

'We all understood each other last night, even though no one there would understand modern English, and I certainly don't know Old Danish or William's version of Scots.'

'I wondered when you'd notice. It's part of the structure of Sanctuary: as long as you're here, conversation is natural.'

The inscriptions on the stone glimmered in my mind.

'Another question?' Rowan asked.

'No, I was just thinking about something I once read, about advanced technologies looking like magic to people who haven't seen them before.'

'There's no technology at work here, at least as I understand it to mean a mechanical contrivance. But they're right if they mean that "magic" isn't a helpful way of trying to explain things you don't understand.'

My walking boots and clothes felt strange. Rowan had already packed everything into my rucksack. I gave her my *Guidebook to Scotland* and Ordnance Survey map. Whatever I did with the remainder of my sabbatical, I doubted I'd need either again.

I tried not to look back as we left her house. The path to Strathmore and Ingrid's broch gave us a good view down the length of Loch Hope. The loch's water was lower than I remembered from the pictures in the guidebook, as if there'd been a prolonged drought. A distant wisp of smoke rose into the still air, from an unseen camp fire perhaps, or one of the other inhabitants I hadn't met. Rowan hadn't said how many others lived there.

'Will I really be able to come back?'

'I don't think we've seen the last of each other.'

'Why's that?'

'Because of how you got here. Because you got here at all.'

'There's a reason for everything, you mean?'

'No. Not everything has a reason. In fact, most things don't. Do you want to come back?'

'I think so. But, you know, it's that pleat-within-a-pleat thing – I don't even know where *here* is to come back to.'

'Time will tell, then. Time will tell.'

We walked on in silence, companionable. Ingrid and Cathal or William should have been out and about, but I couldn't see any of them.

'Where does Ingrid keep her hives?'

'Hives?'

'For the bees, for her mead.'

'She uses wild honey from the birch woods. Isn't that common?'

'No: disease is a problem with wild bees.'

'How can that be?'

'Humans. You asked about the population, the five and a half million in Scotland. There are nearly eight million million humans in the world, and we're destroying it. Our filth is everywhere. We're pushing things to extinction, like the wolves in Scotland, but much worse.'

'I can't imagine a world without wolves.'

'You know, when I first heard them on the road, instinct took over and I ran away, but when I heard them yesterday, I found them comforting.'

Her look was sharp.

'Yesterday?'

'Yes, just as I was drifting off for a nap.'

We were on the route where the old road would be on the *outside,* barely a track through the grass, interrupted by the occasional stream running off the slopes of Ben

Hope. The river broadened into Loch Hope, that Ingrid called Arnaboll.

'Who's Lallig? He didn't come last night.'

Rowan kept her eyes on the track and her voice steady, though her arm, still through mine, tensed.

'He's a recluse. He does what he wants and we leave each other alone.'

'Cathal said he lives in the forest south of here and talks in verse, like that voice I heard just before I came here.'

'Did he? We're almost at my boundary.'

'I don't see it.'

'Nevertheless, it is there. I have to tell you something important before you go: you can't come here, even for a short time, and not be changed. Just knowing I'm here changes things, even if your conscious memory of me fades.'

'How could I forget?'

'You will. I like to think that's why people don't come back, because they forget me.'

That seemed a profoundly melancholic thing.

'Is this the only way back, along this road?'

'Oh no. Remember where I said the boundary is?'

'Six miles in all directions from your house.'

'In the *outside*, yes. You can cross the boundary at any point. There were other ways, but they're not easy to find even if you know where and how to look. And here we are. I can go no further.'

'Can't, or won't?'

'Both. My borders are closed, even to me. At least, I thought they were. I don't know what would happen if I left for more than the odd hour or two every so often – and I haven't done that for a long time. What if Sanctuary collapsed and the others all turned to the dust of their years?'

'You avoided my question about Lallig.'

She nodded, but didn't offer any more information. I wanted to go then, to make as quick an exit as I could. I hugged her, and she seemed like a different person, younger, more potent. *What is she, that she can make a place like this?*

'Thank you,' I said. 'For everything.'

The hills and loch behind her faded. The air grew thinner, the sky pale. Shadows shifted as light coalesced around and within her.

'Change is coming. It's in the smell of the water and the taste of the wind. Until the next time.'

And she was once again the Rowan I thought I knew, waving as she receded into an indefinite middle distance. Wolves panted and sang, patrolling the border. This time, I had no fear and turned to walk between the worlds.

CHAPTER 5

Dim light. Duvet. Smell of chicken cooking. I was in my underwear. No saline drips, no bleeping machines monitoring me, no bustle of nurses, no smell of antiseptic. Not hospital, then.

'Welcome back to the land of the living.' A stranger sat by the bed. 'I'm Dr Baynes. How do you feel?'

'Like I slept in too long. My mouth tastes funny. Where am I?'

'You're in Katriona Mackay's guest room. You've been quite ill. I'm just going to check you over, if you don't mind.'

She was old-school, nearing retirement I guessed. I'd met doctors like her before, their shrewd diagnostic sense honed by years of general practice in isolated communities. She put a stethoscope to my chest and back, took my blood pressure and temperature, looked at my eyes and tongue, and declared I was on the mend.

'Mind, I'm waiting for the results of the bloods I sent to Inverness – they should be back tomorrow. Your temperature's still up, but not enough to worry about. What do you remember?'

My mind was blank, just impressions, traces.

'It's fuzzy. I got to my rented cottage, then went out for a walk. When I got back, I didn't feel well. I remember my fingers curling tight into my palms and I couldn't stop them.

I must have fainted, I suppose. I had weird dreams.'

'I'm not surprised: you were delirious for a while, and quite dehydrated by the time I got here.'

'What happened?'

'Quite a lot of people want to ask you that same question, but you're in no state for any excitement yet.'

'Can I get up? Get dressed?'

'Yes, but take it easy. You'll probably feel quite weak for a while. Katriona's got chicken soup and fish on the go. Eat what you can and drink plenty of fluids, and I'll check in again tomorrow.'

Chickens, at a cottage. Why does that mean something?

'It's a shame we don't have any of Katriona's nan's honey. That cured everything and anything,' she said.

'There was mead in my dream.'

'Was there? I like a drop of that myself. But no alcohol for a day or so yet.'

The soup and fish were excellent. Mrs Mackay and I sat in the conservatory, not quite sure what to say to each other, looking out at the distant white triangles of yachts in the open water of Loch Eriboll.

'Thank you for having me.' Hardly sparkling conversation, but I wanted to break the awkwardness.

'Nan would turn in her grave, God rest her, if I turned you out to a bed and breakfast.'

'But I've a long let on the cottage.'

'You did have, but that all changed, didn't it? I suppose police and newspapers and TV people will be all over us again now you're back.'

'I'm sorry, what?'

'All that time and no one could find you. Everyone thought you were dead. You were on the telly and everything. Then you just showed up like nothing had happened and fell over.'

'All what time?'

'You got here last November and turned up again on the 1st of May.'

'Get away with you. Where would I go for nearly six months?'

I flopped onto the settee, shivering though I wasn't cold. My arms, legs and shoulders ached, as though I'd picked up a virus. A thick blanket was draped over the back of the settee, and I wrapped it around myself, curling my legs beneath me. The folds of the blanket didn't look right – like pleats that hadn't been ironed properly, curling in on themselves. I felt dizzy, groggy. Mrs Mackay brought me a hot tea, but it tasted strange and bitter. Why was there no mint?

I had the strangest feeling I'd forgotten something important, forgotten somewhere I wanted to be. The cottage was wrong: the light switches, the sound of the radio, the electric cooker, the kettle, the hum of the fridge.

Where are the peat fire and candles?

'You don't look well.'

What's happening to me?

'You just settle down for a while. You're still not right.'

I woke up with a duvet on top of the blanket, a pillow under my head. The evening light played across the distant summit and flanks of Ben Hope above Sanctuary.

Sanctuary. Where did that name come from? Why was it important?

'What was that?'

'Pardon?'

'You muttered something.'

'A' Chomraich.'

'You have the Gaelic? That's a long way south, down at Applecross. Did you go all the way down there?'

'Last thing I remember, I was on the road to Yrreddell.'

'Where's that?'

'The old broch at Dun Dornaigil.'

'They searched there.'

'I went into the hills for a bit. I had my tent.'

'For all that time, in those blizzards?'

Blizzards?

'Were the newspapers and TV a problem?'

'Och no, not for the most part. I think there was only one that was a nuisance, said her name was Hartley – you know, like the jam. There was something not right about her, like those New Age weirdos we used to get.' She sniffed. 'Nan would never have stood for it. She used to say that road played tricks on you, played games. Some days, she said, it liked to be three or four miles longer than it needed to be, just for the mischief of it. She had the Sight, of course.'

There was something about the way she said *the Sight*, like she was trying to tell me something without coming out and saying it.

'Nan said the Sight was a curse, not a gift, that she never wanted it, never wanted to know who would die, who would never have a bairnie of their own. Daddy said the Sight skipped generations, that I might have it too, but I don't want it either. You should be careful what you say when they ask you questions. Can't have them thinking you're not right in the head.'

No. Can't have them thinking that.

'Where's my car?'

'The police have it. They'll be wanting to talk to you. That nice bishop as well.'

'I should call Venny, too.'

Why did I think of her?

'Who's that?'

'Someone I used to know.'

The Rt Rev Dr Sydney Hair and I had last met to agree that my leave of absence should be described as a sabbatical, for personal reflection and study.

He's an odd man, unprepossessing, with a handshake like wilted lettuce. His doctorate is honorary, but he likes to use the title, I think because he wasn't able to do the real thing for reasons I've never asked. His official residence sags under the scattered detritus of years of compromise, an agreeable reward for a life spent not making waves, though he sometimes shows glimpses of the intellect for which he was known as a student.

His door is opened in working hours by a pair of stout, sensible shoes containing a stout, sensible housekeeper called Dorothy, who favours me with the special sniff she keeps for those of whom she disapproves. We know who we are, we who are offered the supermarket teabag in a mug rather than Ceylon leaves mashed in a warmed porcelain teapot.

Sydney, never Sid, likes to meet on ground of his own choosing, often his drawing room lined with volumes of aggressively German theology. He and his partner Geoffrey, whom we weren't supposed to talk about, had furnished the room from a 1920s catalogue of ecclesiastical chintz without any concessions to modernity. All electronic equipment was banished to the office across the corridor, and I took care to set my phone to silent whenever I went.

When I'd gone to see him about taking a sabbatical, I'd sat on a worn settee facing a high-backed leather chair on which Sydney had perched in episcopal splendour. I'd fished the teabag out of the mug as we exchanged the usual pleasantries, the phony war before we got down to it.

He hadn't said as much, but he didn't seem surprised that I wanted a break. He'd already made contingency plans: a locum was rustled up with disconcerting ease. The only sticking point was money. He'd wanted to cut my stipend in my absence. I'd held out for full pay, pointing out that a sabbatical for prayer and study was hardly a novelty, and referred to recent case law with a specificity that led to him to concede that discretion might be the better part of valour, and certainly better than a public airing at a tribunal, with the attendant publicity. It was all very civilised.

I called him on Mrs Mackay's landline when I was well enough, still coming to terms with having mislaid nearly six months somewhere.

'That really wasn't very helpful, you know,' he said.

'But it was the whole point: to get away from it all for prayer and reflection.'

'You didn't say anything about disappearing off the face of the earth. It's caused no end of nuisance, I'm afraid. Admirable, I'm sure, but hardly realistic in this day and age, and quite irresponsible.'

'Do not be conformed to this world but be transformed by the renewal of your mind.'

'What?'

'Romans 12.2: *Do not be conformed to this world, but be transformed by the renewal of your mind.*'

'Oh Lord, you haven't caught religion, have you?'

'I threw it back into a loch to swim another day.'

'You know perfectly well what I mean. It's not your style, never was.'

'No, Sydney, I haven't caught religion. I was thinking a lot about my vocation.'

'Ah, now you're making sense. When will you be back?'

'I still have a little of my sabbatical to go.'

'I know, and you might be better off where you are, out of the way of reporters and the like, but my advice is to come back as soon as you can. We have to talk about what you'll do now.'

'What about St. Joseph's? They'll expect me back.'

'Oh no they won't, it's not your parish anymore. When we all thought the worst, we had to fill the vacancy. Bridget Halliburton has St Joseph's permanently now.'

'Oh. I mean—'

'Yes, quite. You see? Not helpful. It *would* be helpful for you to come back now and sort this mess out – easier done here than there.'

'But my things – my books and clothes. My other stuff.'

'All in storage.'

'But where will I go?'

'Oh, don't worry about that, I'll put you into Weston House for now as acting chaplain. It's the ideal place to recuperate. You can help look after the students for what's left of term, then we'll have the summer to work something else out.'

I couldn't say I was thrilled by the prospect. Weston House had acquired a reputation since the scandal and investigation. Student numbers were down, and a new principal and vice principal had been put in a year or two back to revive its fortunes, if they could. I'd encountered the principal, David Sharpe-Thompson, at various events but only knew the vice principal by name – Dr Eithne Simpson.

'I'll let you know my plans once I've got my car back from the police and finished up here.'

'Right-ho. That reminds me: your credit cards were all suspended or cancelled. Unfortunate. Dorothy will let the bank know you'll be in touch to get them sorted. Best of luck with the police, can't help you there. You can give some thought to your future on your way down. I've put you on the diocesan prayer list by the way.'

'Thank you, Sydney, that's a great comfort.'

There were two of them: Detective Constable MacKenzie, a no-nonsense woman, a soft Highland lilt to her voice, and her senior colleague, Detective Inspector Buchan, a Glaswegian who looked like he missed the old days. They must have attended the same courses as me on how to have sensitive discussions with unusual customers. They weren't happy when I said I couldn't remember where I'd been. They sat back on Mrs Mackay's settee, scepticism all over their faces.

'How could you be away for six months without noticing there was a search on?' said Buchan. 'It was everywhere.'

'I came here to get away from it all,' I said, squirming.

'Lots of people do, but they don't disappear off the face of the earth. Your phone dropped off the grid, and wherever you were you'd need food, so you'd have to shop or have someone do it for you, so the headlines in all the papers should have tipped you the wink, no?'

I shrugged, helpless.

'The thing is, Reverend Cant, there are some checks we do as a matter of course and one of them is bank records. You paid Mrs Mackay seven months' rent in advance, and you bought groceries in Tain, and petrol, but then nothing at all. That's why we thought a walker would probably find your remains in a remote glen one day. That, and the weather.'

Shit! They'd probably pulled my internet history, and seen all my searches about mental health. They'd have trawled my medical records too.

'I'm in some difficulty, Inspector.'

'We're all agreed on that, Reverend.'

'My job encourages, requires actually, reflection and meditation. Some of us can do that in the middle of the city, but I can't. I need peace and quiet and no distractions.'

'Like those monks who used to live in the desert?'

Copts.

'Less extreme than that.'

'Well, I'll put that on the file, but I have to warn you that it might come back to haunt you. The thing is, if anything else should happen to you in the future, we could be less inclined to investigate if we thought you were off on pilgrimage somewhere.'

'Retreat, not pilgrimage.'

'Whatever, you understand me, I'm sure. We don't like wasting police time and money, and you've wasted a lot of my time and an awful lot of the public's money with your *retreat.*'

I put on my contrite face.

'Point taken. If I've learned one lesson from all of this, it's to leave a note with someone what my plans are.'

'That would be just grand, Reverend, and would save a lot of fuss and bother. There's something else, and it might cause offence.'

'Ask away.'

'Is there anything about where you were or who you were with that would compromise you, something you're not telling us?'

'I'm sorry?'

'Your story makes zero sense, frankly. I don't believe you're telling me everything you can, and that pisses me off. Naturally, because it's my job, I wonder if you've got something to hide. You must have been somewhere, and to be there without using your bank cards means someone else did all that for you. Someone whose identity you might want to hide due to the, ah … nature of your profession.'

'You mean a secret love nest? No Inspector, I can say with a completely clear conscience that there is nothing like that.'

His face gave nothing away.

'Thank you, Reverend Cant. I'm sorry to say you'll likely be hearing from us again.'

I left three days later for the long drive south. In my mind, it was only two and a half weeks since I'd got there. I hadn't paid much attention to the scenery on the trip north, I'd kept my eyes on the road and my ears on the music mix I'd put together.

Driving south wasn't like that. I kept looking in my mirror, haunted by a feeling something I'd forgotten was tailgating me, but there were only campervans and motorcyclists. And it was weird to sit in my old VW again. Normally I felt comfortable in it, used to its little quirks, but I felt self-conscious behind the wheel, as though I were still a new driver, flinching at the cars and lorries on the other side of the road, stopping regularly to let traffic behind me pass.

The journey stretched, and it was as if someone else was behind my eyes, someone who noticed the junk scattered across the landscape, the sandwich packets and drink cans on the verges, the metallic foliage of burned-out cars, rusting rotovators and discarded washing machines, the tumble-down buildings with sagging roofs and smashed windows, every available surface daubed with graffiti. The outskirts of towns, next to ring roads and service stations, were full of dull grey people and dull grey houses in dull grey estates under a dull grey sky, patronised by the dull grey intellects of dull grey politicians. Mechanical excavators trenched the remnants of the landscape, sowing the seeds of a future harvest of industrial failure and dereliction.

As the light faded, pools of blackness multiplied, deep shadows cast by absent light. Every town and village had people shivering in shop doorways, wrapped in damp sleeping bags, coughing into their hands.

I knew these places. I'd worked in them, and tried to find God in them. Shadowlands, C.S. Lewis called this world, the places that aren't Narnia, like St Paul seeing through a glass darkly. The thought resonated and I didn't know why.

How do you lose six months? What just happened?

I spent the night in a cheap hotel south of Newcastle, and arrived at Weston House the following afternoon, driving between wrought-iron gates and into the parking place marked *Chaplain.*

The college was a mish-mash of mid-Victorian and faux-Gothic, with 1960s concrete additions, best described as low-budget modernist, that I suspected would be damp and ghastly to live in.

Blurred faces in shadows behind windows waited for their first glimpse of this new specimen dropped into their lives, wondering who I might be, what I would bring with me, what I could offer.

I couldn't answer.

CHAPTER 6

Christine, the college secretary, walked me through a decent-looking library to a back stair leading down to the basement flat that was my new home, apologising for the noise the old stairs made. There was a pronounced creak and squeak from the fourth step from the bottom.

'Father Sharpe-Thompson and Dr Simpson asked me to pass on their apologies. They're both out this evening but look forward to meeting you tomorrow. You have a hall and main door through here. The telephone is old, but it works. It's 9 for an outside line, and press one of these buttons for Father Sharpe-Thompson, Dr Simpson or me. They light up if one of us calls you or if their extension is in use.'

Like every Church property I'd ever lived in, the flat had a musty smell, but Christine assured me that the heating worked and had been recently serviced. In the living room and spare bedroom were the boxes and packing cases that contained all my worldly possessions from St Joseph's vicarage, only two miles across town, but a world away from the college.

'All the keys are in the kitchen by the kettle, and I keep duplicates in the office if you mislay them. Evening meal is at six and breakfast is between seven and eight-thirty in the refectory. Just go back the way we came through the

73

college, straight on, turn right and follow your nose down the stairs. There's usually a buffet lunch set out from twelve. Do you mind if I dash off? I have to get the kids to music lessons and I'm late already.'

How on earth had I come to be a college chaplain? I hadn't applied for the post, had no particular training for it, and had no idea what the job involved. I fetched my bags from the car and left them in the main bedroom. Someone had made up the bed for me. There was neither tea nor coffee in the flat, but there was toilet paper. I did what I always do in a new place: I went for a walk.

The streets were busy with the last of the Saturday shoppers making their way home, masses of bodies moving on multiple trajectories, arcing around me. The hair and flesh and clothes, the smell of perfume and deodorant, the coughs and sneezes, were a physical assault. The constant noise of traffic, of canned music blaring from shops, buffeted me. I wanted to be somewhere else.

I bought a coffee and muffin from a stand near the entrance to a park and sat on a bench in a quiet spot by a rain-swollen river. When I was little, I'd have crouched by its edge with a toyshop fishing net on a cane, looking for minnows or sticklebacks. Now the banks were fenced to keep children out, though not old supermarket trolleys and bicycle frames. Drinks tins and plastic packaging lined the muddy shore.

One or two people sat on the other benches: a mother with a small child, an old man feeding unshelled nuts to grey squirrels. A dog ran to the water's edge through a gap in the fence and barked at ducks on the opposite bank. Across the park, two tents were erected. I pulled my collar up and drained the lukewarm dregs of my coffee.

The bench was uncomfortable and chilly out of the sunlight, but I let my mind roll with the brown rolling river.

The muttering of traffic and people faded behind the soft syllables of the water. Whatever else was happening in my life, at least I had a roof over my head, regular meals and money in the bank. I wasn't down the pit like Dad's ancestors or already dead of typhus in a Westmoreland slum like my four-times Great-grandmother Margaret. And I wasn't living in a tent in the park.

Although other benches were free, a man sat beside me, putting down his supermarket bag, making sure his sliced white bread and full fat milk didn't spill out. He didn't look at me, but leaned forward, chin on thin-veined hands, hands on the crook of his walking stick.

'Fucking wasters, eh?'

'I'm sorry?'

'Over there. Fucking wasters, the lot of them. Should have been smothered at birth. Would have been a kindness.'

'What on earth are you on about?'

'Those inadequates over there. The police should do something about it, but they won't, just spout politically correct bollocks about community outreach and social care. Waste of fucking time, they just breed and breed and breed and get their benefits and keep decent people out of houses.'

'Decent people ...'

His tight face knotted around the discoloured skin of his nose.

'You know, like you and me, living in the real world. Hard-working, with families.' He leaned closer and dropped his voice to a conspiratorial undertone: 'White.'

I thought about mentioning my Kenyan great-grandfather, asking how people in tents keep anyone out of a house. I walked away instead.

The kiosk was closing but I bought four coffees and a bag of sandwiches that were about to be thrown out. The tents looked cheap, probably from a supermarket. They would be shower-proof but I wouldn't want to overnight in one in heavy rain. A makeshift washing line ran between them, good quality, but tatty, underwear drying, presumably rinsed in the river hung from it. Someone took care of themself, then.

There were two women and two men, of mixed ethnicities. One of them, a striking-looking Black woman in old jeans and a hoodie with the hood pulled up, still in her teens by the look of her, and in a tent to herself, watched me approach. Her look was suspicious but not hostile. The others, their tent flap open, were out of their heads on something.

'Sorry to intrude; I just brought you some coffee and sandwiches to keep away the chills. Sorry I can't do more. How are you for hot food?'

'We'll get food on Sunday down the Mission.' Her voice was soft, a Wiltshire accent overlying a Caribbean lilt.

'Where's that?'

'The old church hall behind the Eastgate. They do a hot meal on a Sunday.'

'Are your friends OK?'

She pursed her lips, shrugged.

'Probably.'

'Right then, if you're sure. Have a good evening.'

The man who'd sat next to me walked past, glaring, knuckles white on his stick.

'Fucking do-gooders,' he muttered.

'What's wrong with doing good?'

I checked the map on my phone and went to find the Mission in case anyone was there. The door was open.

'Sorry, we're closed.' He wore jeans and a well-worn sweatshirt, and was setting up trestle tables. His hair was tied back but strands had slipped over his spectacles. He kept sweeping it aside as he talked.

'That's OK, I wanted to ask if you could use any help. I believe you feed people here on a Sunday.'

'Oh! What can you do? Can you cook?'

'Not for a crowd, but I can clean and tidy and wash dishes or whatever's needed.'

'Can you be here Sunday morning around eleven? We open the doors to feed people at twelve-thirty. I'm Davy by the way.'

We shook hands.

'Eleven it is.'

The streets were empty of shoppers now, the office workers on their way home. It was the turn of the early birds at the pubs, getting tanked up for clubbing, voices loud, clothes louder: no tin of cheap beer and a smoke in a tent for them, these were the middle classes, intent on spend, spend, spending until they were out of their heads on designer spirits, angling to go home with any willing stranger.

The pubs and clubs were fluorescent splashes in the half light, guarded by burly Cerberuses with earpieces and black suits, muttering into radios. In dark spaces between the neon, people settled down in damp sleeping bags in shop doorways, hoping it wouldn't rain, hoping it was just a cough, hoping they'd wake up in the morning.

I stocked up on basic toiletries and groceries in a corner shop. The college was on the fringes of the city, ten minutes' walk from St Agatha's, the massive cathedral that, as the diocesan annual report and accounts always made clear, cost a fortune to heat and maintain but could never be sold. There was a commotion in the cathedral grounds, where someone was being ejected into the twilight through a side door.

'You were told before. Next time it's the police.' A late-middle-aged man was glaring at a woman who wore a tatty coat and carried half a dozen supermarket bags stuffed with blankets and clothes. He was balding and red-faced, and wore a black cassock with a large wooden cross on a leather thong around his neck.

'Is there a problem?' I said.

The man looked me up and down, taking in my cargo trousers and the old jumper beneath my waterproof jacket.

'Just asking our friend here to leave. This is the House of God, not a doss-house.'

'Huh. Is she a moneychanger?'

'What?'

'Matthew chapter 21: the cleansing of the temple.'

'Don't come the smart arse with me. I know your sort.'

'Do you now?' I took the packet of sandwiches and apple I'd bought for my supper out of my carrier bag and gave them both to the woman.

'Here. It's the best I can do just now.' I felt in my pocket and pulled out a ten-pound note. 'I hope this helps.'

'Idiot: it'll just go on booze and drugs.'

I ignored him. 'I'm sorry I can't do more, but I've only just got here. Go in peace and be well.'

The man tapped my shoulder with more force than I thought polite.

'Who the hell do you think you are, interfering? This is Church business, none of your concern.'

'I'm the new chaplain at Weston House, and I'll decide what's my concern.'

I slept well in my new bed and had my first rinse under the tepid shower. Christine buzzed through to ask if I'd accept a call from a journalist. I said no, I hadn't had breakfast yet, but asked her to take a message.

Call me naïve, but I couldn't think why the press would be interested in me: where was the story? Someone who was assumed to be missing turned out not to be. I wandered through to my small kitchen and made toast and a mug of tea. An ancient transistor radio sat on the windowsill and I switched it on for the news headlines, but couldn't engage with anything. I busied myself unpacking the boxes in the living room for a while, but my mind wouldn't settle and my body was listless.

There were plenty of second-hand bookshops in the city. Long experience had taught me that I could lose myself there for several hours, especially now I'd sorted out my bank accounts and had a live debit card – and my back pay had come through. It was in the third bookshop, deep in the antiquarian section, my mind far away, that I wondered how the journalist had known I was at the college.

Back at the flat I found phone messages from the bishop and David Sharpe-Thompson. Sydney wanted me to check in with him when I got a chance. He meant on receipt, but I didn't feel like it. David asked if I could drop round to his office after supper.

A note from the journalist asked if I would care to talk about my 'disappearance', given the significant public interest at the time and the 'wall of silence' since my return. It gave her email and mobile phone details, and her name: Martina Hartley. The name sounded familiar, but I couldn't think where I'd heard it before.

Whoever packed my things had simply stuffed them in wherever they would fit. There were items I'd forgotten, stuff I'd taken away when I'd cleared my parents' house and never looked at since. Toys and books, of course, souvenirs they'd kept on the old sideboard in our living room, and photo albums of relatives I didn't recognise. There were school photos of me, almost all with Venny somewhere in the background, on my arm or clowning, the early ones in school uniform, the later ones when she discovered punk. She'd so much wanted to look like Patti Smith, but she was too short. It made me smile even after more than forty years. I should get in touch with her, it had been on my mind to do that since I'd woken up in Katriona Mackay's spare bedroom, but what would I say? It was so long since we'd talked, since the night we fell out, and I didn't have up-to-date contact details for her anyway.

The thought nagged, nonetheless, that I could at least look for her online, see if I could find out what she was up to.

I put the photos away and lost myself in setting up my HiFi, isolating components, cleaning connections, adjusting the position of the speakers and the settee to establish a decent listening position. I checked my turntable hadn't been damaged in packing and carriage, then found my spirit level, digital scales and cartridge protractor to set it up properly.

I considered putting on one of the clerical shirts and collars I'd unpacked, and donning the uniform for supper, like the man at the cathedral in his cassock and cross, who would never have dreamed to speak to me like that if he'd thought I had any authority or status. *And is that what being a priest means, authority, status?* The question buzzed around my head until I threw all my collars and stocks and clerical shirts into the kitchen bin and went to supper without a second thought.

It seemed to me that the best way to get to know the students, ahead of any formal meetings, would be to chat with them in easy settings. The students I sat next to kept their questions about my recent history to themselves, and conversation was more by way of gentle sparring to size me up. I did the same, trying to figure out how fiercely intellectual they were, who might be hiding undiagnosed depressive issues, who looked like they'd do well in a parish, who might find it difficult, who was open, who was closed.

They talked about the parishes they had placements in. They worried about how to talk to teenagers and pensioners, how to communicate with people with whom they felt no connection.

'Let me tell you about Miss Boards,' I said. 'Betty to her friends. Betty says she was eighteen or nineteen when she saw Pink Floyd and Soft Machine in the UFO club in 1967. She was a secretary at a music publisher in Soho, and over the next decade saw every major rock band on the scene, and slept with most of them. She was at the Isle of Wight in '69 and '70 and Glastonbury Fayre in 1971. If she really likes you she'll show you the cast of an erect penis she keeps at the back of her drinks cabinet. She says it's Jimi Hendrix and a gift from Cynthia Plaster Caster herself – best not use a college computer to search for Cynthia, by the way. Betty grows dwarfed cannabis plants in her greenhouse between her heritage tomatoes, courgettes and cucumbers, and her home baking is the first to sell out at parish jumble sales. Her main complaints about modern living are that she can't get good acid anymore and there are executive homes where her favourite mushroom field used to be.

'Last time I saw her, she was working through downloads of the Grateful Dead's 1972 European Tour, which she saw in Paris, London and Bickershaw, trying to decide on her favourite version of "Dark Star". So, lesson number one about pensioners, like any other parishioners, is don't deal in stereotypes, talk to the person.'

I surprised myself: maybe I did have a role to play in their education, a pastoral role quite separate from my personal struggles with belief. I said so to David Sharpe-Thompson over a glass of sherry later.

'Oh, good. The thing is, you see, and I might as well be up-front, Dr Simpson and I weren't consulted on your coming here.'

'Neither was I. I thought I'd be back at St Joe's. It's all happened very fast.'

'Yes. St *Joseph's.*' The heavy emphasis was to correct my informality, I guessed. 'Look here, I ought to tell you it wasn't an entirely popular decision. And there's a journalist nosing around too. We really don't need any more publicity: we're trying to steady the ship, don't you know.'

'She called asking if I wanted to talk. I don't. I have nothing to say. I don't know how she found out I'm here.'

'An ear to gossip probably, it wasn't a big secret. Look, I'm not sure quite how to ask this, but is there anything I should know? Anything that will cause a problem?'

I hadn't taken to Sharpe-Thompson on previous encounters. I'd found him oleaginous around people he wanted to impress and condescending to everyone else. I remembered him on the fringes of diocesan synods, arguing with unusual passion against the ordination of women, then undergoing a remarkable reversal of opinion when he saw the way the ecclesiastical winds were blowing. He was known for the precision with which he celebrated Eucharist, his grand theatrical gestures and movements, his scowling at trivial errors in ceremonial when others officiated. I couldn't imagine why he was put in charge of ordinands, especially in Weston House. The scuttlebutt was he was hoping for a hat and stick in a quiet diocese somewhere, and had friends in high places who could arrange it.

'Any improprieties, you mean? No. I can say hand on heart that there's been nothing improper. I just needed to spend some time off-grid.'

'Well, do let me know if the need strikes you again.'

'I might as well be honest and say it could. I took the sabbatical because I was unhappy in the parish, so being here is an unexpected blessing in a way. I'm sixty and need to plan for retirement. My trip helped me think.'

'I heard there was some trouble at St Agatha's last night?'

Gossip travels fast.

'No, no trouble. I helped a woman who was getting thrown out. I gave her some food and cash to see her safe.'

'I heard you ranted and raved and quoted scripture. Poor Martin was mortified when he found out who you were. It was quite unfair of you.'

I sipped the sherry. It was terrible.

'Did you ever hear of Roland Walls?'

'No, who was he?'

'He turned up one day at my college when I was an ordinand. I thought he was a tramp and fumbled for small change. But Roland was the guest celebrant at the Eucharist that evening. He was a priest, and a lecturer in theology, and formed a religious community outside Edinburgh at Roslin: the Community of the Transfiguration, they called themselves. They adopted a life of poverty. I've never forgotten him or the lesson I learned that day: you never know who you're talking to. That poor woman was homeless and hungry and in need, and for all I know she was a priest too, not that it matters. I did what I could for her.'

'Well, that's all very charitable and noble, but you must be more careful now you're here and working for me. Things are very sensitive, and we're trying to keep a low profile, if you get my meaning. The last thing we need is for people to take an interest in us. It wouldn't be fair on the students.'

'You're saying I shouldn't minister to the poor where I find them?'

'That's unfair. I didn't say that, but there's a time and place, you understand, a time and a place and proper procedures. There's a diocesan charitable trust that's always looking for board members, for instance. They do good work for the poor. Always on the lookout for new trustees.'

'Didn't it invest a lot of money overseas in sweat shops?'

'Everyone makes mistakes. Still, a good return to the fund, I shouldn't wonder.'

'Indeed. I'm sure lessons were learned going forward.'

He gave me a look, not sure if I was taking the piss.

There was a knock at the study door, and a petite woman entered, wearing a pastel-peach clerical shirt with collar and a business-like trouser suit, her prematurely salt 'n' pepper hair pulled into a bun. She introduced herself as Eithne Simpson, the vice principal of the college, and declined a sherry, no doubt because she'd tried it before.

We spent the next half hour or so working out roles and responsibilities. I agreed to talk to each of the students over the next few days and get to know them. I had no teaching role for the remainder of the academic year. David tutored in liturgy and ritual, and Eithne taught Christian Ethics part-time at the local university, specialising in the sociology of cults and sects. Neither had recent experience in a parish.

'Have you any thoughts on what you might teach next year, if you're still here?' Eithne asked.

'All the things we weren't taught as ordinands, I think. Something more relevant.'

They exchanged glances.

'Such as?'

'We were taught liturgy and ritual and how to sing Evensong. They taught us how to churn out sermons and fit them around the liturgical calendar so you could recycle the material as the years turned and the congregation forgot that you'd said it all before. They taught us the correct sequence of putting on robes and when to genuflect and how to hold the wafer so it breaks into three neat pieces. They taught us that it's fine to be radical but not radical enough to be an embarrassment – no overturning of the moneychangers' tables or any of that nonsense, nothing to make people take an interest in us.'

I caught a nervous look in David's eye and felt an unworthy flare of satisfaction.

'They didn't teach us about loneliness, the constant regret, the unshakeable self-doubt and imposter syndrome, the sexist comments and letters, or the never-ending pointless meetings that achieve precisely nothing. They didn't tell me what to do when, after thirty years, I stood in front of a congregation wondering if they even cared just how hollow I felt inside.'

They looked at the carpet. David sipped his dreadful sherry in silence. For a moment I saw through his façade, saw him as someone alone and lost. Haunted, almost.

'Um, we were thinking you could maybe lead a class on spirituality? You know, maintaining a personal faith in the parish context? Something like that? And practical ceremonial,' he said at last.

'Ceremonial?'

'Yes, the correct words and gestures of the Eucharist, getting it right.'

'Why is that important?'

'Isn't that an important part of liturgy, getting the ritual right?'

'No, that's cultic thinking imported from pagan Rome, the notion that if you say the magic words and dance the little finger dance God will snap to and do as we ask. That's ritual as magic, not ritual as participation.'

'I must say, I find that a particularly unhelpful attitude. You should meet our sacristan, Gavin, when you get a chance, by the way. He's very good on this sort of thing.'

Later, David took me aside and lowered his voice as if letting me in on an each-way certainty at Newmarket. 'Listen, I don't want to be rude, but I wanted to have a word about your attire.'

For most male clergy a black clerical shirt and collar with an off-the-peg High Street suit was the norm, but Sharpe-Thompson invariably dressed with a fetishist's eye for exact detail. He was one of the few people I'd ever seen wearing a full, hooded clerical cloak.

'Here's the thing: I know you had a certain reputation in the parish, but I think it's important we maintain a standard of professional decorum, you know? Clerical collars and formal wear, set the students a proper example.'

'Well, thank you for the advice, David, I'll keep it in mind.'

'I'd rather we used formal titles too. I encourage the students to call me Father Sharpe-Thompson, and Eithne is Dr Simpson, of course. Would you mind if—?'

'Yes, actually – yes I would. My name will be fine. Thank you for the sherry.'

I disconnected my phone from the charger in my flat and, without thinking, turned it on. Twenty minutes later the device had downloaded 2,674 emails and 573 text messages, many to advise that my voicemail was full.

I turned it off again and went through to the living room and found my CD of Bruckner's *Mass in D Minor*. Sorting the CDs and records into alphabetical order was an urgent task for the next day. I wanted a single malt, but had none. I'd left an unopened Ledaig I'd saved for a rainy day in the vicarage, but it had disappeared. I thought about searching online for Venny – why wouldn't that thought go away? – but decided it would wait until morning. Another day wouldn't make any difference after all this time. I sat in the sweet spot in front of the speakers and allowed myself to drift, until I woke up in the same place at two in the morning and went to bed.

I woke in the night with my sheets and duvet in a tangle, with a fading memory of wind and rain and a dream about wolves; of uncials floating in a bog, majuscule and minuscule without context or order, their meaning fluid; of letters rising up a chimney from the ashes of paper. My legs ached, as though I'd been out on the hills. I looked around my bedroom, not knowing where I was or why there were walls around me, or why a taste of fresh blood lingered at the root of my tongue.

CHAPTER 7

A bundle of letters was in my pigeonhole, redirected from St Joseph's. Among the offers of insurance and invitations to seminars on pension planning were letters from my occasional stalker and from the Health Board chiding me for missing my annual check-up at the oncology unit. I thought I'd cancelled the appointment before leaving for Sutherland, but I was still registered with my old GP and made a fresh appointment, then went to the pharmacy for a urine sample bottle.

The stalker's note was more of the usual:

Dear Miss Cant.
I've had the great pleasure of observing, many times, how prettily you fill out a cassock, for an older lady. If you ever want a good hard cock inside you, I'll be happy to oblige.
Yours in anticipation
An admirer.

It went into the bin, too routine now to cause upset.

Sydney called about the journalist.

'I'm going to politely decline. Sleeping dogs, and all that.'

'Your call, of course, but you wouldn't want her thinking there's something to hide, eh? Anyway, I won't influence your decision. While you're on, I heard there was a fuss at the cathedral the other night.'

Is this going to haunt me?

'Nothing in particular, just a woman who deserved better.'

'You gave Martin quite a fright when you told him who you were.'

'It shouldn't matter.'

'Quite. But still, maybe time to dig out the collars now you're back in harness, eh? Save any more misunderstandings. And be gentle with David, too, he has enough on his plate.'

'I'm sorry?'

'Something about not helping the poor? Best not rock the boat, it was a rush job to put you there and I'm sure it'll take some getting used to for everyone.' *What's he trying to tell me?* 'David tells me that you're interested in the charitable trust – he's been trying to get out of that for ages, ever since that dreadful faux pas with the child labour in Malaysia.'

'Probably best to hold off on that front until I'm a bit more settled and can make longer-term decisions,' I said.

I was bombarded with system messages telling me that everything on my laptop was out of date. I left it to do its thing and went to the kitchen bin. I emptied used tea leaves over the dumped clerical shirts and collars, sealed the bag, and chucked it in the college bins. I rummaged through the cases in the bedroom until I found my battered old M-65 field jacket with a woodland camouflage pattern, and hung it on a hook by the back door, determined to wear it for as long as possible before summer made it too warm. *Formal attire*, indeed. I pinned a Grateful Dead badge, a gift from Betty Boards, to the lapel.

When the laptop was ready, I dealt with the emails by deleting them unread, just as I'd deleted all the texts on my phone. I went back to unpacking and, in a side pocket of my rucksack, I found two glasses cases, one for normal glasses, the other for prescription sunglasses. I'd completely forgotten about them and hadn't missed them, not even on the long drive south. The bridge of one pair looked new – and made of silver?

How could I forget something like that? And why didn't I need them anymore?

My journal was on top of a silk wrap. Two pages of the journal had been torn out, but for the life of me I couldn't remember doing that. There were details of the drive north and the start of my walk to Dun Dornaigil, but then nothing at all. I couldn't find my map or my guidebook either.

Why would I tear pages out?

The silk was beautiful and had an ineffable quality that suggested great age. The pattern looked old too, like Byzantine patterns I'd seen in museums. It was wrapped around something heavy. As I unfolded it, I found that it wasn't a scrap of cloth but a complete scarf. Inside was a gold brooch in the shape of a Viking longship, a dragon head at each end. There were no hallmarks or maker's marks of any kind. The eyes were chips of polished stone, deep blue at one end, green at the other. I ran the tips of my fingers over its ridges and contours.

What the hell?

I touched the silver bridge of my glasses, and something stirred in my memory.

Ingrid. Skarfr.

A shadow shifted behind the HiFi and I felt cold. The rooks nesting in the trees the college grounds cawed as one and rose cackling from their perches, wings rattling.

I turned my phone off and put it in the drawer of my bedside table.

Outside, the air was full of crows. I sat at the foot of an impressive oak tree, out of sight of college windows. The tree was gnarled and knotted, weathered by the decades, and the bark seemed to fold back on itself in places, like pleats within pleats.

I tumbled into reflections and echoes, regressions and refractions. I'd felt like this before, though for the life of me I couldn't remember where. I let my mind flow with it, the multiple oaks behind my back, the many breezes in my hair, the kaleidoscope of crows, the hints of all the choices that had led me here, all the paths ahead of me. And I felt the pull of something else, something I should have done earlier.

Trembling, I went into the small college chapel and surrendered to something elusive but *present*. Someone came into the chapel and walked behind me to the sacristy, as noisy as someone can only be when they're trying hard to be quiet. The chapel air held the remembrance of old incense, and distant echoes of why I got into this in the first place all those years ago.

Christine rang to say Ms Hartley was upstairs in the seminar room and would I care to speak with her. So much for politely declining.

She was in her early forties, I guessed, neatly turned out, not remotely scruffy, but not too flash. The only jewellery I could see was what I first thought was an ankh on a cord round her neck, but was more of a crucifix with the ancient Chi Rho wheel design instead of the upper part of the cross. It hung behind her blouse. I only caught a glimpse when she leaned forward to place a small digital recorder on the table between us and checked the levels.

'Thanks for seeing me; I wasn't sure if you would. It's about your disappearance, you won't be surprised to learn. I'd like to hear what happened from your perspective. There's been so much speculation it would be good to get the truth out there. The bishop said it was OK to ask you.'

Did he now?

'There isn't a lot to say: I took a sabbatical and went off-grid. I had no idea there was such a fuss until I got back.'

'Off-grid is certainly one way of putting it. The obvious question is, where were you?' It was casually asked, but there was something about her voice that made me wary, as if the question was more important to her than she wanted to let on.

'Forgive me, Ms Hartley, this will sound rude, but that really isn't any of your business.'

'But people are interested. A lot of them were worried, after all, and it's no secret you were in the far north of Scotland. Surely there must be something that you'd like to say to them after all the efforts made to find you?'

I'd had a lot of contact with journalists over the years, usually for local newspapers before they became predominantly advertising sheets, and I'd always found them professional and courteous. There was an edge to Hartley's approach that didn't sit right with me, and I didn't like it. My feeling grew that there was more to her questions than journalistic interest.

'It was all a misunderstanding that got out of hand. I'm happy to put it behind me.'

'I'm sure. I believe the police are still looking into things.'

'Then you're better informed than me. They're welcome to come and speak to me again any time. Will that be all, Ms Hartley? I've just started a new job and I have a lot to do.'

'Of course. Been there, done that, know what it's like. I'm a bit surprised you're not cooperating if you've nothing to hide though. And please, call me Tina. I'll be in touch.'

She gave me her card and picked up her recorder, but didn't turn it off.

'What's the best way to get in touch with you?' she asked.

'Through the college switchboard.'

'Not your mobile?'

'Switchboard is best. I may be with students or in the library.'

'Or off-grid?'

'Perhaps. It's liberating, I've found.'

'Like helping vagrants at the cathedral?'

How does she know about that?

'Matthew 25, verse 45, Ms Hartley.'

She could look it up when she played back the recording.

There were missed calls showing on the phone, but no unplayed messages, just one I'd supposedly already played from DC MacKenzie of Police Scotland, asking if I could call her when I had opportunity. The other missed calls were from a number I didn't recognise.

I called MacKenzie. Her voice was business-like but sang with the modulations of the Highlands.

'I just wanted to check something: you said you'd gone off-grid on purpose to take time out from the modern world and think about things. That sounds like a great idea by the way.'

'Yes.'

'The thing is, Mrs Mackay told some friends that when you came back you insisted that you'd had a fall and were only away for a couple of days. Is that right?'

Crap!

'I'm afraid I was confused, and very sick.'

'I understand, and Dr Baynes has confirmed you were ill, but Mrs Mackay was very insistent it's what you said.'

'I can't really add anything else. Sorry.'

'So you're saying she's mistaken?'

'That's putting words into my mouth. I can't answer for how Mrs Mackay remembers our chat, and, to be honest, for all I know I did say it. Whatever I had made me delirious and put me in bed for a week. Frankly, I could have said any old nonsense and not known what I was saying.'

'Right. Well, thank you Reverend Cant. I may have to call you again. Is this the best way to get you?'

'Yes, but my phone is often off if I'm busy with other things, and it's acting a bit peculiar anyway. It's only by chance I got your voicemail.'

'How's that?'

I explained about the messages.

'Could anyone have used the phone while you were out?'

'It's possible, but it's quite a modern phone that needs a code to get into it.'

'Do you have a password on your voicemail?'

'No, it's just as it came when I bought the phone.'

'Have you downloaded anything recently? Any apps?'

'No, nothing like that. I've barely used it recently. Why?'

'Because I don't like that my message was flagged as listened-to when it wasn't. If I were you, I'd put a security code on your voicemail without telling anyone about it. We can ask your service provider to check things out too if you'd like.'

'Well, if you think that's really necessary. Should I buy a new phone?'

'You might want to think about it. You always want to think about security. I'm sure in your position you get lots of messages people want to keep private. It's like all that stuff that came out at the Leveson Inquiry about phone hacking by journalists, and you certainly attracted the attention of a few of them.'

'Journalist? I just had one at me half an hour ago, name of Martina Hartley.'

'Who does she work for?'

'Hang on, I'll check her card ... It doesn't say anything about where she works – freelance I suppose. Oh! Hang on ...'

The number on Hartley's card matched the unknown number in my message log.

'Well there's a thing – those calls either side of yours were from her.'

'Right. We'll look into it. And maybe doing something about your phone isn't a bad idea. How do you spell her name again?'

'Like the jam.' Memory stirred. 'Do you know, I think Mrs Mackay mentioned her, too – said she'd been a pest, or especially persistent, or something like that.'

After MacKenzie hung up, I assigned the Imperial March from *Star Wars* to Hartley's number as the ring tone, and said to Christine that, if Ms Hartley phoned again, she wasn't to be put through to me but asked to leave a message.

I turned the phone in my hand as if it were an artefact from another time. When I was little the idea of portable communications was something for *Thunderbirds* and *Star Trek,* an imagined future where we could communicate with each other in an instant. But the imagined future didn't include spam, malware and cold callers. Presented with a technological marvel, we found the basest ways to abuse it, and then to monetise the abuse. Yet we carry them around in our pockets or bags and jump to answer their blips and buzzes and tones – smaller than a pyx, twice as venerated and just as mysterious.

I looked at the screen and the floating symbols, icons, sacred images focusing our attention on the immanent, inviting our touch, promising revelation.

Indistinguishable from magic.

I randomly opened and closed apps, finding the technological marvel empty, a false prophet, a dead weight in my hand, until I opened my photo gallery and found it full of photographs I couldn't remember taking. I expanded one of the images: it looked like a manuscript, the script a curious mix of what looked like Greek and other characters I didn't recognise.

When did I take them, and where? They were linked to the brooch and scarf, I thought, but I couldn't make the connection.

Eithne waved me over to join her at lunchtime.

'Penny for them.'

'Sorry?'

'You look a million miles away.'

I didn't know Eithne. I'd only met her for the first time the night before. I wanted to fit in but didn't want to have to fend off potential questions about Sutherland. On the other hand, she was ordained into the same ministry as me, and I could do with some friends, so I told her about my conversation with DC MacKenzie and her mention of Leveson.

'Why would anyone want to hack me, though?'

'Well, have you done anything to attract press attention recently?'

Heat rushed to my face as I blushed.

'Apart from sparking a nationwide search for my whereabouts?'

'Apart from that.' The corners of her lips twitched and her cheeks dimpled. 'My grandmother was from up there, you know, from Applecross, but she always called it something else, something Gaelic.'

'A' Chomraich.'

'Yes! That's it exactly, even her intonation. Do you have the Gaelic?'

'No, sorry. I just read up on Applecross in a guidebook.'

'What does it mean?'

'It means a sanctuary, a place of safety. It's because there used to be a monastery there.'

'I used to love it up there. I remember Dad driving way up high into the hills then turning off, and the road winding, winding, winding down towards the sea. Gran's croft was in the family for years, or I think it was a croft, I'm not sure now. She used to tell us stories of shipwrecked sailors from the Armada making homes up there, having families. She had a tree by the gate that had the most amazing red berries in the autumn, said it was to keep the witches away. What was it called now?'

'Rowan.'

The refectory faded. I sat on a stone looking over Glen Golly with chuckling chickens in the coop, windows that defied time and space, a library with an ancient lectern and, somewhere upstream, a waterfall and an ancient pine tree near which a Coptic monk once made his home.

The missing months made a sort of sense – kind of – and I knew what the photographs on my phone were.

'The university is pretty hot on security – you could ask there.' Eithne scooped the remaining yoghurt from a plastic tub with her spoon; I couldn't remember what we were talking about.

'I'm sorry? What?'

'Your phone, security. Are you OK? Your face just went completely blank, like you weren't here. Are you about to be sick?'

'Probably a hangover from that bug I had in Sutherland. I'm not on the university faculty.'

'That's OK, I know the IT team from putting modules together for distance learning. You should speak to Sally Barratt. I'll take you along and introduce you this afternoon if you want.'

'I hadn't really thought to do anything so fast, but yes.'

'Right, I'll see you at the front door in thirty minutes? If you want, I can get you set up with some kind of associate staff status as well. The Divinity School has a fantastic library.'

'How are they on Coptic?'

'Coptic? I don't know. Danny Richardson is a rising star in early Christian thought and North Africa is his speciality. He's your man. Do you read the language?'

'Not at all, but I came across some stuff that intrigued me and wanted to know what it said.'

'I'll fix something up: Danny owes me several coffees. In fact, I'll call him now. Hacked phone, Gaelic and Coptic, eh? Not how I expected this chat to go, to be honest. Do you need to get changed?'

'Sorry?'

'You know.' She fingered her dog collar, nodding to where mine wasn't.

'Oh! No. I threw them all out. See you in a few.'

I copied the photos from the phone to the laptop and dropped them into a file I used for notes for sermons and related odds and ends of research. I backed the file up to a blank flash drive and also to an external hard drive. I put the hard drive with the rest of the electronics by the HiFi; the flash drive went into the pocket of my old M-65.

Sally Barratt tried hard not to be rude about the phone, though her face spoke volumes. She connected it to her laptop and ran tests that looked like a lot of random white code scrolling across a black screen.

'Well, the good news is the phone hasn't got any viruses.'

'Well, that *is* good.'

'Right, but the bad news is it would be easy for me to compromise it if I wanted to.'

'Just as well you don't want to, then.'

'What makes you think that? Did you understand any of what I just did?'

'Not a thing.'

'So how do you know I didn't do anything nasty? You don't. But believe me, with something this old I could have, easily.'

'But I've only had it a couple of years.'

'This stuff gets older by the day, not the year. Why do you think someone tried to get into it?'

'The police mentioned Leveson, and thought someone might have got into my voicemail. There's a journalist sniffing around.'

'The police, huh? They suggested that?'

'Yes. They also asked if I'd downloaded any apps recently.'

'And have you?'

'No, it's just as it came with the contract.'

'Do you ever connect your phone to a computer?'

'Just to transfer photos sometimes.'

'Right. Maybe best not to if you're really paranoid.'

'How paranoid should I be?'

'If you're like me, very paranoid indeed, but that's my job. Cautious is good though. OK. Well, it's none of my business why the police are involved, but it's damn near impossible to protect a consumer device from someone who knows what they're about, someone like me for example. But there are some basics you can do, starting with a new phone.'

'Any suggestions?'

'Yes, something hardened to government security standards and operated over a secure network, but that ain't gonna happen. If you come back about three, I'll have some basic stuff written up for you.'

The university had ancient origins. It liked to say late medieval but early modern was more like it, rebuilt by the Georgians and expanded by Victorian grandees and country vicars keen to reinvest the compensation for loss of their slaves. It was impressive enough, imposing faculty buildings built around quadrangles and courtyards, linked by alleys and passageways, heavy with the learning of the centuries and the whitewashed stain of African blood.

Eithne led me across the yard outside the security office, through a sequence of corridors and lecture-theatre concourses. Danny Richardson was waiting in a coffee shop. We did the introductions and she went to the counter.

'Eithne says you have something you'd like to have translated from Coptic.'

'Yes, on here.' I took the flash drive from a pocket and handed it over.

'What is it?'

'Photographs of a document I came across in a private library in Scotland.' Eithne looked more intently at me as she placed a tray of coffee and muffins on the table.

'A private library?' she asked.

I kicked myself.

'Yes. The owner would very much prefer not to let its whereabouts be known. I'm curious about what it says.'

'Have you any idea what it is?' said Danny.

'Only in outline. I believe it was written by a Coptic monk called Antonios and tells how he left Egypt and travelled to Ireland and thence to Scotland.'

Danny looked at me for an uncomfortable period of time.

'Do you know when he might have written it?'

'I believe in the mid-fifth century, but have no way of verifying that.'

'No way of verifying it. No. Of course. Ireland and Scotland?'

'Yes. Why?'

'I have a horrible feeling someone is playing a prank on you.'

'Why?'

'Because to my certain knowledge no such document has yet been found in Ireland or Scotland.'

'What was that one they found in a bog?' said Eithne.

'The Faddan More Psalter? That's three centuries later, give or take.'

'What's that?' I asked.

'A book that lay in a bog in Ireland for a thousand years or so. When they examined it they found papyrus in the binding, suggesting a link to Egypt at some point. And Theodore and Hadrian brought early North African fragments to England with them, probably, but that was seventh century.'

'So you think my document is a fake?'

'I would be very surprised were it genuine. Look, there's not a lot of doubt about connections between North Africa and the early Church in Ireland, and maybe England. But a personal document written by a Coptic monk in Scotland in the fifth century would be unprecedented. Can you tell me any more about its provenance, and how you came by it?'

'Not without compromising my source, but I have no reason to believe the owner is lying. Could you at least let me have a rough translation, if only to satisfy my curiosity? If it's a fake then the joke's on me.'

'You only have copies, no physical fragments?'

'Just photos taken with my phone.'

'What did it look like?'

'It was written on folded sheets of stretched goatskin stitched into stiffened leather binding. The stitching was lovely, like a cable stitch.'

'You could see the ends of the pieces? There wasn't a spine on it?'

'No, nothing like that, just the stitching. I think it was hemp with some thin leather twisted in. Why?'

'That sounds like an old style of Coptic binding, associated with the Nag Hammadi codices, so middle fourth century or thereabouts. OK, my curiosity is piqued. I'll give the copies a once-over, but it'll probably be a couple of weeks before I can get anything back to you. How do I reach you?'

I gave him my mobile number, went to collect my instructions from Sally Barratt and made my own way back to college while Eithne was teaching. I stopped at a specialist Middle Eastern store and bought very finely ground coffee and rose water. I went to a high street branch of my network provider and sorted out an upgrade, selecting one of the phones on Sally's list. Perhaps some of her paranoia had rubbed off on me: I could have sworn I saw Martina Hartley's grey Astra drive past the shop while I was waiting. Twice.

I got back in time for the evening service and slipped into the back of the chapel. It was the first service I'd attended since I'd left St Joe's. No matter how much I concentrated, something about it wasn't right, as if the words got in the way of meaning.

Rowan's words came back to me. *You can't come here, even for a short time, and not be changed.*

Danny Richardson called after supper.

'I took a quick look out of curiosity. The text is quite irregular, but there's something about its style that intrigues me. Would you mind if I made some discreet queries of colleagues? I'd like to find out if anyone's seen anything like this outside the usual sources. I'm thinking of some archivists I know at the Vatican Library and in Alexandria, and some German colleagues after that.'

'To be honest, I promised to keep this quiet and not attract attention. The owner is a very private person.'

'I understand, but there are fundamental issues of professional ethics here for me. Any number of fake texts have appeared recently. Provenance and circumstances of acquisition are crucial, and you can't provide either of them, so there's an operating presumption that it isn't genuine. I need to dig a bit.'

'Then you think it's a fake?'

'I didn't say that. I said there is a presumption that it's fake in the absence of provenance, and the number of fakes in circulation is something we're keeping an eye on. On the other hand, if it's a fake, it's a jolly interesting one. But you know, this isn't the stuff of headlines, it's just low-level chit-chat between scholars. There's no chance of any comeback on you.'

CHAPTER 8

David collared me after breakfast to let me know Sydney had decided to make the regular Friday Eucharist in the chapel that evening a formal welcome for me. Sydney would be celebrant, but would I mind saying a few words in the form of a short sermon?

I should have expected it, and could hardly refuse.

'Good-oh. I'll let the bishop know. Do you know where the robes and things are downstairs?' He screwed up his eyes in distaste at my casual clothes.

'I have a cassock-alb – would that be appropriate?'

'Splendid. Have you any thoughts on what you might say?'

'I'll follow the readings. Let me check the lectionary and take it from there.'

By happy coincidence the reading of the day was Matthew 21.12 and following: Jesus's cleansing of the temple.

The Friday Eucharist was in the full bells-and-smells tradition of High Anglicanism, cosplay as ritual, or maybe vice-versa. I don't mind that: the theatricality is entertaining in its own way and, done well, there is a regularity and momentum that carries you through, like a well-executed Dashing White Sergeant or Strip the Willow, but without kilts or whisky.

Gavin Surtees, the college sacristan, was in his element. I'd met him earlier that afternoon, one of several meetings I'd arranged with the students to get to know them a bit more formally.

He was a strange one. He'd worn a cassock to our meeting, which caught me by surprise, but suited his role, to which he'd been elected by the other students. When I'd seen him around the college from a distance, I'd thought him older than he really was, but that was an impression he was trying to project. Up close, I'd put him in his early twenties but tending already to middle age. He took care to ensure everything was exactly as it should be in the chapel, bustling around with expert intent.

We entered on clouds of incense, overwhelming in the small space, and took our places at the front of the congregation, mainly students but with a smattering of the priests of the diocese. Sydney was in his finery and his element, his voice sonorous, gestures precise, straight from *A Directory of Ceremonial for Pedants*. After the readings, he offered some words welcoming me to my new post, not mentioning recent controversies, and I was on.

'I want to begin by thanking you all for the warm welcome you've given me over the last couple of days. I look forward to knowing you all better as time goes by, and serving you as best I can.

'In Jeremiah chapter 24, the prophet looks at two baskets of figs in the temple, in the sanctuary of the Lord. This is after the beginning of the Babylonian exile. In one basket, the figs were very good, in the second, too bad to eat.

'God spoke to Jeremiah and said She would treat the exiles as good figs, would restore them to their land, and build them up. They shall become my people, She said, and they shall come back to me. But She would treat the King of Judah and his officers and the survivors in Jerusalem

105

like bad figs, make them repugnant, and send sword, famine and pestilence against them, until they vanished from the land.

'I mention this because tonight's Gospel reading, Matthew's story of the cleansing of the temple, is followed by the story of Jesus cursing the fig tree.

'Parishioners sometimes asked me what Jesus had against figs, and the clue is the association in both Mark and Matthew of cursing the fig tree and cleansing the temple.

'Matthew has it that Jesus entered the temple, drove out the merchants in the temple precincts, upset the tables of the moneychangers and the seats of pigeon dealers, and shouted that the temple was a house of prayer, not a robbers' cave. Then He healed the blind and crippled, and the chief priests and teachers of the law were indignant. The next morning, according to Matthew, Jesus could find no fruit on the fig tree, and He cursed it, saying it would never again bear fruit.

'Mark says that Jesus found no fruit on the tree because it was not the season for figs, and cursed it before going to the temple, and they found the tree dead the morning after.

'Matthew and Mark each want us to understand that condemning the tree and cleansing the temple are the same thing. Just as Jesus got no physical nourishment from the fig tree, so he got no spiritual nourishment at the temple; he is condemning the priesthood.

'And so the story isn't about figs at all. It's about the people of God and the nature of priesthood and worship, subjects I hope to explore further with you in the weeks and months ahead, bearing in mind that, for Jesus, the thieves were the priests, not the merchants. Amen.'

David leaned over when I sat down.

'I say, that was edgy for an opener.'

The inevitable sherry reception followed in the common room before supper. I had water. Everyone made polite small talk while avoiding what they really wanted to ask, and I fended off a couple of students keen to skewer my exegesis.

Sydney was friendly, accepting deference with practised ease.

'Jolly good, yes, I enjoyed that, proper Anglican: no lengthy exposition, just something to think about. Robbers' cave, ha! Yes, and teasing us with the feminine pronoun. A good start. I approved your expenses claim for that replacement phone by the way. Something to do with the police, you said?'

'They suggested I should have an up-to-date one with journalists around, and Eithne got the university security team to give me some advice.'

'The journalist was fine?'

'I was polite but basically said "no comment".'

'Wasn't that a bit unhelpful? Couldn't you have given her some kind of story? I like to keep good relations up if I can.'

'I didn't like her manner – there was something about her that rankled with me, and David says he wants to keep the college out of the public eye, that it wouldn't be fair on the students to have the press around.'

'Of course. Well, jolly good. Look here, you must give a sermon at St Aggie's some time. Short and sweet: they'll like that.'

'Isn't it a bit soon for the cathedral?' David asked, a frown on his face – I hadn't noticed him behind me. 'Plenty of time for that later, isn't there?'

'Strike while the iron's hot, is my motto. Yes, that's a plan. I'll arrange it.'

After supper I went to a local pub with some students. It wasn't raucous, just decent cask beer and a solo jazz guitarist who was rather stronger on chord progressions than finding melodies to link them. I made my excuses once I'd bought my round, pleading tiredness after a busy week. I was delighted to have a free weekend, with no services to take and no college duties.

I went down to the chapel and sat in the glow of street lights through the stained-glass windows and the lingering smell of incense. I fixed on the crucifix in the alcove with the reserved sacrament, the body nailed there. Memory stirred in the half light.

Haily blood bled on bloody banners
His body lies broken, in bondage biding

The lights came on. It was Gavin.

'Oh, I'm sorry, I didn't know you were down here. That's twice I've disturbed you now. I'll let you be.'

'It's fine. I was just reflecting on the day. Can I give you a hand with anything?'

'I'm just making sure everything is put away properly. Father Sharpe-Thompson is a stickler for detail, as am I.'

There was an earnestness about him that I found disconcerting.

'We're not like your usual parish, I suppose. Miss Boards, wasn't it?'

'You heard about that?'

'I should think everyone has by now.'

'Ah. Well, Betty's one of a kind, but people are people and that doesn't change because they're ordinands. Or priests, for that matter.'

While we talked, he tidied the sacristy with a precision that approached the obsessive, checking every drawer in the robe chest to ensure everything was in its proper place. I said goodnight and left him to it.

The guitar player in the pub had put me in the mood for jazz on LP, but not that sub-Joe Pass chording.

It's hard to explain records to children of the digital age, even harder to the hip who try to claim their 'vinyls' as an external signifier of inward virtue. It isn't about second-hand emotions or an urge to assert an older technology as somehow more authentic, nor is it an atavistic urge to stand firm against evil modernity. It is bound up with who we are when we first learn how to be, a set of signs we share as common experience. It's not a borrowed persona, it's part of our identity.

A gatefold sleeve on your lap with art by Roger Dean or Hipgnosis, or a Blue Note original, or a Deutsche Grammophon, reading sleeve notes while the disk spins at 33⅓ rpm, getting up every twenty minutes or so to turn it over, is sound, touch and vision combining to a whole greater than the parts. There is a thrill in the old Vertigo label pulsing around the spindle, in finding *A Porky Prime Cut* etched into the dead wax, in reading the sacred text: *This stereo record can be played on mono reproducers provided either a compatible or stereo cartridge wired for mono is fitted. Recent equipment may already be fitted with a suitable cartridge. If in doubt, consult your dealer.*

The LP record was a talisman, binding communities in an occult embrace. My copy of Pink Floyd's *Meddle* carried the psychic residue of every cigarette paper that ever rested on it, every stray fragment of bud or crumbled resin, every torn cardboard roach. *Rastaman Vibration* dances to its own backbeat and the rhythms of women and men I've slept with, the feel of their flesh against mine, the taste of their tongues, the surrender of self in moments of intimacy.

It occurred to me that I still hadn't looked up Venny's contact details, though why she'd want to hear from me after all this time – and why I couldn't get the idea out of my head – was beyond me. I checked my watch and decided it was too late.

I selected Eberhard Weber's *Yellow Fields*, the original ECM LP, and relaxed as the music washed out of my vintage speakers. Charlie Mariano's sax snaked a melody over Weber's liquid bass and the darkness in the corners of the room shifted, coalescing and diffusing, forming deeper pools of black that looked back at me through eyes of deer at the treeline. There were no vocals, and yet I heard voices, scattered plosives and fricatives, never quite forming syllables but not random, heavy with implied meaning.

A breeze drifted through the room: it whispered in my hair, and smelled of wild places, of birch sap and peat smoke and venison roasting in a great hall, leaving behind a taste of spiced mead. The pulse of 'Sand-Glass' transported me to pleats within pleats in a house with many mansions, many rooms. Elizabeth Boards was evicted from each room by a fat cherub in a cassock saying *this is a house of God not a doss house*, and in the cathedral grounds a dead fig tree drooped, draped with discarded dog collars, dripping in a tea-leaf rain.

And the speakers sounded the rhythmic *tht … tht …* of the stylus at the end of the run-out groove.

CHAPTER 9

My phone woke me: two early emails from Danny. The first had a translation of Antonios's document attached, full of health warnings about how it was very rough and provisional, with several meanings glossed for ease of reading, and some of his notes left in the text. He'd added punctuation that seemed to make sense.

The second email was an update on the replies from his colleagues. The Vatican Library, no less, was extremely keen to know more about the document's provenance and when it would be convenient to inspect a copy. The office of a Coptic bishop had replied almost immediately, and shortly after that the vice principal of the university texted about the significant discovery he'd heard about on the grapevine, and asked to be kept in touch with developments. A private museum in the States was excited to learn more.

He said he'd thought Antonios's text was an elaborate work of fiction until the queries came in, and now he didn't know quite what to think.

Bleary-eyed, I wandered to the kitchen in old jogging pants and a worn, faded sweatshirt. I mixed Turkish coffee and cold water in an old *cezve* I'd bought in Egypt and heated the copper minaret on a low heat until its first rise, then poured the hot liquid and foam into a demitasse, adding the least drop of rose water. I took it to the sitting room and opened the translation on my laptop.

IN THE PEACE OF GOD! May His holy blessing and the blessing of all the saints come upon us and may we all be saved. AMEN.

This is how I found [Sanctuary? obscure] *at the ends of the earth and how I came to carry the most Holy relic I now leave here, until I return from far* [Thule] *or such day as the Lord appoints.*

I was born in Alexandria on the day of the great wave [365CE?]. *My father traded goods from Albion and Hibernia in the West, to the farthest ports of the Bosphorus in the north, to Andropolis and thence Africa and, with the monsoon winds, India. His cargoes were tin, wine, olive oil, spices, pearls, silk, diamonds, or any other thing* [that turned a] *profit.*

Father's philosophy was to be neither enthusiastic nor neglectful, and to never express an opinion. Better to go about business and not draw attention [because] *opinions can deprive you of your life or, worse, trade.*

As son of my father I was trained in the arts and skills of business and obliged to join one of Father's partners' ships in the lowliest position. When sailing skills were mastered, I could perform my duties while my mind was elsewhere. This was the beginning of meditation.

[In this way] *the Lord prepared me for what was to come, how to take care of my body and mind. I saw many peoples and their many beliefs, and thought on matters of faith, of how I came to be, and, as I navigated by the night sky, what guides the stars that guide us.*

When the great council in Constantinople decreed all in the Empire [to be] *Christian save only the Jews* [381CE], *the streets and alleys of every port overflowed with those professing secret teachings of Christ and sacred mysteries known only to elites, though our Lord said, I have said nothing in secret* [John 18.20–21? Anti-Gnostic?].

The Manichees teach we are but fields of battle on which the armies of God and Satan meet, our souls pulled to the darkness of the physical world, or to rejoicing in spiritual light. They say we must embrace virtue and put aside vice and the pleasures of the world. I found this unconvincing, but [nevertheless] *felt a call to the way of the ascetic.*

There was a man in Alexandria with excellent Latin and Greek, but his speech was of Albion or Hibernia. Like the desert fathers and mothers, he lived a life of chastity and poverty. We discussed the doctrines of the Manichees and the sinfulness of souls.

He said, 'Who knows our strength except Him who gave us it? He is righteous and does not ask the impossible. We are given capacity to choose and are weighed on the balance of our choices. [If we] *choose virtue and eschew the temptations of the flesh, we can rely on His Grace.'*

I heard the truth of his words, and I thought of them on the long voyage from Cana to Muziris. We carried figured linen, coral, metals, realgar and orpiment and expected to return with pearls, ivory, spikenard, malabathrom and the like, perhaps even tortoiseshell from Chryse, but I found far greater riches in my heart.

In Muziris I sought the Christians of the Church founded by the Blessed Apostle Thomas, and there apprehended the majesty of Our Lord and was baptised into the Community of the Saved. I rose from the water a new creature, washed clean of sin. I shared a joyful meal with the community there, and we asked the Holy Spirit to come upon us and bless our offering of ourselves to His service. A cloud of light descended and from within the voice of the Lord commanded me to go to Egypt and forsake the world and the ways of the flesh, and I would be named Antonios and a great deed would be entrusted to me.

Thirty years I served the Lord, tending our small collection of documents, repairing bindings, wondering what great deed I would be called to do. A time came when the risks to our lives from bandits and thieves became too great. We are called to sacrifice, but that does not mean embracing the [cult of suffering?] or [glorying] in martyrdom when Our Lord has taken that path [for us?]. News came of the murder of Hypatia [415CE] on the day Apa [Father] Archeleos summoned me.

He knelt before a small package wrapped in ancient leather tied round with leather cords. He instructed me to take this most holy relic to the ends of the Earth and hide it from the eyes of thieves and idolators, saying, I give you the same warning given to me and other keepers of this great treasure: do not open or *examine the package, however much Satan himself may tempt you, but carry it with you and trust in the Lord's Grace to keep you strong and guide your path.*

'Father,' I said. 'What is this treasure that I should take such care to protect it?'

'I know not, for I have not looked. I know only that it came to Egypt from India and was blessed by our Lord Himself. Find the ends of the Earth with his guidance and blessing.'

In Father's library was the ancient journal of Pytheas of Massalia, recounting his voyage to Tintagel in Britannia, that we now call Albion, and thence to the sacred isle of Iouernia, where the Scots are, and yet further north, to a land where the natives are tattooed from skull to toenail. Thence he voyaged to Orkas, and beyond even to the mysterious [Thule], [where it is] *so cold that land, sea, air and ice congeal together and are indistinguishable. Truly the ends of the Earth. And a voice said this was my great calling.*

I took passage to Gaul and thence to Tintagel and Iouernia, where I found my brothers had been before me, preaching the word of God. The Lord led me the length of that land until I came to a place where a boat sailed north for Εβουδαι [Hebrides? Ptolomy's name. cf Pliny et al.]. *A great storm arose on the water, and we were cast ashore at a place surrounded by green hills where a river ran into a bay. I set* [out on foot] *thanking the Lord for my life, with only my pack and the treasure, unopened, until a strange* [quiver?] *ran through my senses and a fog fell around me and—*

115

[Two lines obscure. Parchment appears damaged, gall ink? Final lines added later? Ink colour different, rounder hand?]

—*I will take a small boat and cast myself into the hands of the Lord, even unto* [Thule] *itself, but my holy treasure I leave here with this my testament, for as I have come to know this* [place?]*, I know none safer for it to rest until the end of days, or the Lord wills otherwise.*

Through our Lord Jesus the Christ, our Saviour, unto Whom be glory, and unto his Good Father, and unto the Holy Spirit.

Amen.

Aside from the historical importance as a record of an Egyptian monk making a trip to Ireland and Scotland, I couldn't see anything that excited interest until the transport of the holy treasure, presumably a relic. I knew enough about relics not to read too much into that. The early and medieval Church, right through to the Renaissance, did a roaring trade in fragments of the True Cross, saints' bones, and other exotica, all supposed to have magical powers. Joseph of Arimathea was said to have brought the Holy Grail to Britain and even, in some accounts, the young Jesus himself. The internet and bookshops are full of this stuff, elaborating myths upon fable, fiction, fabrication and fantasy, pretending to uncover elusive 'truths'.

Rowan hadn't mentioned a relic when she'd talked about the manuscript. Did she know about it? She'd said she could read the text, so she had to know. Of course, she'd had no reason to mention it to me.

I saved the document in a folder full of sermons on my laptop and called it 'random research'. I put a back-up copy on the external drive I'd put in with the HiFi, and deleted the emails. Some of Sally Barratt's paranoia had rubbed off on me, and I didn't like all the interest Danny had generated.

In my childhood, Sunday streets were deserted apart from families walking to church in their good clothes. No shops were open, and there was nothing interesting or entertaining on TV, for fear of offending the faithful, fear of questions in the House, fear of bishops intoning their dismay at the evils of secularisation and the steady decay of moral standards. On the whole I prefer things as they are now: the faithful do what they want without impinging on the choices of others. These days the streets have a good number of tourists finding things to photograph – usually the same things that every other tourist photographs. They buy cheap tat from souvenir shops, look at maps and block the footpath, pretending they aren't lost.

Davy introduced me to three other volunteers at the Mission – Anna, Chris and Mohammed – who pointed me towards boxes full of donated crockery and cutlery, most of it carrying logos and branding of long-closed restaurants and hotels. I counted up quickly: there were seats for about a hundred and fifty.

'That many?'

'It's about right for a usual Sunday,' said Chris, a student. 'We get between eighty and a hundred and sixty, depending on the weather. Numbers are heading up again.'

'Why is it called the Mission?' I asked Davy.

'It used to be run by the Church. They wanted people to pray as the price of a square meal. They're long gone, but the name stuck.'

'Where does the food come from?'

'Donations. Some from supermarkets and retailers who'd throw it away if we weren't here. We get yesterday's bread and rolls from a couple of bakeries, and the Sikhs and the local mosque are always generous.'

The doors opened at twelve-thirty and the hall filled in next to no time. Lines of tired-looking people, mostly under thirty though it wasn't always easy to tell. Several had dogs, who all got bowls of food and water. My job was to go round offering water, tea or coffee, and clear away dishes. The girl from the park saw me and flashed a smile and a thank you. She was alone, her hair wrapped in her hood. I should have asked her name.

There was enough left over for Davy, Anna, Chris, Mohammed and me to have a meal together before clearing up. I volunteered to wash dishes and set to it, the others drying and packing, loading everything into a van until next week. I asked Anna how she'd got involved.

'My Great-Aunt Julie was Romany. When I was a little girl she used to tell me about a woman who refused food to a beggar and was turned into an owl. I don't want to take the chance.' She laughed.

'Will we see you next week then?' asked Davy as I slipped into my battered field jacket.

'I hope so, but I'm often tied up on Sundays.'

'Oh, right. What do you do?'

'I'm a priest.'

All four looked surprised.

'Oh! But ... Sorry. I didn't expect that,' said Mohammed. 'Shouldn't you be at Communion or something?'

It was Pentecost, a Sunday when I would normally be resplendent in red vestments celebrating the coming of the Holy Spirit. One of the readings for the day, the Song of Ezekiel, ran through my mind:

I will give you a new heart and put a new spirit within you;
I will take the heart of stone from your body and give you a heart of flesh.

'I think I was.'

Something had hit home that I'd sort-of known but hadn't fully appreciated – just how many people were on the streets. It didn't used to be like that. I'm not idealising the sixties and seventies, but something had gone terribly wrong since the days when our future was in the stars, not the gutter.

My reply to Mohammed was glib, but as soon as I said the words I knew they were true. I was certain it was more important to serve and feed the homeless than to put on vestments and go through the usual routine of a Sunday service. *Do this in remembrance of me.* That's your anamnesis right there, but what do we do in remembrance of Him if we only eat dry wafers and drink cheap wine? What, exactly, is it we're expected to do?

Later that evening, I slipped into the back of St Edmund's parish church, supposedly built on a Norman site, though you wouldn't know it now. The building itself is certainly old, the exterior stonework slowly rotting from modern pollution. Inside, the plain architecture and simple appointments fitted my mood, down to the worn and faded hassocks on the floor, bearers of generations of knees. I was in jeans and trainers and an old sweatshirt, wrapped up in the field jacket.

I didn't know the priest, Walter Cunningham, but I'd heard he clung to the tradition of sung Evensong. The choir at St Edmund's was not strong or especially accomplished, but it was committed, as were the regular congregation. Fiona Montrose, a final-year student at Weston House, led the service.

Evensong had often been a source of comfort for me, but I reacted against it that evening. I paid attention to the words, to what I was saying and hearing, and I didn't find any comfort at all.

But thou, O Lord, have mercy upon us miserable offenders; Spare thou them, O God, which confess their faults ... That we may hereafter live a godly, righteous and sober life.

God, how dreary. Where was the joy in this litany of misery? Where was the hope?

He hath shewed strength with his arm: he hath scattered the proud in the imagination of their hearts. He hath put down the mighty from their seat: and hath exalted the humble and meek.

Really? Even calling this stuff metaphor pushed the limits of meaning.

Then the *Nunc dimittis* and its talk of Gentiles and Israel? Well, Luke would write that, wouldn't he? That was his thing after his voyage with Paul. But the origins of Christianity are in a radical Jewish teacher.

I didn't read the Apostles' Creed out loud: I couldn't. I looked at the words on the page in front of me, words I'd recited countless times, and was as certain as I was of anything that I didn't believe a single one of them.

Then the third collect, the poetic glory of the service – *Lighten our darkness, we beseech thee, O Lord; and by thy great mercy defend us from all perils and dangers of this night; for the love of thy only Son, our Saviour, Jesus Christ. Amen* – before a bunch of prayers for the royal family.

I slipped out without giving Walter or Fiona a chance to recognise me. I drove round the bypass and out of town, onto an old road that went up and over open moorland. I found a spot where light pollution wasn't too bad, and waited for the stars to emerge behind the running lights of aircraft.

When I was very young, Mum's brother, Alan, tried to teach me the constellations. Most of the names didn't stick, but I remember looking at the Pleiades through a telescope, profoundly moved when, for a moment, something of the immensity of the universe became real for me in those globules of energy hanging bright in the blackness. I'd connected with *something* under the stars in Sanctuary, maybe the same thing I'd connected with as a child.

My reaction to the Pleiades was my first experience of the numinous, the thing that suggested to me that there is a God. Years later, my cousin Joanne said the same view of the Pleiades, the same sense of the vastness of the cosmos, convinced her that there is no God. How odd that the same experience should produce different reactions in Jo and me. She thinks my belief is a delusion.

The thinking part of me, the part that asks people to define spirituality, tells me there are hidden premises behind our different reactions, and that it's always the hidden premises that make the difference. But where did that leave me? How could I reconcile the remnants of my faith with a rejection of the forms and orders of the Church into which I was ordained priest?

'Well there you are,' said Eithne when I got back. 'You didn't answer your mobile. Danny called. His office was broken into. Ransacked. Completely turned over. He's in a proper state. The police are there.'

I had a horrible feeling about where this was heading.

'How is he?'

'Upset. Confused. Angry.'

I closed my eyes, letting out a long breath. Eithne made herself a coffee and changed the subject.

'Where did you go to worship this morning?'

'I helped out feeding the homeless at the Mission in town.'

'Really? Did you clear it?'

'No, of course not. Why should I?'

'Well, after the fuss at the cathedral?'

'There wasn't any fuss at the cathedral, just a woman who needed help and got the bum's rush.'

'Well, she was trying to sleep there, I heard.'

'She was. And the gentleman who threw her out said it was because it was a house of God, not a doss-house. But you know, on the whole I think you're rather more likely to find God in a doss-house than a cathedral.'

Eithne smiled at that, at my little joke. Then she saw my face.

'You're serious, aren't you?'

'It's as well there isn't a fig tree in the cathedral grounds, don't you think? It would have withered long ago.'

I understood in that moment that Rowan had asked the wrong question: what mattered wasn't what I was running from, but where I was running to.

I dreamed of wolves again that night. Wolves hunt in silence, said Rowan, as packs of stars roved the skies, coalescing into constellations before shifting, sliding in uncertain motion in cassocks and Pentecost-red chasubles, lightening the darkness. And the stars noticed me and waved, before they went their own ways, out, out, out into the nothing-at-all.

CHAPTER 10

'I do wish you'd take formal attire seriously. A chaplain should lead by example, don't you think? Eithne tells me you chose not to attend Communion yesterday. Surprising at Pentecost, I'd have thought. An aspect of priesthood perhaps? More ministering to the poor?'

His eyes lingered on my absent collar. I wasn't in the mood for his sarcasm so soon after breakfast.

'I was serving the homeless at the Mission.'

His eyes narrowed, and he retreated to his office.

Sydney called to tell me he'd slotted me in to give the sermon in a couple of weeks' time, the second Sunday after Pentecost, which was fine with me.

'Jolly good. How are things with David and Eithne?'

'It's only my first Monday in post, so early days yet; but we'll get there.'

'Any more word from that journalist, Harling or whatever her name is?'

'Hartley. No, nothing else.'

'Good stuff. Look, I have something I'd like you to think over. I know I said it was a rush job putting you in Weston House, and you've only just got there and you're probably itching to get back to a parish, and I couldn't blame you, but I want to float the idea of you staying on full-time, as a permanent part of the team?'

'Have you spoken to David yet?'

'I wanted to sound you out first, so mum's the word, eh?'

'I'd be more comfortable if he and Eithne were involved in the decision.'

'Quite so, and if it comes to that they will be, but first things first. This way is less embarrassing if you say no. Anyway, a bit of creative tension in the team does no harm.'

What does that mean?

'Sorry it's all a bit sudden. I've had it on my mind to strengthen the team for a while, and there's nothing like the bold approach, eh?'

'I'll give it some thought. I don't want to get too formal, but it would be helpful to have a better idea of what I'm expected to do. When do you need a decision?'

'No tearing hurry, but if you could let me know when you come to give that sermon, that would be ideal. We can sort out a job description after that.'

'There's a Father Adrian Coulter calling for you,' Christine said. 'He says it's about an ecumenical matter.'

'Never heard of him, but better put him through.'

There was a pause and faint variations in the quality of the silence on the line until the call connected.

'Thank you for taking the call. I appreciate you don't know me.'

'Not at all, a pleasure. It's about an ecumenical matter, I gather?'

'In a manner of speaking. It's about a manuscript written by a Coptic monk and found by you while you were missing, and I would prefer not to talk about it over the phone. Would there be a convenient time to meet?'

Whoa, what?

'I think perhaps you've got the wrong person. I'm acting chaplain at Weston House Theological College. I don't do manuscripts.'

'I know very well who you are, you were all over the news, though you managed to keep your return quiet.'

'I can tell you with complete confidence I have no such manuscript.'

'No doubt, but I think you know where to find it. This is a matter of some importance: my brothers have tried for a long time to find out what happened to Antonios and the relic entrusted to him. When word of the manuscript got out, naturally we became excited to find out more.'

'I'm sure, and it all sounds fascinating, but I'm interested in today's ordinands, not yesterday's monks, Father Coulter.'

'Well, so be it. I have to tell you that this won't go away: your Church has its structures and rules, as does mine. I hope that when we speak again it will be in better circumstances.'

Two students, Robert Graham and Helen Ayanwole, were in the library, sitting as far apart from each other as they could. I knew from chatting over meals that they were very different characters. Robert's first degree was Law. He'd tried to use his thick beard to hide his disdain when I mentioned Paramhana Yogananda's *Autobiography of a Yogi* at breakfast. Helen was from an upper middle-class Nigerian family. She was intensely intellectual and academic, with a first-class honours in History and a liking for Liberation Theology, but not much in the way of social life. Both of their placements had finished ahead of exams, so

I suggested that if they were free the next Sunday they might go down to the Mission and say I'd sent them.

The reading for the second Sunday in Pentecost was the end of Mark chapter 2 and the beginning of chapter 3, Jesus arguing with the Pharisees. I photocopied the passage in the library. Remembering my conversations with Rowan and William, I copied the Greek text as well, to see what I could do with it, if anything, with a dictionary and an online copy of a literal translation.

Eithne was at the copier too.

'Did Father Sharpe-Thompson speak to you? He was incandescent about that parishioner you talked about.'

'Was he? He hasn't mentioned it.'

'He's telling everyone he meets that he didn't think it appropriate for tender young minds.'

'The tender young minds didn't object and needed to be disabused of their preconceptions. I should invite Betty along to a college supper one night, she'd be a riot. How's Danny?'

'Trying to put his office back together. He's not the only one having problems: Sally Barratt was in all weekend as well, some sort of security alert with the university's systems. Listen, I was thinking about what you said about the cathedral and the fig tree: is that what you really think?'

'Honestly? I'm still working through it, but one of the reasons for my infamous sabbatical was to consider my vocation after all those years in parishes. A lot of things that once seemed important now seem inconsequential, and vice versa. One of my tutors at University was Italian, originally a Roman Catholic priest. I remember him saying, *all of human knowledge is provisional and theology is no exception: take God seriously, theology not so much*. I was young and didn't think too much about it at the time, but it makes sense to me now.'

'But if you don't take theology seriously, how do you avoid drifting?

'His point was to keep your eye on the main thing. But you know, it isn't as if academic theology hasn't paddled into strange waters over the centuries, and notions of heresy or error depend on some agreed notion of truth. You don't even get that in the canonical New Testament, let alone the Apocrypha. Several of the Apostles seem not to have followed Paul's line at all - they argued about it amongst themselves in fact. By the time Paul sailed to Rome and the Gentiles, Thomas was already in India preaching to Jewish merchants.'

Eithne was smiling.

'What?'

'Nothing. It's just that when Sydney said you were coming, I didn't know what to expect. You know, for all you give the impression that you don't take this seriously, you do, don't you? Take it really seriously? I think you might be just what this place needs. It's a shame it's only temporary.'

I couldn't see how to accept the position as full-time chaplain with a good conscience, and it was time that I looked for an alternative, even though I didn't know where to start. I needed someone to ask. I'm not very good at asking; it's easier to be the listener, to let other people reveal themselves to me. And Coulter's call had disconcerted me; there'd been no messing about and he would know my replies were a smokescreen.

The problem was, I'd had no one to talk to for a long time, not to *really* talk to, the way that leaves you exposed, with a person who doesn't just listen but also opens themselves. The only person I'd ever had like that was Venny, and I'd messed that up.

Times and lost teenage loves get idealised by memory, but Ven had a quality you might call fey if you didn't know her, and very few knew her. She could wear a Laura Ashley floral A-line dress and still be a radical Earth goddess. She had a complete sense of self, even in her teens.

I could think of a hundred and one reasons not to call her – it wasn't as though I'd made any effort to reconnect before, and I'd no idea how she'd react to my calling now. She might not even remember me: for all I knew she'd moved on with her life and long ago put me out her mind. That was my biggest fear: that I didn't mean to her what her memory did to me. Maybe not knowing was better than being told to get lost. I was back at my own cowardice again – knowledge of the lie negates the possibility that you are deceived by it.

I opened the laptop and searched for a street view of our old houses, then searched her name. One of the hits was the electoral register, and there she was, Ravenser Odd, sole occupant of the house she grew up in.

I rehearsed all the reasons I shouldn't call her, while my fingers dialled the number I didn't know I remembered.

'Hello?'

The same voice: breathy, guarded, deeper with age, her accent unchanged.

'Ven? It's me, Canty.'

'About bloody time, ducks. I were just thinking about you.'

'I didn't know if you'd even remember me.'

'Silly bugger. And all that fuss in the news and your picture everywhere when you disappeared. I didn't tell 'em owt, mind.'

'Who?'

'Reporters mithering your old school friends. I told 'em to fuck off.'

'Sorry.'

'Don't be. Anyway: yes.'

'Yes what?'

'Yes, I want to see you. When are you coming?'

Don't hesitate.

'I'll have to get a couple of days off. And I'll need to find somewhere to stay.'

'Silly Canty. There's room here. I've missed you.'

'I don't know what to say.'

'Just let me know when you can come. You dunner 'alf talk funny by the way, has anyone told you?'

I rang off, elated. I tried to remember past times, talking about music, her championing of Patti Smith and punk, calling me a boring old fart for my Yes and Jethro Tull albums; giggling under her candlewick bedspread as we experimented with kisses and more, desperate that no one heard or found us. And why did she say I talk funny?

I needed a walk. I decided to see if I could wangle a reader's ticket in the university library while Eithne was trying to sort out associate status for me, and maybe fit in some second-hand bookshops on the way back. It was a perfect spring day for it, warm, not humid, with the lightest of breezes, and I was high from talking to Venny. Eithne stopped me as I left the librarian's desk, my new ticket in my pocket.

'Sally Barratt wants to speak to you as soon as you can.'

Sally was surrounded by monitors and harassed assistants, and looked like she was surviving on caffeine and adrenaline. She grabbed a laptop and took me to a private room.

'Have you got your phone there? Would you mind if I just ran a quick test?'

She plugged a cable from the laptop into the phone. The usual lines of code and text rolled across her screen.

'Did you hear we had network problems over the weekend?'

'Yes, Eithne told me.'

'It was a very specific problem, and it took me a while to figure it out until I heard about the break-in at Danny Richardson's office. Someone was trying to get into Danny's files. They didn't succeed, but they had a damn good crack at it. I had a quick look at his email logs in case there was any attempt to upload anything nasty that way, and I saw he'd sent something to you at a private email address.'

'I'm not on the university network.'

'Right. Anyway, whatever he sent, you need to know that once it's outside the university network it might not be secure.'

'Which means ...'

'It means I can't guarantee your email provider's system is as secure as mine. And since you said you had a journalist nosing around your phone messages, I thought you should know. There's a chance someone else read it, and even if they didn't, they might have your name as someone Danny contacted.'

'Who else knows?'

'No one yet, but there's an audit of the logs happening right now, so it won't be long.'

'Who sees that?'

'The Audit Committee and the senior team, though they only get high-level summaries. But my professional recommendation will be to refer everything to the police as linked to the burglary.'

The muted thump of fingers on keyboards carried from the room next door, the chatter of a printer, the laughing of students in the quad. Gravity pulled at the pit of my stomach.

'Are you OK?'

'Sorry?'

'You looked like you were about to be sick.'

'I'm just thinking how much I could do without this, and what Danny must be going through.'

'I don't suppose you can tell me what's going on?'

'I wish I could, but I don't know either. All I can say is it seems to be something to do with a manuscript Danny translated for me, but that's so bizarre. That stuff doesn't happen in real life.'

'Right. I'd never mistake Danny for Tom Hanks or Nicolas Cage.'

'Pardon?'

'You know, conspiracy theory movies: ancient artefacts and secret societies, obscure monastic orders, that stuff.'

'Oh. Well that's what I mean. It's Hollywood fantasy, action movies and thrillers, not what happens to the likes of me.'

The likes of you, who walks into a hidden part of time and space and loses six months of your life feasting with Danish warriors.

'When will the audit people will be finished?'

'The police will know in the next couple of hours, and they'll give us ten kinds of shit for not telling them sooner.'

When I got back to the flat, I went to the HiFi to retrieve the hard drive with the copies of the photos and Danny's translation, but it wasn't there, nor anywhere else I looked.

How many times could the same few square metres be searched? There was nothing odd or out of place, and no indications that anyone had searched through my things. The main door and windows had no damage that couldn't just be normal wear and tear. There were no signs of damage or forced entry to the upstairs door leading into the college.

Could I have left a door unlocked? It was possible, but whoever had taken the hard drive would have needed to know what to look for, and no one knew about it apart from me. Call me slow, but it was only then that it occurred to me to check the laptop, sitting where I'd left it on the coffee table in front of the settee. It was on, but hibernating, which wasn't unusual. It was password protected, and the password was a variant on the name of an Old Testament prophet rather than my mam's maiden name or anything obvious.

I called Christine.

'Has anyone come down in the flat, do you know? Cleaners maybe?'

'Not that I know of, why?'

'I've mislaid something. It's possible it was picked up by accident if someone was down here.'

'Is it important?'

'An old hard-drive with a lot of my old research and notes on it. I wanted it for a sermon the bishop has asked me to preach. I've looked where it's supposed to be and then everywhere it shouldn't be, so I'm stumped.'

'I'll ask around. I'm sure it'll turn up. While you're on, the police called – something about a break-in at the university.'

Shit.

I felt the weight of Ingrid's brooch in the front pocket of my jeans and took it out, running my thumb over its talismanic surface, looking into the deep-blue and green stones of its eyes. I could taste mead. The scent of peat smoke whispered through the indoor air, the iodine tang of spray fizzing over the bows of a longship, *Skarfr* perhaps, as she tacked against the wind.

I stood in a field leading off to an indistinct horizon. I shivered, hairs on my forearms and the nape of my neck rising. Wolves paced unspoiled ranges, panting, padding, calling, snarling. I recognised them, welcomed them.

A man stood in front of me, unable to make up his mind if he was old or young or both at the same time. His clothes were rough, though the stitching and cut hinted they were once of good quality. His feet were bare and gnarled, ligneous, like exposed tree roots; his eyes were washing blowing wild in the wind.

> *Daughter of Maedhbh*
> *Lark of the morning*
> *Sing to me of magic*
> *And times to come.*
>> *Brave brother*
>> *Bold you were in battle*
>> *The bloodied bodies of Gwrgi and Peredur*
>> *Tell the underworld of your prowess.*

Ingrid's brooch was heavy in my hand; I held it tight against my chest, by my heart. What would Ingrid do if she were me? But I didn't really know her, wherever she was, lost in her pleats in the warp and weft of the world.

I woke up on the settee, cramped, with a stiff neck, and went to bed early. I had a doctor's appointment in the morning. My sleep was deep, with no dreams I could remember.

CHAPTER 11

Someone had made a valiant attempt to de-stress the doctor's waiting room since I was last there, with soft pastel walls, comfortable chairs, and a toy corner for children. An old couple sat in one corner, he on a gentle spiral towards death, she with the patience and concern of a decades-old love, words unnecessary. A young mother of two, with an infant squirming and angling for her breast, and a toddler smashing building bricks together in the play area, glared when I was called first, looking me over for obvious signs of infirmity.

I'd seen the look on her face before – the same one she'd worn the first time shed sent me for cancer tests, the same composed face and controlled, professional tone. And even if I hadn't been there before, I'd had years of sitting with doctors and parishioners in hospital and hospice with the tragically young, the stoic, the frightened, the elderly, going gentle or ungentle, but going all the same.

We negotiated the preliminary skirmishes: any need to pee more often? Had I ever smoked? Any recent urinary infections? Any lingering effects of that illness? Then we got to the haematuria in my last two urine samples.

'It could be a number of things,' she said, hedging bets, leaving room for hope. 'But after the last scare and at your age we need to check it out, just to make sure.' On her computer screen was the suspected cancer pathway protocol. 'I'm making a hospital referral.'

She took some blood and said I'd get an appointment at Urology at the hospital for a cystoscopy within two weeks. She also said it was possible I'd have what, in my numb discomfiture, I thought she called a turbot, and I couldn't work out what flatfish had to do with it. Later, the internet told me she said TURBT. The fish sounded preferable.

She listed the things it could be, but I heard cancer in the way she carefully didn't say it.

The moors were a quite different place in daylight. I wanted bleakness, but the quiet beauty of the swaying grass in the breeze, the play of sunbeams through the clouds rippling across the contours, denied me my melancholy. I was calm in the clean air and the whispering of the breeze on my skin. The light danced over the land and I was taken unawares by joy. The roving shafts of light flittered over me, bringing a second or two of perfect warmth. I was consumed by the now, by *being*.

Rabbit scuts flicked white, scattering at my footfall. A kestrel hung in the air. Indolent sheep followed my progress. The breeze that ruffled the kestrel's feathers skipped through the heads of tall moorland grasses, tickled my cheek. The shifting angles of the falcon's pinions, the bending and twining of the grass stalks, the translucent wings of insects, were shockingly clear, all interconnected. It was much more real than the faith I once professed.

I held the simplicity of the moment for as long as I could, transfixed by the overwhelming *rightness* of it all. And in the moment found someone to call *me*, the same me that had felt heaven under the stars of Sanctuary.

I fumbled for my phone and called the diocesan office for an appointment to see Sydney.

I got there early and found a spot in the cathedral nave, half a dozen rows back from the transept. The choir rehearsed the Credo of Tallis's *Missa Salve intemerata*. The voices swirled up through the tall air, ruffling faded flags hanging limp on either side of the war memorial, finding the ears of the stone heads carved high above the chancel.

> *Credo in unum Deum*
> *Patrem omnipotentem,*
> *factorem caeli et terrae,*
> *visibilium omnium et invisibilium*

But did I? One God, Father almighty, maker of all things visible and invisible in heaven or on earth – that's quite a thing, even without the gendered language. I believed in the sense of *being* I'd had on the moor, the ecstasy of consciousness, but all the rest? The beauty of Tallis, of the voices, of the vaulting architecture, all spiralled up towards elation and beauty, but it was the beauty of human hands and minds and voices. On the moors and under the stars of Sanctuary I'd heard the antiphonal call and response of the sublime. I couldn't any longer see a need to personalise it and call it the Divine, but I couldn't trivialise it as a passing aberration or a meaningless psychological category. It felt very real, even if I no longer wanted to call it God.

> *Et expecto resurrectionem mortuorum*
> *et vitam venture sanctum saeculi. Amen.*

Ah, there's the rub: the resurrection of the dead and the life of the world to come – a bit on the nose, that; one for another day. *Everything dies, that's how the universe works, you can't change that,* Rowan had said, and she was right. It's just that an intellectual appreciation of transience isn't the same as a physical symptom of it.

'It could turn out to be nothing at all, like last time. But I thought it was right to tell you before you made any long-term plans.'

Sydney's look was compassionate, and I was grateful he didn't reply with any over-emphatic expressions of concern.

'The offer stands, of course. If the tests are negative then no harm done, and if they're not, well, we'll deal with that when we have to. Have you told anyone else? David or Eithne?'

'I'll speak to them when I get back.'

'Are you sure? Until the tests are done, I mean. You don't want to be too hasty in case it turns out to be another false alarm.'

'I'll have to take time out to visit the hospital and stuff, so it's right that they know why I'm not there. I'd prefer it not to get out generally, though. And I don't want the students to know.'

'Understood. Thank you for letting me know so soon. You only heard this morning, you say? Must have been a shock.'

'Yes, but it put a lot of other things in perspective.'

He coughed, and looked embarrassed. 'I know this is poor timing, but I need to ask you about something while you're here: I've had stories about a manuscript come my way.'

Oh Christ, what now?

'What have you heard?'

'A bit of a jumble of things, about you finding something important and then a burglary at the university. And I got

137

a strange enquiry from Canterbury too, about Vatican interest.'

'This is getting out of control. I asked one of the faculty at the university if he could translate something I came across in Scotland. He thinks it's probably a fake but made some enquiries with colleagues. His office was burgled soon after. The police are involved.'

'Is it just smoke or is there fire?'

'Not even smoke as far as I know, but it's taken on a life of its own.'

'What's the manuscript?'

'Supposedly the story of a Coptic monk travelling to Scotland via Ireland in the early fifth century.'

'Really? Sounds jolly interesting. I can see why academic types might get excited – years of papers and conferences and PhDs in prospect. You've read it?'

'Only a rough translation. I don't know if there'll ever be a final one if it's a fake.'

'Right-ho, thanks. And I hope I wasn't too insensitive bringing that up, what with, er, you know ...'

'It's fine. Really. And they're just tests.'

'Do you have anyone to help you through this, to talk to?'

'I'm taking a long weekend with an old family friend.'

David and Eithne were talking in the vestibule of Weston House when I got back. I told them the news, making it clear there was no diagnosis, just a set of possibilities and the tests were to rule things out. I don't think either knew what to say. I felt sorry for them: they barely knew me and would look at me now in a new way, be anxious not to say the wrong thing, not to be *insensitive*.

The Imperial Death March played.

'Miss Hartley, an unexpected treat. To what do I owe the pleasure?'

'I wanted to ask you about a burglary and a security breach at the university. The target was Dr Danny Richardson. Do you know him?'

'I've met him, but I'm not sure why you're calling me.'

'The tick-tack is that he's made some kind of discovery, a manuscript, that's stirred up international interest.'

'That must be very exciting for him.'

'Yes, probably. Anyway, the problems at the university seem to be linked to his discovery, and here's the funny thing: your name cropped up. The rumour is that he got the mysterious manuscript from you. Do you have a comment?'

'I'm afraid I'm destined to be a perpetual disappointment to you, Ms Hartley.'

'Tina, please.'

'Sorry, I can't help you.'

'It's an eventful couple of weeks for you so far, isn't it?'

'Is it?'

'You know, unexplained disappearance and return, losing your parish, and now controversy when you start your new job, more controversy I should say. Abusing the staff at the cathedral on your first day was hardly a great start, was it?'

'I think this conversation is over, Ms Hartley. Please don't call me again.'

I cut the call and blocked her number, just as two police officers rang the doorbell.

'Oh, hello. Is this about the problems at the university?'

If they were surprised they hid it well.

'As a matter of fact it is, Reverend Cant. How did you know?'

'Because I've just had a journalist on the phone telling me my name has come up in the investigations. You'd best come in. Tea?'

I'd had lots of dealings with the police over the years, mostly to do with deaths and funerals and talking to the bereaved, sometimes for community relations. I thought I had a good working relationship with them, when I wasn't avoiding questions about disappearing for six months. They do have a knack of making you feel guilty even if your conscience is, mostly, clear, though. I daresay they know this and cultivate it, or at least don't disabuse you of it.

Like all representatives of officialdom, and all doctors and dentists these days, they looked like recent school-leavers. They flashed their ID and introduced themselves as DCs Gretton and Connor, and made themselves at home with my teapot. They brightened up when I brought out the chocolate digestives.

DC Gretton took the lead.

'We're hoping you can help us with the timeline leading up to the break-in. We'd like to establish the nature of your contact in your own words.'

DC Connor, eyeing my bookshelves, said: 'This was the same journalist you mentioned to DC MacKenzie in Sutherland?'

So they've checked me out.

'Yes, Martina Hartley.'

'And she just called you? From the same number?'

'Yes. Why?'

'Because we can't trace a freelance journalist of that name from the details you gave Police Scotland.'

I showed them the record of the call on my phone.

'There you go, the same number.'

'How do you know Dr Richardson?' Gretton said.

'Through a colleague: I only got here a few days ago and

met several people while settling in. Danny's one of them.'

'And you say Dr Richardson emailed you?'

'Yes. He'd been looking at some old material I'm interested in.'

'Would it be possible to see that email?'

'I'm afraid not, I deleted it. My email was so full when I got here that I deleted everything and have kept my inbox empty ever since.

'Do you normally keep it empty?'

'A lot of my old parish stuff was confidential and had to be deleted now that I'm here, so I just decided to delete the lot and start afresh. Same with texts. I reckoned if it was important enough they'd get back in touch. If Martina Hartley doesn't exist, who did I speak to?'

'Can we deal with Dr Richardson first?' Gretton said, glancing at Connor. 'It saves jumping around. Can you tell us anything else about your contact with him?'

I had to assume Danny and perhaps Eithne had told them everything about me and the manuscript. I offered more chocolate biscuits.

'There's not much to tell. I came across an old document, or what appeared to be an old document at any rate, written in Coptic – that's an old Egyptian script – and as it's Dr Richardson's specialist field I asked if he could let me know what it said.'

'When was that?'

'Last Thursday.'

'The 17th?'

'That sounds right.'

'What did Dr Richardson make of the document?'

'His impression was that I'm the victim of a hoax. He called it an "interesting fake", or words like that. He sent me a very rough outline with the warning that it wasn't a proper translation.'

'And this is the email that you've deleted?'

'Yes.'

'Why did you delete it?'

'Because it was just a rough, like I said. I'll keep a finished translation if he ever sends one, but it's a bit pointless if it's a fake.'

Sounds a bit thin, even to me. Keep breathing.

'You also met Sally Barratt of the IT security team. Why was that?'

'DC MacKenzie let you know about my phone?'

'It's recorded on the system, yes.'

'Eithne suggested Sally Barratt would be the ideal person to take a look at the phone and give me advice.'

'And did she?'

I fished in my pocket again.

'New phone,' I said, holding it up. 'She gave me advice on passwords and backups and securing voicemail and transferring my contacts. DC MacKenzie was going to look into my messages being read. Did anything come of that?'

They glanced at each other.

'Unfortunately, other matters assumed a more proactive status in the ranking of our operational priorities. The problem with Ms Hartley makes it more interesting to us, particularly what you just said about her call. There was a Martina Hartley who was a freelance journalist in Lincolnshire, but eventually gave up and went into PR and Event Management about four years ago. She died in a road accident in Portugal two years back. This is her.'

The woman in the picture Gretton showed me was carefree and laughing in a beach-front bar. I shook my head.

'When did Ms Hartley first contact you?'

'Not long after I got here. She said she was writing a public interest piece on the return of the disappearing vicar, although I'm told she was up in Sutherland, too, while the search was on.'

'Who told you that?'

'Mrs Mackay, the owner of the holiday cottage.'

'You've only had phone calls?'

'I had one meeting.'

'Can you describe her?'

'In her forties I'd guess, neat, professional, brunette. Shoulder-length hair, simply styled. She wore a necklace with a stylised crucifix. Drove a newish-looking grey Astra.'

'Short? Tall?'

'About my height.'

'Any accent?'

'Not that I noticed. Not RP but not obviously regional either.'

'Thank you. What can you tell us about the call you just received?'

'She knew Danny was looking at something for me; she was fishing. She got quite unpleasant actually.'

'In what way?'

'On my first day here I had a disagreement with one of the cathedral staff who was chucking a rough sleeper out of the cathedral. Somehow she'd heard about that and implied there was some controversy or ill feeling about it. I hung up on her.'

'Why?'

'I don't need a tabloid splash full of innuendo. It would make life awkward for the other staff and especially for the students.'

'Have you told anyone else about the call?'

'Not yet. I'd only just hung up when you appeared. And I'm new here, so I don't really have anyone to tell.'

'Can you think of any reason why someone should be

interested in the document you passed to Dr Richardson?' DC Gretton asked.

'That's beyond me, I'm afraid, especially if it's just an old hoax.'

'Thank you. Can I just confirm that I've got everything correct?' She read back her notes. 'Thank you, Reverend Cant. I think that's all we need for now, but we may have to be in touch again, especially if we find out any more about Martina Hartley.'

'I'm here tomorrow meeting students for most of the day, but I'm going away for the weekend on Friday. Do you want me to let you know if Ms Hartley calls again?'

They each left me a business card and I gave them what was left of the packet of biscuits as they went out into the evening – a votive offering, sacrificial, a prized axe head dropped into a sacred well.

CHAPTER 12

I parked in a bay a couple of hundred metres or so from Venny's house. Now I was there, my confidence was ebbing. What if my old friend was as long gone as space hoppers and clackers and Alvin Stardust on *Top of the Pops*? All Venny and I had was a shared adolescence. We'd never known each other as adults, never became what we flirted with under that candlewick bedspread. What was I thinking, coming back after forty-odd years?

This street was my whole world then: tightly terraced red brick houses, built for railway workers, with blue brick details in the masonry and a frontage onto the main road. I walked through memories of *Stingray* and *Fireball XL5* on telly, of 'Sparky's Magic Piano' on *Family Favourites* on the radio, of *Yellow Submarine* at the cinema – so good we stayed in the dark and watched it twice.

The world changed all around us in the sixties, as the generation who'd fought the war kept working to build the peace. While everything swung as a pendulum do, rosy-red-cheeked little children like me never noticed. No turning on and dropping out for me – I was safe in my cocoon of *Stig of the Dump*, *The Wolves of Willoughby Chase* and *The Children of Green Knowe*, until the Christmas that Borman, Lovell and Anders orbited the moon. We all waited the long fifteen minutes for their radio contact, then Jim Lovell said,

145

Please be informed that there is a Santa Claus, and Dad said Santa and Rudolph would have to watch out for traffic jams in space. Seven months later we all gathered in the school assembly hall to watch flickering ghosts walk on the Sea of Tranquillity, and each and every one of us who saw the giant leap for mankind thought our future was in the stars.

I toyed with finding somewhere for a coffee and a scone to pick myself up, but didn't get the chance. She'd watched for me from her front window and was out of her front door by the time I got there, all five foot one of her, crimson cropped hair and faded jeans and vintage cheesecloth top and a huge grin on her face.

It gave me such vertigo that I wanted to sag to the pavement. God, she was gorgeous.

She smelled just the same, of soap and sweetness and medicated shampoo, and she looked a good ten years younger than me, though our birthdays were only two weeks apart. She was light in my arms as we hugged, but her arms around my middle felt strong, as if she weren't squeezing as hard as she might for fear of hurting me.

'No dog collar?'

'I gave them up: stunted my growth.'

Her grin seemed to get bigger, though I didn't see how that was possible.

'In you come, tea's mashed.'

The house smelled of memories. I breathed in joss sticks, damp dog and books. Books were everywhere, on shelves, in piles, balanced on every surface, stacked under side tables and wooden furniture. Half a dozen tatty Barbara Cartland romances were bookended by *Wuthering Heights* and Hesse's *The Glass Bead Game*. *Pan Horror Stories* selected by Herbert van Thal butted against Delia Smith and a hardback edition of Geoffrey Elton's *The Tudor Constitution: Documents and Commentary*.

I dropped my bag in the hall and walked into the sitting room, almost unchanged from when I would come as a teenager. The glass-fronted mahogany cabinet was just where I remembered it, glass shelves holding her gran's collection of Royal Crown Derby porcelain, mostly Imari but with a nice-looking Posie tea set on the bottom shelf.

There was no TV, just a digital radio on the old sideboard. Two settees were arranged in an 'L' about a low rectangular coffee table in front of an open fireplace. Kindling and paper were in the unlit hearth. The carpet had been changed at some time in the intervening four decades, but somehow didn't look much different. The 1970s brown-patterned wallpaper I remembered had given way to pastel ivory paint that presented the art on the walls well.

The paintings were deftly executed, with a canny eye for composition and style, and all signed by Ven. There were a variety of scenes of the esoteric and occult in pastoral settings: someone standing in the rain with arms outstretched; a wild figure, warrior-like but dishevelled, standing on a cliff overlooking a river; a coven dancing sky-clad in a stone circle on a lonely moor; a Pan-like figure standing against a darkening forest. The centrepiece was a mountain landscape, a hillside at sunset with a shockingly familiar ruined broch in the foreground.

She was close all of a sudden, slipping inside my personal space like it was her own.

'I saw that place in a dream I had about you and had to paint it. It messed my week right up, I can tell you: I had lots of other things to do. Where is it?'

'It's Dun Dornaigil, near the foot of Ben Hope. I went to a party there.'

Ingrid's brooch pressed heavy against my leg.

'While you were missing?'

'Yes.'

'I bet it was some party.'

'You have no idea.'

'You *will* tell me?'

'Yes. Yes, I will. I think you are the only person I can tell. Look, I need to say sorry. You know, for not coming back.'

'I were mad at you for long enough, but then I wasn't. And things got weird, and then you called and now it's all good. And, you know, I could have called or written too.'

She opened the kitchen door and a ridiculous bundle of fur and tongue bounded out, barking, jumping up my legs.

'This is Herbert. Say hello, Herbert, and I'll get you a biscuit.'

It was a relief to tell someone everything. Venny sat, silent, asking no questions. Her eyes never left my face. Her tea got cold.

Herbert lay across my feet, shooting occasional sly glances at me. He was a cross between a terrier and a feather duster, his white ruff and black-tipped ears contrasting with his brown fur.

I put the heavy brooch into her outstretched palm. She felt the weight of it, examined it, looking into the blue and green chip eyes of the twin heads, running the tips of her fingers over the moulding, just as I had done.

'My God. It's the real thing isn't it? It feels like solid gold. What're the stones for the eyes?'

'I don't know. It's not the sort of thing I can wander into a museum and ask about without drawing attention.'

'She made it?'

'I think so. She wore another just like it.'

Venny sipped her tea and grimaced. She went to make a fresh pot. I left the brooch sitting on a six-month old copy of *Fortean Times* on the coffee table.

'I knew something weird happened while you were away,' she said when she came back. 'But that's something else.'

I couldn't take my eyes off her when she walked, as she sat down beside me, the easy naturalness of her movement. I hadn't felt like that about anyone in years.

'You believe me?'

'Oh yes, me duck. It's a common motif, associated with fairy mounds in Scotland and Ireland. And Rowan sounds familiar too, as a kind of archetype. Rowan isn't an old personal name, though, I mean distinct from the tree. I think it's Scandinavian, or Germanic, or something, not Irish. And the Norse, *Reynir*, is usually masculine. Interesting trees, rowans, they're supposed to ward off evil and protect against witches.'

'Best not say that if you ever meet her – she won't have the word "witch" used in her presence.'

'Oh? Why?'

'A lot of the women she spoke with when she was more active in the world were burned as witches.'

'Really? Oh, that's interesting. In Scotland?'

'I think so. Why?'

'Because there is a lot of overlap between the accusations in the Scottish witch trials, traditional fairy belief and pre-Reformation culture generally. No wonder I couldn't sense you if you were in Faerie.'

'You're losing me here.'

'Scotland had a fantastic heritage and the zealots of the Kirk damned near wiped it out.'

'No. Go back a bit: you said *Faerie*.'

'Don't let the word put you off, there's quite a history goes with it; a deep mythology.'

'And myths contain a kernel of truth?'

'Mostly they're just bollocks, ducks. Unless you disappear and come back six months later with a solid gold brooch made by a Danish warrior who should be a thousand-years dead. Then maybe there's some truth in it. It depends on what you want to believe.'

'I haven't told you why I went up there in the first place. Remember all that stuff you said before I left? Well I do, even if you don't. You were right. I should never have chosen this life.'

'If you hadn't, you wouldn't have had to get away and then you'd never have got pissed with a Viking and I'd never be sat here holding that brooch in my front room.'

'What's your story then? What did I miss?' I asked.

'Mam and Dad left me money and the house, so I've never really wanted for anything. I was a secretary for a bit – admin assistant, that kind of thing. And I've travelled about. Not much to tell, really.'

'What did you mean about "sensing" me earlier?'

'I've known what you're doing and how you're feeling for a long time. I kind of know where you are too, like a compass in my head pointed towards you.'

Well that's unexpected.

The room was dark now the sun had dropped below the rooftops opposite. People passed by outside, dark shapes against a dull background, walking who knows where to do who knows what. I shivered.

'How long?' I asked.

'1983.'

I thought back. That was after my degree but before I was an ordinand. I had a clerical job in the Civil Service for a while as I worked out what to do with myself.

'What about when I was in Sanctuary?'

'I felt you disappear from my head, but I knew you weren't dead. And then one morning you were back.'

'This is what you call not much to tell? That's weird.'

'It's all bloody weird, ducks. Do you remember John

Dawson? Sat behind us in Chemistry, played bass in the school band. He was in a History night class I did and we went to the pub a few times. He was into all sorts, *Supernature, Chariots of the Gods*, that stuff. He had this big book his mam got him from *Reader's Digest*, with maps and articles about folklore and myths of Britain or something like that, and he went out at weekends looking for ley lines. He'd try and link places up with a ruler on the map and go and see how they looked on the ground. So I went with him. It was fun, and we got to stop in lots of country pubs, and sometimes go for a long weekend with a tent and stuff. He'd borrow his dad's car and we'd disappear. Then he got too serious, and that was that.

'But we'd meet up with others interested in the same sorts of things and soon we all knew each other. I got friendly with one who wanted help cataloguing and sorting out his stuff. He had this big house in its own grounds in the middle of all the new estates. His name was Edmond Boulton-Lane, and he was quite posh, or he liked to give that impression anyway.

'He were right self-absorbed and could have done with a bath and a trip to the dentist, and I've seen more fat on a chip, but he was OK – not a creep. He had this big collection of photographs and negatives, journals, artefacts, books and ephemera he'd collected over years, mostly to do with battlefield ghosts and miracles, and the restless war dead, mainly World War One. But he kind of branched out into anything that caught his eye: plague villages, Civil War battlefields, folk tradition. He was a keen Morris dancer with a sideline in Yorkshire Long Sword and didn't have time for what he called Sunday-supplement feyness for the Aga and Volvo crowd.

'I thought he was just a harmless old bloke with more money than sense, but he wasn't. He got interested in Faerie and faerie-lore: the good folk, you know? One of his stories from a trip to the Scottish Borders had something different about it, like he'd met something.'

'A fairy?'

'They don't like that name, and can get quite unpleasant if they hear you call them that. The good folk is safer, or the good neighbours, the fair folk.'

'You're serious?'

'You tell me, I'm not the one who went to Sanctuary. Anyway, Edmond concentrated on the good folk after that, and collected lots of recent stories too – more than you'd expect.

'Then one Friday I went round after work and this other bloke were there. Edmond had gone to Sussex in his old Morris Minor Traveller, with red leather seats and wooden framing and split windscreen, which he somehow kept on the road. He came back with a big bag of notes and half a dozen exposed rolls of film and a new housekeeper, clerk, butler and general help rolled into one.

'That were Master Dobson, never Mister, always Master. He were a right funny one: tall, austere, with a mop of greying hair and huge hands with long fingers. He always had on the same suit that were too big for him. I knew there were sommat strange going on, but you know, Edmond never tried it on with me or anything like that, I'm not sure it ever even occurred to him, so I just thought him and Master Dobson were, you know— Are you OK with this, by the way? You're not hungry or anything? I can make another pot of tea.'

I was hungry, but I was lost in her voice, her scent, and she'd opened a door that I wasn't about to close.

'Master Dobson and I sort of danced around each other for a while. One night I saw him out on the lawn in torrential rain, face up to the clouds, eyes closed, arms outstretched, like those Jesus freaks you used to hang around with.'

I glanced up at the painting I'd noticed earlier.

'Yes, that's him. He wanted to know what I was up to. He made it his business to get the whole house immaculate, everywhere except the room I worked in; that irked him.

'Anyway ducks, long story short, they were both awfully sweet when I finished the cataloguing. They had a small tea party, and Edmond asked what I would do next, and I said I didn't know but probably I'd keep up the day job and find a new hobby. And they asked about my friends and I said I'd lost touch with a lot of people but I wished I knew what you were up to, and Master Dobson looked at me in the most peculiar way. That night I dreamed about you and when I woke up I knew what you were doing, and always have ever since.'

She leaned into me and I put my arm around her shoulders. She snuggled in like a Labrador puppy.

'Did you keep up with them?' I said.

'I went round to see them one day, but it were all gone. Everything. The trees were chopped down and the roots dug up, and where the house should be was a building site, with new foundations in a big hole in the ground. I tried to find out where they'd gone, looked in the newsletters, even wrote to them, hoping the Post Office would forward it. I got nowhere – no one had ever even heard of them.

'I tracked down the Morris side Edmond had said he danced with in Oxfordshire, but the dancers all died together on the same day in the First World War, and the side never revived like a lot did in the seventies. There were old pictures of the dancers in their kit on the walls of the village pub. The older locals could name them all but when I pointed to Edmond none of them could see him, and said the faces were just a trick of the shadows.'

I glanced at the *Fortean Times* on top of the coffee table, the back issues on the shelf underneath.

'Hence the whole weird Britain thing?'

'Oh yes. I even tried all the local estate agents to find who'd sold Edmond's house and spoke to a lawyer for the builders. They said the place had been derelict since 1943 and they'd banked the land years ago. They hadn't built on it before because everyone who'd gone on the site was creeped out and refused to go back. Clods of earth came out of nowhere, and birds would divebomb people. Local kids used to camp in the grounds sometimes for a dare, but never made it to morning because of the voices and the noises from the trees and the guylines getting cut in the night.'

'So it was all—'

'I tried to figure it out for years, ducks. It didn't do my health any good, you know, up here.' She pointed to her head. 'Especially when Mam and Dad were dead and I was by myself. What do you want to do for tea? I can cook or we can eat out or the old chip shop is still there.'

'Chipper. Is it still as good?'

'Same family, next generation. Hasn't changed in donkey's. Herbert needs his walk too.'

'My treat then.'

Venny laughed.

'I just remembered a night I went to the chipper on the way to Edmond's house. They were right confused when I got there: I don't think they'd ever seen food like it in their lives. They didn't have the right stuff in the pantry, so we all had balsamic vinegar on our pea mix. After that, every so often one would sidle up with a kind of pleading look on their face and I knew what they were after.'

After supper, we tidied away the remnants and opened a bottle of supermarket Malbec.

'So,' said Venny. 'This manuscript, then.'

'Yes. Would you like to read what it says?'

The strangeness of sitting in Ven's living room, chatting away as if we'd never been apart, washed through me. The house I grew up in was by the old canal, overgrown with rushes and algae, blocked with old prams and bicycles, home to rats, although Mam said it was once clean enough for Grandad to swim in. The towpath led from by our house to lock gates, corroded and rotting. The cut's filled and concreted over now, like my childhood. My car was parked next to it, a safe route for cyclists and joggers, a highway for foxes. The fields, golden with corn in my endless childhood summers, are all undersized houses and oversized German cars.

I flicked through one of Venny's magazines and tried to lay the memories to rest. It didn't work. My past wanted to reclaim me, but it was as alien to me now as Sanctuary, as the Church, and just as mysterious, inhabited by memory and loss and people long gone. My family clamoured for attention: I saw their faces, heard their voices.

There was Uncle Stan, who never married. At his funeral we found out he was awarded the Military Cross in North Africa; he'd never mentioned it to anyone. Mam found the medal after he died, stuffed in the back of his sock drawer with fading snaps of young men in and out of uniform, skylarking, posing in singlets and shorts on a Bren Carrier. I didn't know the adult code then, *confirmed bachelor*, still a criminal offence when he died. Did that poor, lovely, brave man spend his life in constant fear of imprisonment and ridicule in the new country fit for heroes? Lung cancer got him in the end.

And Aunty Bessie's husband, Henry, who was always away on business for three- or six- or nine-month stretches.

Mam and Dad kept their distance from them, though I remember Bessie at a leaving party for Uncle Robert and Aunt Patricia when they sailed for Canada and a new life, getting plastered on Mackeson Stout and sherry chasers while Mam cried.

Venny's voice dragged me back.

'Wow! A treasure out of India and Egypt, eh? And blessed by Jesus himself. No wonder people are excited.'

'But it's all bollocks, isn't it? There was loads of this stuff about: pieces of the true cross, various bits of martyrs.'

'Whoever's after it doesn't think so, ducks.'

'There's no one more gullible than someone who wants to believe.'

'I know that as well as you do. But you're missing something.'

'What?'

'Provenance.'

'Danny mentioned that too; he's unhappy there isn't any.'

'I don't mean it the way that academics mean it. D'you believe Rowan told you the truth?'

'You know, I've never thought about that, I just took what she said at face value. I suppose I've no reason to think she was lying, even if she left a couple of things out.'

'Right. Well, just the fact you got it from her would be enough for some. Or even that you produced it after you went missing in *that* valley. It doesn't matter what you think of them or what they believe, just so long as it's real to them. It doesn't matter if it's so-called respectable belief, or out-there Looney Tunes conspiracy nonsense or whatever. Trust me: there'll be consequences. Wait here a mo.'

I watched her in motion as she wandered into the hall, returning with an ancient Bartholomew's *New Reduced Survey Map for Tourists and Cyclists of Tongue and Cape*

Wrath. She spread it across the coffee table, brushed against me, her heat warming my arm. The map had sticky notes fixed to it, and various annotations, all centred roughly on Dun Dornaigil (shown as Dun Dornadilla). She pointed to the dark brown contours of Ben Hee.

'What do you know about this one?'

I remembered Rowan and Cathal mentioning it but not what they'd said. And I'd used it as a sighting point when I'd oriented the map I'd left with Rowan.

'Doesn't it have a different name in the Gaelic? Like out of *Star Wars*, Ben Sith or something?'

'Close. It's Bheinn Shith, meaning Hill of the Fairies, or Fairy Hill. There's loads of places in Scotland and Ireland with a similar name, all from the same root, meaning mounds or fairy mounds, with stories about people falling asleep there and waking up decades later, all dismissed as myth and superstition of course.'

'Oh.'

'Quite. There's a Chinese version where the protagonist doesn't fall asleep but watches a game of *Go*. Where did you say Rowan's home is?'

I pointed to the general area. Venny took a pair of compasses from a drawer in the sideboard and measured off the distance from Ben Hee.

'That's pretty much six miles exactly from the summit,' she said.

'Her *termonn*. Her *chomraich*. That's what she called it. I've just remembered, Cathal said something about Ireland, about hearing tales as a boy of fairy mounds and the Tuatha Dé Danann. Rowan looked at him in a strange way when he said that: watchful.'

'Did she, ducks? Well, that was the first strand of all the lore around places with that name. But there's lots of stories in private archives of walkers and wild campers hearing voices, of bee stings when no bees are around, metal detectorists reporting their machines giving spurious readings, or just not working at all.'

'Mrs Mackay, who I rented the cottage from, said her grandmother had the Sight and said there was something odd about the road, that it played tricks on travellers; some days it would decide to be a mile or two longer or shorter on a whim, like it couldn't make up its mind how long to be. She told me her nan used to walk out to abandoned townships and play with the ghosts of children buried there.'

'Has she got the Sight herself?'

'She said she didn't want it, which is a bit ambiguous, now I come to think about it.'

'I'd like to meet her. The travelling folk had stories and songs about that place too. They shared a lot with folklore collectors in the fifties and sixties, but not everything. You can hear it on the recordings: someone starts a song or story and stops themselves, or someone interrupts them.'

'That's not common knowledge though, is it?'

'It doesn't need to be, it just needs one clued-in person to join the dots. It didn't take me long to put two and two together. So when your friend Danny put the word out, I reckon ears pricked up, and word travels fast in those circles.'

'Maybe before that, even.' I told her about Martina Hartley, and brought her up-to-date with everything else, almost.

'She's just first in line, you mark my words. Come to think on it, there's a good chance she already knows that there's summat up there, so when you disappeared there she'd be interested, then when you came back, carrying an ancient text, she'd certainly want to know more. This is strange shit. I mean, I've seen weird stuff, but that's hardcore.'

I was sitting forward, shoulders tight, body tense. I topped our glasses up and fell back against the back of the settee, forcing my shoulders to relax.

'So what did you do, after the thing with Edmond and Master Dobson?'

'I wrote articles under a pen name – Suzanna Radclyffe – in mail-order zines, then online.'

'I searched for you online last week, but I only found you on the electoral register.'

'I never used my own name, right from the early days when it were normal to have a different online handle. And I never use social media at all. What will you do about that?' She pointed to the document on screen.

'I can't see a way out. I'm tangled up and don't know how to move on without getting more and more wrapped up. What a mess.'

Her arm slipped round my waist, mine round her shoulder; she wriggled in closer.

'You needed someone to talk to and you found me. We'll get through it.'

I looked at the table, thought about the tests I needed to schedule at the hospital.

'What? What else?'

'I was at the doctor's a couple of days ago. They want to test for cancer. Again.'

She was quiet at first, then laughed.

'Fuck me, Canty. You 'aven't 'alf chosen a great time to come back to me. What are we going to do with you?'

I poured the last of the wine.

'I ought to sort out my stuff. Which room am I in?'

'You can have my old room, I made it up for you.' She hesitated. 'Or you can sleep with me.'

CHAPTER 13

First light ghosted through the curtains, haunting the contours of her body, the shock of red on the white pillowcase, the subtle changes in her face as she woke up, the slow smile when she opened her eyes and saw I was still there.

The way she moves around the kitchen, the angle of her arms, the shifting set of her hips, the way she pushes her fingers through her hair. The words rolling around her mouth, across her lips, the ripple of vowels and consonants over her tongue. Everything about her looks different, sounds different, smells different.

'So what do you want to do today?' I asked

She gave me a look as salacious as it was seductive.

'Apart from that. We could go out somewhere, take Herbert for a walk?' I suggested.

'Spoilsport. Good idea though. And I need to clear my head of that wine from last night. Why don't you get the first shower?'

I'd just frothed up the shampoo in my hair when she joined me under the hot stream.

It was eleven o'clock by the time we parked my car and set out along a towpath. Herbert ran ahead, barking at mallards and goosander, looking for any excuse to dive into the canal. A steady procession of lovingly painted and maintained narrow boats passed in each direction. There weren't many other walkers out yet, and we had the path more or less to ourselves.

Venny's memory of school was better than mine and she tried to get me to remember events and people, with little success. We walked close but I was too self-conscious to take her hand in public, and hated myself for it.

The path was well maintained and litter-free. Every so often a laminated map on a noticeboard showed the routes of waterways in the area, the locks and towpaths, with pictures of wildlife we might see. We were aiming for a lock complex where we planned to get a pub lunch. I stopped to get a photo of the sunlight filtering through trees lining the opposite bank, glittering on the water, and saw a familiar figure a couple of hundred metres behind us.

'Hello, that looked like Martina Hartley, backing behind that bush.'

'Do you want to say hi?'

'No, I really don't.'

After half a mile or so we turned a bend and came to a bridge over an old, unrestored cut.

'In here, quick.'

'Where?'

Venny slipped into shadows. The towpath disappeared beneath tangled roots and foliage, by brackish water stagnating under a quilt of bright green algae. We were invisible from the main towpath after only a few yards, though we could see it through gaps in the dense leaves.

'How did you know about this place?'

'Keep your voice down. I've been here before – before the cut was cleaned up. Now shush.'

A couple of minutes later Hartley passed over the bridge. I only saw a partial profile, but it was her. She hurried on.

'What if she tries to phone you?'

'It's on vibrate and her number's blocked.'

'Clever Canty. So, we can follow her, or go back the way we came and go somewhere else.'

'Back. That's spoiled the walk for me anyway. I wonder how she knew where we were?'

'She followed you, or someone did. Did you tell anyone you were coming?'

'I told everyone I'd be in Bristol, not Derby.' She giggled, and reached her hand towards mine, just as Herbert bounded up in triumph, a dead rat in his mouth.

There weren't any grey Astras in the car park. I kept checking the mirror to see if anyone followed, but, after half an hour of back roads and country lanes, we decided we'd lost her. We stopped at a pub set back from the road, with a car park round the back and a sheltered, south-facing beer garden at the side. We sat out for a whole two hours while Herbert slept under the table and Venny talked about the stuff she investigated and wrote about as a hobby. They included Nessie and other monsters, mythical wyrms, holy relics, UFOs, Alien Big Cats and zoological anachronisms, spatial and temporal rifts, stigmata, Arthuriana and the Holy Grail, spontaneous combustion and ecstatic visions.

'I want to file it all as somewhere between delusion and error and silly buggers, but I can't just reject it all in case I miss something like Edmond and Master Dobson, or you and Sanctuary.'

'Have you found anything genuine?'

'I've met plenty who've had weird experiences and believe they're genuine. They're compelling when they talk, artless, not given to hyperbole – and embarrassed a lot of the time. What about you? You said summat about not knowing what to believe.'

'I'm still working it out.'

'Don't brush me off.'

I touched the back of her hand, let my fingers linger.

'I'm not, I just haven't put it into words yet. It's easier to say what I don't believe, and that's not enough, is it? And it's too wishy-washy to say I'm searching. The main thing I'm sure of is that I can't be a priest any more. I haven't said that out loud to anyone before, but I can't pretend to be something I'm not.'

Something inside me cracked; letting the words out made the fracture real.

'That's a hard decision.'

'No, it's an easy decision. It's the consequences that are hard. I believe ...'

But what did I believe? Back to that again. If I stripped away everything, washed away all the clart, what was left? It was the same question I'd asked myself in the cathedral and on the road to Dun Dornaigil.

'I believe in life, in existence, in joy and love. I believe we can be more than we are, and that it might be possible to describe that in terms of transcendence. I believe the usual language of Church and religion carries too much baggage. And I think the problem with Jesus and Gautama Siddhartha and all the rest was their followers made religions out of them. Sorry. That's so unoriginal. I'm supposed to be a professional at this. Give me a while and I might articulate it better, but it's why I can't be a priest. And I don't know what's left for me.'

'There's me – I mean, if you want me, that is. I'm here.'

I leaned across the table and kissed her.

'I'd like that very much.'

All these years alone and suddenly this, out of nowhere. Could we have had it earlier? We could have had something, but not so much in the Church. The stigma has lessened there, but it hasn't gone. Oh, there's 'tolerance,' but tolerance isn't the same as acceptance and celebration; it's implicit in 'tolerance' that there's something dodgy or transgressive going on.

I drifted off, imagined I was on top of a mountain above the clouds. The sky was empty of birds, but I saw other people, all on their own mountains. I shouted and waved, and a multitude of others, waved back, all of them me.

'Hey!'

I started back to reality.

'What?'

'You were somewhere else for a moment, somewhere that wasn't here with me. Venny's new rule from now on is you dunner go anywhere like that without taking me as well. Got it?'

She brushed stray hairs from my forehead with gentle fingers.

'Oh! Where'd you get that?'

'What?'

She dug into her bag and handed me a makeup mirror. On my scalp just above my hairline was a small, thin scar, stained, as though not quite healed.

'That's where I ran into the tree. Rowan said she couldn't get all the dirt out when she patched me up.'

'Could be worse I suppose, could be a zigzag scar across your forehead.'

'Pardon?'

'A zigzag scar, like … You don't know what I'm talking about, do you?'

She gave me a look I remembered from school.

'What will I do with you?'

'I've just thought: if Hartley's here, there might be someone watching your house. Shit, someone might have broken in.' I felt the comforting weight of the brooch in my pocket, safe from burglars.

'Best of luck to them.'

'Why?'

She looked at the table top.

'I didn't tell you the whole truth about Master Dobson. I didn't lie, I never have seen him again, but I sometimes think he's watching out for me. Someone did try to break in once, a few years back. Didn't get further than the hall. The stories he told the police in hospital had them convinced he'd swallowed a bag of mushrooms. Lucky I were out of town so the neighbours couldn't blame it on me.'

'Why would they do that?'

'They'd love a chance to have me turned over: they're too straight and I'm too strange. They'd like nothing better than for me to Bobby off someplace else. You watch the curtains twitch when we get back. I bet they dobbed you in to Hartley.'

'Is there anything else you need to tell me?'

'Oh, lots and lots. I've just thought, who were the others you said were in Sanctuary?'

'I only met Rowan, Ingrid, Cathal and William. Rowan said there were others.'

'Did you try to research them?'

'No.'

She shook her head.

'Well, why not? William's family were executed in the early seventeenth century?'

'That's what Rowan said.'

'You could have a look and see if there's owt there. A lot's been done on Scottish witch trials, you never know what you might come across. Nasty stuff. The archives in Edinburgh are good: have you ever been?'

'A couple of times. A Church of Scotland minister invited me up for the Dora Noyce Memorial Barbecue they hold every year during General Assembly week. Nice place.'

'Horrible history though. Walk up the Royal Mile and it's like the ghosts of the Old Town walk with you, like a great pageant of the dead. Pity it's overrun with tourists now, like Skye, destroying the reason people want to go there in the first place. Shame.'

I knew what she meant: I chose to go to Sutherland in November to escape the mass of tourists driving the North Coast 500.

'Right, then: research it is.'

'I haven't told you about Mam and Dad.'

I remembered them well because I was round at the house so often. They were good to me, and I liked them. Bob was an electrician with his own business and did OK for himself. Ruth did lots of jobs without ever sticking to one, just enough to bring in a bit of extra money and get her out of the house, she said.

'You remember I'm adopted?'

'The car crash, yes.'

'No: it turns out that's just what we were told when we were kids. My real mother was Mam's sister. She killed herself. Mam and Dad told me on my twenty-first, after you'd gone.'

'Holy shit. I'm sorry.'

'They took me to Rome for my birthday and told me there. Have you ever been to Rome?'

'Yes, lovely city. Had some odd experiences around the Vatican.'

She smiled.

'The singer out of Slipknot?'

'What?'

'Never mind. Anyway, it turns out my genetic father is a Roman Catholic priest.'

'Oh, Christ.'

'Hardly, ducks, but yeah.'

'Dead?'

'No. The bastard's alive, ninety-three now, but he's never wanted to meet me, ever. Guilt, probably.'

'Breaking his vows would be—'

'No, about Mam. She'd just turned sixteen when she had me, miles away from home. She were besotted with him, apparently – would do anything for him. From aged fourteen. The car accident was made up: they always knew it wouldn't stand up if I ever investigated, but I never did; never needed to. And the Church looked after him, kept it very, very quiet, put him overseas for a while, then brought him back to the south coast.'

'A regular parish?'

'Yup. Never a word said. Maybe they kept an eye on him, maybe not. Who knows?'

'Did they look after your mam too?'

Herbert lifted his head and looked between us in the silence, sensing a change in atmosphere. I reached down and scratched his ears; he twisted his head and licked my hand.

'When she worked out she was yesterday's rubbish she hanged herself. They found me crying in my cot by her body. She left a note saying she loved him and would see him again in heaven.'

Ven was detached, as if she were telling someone else's story.

'I've never talked about this before. I went to see him once – Father Alexander Hepburn. He looked at me for a while on the doorstep of the parish house, then said sorry but I was a mistake and he had repented and moved on and would I please go away and not cause him any more trouble.'

'Oh, Ven.'

'It's the best thing the bastard could have said. I am no bugger's mistake.

'The Church gave Mam and Dad a lot of money to keep their mouths shut and look after me. They didn't need the money, didn't want it, said it was tainted. But they weren't daft, they put it all away in the bank. That's how I've always had enough to live on, without really touching the capital. I can do whatever I want. I'm not fond of the Church, but I've had a decent life living on their guilt money. I'm just telling you now so you know – for the future, like.'

We sat, her head on my shoulder, watching the shadows cast by the early evening light drift across the wall opposite us. A shaft of light lit up the painting of Dun Dornaigil. The red light reflected off ridges and furrows in the brush strokes, candle flames around the broch. My arm was numb, but I didn't want to be the one who broke the contact.

'Are these all from dreams?'

'The broch is, and this wild man on the cliff is. Pan was done for someone who didn't want it when they saw it. You already know about Master Dobson in the rain.'

'And the dancing in the stone circle?'

'That's from memory. See if you can work out which one is me. The spare room is full of paintings I don't know what to do with. I used to sell a few but haven't bothered for a while.'

'Why are you naked in this one?' I pointed to the dancing in a circle. 'Something to do with the ritual?'

'Oh no, we didn't *have* to be starkers, it's just more fun that way. Don't you do that in the Church of England?'

She led me through to the kitchen.

'Do you want to butter some cobs? I'll feed Herbert and cook up some bacon, eggs and tomatoes.'

'Train smash,' I said.

'What?'

'Cooked tomatoes and bacon. Dad called it train smash, every time.'

'I always liked your dad.'

'He liked you too. Said you were good for me.'

'You should have listened then, shouldn't you.'

'Venny, I—'

She turned and rested a finger against my lips.

'Not a word. Don't spoil it. Accept it for what it is.'

'And what is it?'

'Us.'

I woke first. Ven's face was turned towards me, at rest, her spirit poised to dance across her eyes and lips. *Us*, she'd said: what were we? Lovers, yes. A couple? I wanted to think so, but once I committed to her, I could never break her heart by stepping back again. I hadn't come here for this, hadn't even considered it. Could I be falling out of love with the Church and into Ven's bed on the rebound? I didn't think so, but I'd had no time to take it all in.

And there was the other stuff: getting back to the college, bringing a lover back to the flat. I was certain that if I took Venny to Weston House she'd damned well be on my arm, not snuck in while no one was looking, as though she were something to be ashamed of. I certainly didn't want to end up like Sydney and Geoffrey, putting up a façade to the world and hiding the joy they should be building their lives around for the sake of show, in the name of 'propriety' and 'decency.' I wondered what Geoffrey thought about that.

'Stop it.'

I hadn't noticed her wake up.

'What?'

'Churning things in your head, looking for ways for it to go wrong.'

She pressed herself against me, tangled her legs in mine, snaked an arm across my stomach.

'It's just that I didn't expect this, at my time of life, *our* time of life, in my situation.'

She raised herself up so her face was above me.

'Is it a problem?'

'No. It's just—'

'Consequences. You said that before: not the decision but the consequences: how you change, how people see you. Me too. I used to be an eccentric single woman with a yappy dog, now I'm a seducer of priests.'

'This will sound silly.'

'Bet it doesn't.'

'Well, I've spent all these years talking about love: God's love, the love of the couples I married, the love of a widow for her dead husband, the love for the babies I've christened. But I've never actually been in love.'

'That's not silly at all.'

'Have you? Ever been in love, I mean.'

'Only once.'

'And?'

'And you've come back. No!' She put her finger to my lips. 'Don't say anything you aren't ready to say. Don't say what you think I want to hear. That's not how this works.'

'That's just it, Ven: I don't know how this works. I don't think I've ever known how it works.'

She rested her chin on my breast bone, ran the fingers of her left hand gently down my side to my hips. It felt good. I lost myself in her lips.

'We'll work it out. Just you wait and see.'

'I can't stop thinking I've screwed up my whole life, and I'm only finding out too late.'

'Don't you dare.'

'What?'

'Come out with any crap about how you don't deserve me or how I deserve better or any of that shite. Don't go anywhere near there.'

'I wasn't.'

'You bloody were. I know you, remember.'

There was no point arguing. She was right.

CHAPTER 14

Venny took the esoterica and I got to work on William's family. Rowan had said they were executed when James VI of Scotland became James I of England and united the crowns. That was 1603. There would be a record of the trial somewhere, and the obvious place to start, according to Venny, was Pitcairn's *Ancient Criminal Trials in Scotland*, online at the Internet Archive, but Pitcairn hadn't included anything that matched the little information I had.

I spent all morning wading through pages and pages of junk thrown up by search engines. I kept at it while Venny took Herbert for a walk and picked up more milk and bread at the corner shop. I tried not to pay too much attention to the pages of notes she'd made while I'd got nowhere.

After hours of trawling, I found the transcript of a trial at the High Court of the Judiciary in Edinburgh in November 1605, in the appendices to a PhD dissertation from 1975, digitised by an American university.

'This might be it.'

'What does it say?'

Mr Williame Hairt of Preſtoune, Justice-Depute
Nov. 8: Jonet Wilkie, ſpous to William Maxwell in Edinburgh.

Dilatit of the vſing of Sorcerie, Witchcraft, and

Incantatioune, with Invocatioun of spretis of the devill;
continewand in familiaritie with thame, at all sic tymes
as sche thocht expedient; deling with charmes, and
abusing the peple with devillisch craft of sorcerie foirsaid,
be the meanis eftir specefeit; In the first, That fforsamekle
as the said Jonet being demandit, be quhat art and
knaulege sche culd haillit seik persounes? Ansuerit and
declarit, that sche hirself had na kynd of art nor science
swa to do; bot diuerse tymes, quhen onye sic persounes
come ather to hir, sche wald inquire at ane Roan, quha
wald tell hir, quhen euir sche askit. In the 2nd That
fforsamekle as the said Jonet being demandit, be quhat
art and knaulege sche culd schaw diuerse persounes of
thingis to cum? Ansuerit and declarit, that sche hirself
had na kynd of art nor science swa to do; bot diuerse
tymes, quhen onye sic perounes come ather to hir, sche
wald inquire at ane Lulach, quha deit in tyme lang
bygane, wha wald tell hir, quhen euir sche askit.

'Bloody hell, that's hard work,' I said.

'At least it's printed. You should see what the originals look like. Isn't there a transcript in modern English?'

I looked through the contents page of the dissertation and checked the footnotes for sources, which were shelf references for the original process papers. I noted them down.

'Some bits are transcribed and some aren't. Go and put the kettle on and I'll see what I can copy and paste and print out.'

ITEM, for frequenting and associating with the good
neighbours and Roan, who denied she was Queen of
Elfame, confessed said Jonet that she would be [well
and active] *in her bed and would not know where*

*she would be in the morning: And that she was seven
years in the Court of Elfame and had kind friends
there, And that it was [those] good neighbours that
healed folks under God: And that she was coming
and going in Edinburgh in healing of folks these many
years bypast. ITEM, that she saw the good neighbours
make their salves, with pans and fires; and that they
gathered their herbs, before the sun rising, as she did.*

'Do you think that *Roan* could be Rowan? And there
was another name in the first bit, Lulach – could that be
the Lallig who Cathal told me about? This next bit isn't
modernised.'

*ITEM, of hir confeſſioune maid, ſaid Jonet ſpeikit a
prayer and conjuration quhene ſche haillit ſeik folkis
leirnit fra Agnes Sampsone, brunt in aſſis as a wich
in tyme paſt quhairof the tennour followis.*

    All kindis of illis that ewir may be,
    In Cryſts name, I coniure ȝe;
    I coniure ȝe, baith mair and les,
    With all þe vertewis of þe meſs,
    And rycht ſa, be þe naillis ſa,
    That naillit Jeſus, and na ma;
    And rycht ſa, be þe ſamin blude,
    That reikit owre þe ruithfull rwid;
    Furth of þe fleſch and of þe bane,
    And in þe eird and in þe ſtane.
    I CONIURE ÞE, IN GODIS NAME

'Is that an actual spell?' I asked.

'It's what the prosecutor wrote, not necessarily what
Agnes Sampson or Janet said, but a verse like that isn't an
obvious thing for them to make up. The alliteration sounds
like a much older style.'

'Right, but why does she call on Christ and the nails from the crucifixion? Why *in God's name*? That doesn't make sense.'

'Maybe not to you or me, ducks, but you can't put a modern spin on it. You have to get your head around it in its context. I bet it's a remnant of something much older – pre-Reformation and then some.'

'There's a load more here about Roan and Lulach, but not in modernised English. Let's see: *Sche being inquirit, quhat kynd of creatour this Lulach was? Declarit: He was ane vile vnworthie wretche quha had vnkemmit hayre, and had ane roughe sark for his coitt and na brekis na ony maire claithes or goodis bot ane quhyte wand in his hand. Than Lulach went away fra me, and I thocht he gait in at ane schaddow in ane wall nor ony erdlie man culd haif gane throw: This was the first tyme that Lulach and Jonet forgadderit.* Hang on, this is clearer: *She saw a company of twelve riders on snow-white horses who were very seemly to see. Asked if she knew their name, she answered that they were seelie wychtis of the Court of Elfame; who came to desire her to go with them.*

'What's that got to do with witches? It sounds like a ballad, like *Tam Lin* or something.'

'Remember what I said about Scottish witch trials? That's them all over: fairy belief and pre-Reformation culture. For the hardcore Kirk, pre-Reformation folk beliefs were stories from the Devil. Loads of what we know about older beliefs comes from records of the Kirk trying to stamp them out.'

'Here's another rhyme,' I said.

Interrogat, gif Lulach, at his awin hand, had send to ony persoun, to schaw thame thingis to cum? Declarit,

*that he ſend hir to na creatour in middilyerd, bot ſpaik
and propheſiet thingis to cum to her in versis, videlicet*

> *Quhan Ieſuis twynne in Ynde gangand
> And hailly goſpel proclamand
> He Ioſephis gyfte giftit awa
> Til Egipt þyns til Scottis ſchoir
> Quhair Lanwethis twynne ſchall tak na ſleip
> Quhyle Ioſephis gifte in gombraich keip
> Fals Noſtradam and Hercyldoun
> Fra hie renoun be nacht caſte doun
> Til ſic daye he maun dree his weird
> Betuixt Elfame and Middil-ȝeird*

'That rings bells,' said Venny, leaning forward to look closer at the print. 'Some of the names that crop up, Lanweth, Nostradamus, Thomas of Ercildoune. They don't mean anything to you?'

'Nostradamus: Al Stewart wrote a song about him.'

'I'll take your word for it. Thomas of Ercildoune is Thomas the Rhymer, or True Thomas, supposedly a great magician and seer long before Nostradamus. I've seen Lanweth's name somewhere, but can't remember where.'

'It's strange poetry.'

'It's a prophecy, but I think something's missing. Is there much left?'

'Not really. Oh, I don't like this bit.'

*ITEM, she confessed by her Disposition that her own
lawful daughters by said William Maxwell, viz. Beatrix
Maxwell, Christiane Maxwell, Annabel Maxwell and
Marioun Maxwell, also continued in familiarity with
the said good neighbours and said Roan and Lulach
and they also dealt in charms and healed diverse
persons that were sick in the manner aftermentioned
though said Marioun Maxwell is but a bairn. Asked*

if her husband, said William Maxwell, knew of the said crymes of sorcery, witchcraft and incantation, answered, denied as her goodman was away in service of His Majesty's secret council.

'Oh shit.'
'What?'
'The next sentence.'

For which crimes the said Justice depute ordained the said Janet, by the mouth of James Henderson, doomster, as culpable and guilty thereof, to be taken to the Castle Hill of Edinburgh and there bound to a stake beside the fire and worried [strangled] *thereat* [until] *she be dead; and thereafter her body burnt in the said fire, and all her movable goods escheated to our Sovereign Lord's use.*

A marginal note added: *conuicta et combuſta.*

High clouds drifted in front of the late-afternoon sun. A stiff breeze ruffled stubby grasses beside the path. Herbert ran ahead, yapping. The path topped a rise and led a further three-quarters of a mile or so to a group of megaliths, enigmatic in their isolation. Were people sacrificed here to some forgotten deity? Men, women, children, virgins meeting an abrupt end to maintain the cycle of the seasons, for death and fertility? Was it an honour, to be embraced gladly? I placed the palm of my left hand against the tallest stone, wondering if I'd feel anything – any energy, any resonance of the beyond. Herbert cocked his leg and peed against it.

'You OK now?' Venny asked.

'It could've been me,' I said. 'It could have been me, telling them how I was spirited away to talk to people in a parallel existence, or however you want to describe it, then hauled off and before you know it *convicta et combusta*. All my life I've accepted without really thinking about it that the so-called witches were delusional or coerced into confession by torture, or had issues we pathologise as some kind of mental illness. But what if some of them told the truth?'

I imagined Janet's final moments, her children killed, the crowd cheering and jeering her into eternity in the name of the same God I'd dedicated my life to, just as women and men are slaughtered around the world by Christians, Hindus, Buddhists, Muslims, atheists in the name of some higher power or ideal; killing our precious babies to appease nothing as the seasons come and go.

'I found Father Adrian Coulter, by the way,' Venny said as we drove back. 'At least, I think so. His name cropped up in some archived Usenet threads from old conspiracy-theory newsgroups. Not his full name, just passing references to *Rev. Coulter* and *Father Adrian*. I had to juggle hints to get anywhere, and that wasn't very far.'

'What kind of conspiracy sites? UFOs? Illuminati?'

'Nope. Good old King Arthur.'

'Right. Arthur and Merlin and the Grail and the round table and all the rest of it. Do people take that stuff seriously?'

'Very seriously, and not always in a good way. It's like the pyramids: there are your proper Egyptologists, then there are the others. Same with Arthur: historians who pick through myth and legend for some hint of a historical figure, if he ever existed, and the others go the whole hog for Avalon, Excalibur and the return of the sleeping king.'

The sky glowed in the west, lighting the fringes of clouds gathering to bring overnight rain.

'Biblical scholarship has that too: the quest for the historical Jesus, trying to find the man rather than the Messiah,' I said.

'Coulter crops up whenever anyone gets a whiff of anything more tangible than outright fantasy. So I looked to find out why a priest might be interested in Arthur, beyond a hobby, like building a model railway in the vicarage. Long story short, I don't think he's interested in Arthur at all. Every time he crops up it's to do with the Grail myth – to Joseph of Arimathea bringing the cup from the Last Supper to Britain.'

'Jesus, I'm in an Indiana Jones movie. It's all bollocks, you know, that Last Supper stuff, a liturgical readback, if it ever even happened. You'll be telling me next there's a secret order operating out of Rome trying to control esoteric knowledge and sacred relics.'

'There are several.'

'Fucksake, Venny, I was joking.'

'But I'm not. You never know where you might find a clue.'

'Do you know what apophenia is? It's finding patterns in random data, like economists do, or like Schiaparelli seeing canals on Mars, or people seeing Jesus's face in their tea leaves. *Finding a clue* assumes there're clues to be found; it all gets circular and self-reinforcing.'

'We have to start somewhere.'

'I know, I'm just … I'm trying to keep the weird at bay, I guess.'

'Oh no, you mustn't do that. You have to *embrace* the weird, or you miss half of what life has to offer. And it isn't really weirdness at all, just an expanded idea of the normal. You're surrounded by weird shit, Canty, and you need to stop ignoring it.'

I thought of Yrreddell, and Ingrid's gentle but determined questioning. The smell of roasting venison was in my nose, the taste of spiced mead on my tongue. I was in a wood-beamed hall with gleaming swords on the wall and a great fire in the middle, too hot to stand near. Cathal was there, his back to me, but he straightened and peered all around the hall, as if he sensed me, as you might sense a ghost in the attic.

'Is somebody there?' he asked.

'You're doing it again!' Venny said.

I was strapped into a metal cage with trees rushing past. Herbert lay on the back seat, head raised from his paws and tilted to one side, ears pricked, staring at me.

'Where were you, and why didn't you take me with you?'

'I was in Yrreddell in the great hall. It smelled of venison and mead. Cathal was there and sensed me but couldn't see me. I was thinking of a question Ingrid asked, about why I thought of this as the real world and Sanctuary, by implication, as somewhere not real.'

'And if I gave it another name, Faerie or Elf-Hame, say, would it be any less real?'

'Where are you going with this?'

'Embracing the weird.'

'Right, and Joseph of Arimathea and the Holy Grail.'

'Look, Canty, it's what I said before: the point isn't what the rational you thinks about it, or how bizarre you think it is. The point is what your Father Adrian Coulter thinks about it. He obviously knows enough about the manuscript and about Antonios to connect them to you and track you down as soon as he heard about it. If it makes you feel any better, we'll call it a working hypothesis, a straw man to be knocked over. Did you get his phone number?'

'He came through a switchboard, number withheld.'

'If it's that important, he won't give up. I wonder, though. The response to Danny's query was really fast: Coulter, the Vatican, a Coptic bishop, and the Archbishop of Canterbury's office as well as the university vice principal. Maybe they're all connected,' she said.

'You'd think if they were connected they'd come through one channel, not five. And what about the mysterious Martina?'

She checked her mirror, but there was no traffic behind us until we joined the main road back to town. We parked behind her house and moved my car to a spare parking space beside hers, then went for a late pub meal of pies and shandy.

'What about Edmond's house?' I said.

'What about it, ducks?'

'We were talking about the idea of the real world and whether Sanctuary was part of it. So where were you when you were inside Edmond's house?'

'Thinking about that did my head in, remember?'

'Yes, but was it like Sanctuary, or something else? Did it have a boundary in its own reality, or however you want to describe it, or was it as big as it needed to be? Was it part of Rowan's pleat, or a different one?'

'Short of asking them, I don't know where to even start with that. And the question might be meaningless,' Venny said.

'Why?'

'Well, the pleats within pleats thing is a metaphor isn't it, a way to describe something you couldn't grasp in terms of an image you could.'

I picked at the remains of my chips, put out by having to be schooled about metaphor.

'You know that thing where you stand between two mirrors that face each other and you see yourself receding into infinity in both directions?' I asked.

'Yeah, creepy.'

'When Rowan first mentioned pleats within pleats I had that same feeling, of an infinite regression of Sanctuaries. It made me dizzy. I remembered it at those standing stones. It happened again at the college.'

Later, I tucked my legs beneath me and settled onto her settee. I read the report of Janet's trial again over a hot chocolate. The horror of it hadn't gone.

'What's on your mind?' Ven said.

'Janet's story doesn't add up: she couldn't have gone missing for seven years if she was married with kids, could she? What about you?'

'That prophecy. There's no punctuation, but I think it translates as something like, *When Jesus's twin walked in India proclaiming the Gospel, he gave Joseph's gift away to Egypt and thence to Scotland, where Lanweth's twin shall not sleep while Joseph's gift is in gombraich false Nostradamus and Ercildoun will still be held in high renown. Until such day he must await his fate between Elfame and Middle Earth.* Does anything strike you about it?'

'Chunks of it don't make sense, like it's been half-remembered. The first part matches Antonios's story of a relic coming out of India through Egypt. Jesus's twin sounds like the Apostle Thomas, Judas Didymus Thomas, "the Twin", the Apostle who went to India in the first century.'

'If you say so. What strikes me is what I said earlier: it feels incomplete, it just says that this Lanweth's twin has to hang about while Joseph's gift is in *gombraich*. Didn't you say that was Gaelic for sanctuary?'

'Yes. What's all the stuff about Nostradamus and Ercildoun?'

'I don't know. But there should be something else, something that breaks the deadlock, something that really is prophetic. *Until such day*: well, until what day? I need to see what's in the records in Edinburgh.'

'Can you read the originals?'

'Good point. I've tried to read Scottish Secretary Hand before, and it took lots of time and coffee to work it out. Copies would be better, more time that way, and at least I could try and read them at home without travelling all that way. Or maybe pay someone to do it, that would be easier.'

'What about the other rhyme, the conjuring one with the nails?'

'I don't know, wasn't it a call-back to an earlier trial? I'll add it to my list.'

'Oh! I've just remembered something. When I was looking around Rowan's library there were some bundles of documents in wrap-around folders. I thought they were recipe books but she said they were collections of herbal remedies. I didn't think anything of it at the time, but those women might have given them to her, the ones who were killed.

'Printed?'

'No, handwritten.'

'Interesting: you'd have to be literate to write and read them. The perils of being an educated woman.'

All of a sudden, I grew weary of it all: the weight of the trial, the strangeness of everything, the way it distracted from *us*.

'Can we do something else?'

'Like what?'

'Go out, see a band, something like that. Late-night film at the cinema even?'

'Are you sure? You might be seen if that Hartley woman is around. Scandal of vicar's sordid secret weekend or something.'

'Fuck 'em. Let's hit the town. If you want to, that is.'

'A band, not the flicks.'

'I'm paying. I got loads of back-money for not dying,' I said.

'Are you going like that?'

'Like what?'

'You know – in those old clothes, no makeup.'

'What's wrong with like this?'

'I've got my work cut out, haven't I? Is that your only bag?'

'I dreamed about you, you know, when I was in Sanctuary.'

'Mmmm. Spicy, I hope.'

'I dreamed you were searching for me, that we were bound together somehow, by something unbreakable. I didn't understand it then, but it seems important now.'

'That thing you said earlier, about looking for patterns, apo-whatsitsname.' Her fingers moved in gentle circles on my stomach.

'Apophenia.'

'Yeah, that one. What if you're caught up in the same thing, looking for meaning in your life if you can't be a priest? Looking for patterns in the sky.'

'I don't know. Maybe. I hope not. That's the thing, isn't it? Having a belief, acting on the faith of it. You can question everything, try and justify every premise and conclusion, until you have nothing left at all. Maybe you're right, I should just go with it.'

'What about God?'

'She'll take care of Herself.'

'What about you? Who'll take care of you?'

I pulled the duvet up and over our heads, cocooning us against the world beyond the edge of the bed.

CHAPTER 15

The jamb was splintered. My books were hauled off the shelves, pages torn out, ripped and scattered. LPs and CDs were out of their sleeves and cases, and my few cassettes had had the tapes pulled out from the casing and tangled. The LP sleeves were ripped to shreds; shattered vinyl was strewn amongst the remains of the books. The HiFi was smashed beyond repair and left in a pool of what I hoped was water, though the smell said not. My clothes were shredded, the door ripped from the wardrobe, the chest of drawers ransacked. Everything was pulled from the cupboards and fridge in the kitchen and poured on the floor; my mugs and plates were smashed. I didn't look in the bathroom.

This wasn't a burglary, this was personal, a deliberate assault on all that was mine. On *me*.

Eithne came over as soon as I called her. If anything, she looked more devastated than I felt, horror and desolation all over her face. She slumped beside me on the steps outside the door.

'Have you called the police?'

'Right before I called you.'

'I'll fetch David and Christine.'

My phone rang. A selfie of Venny and me flashed up on the screen as caller-ID.

'What's happened?'

'My place's been trashed, everything.'

'I'm coming to get you right now. I can feel you from here.'

'No. No, don't. I really want you here, but there's nothing you could do except sit around and we would just be miserable together. Best get on with the other stuff while I sort this out.'

'Fucksake, Canty, you can't do everything by yourself. I don't know how you managed to survive this long without me.'

'I know, I … I'm just … Well, I don't know what I am.'

'Call me when you can. Is my present safe?'

What an odd question.

'Yes. It's in the car.'

DCs Gretton and Connor arrived at the front door. Eithne returned with David just after them.

'Holy crap! Er … sorry,' said Connor.

'We'll need back-up on this,' Gretton said, walking out of earshot to use her radio.

'Got to go and talk to the police, Venny. I'll call you.'

'Make sure you do, or I'm down there like shit off a shovel.'

'When did this happen?' DC Connor asked.

'I've no idea. I was away all weekend and just got back. I phoned you straight away.'

'Have you gone in?'

'Only for a quick look around. I didn't touch anything.'

'Good. Best to keep right out until we've had a look. You won't be able to tidy up for a while, I'm afraid. Was there anything of particular value in there?'

'Only my HiFi and some of the LPs.'

It was lucky I'd taken Ingrid's gold brooch away with me –I'd given it to Venny. The silk scarf was in my weekend bag.

I was surprised by the speed of the response. I've known burgled parishioners who had to wait a long time for any kind of forensic examination, and more often than not it didn't happen at all. Connor must have read my face.

'You have a connection to the break-in at the university, and there's the whole business of that journalist. You'll get the five-star treatment.'

She peered through the broken door and grimaced at the remains of chocolate digestives on the kitchen floor.

'Sorry, can't offer you a cuppa. Talking of Ms Hartley or whoever she is, I saw her on Friday.'

'Where was that?'

'Derbyshire. I was out for a walk with a friend, and she was following us.'

'Did you speak to her?'

'No, we threw her off the scent and went to the pub instead.'

'And you're sure it was her?'

I nodded, remembering her profile on the bridge.

'Is that the journalist who's been calling all the time?' said David. 'I meant to have a word with you about her, ask you not to encourage her.'

'Encourage?' I flared. 'I've been doing my damnedest to get rid of her.' David stepped back at the force of my response.

'Excuse me,' said DC Gretton to David. 'You've had contact with Ms Hartley too?'

'It seems like every other day she calls the office and Christine here has to fend her off.'

'Christine? And you are?'

'The college secretary.'

I hadn't noticed her arrive.

'We may need to take a statement from both of you.'

Christine agreed immediately but David's face was a

picture, as he slowly realised that the high ground had shifted from under him.

I sat on a low stone wall outside the flat, chilly in the shade of the college. I longed to be sitting above the tumbling river by Rowan's cottage, or, better still, giggling under the duvet with Venny. Why couldn't everything be that simple? I'd only just got back and was ready to go away again. Somebody must have called Sydney, who arrived in a bustle of episcopal authority.

'I'm sorry. This is all a bit overwhelming,' I said

'Of course. Let's see if we can't rustle up some water,' Sydney said.

'We can do better than that,' said Eithne, walking towards me with a mug of hot tea. In all the confusion I hadn't noticed her nip back to the small bungalow she lived in towards the back of the college grounds.

More police arrived and set about putting on their scene-of-crime gear while Gretton and Connor taped the area off. One or two students had come down to see what the fuss was about. Onlookers were gathering on the other side of the college boundary, mobile phone cameras snapping away, and a smattering of telephoto lenses on DSLRs.

'I think I'd like to go inside, please,' I said, gesturing at the gathering crowd. 'If I have a breakdown, I'd rather do it where the neighbours can't see.' I summoned a smile from somewhere.

'I'll have one of the college rooms made up for you,' Christine said.

I'd driven into the Weston House grounds with a bad case of the blues. It wasn't just all the unresolved things in my life that I had to sort out, not least the hospital tests and how much, or how little, life I might have left. It was missing Ven.

I couldn't believe the sudden, intense physicality with her, or how quickly we'd tumbled into intimacy, or the emotional energy of it all. At my age you don't expect it, grow resigned to its absence, try to move on to that place they tell you about – a later stage in life where the passions of adolescence and early adulthood decay into memory. That's nonsense, of course. And I'm no more immune to the sight of attractive men and women than anyone else. I'd just learned to keep it to myself, to 'act my age', and keep the pangs of lust locked in an untidy cupboard along the hallway of my psyche. Now the cupboard had been flung open and I found myself groping around the shelves for what I'd put aside for a rainy day, relieved to find it serviceable, as muscle memory guided fingers and tongues and hips in the service of desire.

And love.

I had no doubt Venny and I had not just surrendered to late middle-aged desire, but had made love, a squishy, fleshy metaphor, a sacrament. And I'm willing to bet my blood pressure in the afterglow was better than it had been for years.

'Yes, it's all getting a bit busy,' said Sydney, and he, Eithne and I slipped round the corner into the back door of the college and through the refectory.

'I'd best get back to the office,' said Sydney, once I was settled. 'I'm not much use with all this. If there's anything you need, let me know. Oh, I almost forgot. This isn't a good time, but there was someone at Eucharist yesterday asking for you, one of our Roman brethren. Coulter, I think his name was, Father Coulter. I said I'd pass his details on to you. Sorry, not great timing again.' He offered a business card that I slipped into my breast pocket without looking.

'Someone you know?' asked Eithne.

'We've spoken on the phone once, he said he wanted to discuss an ecumenical matter.'

'Like Father Jack?'

I laughed in spite of myself.

'Anything more from Danny or Sally?' I asked.

'All quiet. No news is good news, maybe. How was your weekend? An old school friend, you said.'

The smell of her hair, the touch of her hands, the taste of her kiss, the way she stood when she laughed, her weight on her right leg, hip angled.

'I had a really good time.'

'I never kept up with my school friends. Not on purpose or anything, we just never kept in touch,' Eithne said.

'Me neither, nor my university class. I went to a couple of alumni things, but it felt forced, so I let it go.'

'Did you say Derbyshire earlier? I thought you went to Bristol. You don't have much of an accent.'

'She said I talk funny now – maybe that's what she meant. All quiet while I was away?'

'The usual. What did you say to Robert and Helen by the way, something about the Mission?'

I had to cast my mind back – last week felt so long ago. 'I saw them in the library the other day, just before I bumped into you at the copier. Their placements are up, so I suggested that if they were at a loose end on Sunday, they might go along and feed the homeless. Why?'

'They took you up on it.'

'Oh, excellent. Did they say anything about it?'

'They certainly did, had a blazing row, actually.'

'How can you have a blazing row about that?'

'You'd have thought it was difficult, wouldn't you? Robert, the one you'd least expect to feel comfortable with it, was really affected. He came to see me afterwards: it was so far out of his experience it was a revelation.

It's given him a lot to think about.'

I pictured Robert and his intense, intellectual presence.

'And Helen? It's more her sort of thing isn't it?'

'You'd have thought so, but she was quite worked up about it. She gave us chapter and verse last night over supper and again at breakfast this morning about the disgrace of volunteers doing the work of government, the need to remove structural inequalities, and not colluding with systems of repression and suppression by promoting charity, however well meant, to mitigate the absence of State funding.'

'Oh, hell.'

'Quite. Anyway, Barbara Armstrong had enough. She cracked a raw egg over Helen's head saying *fuck you, Ayanwole*, and strode off.'

'Oh no. Remind me, which one is Barbara?'

'Tall, intense, glasses, cropped brown hair.'

'Oh yes.'

I'd only met Barbara briefly, but she'd seemed open and approachable, and we'd chatted about Buddhist thought. Not an obvious perpetrator of an incident like that.

'So what happens now? How's Helen?'

'Humiliated but defiant. We're lucky we don't have a serious disciplinary issue on the go, and we might end up with one yet. If it had been one of the male students who did it, we'd be right up the creek.'

'Helen's the only Black student, though, isn't she? That's not good.'

'I hadn't thought of that.'

That surprised me.

'I didn't expect her to be anti-charities.'

'I don't know if she'd go that far, and she didn't really get the chance to develop her point once the egg thing happened.'

I should have kept my mouth shut. Everything I did seemed to make things worse. I made my excuses and went out to buy some essentials.

They made up a room for me on the second floor, at the far end of a gloomy corridor. I emptied my bags of shopping, mostly underwear and basics, into a chest of drawers. I'd bought a kettle, a couple of mugs, a box of teabags and a packet of dark-chocolate digestive biscuits. My laptop was on the desk with my phone charger. Propped up against the wall by the wardrobe was Venny's present, given to me just before I left: her painting of Master Dobson in the rain.

I lay on the single bed looking up at the ceiling, hands behind my head. From beyond the door came the hushed voices of people who didn't want to disturb me. I didn't want to see anyone except Venny, but I was expected in chapel and at supper, and I assumed the police would want to speak to me again when they'd finished in the flat.

In all my life I'd never had a place of my own, it was always a house that came with my office, attached to a church, most of them damp and under-maintained. The flat had been my home for two weeks, and was just a basement of the college, but I still felt violated. It wasn't even my books and records and clothes: in the end they were just things. Things I liked and had emotional connections with, things that nurtured memories and moments and meaning, things I would miss, but just things. It was the vulnerability that was the problem. I was a child's balloon that had popped in the street, tattered plastic on the end of a string. A protective membrane had gone forever.

Who would do this to me? Why would anyone want to do it?

It wasn't just random vandalism. Someone was either searching for something or wanted to scare me, or both. I didn't understand it and didn't have a way into it, except I assumed it was to do with Antonios's manuscript. Everything had to flow from that because finding Sanctuary had been an accident – how could it have been anything else? Venny had asked why I'd felt I had to go to Dun Dornaigil, and Cathal had been sure I'd been drawn there for a reason, but the implications of that way of thinking opened the gates of the road to madness.

But what if I were wrong? What if someone had wanted me to find Antonios's manuscript, and the prophecy in Janet's trial did refer to the relic Antonios had brought out of Egypt? No. The idea that I had been drawn there by some mystical force to take a copy of a manuscript and thereby trigger events was manifest nonsense.

The only certain thing was that I had done exactly what Rowan had asked me not to do and, in that moment of arrogance, set things in motion that were spinning out of control. This was all on me. Maybe I should go back to Rowan and tell her what I'd done, go to ground there for a while.

But then I might never see Venny again.

The more I thought about Sanctuary, the less I knew what had really happened. Venny's story of Edmond and Master Dobson was pretty weird too. Do lots of people have similar experiences but never talk about them? Venny thought so, but even though I'd heard some strange things in my parishes, I'd never heard of anything remotely like Rowan or Master Dobson and Edmond, and I'm sure I would have heard stories if they were commonplace. It would be all over the internet, too. Come to think of it, such stories *are* all over the internet, and in podcasts or documentaries made for obscure cable channels. All that happens is the people doing the talking are treated as cranks.

I'd had enough of being noisily left in peace: I had to get out of there.

It was a lovely late spring afternoon and I found myself in the park by the river again, at the same bench, with a coffee from the same kiosk. The river was benign and chattering. The ducks had ducklings now, tiny scraps of feather and beak bobbing in the flow.

Someone sat down beside me at the other end of the bench. I feared it was the guy from last time, but it was the girl I'd met at her tent, then again at the Mission. She was in the same clothes, her hood still up, tight curls straggling around the edge of her face.

'Oh, hello. How are you getting on?' I asked.

'Not great. Still here. You?'

'Same. How are your friends?'

She counted them off on her fingers.

'Jail, hospital, dead.'

'Oh shit. I'm so sorry. Do you need anything? Is anyone helping you?'

'You kidding? I ain't a criminal or a patient or a corpse, so I get nothing.'

'Are you still in the tent?'

'Nowhere else to go.'

'I can't offer anywhere.' As I heard the words leave my mouth, I knew they sounded defensive, dismissive. I saw her accept a familiar rejection.

'It's OK, I ...'

'No, that's not what I meant. My place got trashed. The police are probably still there. I meant, I can't offer you a place at mine, or I would.'

'The guys at the Mission said you were a vicar or something.'

'I was. I'm not now. Not in a parish, anyway.'

'Are you the one who helped Kate at the cathedral, when she was kicked out?'

'Yeah, that was me. Took some shit for that. People are always talking about churches as sanctuaries, but they're not really, just the opposite.'

'Sanctuary. That's like a place of safety?'

'Something like that, or a holy place.'

'It's just a place though, ain't it? A safe place is good, but sooner or later you have to come out. Otherwise it's just another tent in the park. At least my tent is mine. I'm Connie, by the way: Connie Williams.'

'My best friend calls me Canty.'

'Not reverend or anything?'

'No. Titles mess things up. Canty's good.'

'What will you do about your place getting trashed?'

'What can I do?'

'I mean about somewhere else.'

'Oh. I've been loaned a room in a college. I'm supposed to be looking out for the students, but I can't even look after myself. What about you? You can't stay in a tent forever.'

'Like I said: nowhere else to go.'

I thought of having a room made up in the college, and maybe I should have just done it, but I couldn't see it ending well. I didn't have my phone with me to try and arrange anything else, and even if I had, I knew for a fact I would have a hard time getting any of the local parish priests to offer Connie anything, even temporarily. Too much like the thin end of the wedge. They'd say, *they'll all come looking for a place to sleep, and want food and baths, and then where would we be?* That was a good question, but not how they meant it.

'It's OK,' Connie said, guessing what I was thinking. 'I've not been doing this long, but I know what I'm doing, and it's not like it's winter or anything.'

'What about food and money?'

'If word gets out you've got money, you're a target. I wouldn't say no to food though.'

'Right, come on, we'll go and find somewhere.' She shook her head, laughed.

'What?'

'That's not how it works, Canty.' She paused, testing to see if I was OK with the name. 'They'd take one look and tell me to fuck right off.'

'So what then?'

'Get me a burger and fries and some salad and a couple of bottles of water; that'll be protein and carbs and hydration for the night. Then I'll be fine. Oh, and I need some supplies.' She said it as though she thought she was pushing her luck with a stranger, an apologetic query in her rising tone.

'Supplies?'

'You know, sanitary. Some baby oil or moisturiser for my skin, and some new hair bands.' She gestured towards her hair, still wrapped in the hood. 'I have to keep this tied up and the bands keep breaking. I can't take care of it properly in the tent.'

'Right, come on then.' I looked back towards the park entrance I'd entered by.

'Not that way.'

'Why?'

'See him up there?' She nodded towards the man I'd tangled with last time I was there. He was sitting on a bench, leaning forward on his stick, watching us. 'Grade-A perv. Offers money to girls, says he'll get them somewhere warm for the night if they'll go with him, if you know

196

what I mean. Thinks we're available.'

'Do the police know?'

'Do you think they fucking care?'

Connie must have been let down before to be living in a tent; what was her story? I guessed that she wouldn't tell me that. I liked her, and maybe it was mutual – she was putting her trust in me when she didn't have to. But I was on probation, I guessed, tested to see if I was trustworthy. We walked along a path lined with freshly green trees.

'What about your friends? Is there anything I can do for them?'

'Tom's better off inside. I'd like to see Tracy, I don't think she has anyone. And Joe …' She shrugged. 'I don't even know where they took him, where his body is, you know? He's just another dead Black boy.'

'I'll see what I can find out, if you want.'

How easy it is when you have a bit of status, *reverend* in front of your name. How privileged I was, for no reason at all.

Later, Connie, full of burger and fries and carrying her supplies in a plastic bag, asked if I'd be at the Mission on Sunday.

'I can't, I have to give a sermon in the cathedral. But I plan to be there the week after.'

'If it's still there.'

'Why wouldn't it be?'

'There's a rumour it's about to close because the Church wants the building back or something. And that'll be that.'

A note in my pigeonhole said the police were finished for the day but would be back. A letter from the hospital said they'd made an appointment for Wednesday morning. I had three missed calls from Venny on my phone and messages to ring her. I rooted around in my pockets for either of DC Gretton or Connor's business cards and found Connor's number. I explained the situation and about the man in the park, said I was worried about the risk of sexual assault and that I'd like to arrange for Connie to visit Tom in custody and Tracy in hospital. I asked to be kept informed of procedures regarding Joe, to have it noted somewhere that I wanted to conduct his funeral if his family couldn't be found.

Adrian Coulter's business card was there too. I'd forgotten about it, wasn't sure whether to throw it away or hang onto it in case I needed it.

After more tea, I went to view the wreck of the flat. I was surprised by my own calmness. The sense of violation remained, and maybe strong emotion would return, but right then I couldn't summon the energy. And it wouldn't do any good, wouldn't bring anything back. I found myself quite detached, more outraged in the abstract than the particular at the waste of books and records.

And it seemed like an opportunity of sorts, a chance to start again without the accumulated *stuff* of the years. *You can't come here, even for a short time, and not be changed.* Was this one of the changes?

I went to my college room without looking back.

CHAPTER 16

'I've reached a decision,' I said to Sydney over tea.

'About the role at the college?'

'In a way. I've decided to leave the ministry altogether.'
There: more *stuff* gone, and as liberating as the day I finally
told Mam I fancied girls as well as boys and she leaned
over and whispered *me too.*

'Oh dear. I hadn't expected that. No, I hadn't expected
that at all. You've thought about this for a while?'

'The sabbatical gave me the chance to work it through.
Your offer forced me to make a decision.'

'That's a hard choice.'

'It's the right choice. It has consequences, and I don't
know what I'll do, but I can't keep up a pretence. I can't
present myself as something I'm not.'

'I have to ask if you're absolutely sure about this – we
can revisit it in a month or so if you want.'

'I appreciate that, but I'm sure. And you need to find
someone else for the college.'

'Do I? It might be interesting to have someone of your
experience on the staff as a lay adviser.'

It hadn't occurred to me that was even an option. I took
the teapot and poured another cup while Sydney gathered
his thoughts.

'About the sermon on Sunday: I can cancel it if you want.'

'No, I'd like to do it actually, if you're still happy. I've thought a lot about what to say. I suppose it would be a good way to bow out, so to speak.'

'Right-ho. Look, why don't we keep this to ourselves for a while so you keep the place in the college while we sort out some kind of early-retirement package. We can make a quiet, formal announcement later. What about David and Eithne?'

'David won't be too sorry about it: we haven't hit it off.'

Sydney gave an ambiguous sniff.

'No, well, you're very different people. He isn't the type to make the decision you've made, he's too comfortable. That's partly why I put him in Weston House, to spare some poor parish from him. Is there anything specific behind your decision?'

'It's been a long time coming, and I had to admit some things that I've been denying to myself. You know, I went out to Evensong at St Edmund's the other week, Walter Cunningham's place, and it hit me just how much the words didn't express what I believe at all. I was much more at home serving up lunch to the homeless at the Mission. Does that make sense?'

'Perfect sense. The Mission, eh? You know we've had an offer to buy the land from a developer?'

'I'd heard something along those lines. It's a shame, it's needed more than ever.'

'Really? David told me it was poorly utilised. He's negotiating with this outfit, Saint something-or-other, and reckons the money they've offered would help the charitable trust recoup some of its losses.'

Losses?

'They cater for 150 people every Sunday and the volunteers say demand's on the up. They were surprised I was there at all when I said I was a priest – most of their support is from the Sikhs and the local mosque. The Church has little or no credibility with them. Selling the site to developers won't improve that.'

He looked thoughtful, as if he were weighing something up, but he didn't offer hints what it might be.

'I know I'm changing the subject, but can you tell me again about that manuscript thingy?'

'Like I said before, it purports to be the story of a Coptic monk travelling to Scotland via Ireland in the early fifth century, bringing a relic with him.'

'You didn't mention a relic before.'

Shit!

'Didn't I? It's all very sketchy, and Danny Richardson called it an interesting fake.'

'No mention of what kind of relic?'

'No, but it'll be the usual – a couple of splinters of the true cross, a shrivelled bit of something that was once part of someone's body. Why?'

'Canterbury have been on at me again, trying to get more information. They're being quite persistent, and it isn't like them.'

There was a knock at the door and Dorothy came in with the local evening paper.

'You should see this while you're both here,' she said, opening the paper to a grainy photograph of the police scene-of-crime team outside the college in their white coveralls. The headline was *MORE TROUBLE AT CHURCH COLLEGE?* The first paragraph read:

Police were called to troubled Weston House Theological College yesterday morning, responding to a break-in at the flat of one of the staff.

The story called me 'the controversial vicar whose mysterious disappearance sparked a nationwide hunt.' I checked for a byline, but it was attributed to an anonymous staff reporter. The main references were to the issues the college had had previously, and I guessed it was a slow day and they'd been grateful that something had happened, even though it wasn't much of a story.

Sydney let out a distinctly unepiscopal *oh bollocks*.

'I suppose I'd better call David. Can we speak tomorrow, or next time you're free? I need something to tell Canterbury if they pester me again.'

I sat on a bench under the shade of a beech tree in the cathedral grounds and called Venny.

'You took your bloody time about it.'

'Sorry. I got caught up in stuff. I've just told the bishop I'm leaving.'

'How did he take it?'

'Surprised, but pretty helpful with the practicalities of what I might do now. It's been an odd old day; liberating in its own way.'

'How's that?'

'I've just lost pretty much everything I own and I've handed in my notice. I should be despondent as all hell, but I'm not. Maybe it'll kick in later. What've you been doing with yourself?'

'Researching. I put in a request to the National Records in Edinburgh with those shelf numbers you got from that PhD thesis, then tried to find out more about the mysterious Father Coulter, but haven't got anywhere yet.'

'He was round here looking for me while I was with you. He left his business card. And Sydney's had more interest from Canterbury about the manuscript and the relic as well. It isn't going away.'

'Will you contact Coulter?'

'I'm toying with it. He was quite unpleasant, but he might know more about what's going on. I could do with a day's peace, though I've got an appointment at the hospital on Wednesday.'

'That fast?'

'Yeah. And I have a sermon to write for Sunday too.'

'Did you tell me about that?'

'I thought I did, but maybe not. In the cathedral. My last hurrah. Not how I imagined I'd go, but a good way to finish up.'

'Do you know what you'll say?'

'One or two ideas. I'll try to draft it tomorrow, then let it simmer for a bit and finish it off on Saturday.'

'Can I come?'

'Er, what?'

'Can I come? To hear your swansong.'

'I'd like that a lot. But I'm in a small room with a single bed. Maybe I can find you a guest room or something.'

'Won't people talk?'

'Fuck 'em. Remember the other morning when you woke up and told me to stop turning things round in my head and looking for problems? I decided then that if you ever came here it would be on my arm, not under cover of some polite euphemism, or quietly kept in the background like Sydney and Geoffrey. If you're OK with that, of course. I shouldn't presume.'

'Presume away me duck, presume away. Did you tell me about Sydney and Geoffrey?'

'I'll tell you when you're here.'

'Will I need a new frock?'

'Not unless you want to.'

'I'll plan my outfit now. A Siouxsie Sioux theme, maybe, since it's a special occasion. What will you do tonight?'

'Find something to eat, then go to sleep missing you.'

'It's all been a bit fast, hasn't it?'

'Having second thoughts?'

'Not a one. I was terrified, you know.'

'When?'

'When I asked you to sleep with me, in case you ran away. That you wouldn't, well, you know—'

'I was such an idiot. We could have had this years ago.'

'We've got it now. That's enough.'

I'd spotted a local greasy spoon on one of my walks, the perfect place for comfort food and a mug of tea. There was only one occupied table when I walked in and it was taken by Helen Ayanwole, who didn't notice me. I ordered a mushroom omelette and chips and a pot of tea, then walked over to her.

'Mind if I join you?' I saw hesitation on her face. 'It's OK if you want to be alone.'

'No, please. I didn't expect to see anyone, that's all.'

'Yeah, I'm keeping away from people too. Sorry.'

'I heard about your flat. That was awful.'

'I heard about the egg; that was worse.'

'I'll get over it. But all your things—'

'Are just things. I can replace them, or most of them, if I really want to.'

'I don't know if I could be so relaxed about it.'

'I'm not, really. I hate it. But I went down there earlier and I was OK. And I see things differently since the sabbatical.'

'How so?'

'I needed to think some things through, sort out my priorities. Time off the grid forces a change in perspective when you get back.'

'A mystical experience in the wilderness,' Helen said, with an ironic smile.

'That's not too far off it actually.'

'I was joking.'

'Sorry, it's a bad habit I've got. I can be over-serious about things. I should control myself more, or less, or something.'

'That's what people say about me – too serious, too committed, too academic and intellectual. When they're not cracking eggs over my head. I suppose you think I'm in the wrong too.'

I didn't want to make assumptions, but she must have seen poverty in Nigeria, and she wouldn't be an ordinand if she didn't care about it.

'No. I don't. As I understand your basic point I agree. We abdicate to charity what should be a public duty. But the thing is, when faced with hungry people, I can't not feed them.'

'I get that, but it perpetuates the injustice, doesn't it? The more we step in as individuals, the more government is content to let us pick up the slack, and inequality becomes a social norm to be remedied via a Big Society or some crap like that.'

'There's an old saying I came across once – there are arguments about where it came from – *in theory there is no difference between theory and practice, but in practice there is*. That seems about right.'

'That means compromise though, doesn't it?'

'Of course; compromise is an underrated virtue. Parish life means compromise every day until you don't notice that you're doing it. It has to – there just isn't time to fight every battle.'

I was hungrier than I'd thought, and the omelette was excellent. I asked for bread and a pat of butter and gestured to Helen to help herself.

'I was in the park earlier talking to a girl, a woman: Connie. She's sleeping in a tent tonight, like she has for … Well actually I don't know how long. I first met her a few days ago and she had three friends with her. Now she's alone; one of her friends is in prison, one's in hospital and the other's dead. If the flat hadn't been turned over, I'd have given her the spare room and fuck the protocols.'

Helen was startled when I swore.

'As it is, all I could do was buy her something hot to eat and some tampons and try to sort out a way for her to visit her friend in hospital. I'll probably end up conducting the funeral for the dead guy, Joe, too. It's not much, but what else can I do? Should she be living in a tent in the park? No, of course not, nor should anyone else, ever. And there're some real creeps out there.'

I savoured the last of the omelette, finished the last of the tea.

'Sorry. I got carried away again. Have you any plans for the rest of the evening?' I said.

'Only sneaking into the college when no one might see me.'

'Can I give you some advice? About the egg thing? Don't apologise, don't cringe, keep on being you. And don't sneak into college. Things will spin around your head for a bit, and you'll feel like everyone is giving you side-eye. And it'll feel like shit for a while. But that's what it's like in a parish as well, and there's no safety net there, just a protective cushion of privilege.'

She was quiet for a while.

'What you were just saying about the girl in the park: I get you wanted to do something personal to help her – I'd like to think I'd do the same if I could – but do you really not think at all about the structural issues or the "small-p" political side of it? I mean, I get the whole "the personal is the political" thing, but there has to be more, don't you think? What would you do if you weren't a priest? Ignore her, or find a way to help, or get involved in protest, or what? I don't think charity and protest are exclusive options, you know?'

'I could turn that around – how do you restrict liberation theology to a purely intellectual discipline? I don't see the personal as charity so much as discipleship.'

'Right, and that's great for *you*; but what happens if I say something? What happens if I make a fuss? What happens is that the Black woman gets an egg in her hair – my hair! – and nothing more will be said about it. Do you think Barbara will be disciplined? Will *you* do anything about it or say anything? Or will someone just have a quiet word with her and hope it's all forgotten about? Hope that I don't take it further? Hope that I don't make a scene? Have you any idea how hard it is even just to be here? To be the only Black person in the college? To just keep my head down and get on with my studies and not draw unwanted attention or speak out because the others do stuff and are called Christian and compassionate but I'll be called "woke" or some shit?' She stopped herself, although I got the feeling there was much more she wanted to say. 'Anyway: will you be at the Mission again on Sunday?'

Her abrupt change of subject was welcome; I couldn't answer her other questions.

'Can't, I have to deliver a sermon at the cathedral. But after that I'll be at the Mission as long as it's still there.'

'The cathedral? What's the reading?'

'Mark 2.23 to 3.6. An interesting passage. Well, all of Mark is interesting, but this focuses a broader theme from the prophetic tradition, somewhat anti-clerical, anti-ecclesiastical. I'm still thinking about it. I plan to get the first draft done tomorrow, unless something else happens.'

I wasn't quite as blasé as I sounded, but all I had to do was take my own prescription: don't apologise, don't cringe, and keep on being me.

I went to bed early, unsettled by Helen's words, her challenge to my assumptions. She was right – the worst that would happen to Barbara would be a quiet word, maybe a request that she apologise and 'do the decent thing' and then she and Helen could have tea and cucumber sandwiches on the lawn and all would be well.

The wind was getting up, sighing through branches and leaves, whipping round the crenulations and recessed windows of the building, sounding for all the world like the distant howling of wolves. I shivered and settled myself under the duvet. Late evening light glimmered through the inadequate curtains, casting dappled patterns on the far wall against which Venny's painting stood. It was obviously a trick of the shifting shadows, but I could have sworn Master Dobson waved and winked as I settled down.

CHAPTER 17

I sat in the college library after breakfast with a print of the first three chapters of Mark's Gospel from various translations, including a literal translation and an interlinear Greek/English edition. I worked my way through several commentaries, most of them unsatisfactory because they assumed a meaning in the words without looking hard at the words themselves. Maybe I was just demob-happy, but surrendering to my doubt had reawakened something. I kept catching glimpses of meaning, perhaps real, perhaps imagined.

Helen's comments the previous evening were at the back of my mind, bubbling up as I walked the streets, reminded again of all the other Connies who are out there. I thought of the dereliction I'd seen on my drive south from Sutherland, of the people in damp sleeping bags in shop doorways while others were in clubs.

Helen was right: I'd focused for so long on my own little niche, helping the people who were in front of me, and kept out of anything political, telling myself it was to do with my calling. I'd never given much thought to public expressions of personal faith, content to stay in my own world – my White world, as Helen had let me know – to stick with what I thought I knew. It was comfortable in that world, banking my stipend, taking the Church's cash even though I wanted out. I'd earned a pension, and I was

OK with a salary as lay adviser, if that ever happened, but the stipend had to stop.

What would you do if you weren't a priest? Helen had asked. I was about to find out.

I went out to find Connie. Her tent was on the far side of the park, but she wasn't, and I couldn't see her in town. I window-shopped in the spring sunshine instead. The wind had died down overnight and a heat haze shimmered above a slight rise in the tarmac of the road, the buildings and cars uncertain of form and structure, never quite coming into focus. I cursed the trashing of my HiFi when I saw a 180-gram vinyl reissue of Ace Inhibitor's classic, mellotron-drenched prog concept album *The Dawn Dance of the Calcium Antagonists* in a gatefold sleeve, almost certainly with extensive new liner notes written by Sid Smith. Once, long ago, *Dawn Dance,* a quarter of black and a packet of Rizla would set me up for the night.

I'd been at Weston House for two weeks to the day, and had told Sydney that I was leaving the ministry. It was long past time that I should stop reacting and take some initiative on other matters. I took a snap decision and called the number on Father Adrian Coulter's business card. He sounded as surprised to hear from me as I was to be calling him.

'I read about your flat – a terrible thing.'

'Thank you. Look, I was thinking about our conversation last week, and I'd like to talk to you about Antonios's manuscript.'

'Ah! And the relic?'

'I can't help with that; I only know what the manuscript says. To be honest, I'm curious what else *you* know about it.'

'And what do you think that might be?'

'You could tell me what it has to do with Joseph of Arimathea and the Grail myth.'

The silence was long enough to make me wonder if the call had dropped.

'Why do you think I can help with that?'

'The breadcrumbs you dropped online. And an oblique reference to "Joseph's gift" in a seventeenth-century record.'

I could almost hear him leaning forward with eager interest.

'Seventeenth century? Where was that?'

'Edinburgh.'

'I thought I knew all the relevant records, but I have never heard of such a thing. Are you sure it's related?'

'No, of course not, but it's a suggestive coincidence.'

'Well, this is an afternoon full of surprises. I can be there by about midday tomorrow if that suits.'

'I have a hospital appointment tomorrow, but Thursday or Friday are fine. And, of course, you now have my mobile number.'

'Thank you. Yes. Might I ask what brought about this change of mind?'

'Things have happened that I can't explain. To be honest, I hadn't planned to get in touch, but there's a lot going on that I don't understand, and I'm hoping you can help fill in some gaps. I'll give you a print of the manuscript in return, or at least a rough translation. It's all I have, but I think it's a fair exchange. And since you already know about it, letting you have it can't do any more damage than I've already done.'

'Damage?'

'To its custodian.'

'Thank you. I'll be in touch regarding my travel arrangements. My best wishes for your visit to hospital. Nothing too serious, I hope?'

'Just tests. Incidentally, are you aware of anyone else who might be looking for the manuscript?'

'I can think of several people. Why?'

'Because my flat was burgled and someone pretending to be a journalist has been pestering me, amongst other things.'

'I'll make enquiries.'

I called Venny to tell her what I'd done and was irrationally annoyed to get her voicemail. I wanted to hear her voice.

The scent of late blossom was strong and I decided to go again to the moors. I came to a place where the road ran past one of those ambiguous expanses of water, bigger than a pond, not big enough to be called a lake, fed by a stream flowing under an unimaginative concrete road bridge. I parked about fifty metres further on, and grabbed a waterproof jacket from the back seat, just in case, though the sky was blue and cloudless.

The stream emerged from between two low hills, and a rough track ran along its right bank. Trees and bushes, uncut and overhanging, caught my face as I pushed through. A glimpse of vapour trail overhead, a discarded beer tin, a used and knotted condom, were the sole indications of human activity. After twenty minutes' walking, the trees and bushes opened onto boulder-strewn open moor. I rounded a bend to see a small waterfall ahead. It reminded me in miniature of the falls on the path above Rowan's cottage, that fed the burn that fed the river that joined three others to become the Strathmore River flowing past Dun Dornaigil Broch.

A long-forgotten someone had put a bench near the waterfall to enjoy the view, but the seat was splintered and rotten, and the frame turned to oxidised iron bones and vertebrae, reaching from the grass and sedge like dead men's remains on a battlefield. I found a patch of dry grass and lay back, my waterproof rolled up behind my head. Only the waterfall and skylarks disturbed the silence, not even a soughing of breeze through the grass.

The Byzantine scarf was in my pocket. I took it out and felt its softness, remembering the night at the broch. Could I get back to Sanctuary? I'd managed to make some kind of contact with Cathal, but I had no idea how I'd done it. I'd like to meet Rowan again, and Ingrid and Cathal and William: they were kind and welcoming. How strange that I was comfortable contemplating something I would previously have considered impossible, speaking to people living in some other dimension or whatever it was, while rejecting the fundamentals of my faith.

The instructions from the hospital were straightforward. I could eat and drink as normal before the test and I'd be able to leave soon after the procedure, all being well. There was no plan to do anything more than have a look and take samples for biopsy if needed. I wasn't thrilled by the idea of a someone inserting a tube 'down there', anaesthetic or not, but I wasn't thrilled by the idea of cancer either.

I stripped from the waist down behind a screen and put on a surgical gown. I gave a urine sample then sat in an anonymous waiting room, reading the notices several times while staff came on and off shift. I was called to a treatment room where I tried to ignore the nurse setting out sterile equipment.

The doctor introduced herself and the nurses by name and explained exactly what would happen. I listened and nodded but but didn't take in a word she said. I lay on the table, and let her get on with it. I opted not to watch the monitor.

I'd imagined it would take longer than it did, that there'd be a bit more drama, but it was all very matter-of-fact. The doctor kept up a running commentary in her well-modulated voice, calibrated not to cause fuss or alarm. I'd hoped she'd have a look around with a camera and decide there was nothing to see, like an urban explorer who'd stumbled on an abandoned waterworks, but she took several samples for analysis ('might as well while we're in here,' she said).

When she was finished, I rushed to the bathroom to pee, which is difficult when you're numb. The nurse checked I was OK and finished up the paperwork. I asked when the results of the biopsy would be ready.

'Probably a couple of weeks, maybe three. There's a bit of a backlog.'

'I thought it would be quicker.'

'The doctor thinks there's no need to rush yours through.'

'A good sign then?'

'Let's see what the lab says.'

On the way out was a cafeteria and shop. I bought a morning paper and settled down with a flat white and a lemon muffin. I texted Venny, then tried to do the cryptic crossword but I'd lost the knack, and, anyway, I was distracted by feeling odd down below.

It was a busy concourse. There was a constant flow of staff, patients and visitors, DC Gretton amongst them. I didn't recognise her out of context, just thought that I knew her face from somewhere. I figured out who she was at the same time I twigged the woman with her was Connie. I waved and they came over.

'Hey Canty, what's happening? Visiting someone?' Connie asked.

'No, I had to see a doctor for tests.' Her face went from happy to concerned in a heartbeat. 'It's OK. The doc isn't in any hurry to get the results back, so that's probably a good sign. What brings you here?'

'Fi brought me in to see Tracy. She said you'd phoned Beth after we spoke the other day. She came to find me in the park.'

Connie was in clean, new clothes. I nodded to Gretton, who seemed embarrassed, as if getting caught in a good deed were bad for her image.

'How's Tracy?'

'They think it's pneumonia with complications; they're running a whole bunch of tests. She's happy enough, with the free food and everything. I said I'd find her some magazines and stuff.'

'Here, they're on me,' I gave her some cash, and she straightaway strolled over to the shop.

'Off duty?' I said to DC Gretton. It didn't feel right to call her Fi.

'Yes, well. I do have a life. And it feels better than just moving someone along or arresting them, you know?'

Chairs and tables flowed from the cafeteria counter and over the concourse without a separating wall, just a knee-high rope cordon. Along a corridor, two uniformed police officers had an unhappy-looking young Asian man between them, trapped against the wall.

'The grand thing about civvies is I don't usually get recognised,' Gretton said. 'Three people I've arrested in the last couple of years have walked by while we've sat here talking and didn't notice me. You don't wear a collar?'

'No. I don't like how it makes people treat me.'

I finished the last crumbs of the muffin and drained the coffee. It wasn't especially good, but I thought I might have another if Fi and Connie were sticking around.

'I went to the park yesterday, looking for Connie, but couldn't find her.'

'She was at Beth's place – Beth Connor. Beth's got a spare room and we didn't like the thought of Connie sleeping in the park. Nasty shit happens there sometimes. Oh, sorry, language.'

'You see? That's what I meant when I said people treat me differently when they find out what I do. How long has she taken Connie in for?'

'Undecided. We need to let her settle, and we've bought her new clothes, so …'

'Don't get me wrong, but I'm surprised.'

'Yes, well. Don't tell everyone.'

'I meant that I didn't think she'd trust the police, she said as much the other day, about the police not caring about a pervert in the park.'

'She told us the same thing. We're working on it. It's fragile, but so far so good.'

'What about your colleagues?'

'God no! We haven't told them. It would cause problems, you know? And we haven't done anything like it before, so it's new for all of us.'

'If you don't mind me asking, why now?'

'It was the risk of sexual assault that did it: there's a lot of joking and banter about it in the station – the men, you know? It didn't sit right. So we offered; it felt like the right thing to do.'

'What about her friends?'

'Tracy …' Fi pointed in the direction of the general medical wards, 'Tracy's really not well at all, and we're trying to contact her parents. We'd contact Connie's mum if she wanted us to, but she doesn't. Her pal Tom will probably get away with a warning. Beth said you'd offered to do a funeral for Joe?'

Connie returned with a bag containing three magazines. She offered me change, but I told her to keep it.

'Fi and Beth said your place was really badly done over.'

'Well,' I gestured with my hand to take in the hospital, 'I've had other things to worry about.'

'The tests?'

'Amongst other things. Have you guys got plans?'

'I need to see Tracy again, and Fi and Beth are on duty this afternoon. Why?'

'I was thinking about another coffee, but if you're busy, I'll give it a miss. How do I keep in touch?'

'Fi's getting me a mobile after this.'

I wrote my number on a page of my notebook and tore it out.

'Here: I don't always have my phone on, but you can always leave a message. Anytime.'

Danny had just finished teaching a class on New Testament Greek when I caught up with him. He didn't look overjoyed to see me, but flipped a *Do not disturb* sign outside his office door and took my apology for dragging him into my mess with good grace. The office had been put back to how it should be.

'Eithne said your place got turned over too,' he said.

'Everything – books, records, clothes, the lot.'

'Shit. At least everything of mine was intact, just thrown around a bit. Have the police said anything?'

"A forensics team came round, but no word yet. There's other stuff too. There's a priest who called me, who already knew about Antonios and, I think, was alerted when you put the message out on the grapevine. Then there's a fake journalist who's been on my case since I got back from

Scotland and is persistent, and unpleasant, for no obvious reason. And the Archbishop of Canterbury's office is asking the bishop questions about it as well, so naturally he wants me to tell him how to reply.'

'What have you told them?'

'Just what you told me at first, that you thought it was an interesting fake. I've done some digging though: the priest is interested in the relic mentioned in the text. He associates the whole thing with Joseph of Arimathea and the Grail myth.'

Danny groaned.

'So do you think I was taken in by a prank?'

'No. No I don't, not anymore. There's too much drama happened, and I've had the chance to take a closer look at the photos you gave me. I'd need to see the original to be sure, but everything about it looks right. There've been some really good forgeries lately, but they try their hardest to look ancient while this just looks well-preserved. I suppose the original is still off-limits? It actually doesn't matter what I think about it, I really can't do anything without establishing provenance.'

'Sorry. I didn't say before, but I broke the keeper's trust by photographing it in the first place, let alone sharing it. Even if I could get it, I'm too embarrassed.'

'Ah well. That puts it out of the reach of academic study. I've got a slightly better translation if you want it, by the way. No major changes from the draft I sent you, just a couple of obscure passages are a bit clearer. Here.' He opened a desk drawer. 'it's on your original flash drive. The main things are confirmation of a couple of what appear to be proper names. *Thule* is a disputed term that appears in Pytheas of Massalia's account of his voyage around Britain in the fourth century BC, or at least as we know it from secondary sources. Antonios claims he had access to an original. Thule could be anywhere between Shetland and the Arctic Circle. Also, there's that mysterious *Sanctuary*. I won't bother you with the technicalities, but it's obscure.'

'There's a tradition of calling Applecross a sanctuary, in Gaelic, but that's associated with a monastery established three or four centuries later.'

'Really? I didn't know that. So there could be some kind of lost religious establishment? That's intriguing. I could ask Caroline – my girlfriend: she's an archaeologist and might have contacts.'

'Ask Eithne, her family's from up there.' I pocketed the flash drive. 'This is a bit of a cheek, but while I'm here, there's something else you might be able to help me with.'

A wary look crept across his face.

'Not another manuscript?'

'No. I'm trying to make sense of a passage in Mark's Gospel in the original Greek. I wanted to ask you about the conclusions I've come to.'

CHAPTER 18

Father Adrian Coulter was a neat man, a couple of inches shorter than me. At first I thought he was my age, but as we talked I decided he was older than he looked. His face was jovial but his manner was serious and focused, like a comedian rehearsing Beckett. He was as dapper as it is possible to be in a traditional black clerical shirt and collar, a well-cut black suit, and black silk socks inside black Church's Monk shoes. In person he wasn't as threatening as he came across on the phone, and he was polite and solicitous about my health.

I let him read the transcript of the manuscript while I sipped afternoon tea in the hotel lounge where we met. I wasn't in the best frame of mind. I hadn't slept well, and woke up more tired than when I went to bed. I knew I'd had strange dreams and had a vague memory of oddness and something about a lynx and a fox, which at least made a change from wolves. I'd worked on the text of my sermon after breakfast, buoyed by Danny's view that my take on Mark was plausible.

Coulter had a small, leather-bound notebook resting on his right knee and made neat notes with a propelling pencil as he read the text, which he did twice before looking back at me.

'Fascinating. Thank you. It is all I hoped it would be.'

He paused then said, 'the translation leaves questions open.'

'The nature of the holy treasure? The identity of Joseph?'

'Precisely so.'

I set out my understanding that, on the face of it, Antonios was tasked with bringing an ancient treasure that went first to India with the Apostle Thomas before ending up in Egypt. If Joseph of Arimathea actually came to Britain, it would have to have been well before the end of the first century, so Antonios's journey would be at least three and a half centuries after that.'

'Correct. The problem is disentangling centuries of myth, legend and wishful thinking from something that might, in some sense, however loose, be historical. It's a matter of some controversy amongst those of us who take an interest. Then again, mention of Joseph is often a useful proxy for other topics that interest me.'

'You mentioned your Order?'

'My brothers. Order overstates it. It's more accurate to say we're a long-standing special interest group, not even a Society in any formal sense. We're interested in holy relics, and especially relics traceable directly to Our Lord. In all our years we have found nothing we haven't concluded was fake, and yet we keep searching.'

That surprised me, and impressed me too: scepticism is a virtue in my book.

'How did you know about Antonios?'

'From a fragment found in the Oxyrhynchus Papyri – you know about them? Documents found on an ancient Egyptian rubbish dump. One of us spotted the fragment in a copy of the Gospel of Thomas and put it aside for private study. Frowned on, I know, but that's how it was back then. The provenance was unknown, but it recorded that Joseph's most holy gift to Thomas was put into the hands of a monk named Antonios to take to a place of safety until the Lord called it forth again. Of course, it could have been any Joseph, but, long story short, I hypothesised a link to the legend of Joseph of Arimathea and the Grail and have kept an eye out ever since, just in case.'

'That's quite a stretch.'

'Of course, but it's useful to have a hypothesis because in proving it wrong you learn more. You mentioned a document in Edinburgh?'

'A report of a witch trial. I don't have a full set of papers yet, a friend is tracking them down, but it contained an interesting verse, that she thinks might be prophetic.'

I handed Coulter a printed copy.

Quhan Iefuis twin in Ynde gangand
And hailly gofpel proclamand
He Iofephis gyfte giftit awa
Til Egipt þyns til Scottis fchoir
Quhair Lanwethis twynne fchall tak na fleip
Quhyle Iofephis gifte in gombraich keip
Fals Noftradam and Hercyldoun
Fra hie renoun be nacht cafte doun
Til fic daye he maun dree his weird
Betuixt Elfame and Middil-ʒeird

'Oh my word. How do you interpret it?'

'Sceptically. It's from the indictment in a trial for witchcraft and therefore designed to secure a conviction: you'll note the reference to Elfame. Also, I'm wary of reading in things that aren't there just because of a coincidence of elements separated by several centuries.'

'Surely that's taking scepticism too far? This is marvellous.'

'Perhaps, but I'm not jumping to any conclusions. Taking them at face value, the first four lines appear to tie with the story of Antonios; I don't understand the rest of it.'

I caught the eye of the barman and gestured for a fresh pot of tea.

'You said someone is looking into this?'

'An old friend. To be honest I'd hoped you'd be able to shed some light on it and save us some time.'

'Can I ask my brothers?'

'Be my guest, this is from a public source. I'd prefer that my name isn't mentioned, though – it attracts attention. Your brothers don't happen to include someone in the Archbishop of Canterbury's office, do they?'

'No. Why?'

'Because they're putting questions to my bishop.'

'Oh, awkward. You've shared this material with him?'

'Not yet. I'm wondering what to do. It was an unwelcome surprise. Can I be completely frank? When we spoke on the phone you said we're both subject to the discipline of our Churches. I took that as a veiled threat. So I thought the pressure from Canterbury was related.'

'But you called me all the same. Why?'

'To lance the boil. We could have shadow-boxed, but what's the point? I'm not used to this, don't like it, don't have the patience for it, and I have too many other things to do. So.'

'As you say: so. And perhaps we understand each other better, and that's a good thing. It brings clarity. So, in the interests of understanding, there is something about that rhyme I can tell you. Do you know who *Lanwethis twynne* was?'

'No, it's something my friend was hoping to find out.'

'I can help with that. The Grail is best known as part of the Arthurian corpus, and Arthur's right-hand man was Merlin, or so the story goes.'

Here we go, into the black hole.

'Jocelyn's *Life of St Kentigern* says that Rhydderch Hael, king of what's now Strathclyde in the late 500s, had a wife called Languoreth, evidently the same name as Lanweth. Other sources say Rhydderch's wife was Gwendydd. Some enthusiasts say Languoreth and Gwendydd were the same woman, and some say they weren't. The sources are obscure and contradictory of course, they always are, so who knows? And the credulous have confected unicorns about them all over the internet. But one Gwendydd, who may or may not be the same Gwendydd, is said in later Welsh poems to be twin sister of Myrddin, whom that arch-fantasist Geoffrey of Monmouth renamed Merlin.'

The barman brought the fresh pot and I poured. Coulter and I caught each other considering the chocolate biscuits and we both smiled. A connection. Slight, but real.

'So, on that line of reasoning, or misdirection, depending on your point of view, Lanweth's twin would be Merlin, or, as he's sometimes called, Lailoken, or Lallig,' Coulter said, dunking a biscuit in his tea.

'Merlin. Right. Forgive me if I find that, um, heading into the realms of the unreal.'

'As well you might. I'm not advocating it, just suggesting an interpretation. But it makes the verse interesting if it refers to Merlin, reputed to be a prophet, in the same lines as Nostradamus and Thomas the Rhymer, also reputed prophets, though Nostradamus was a notorious huckster and fraud.'

'Assuming it isn't an invention of the court to ensure conviction and execution.'

'Of course. What was the outcome of the trial?'

'She and her daughters were tied to a stake, strangled and their bodies burned.'

'*Requiem æternam dona ei, Domine, Et lux perpetua luceat ei. Requiescat in pace. In nomine Patris et Filii et Spiritus Sancti.*'

'*Amen,*' I added, automatically.

'How did you come to find this, may I ask?'

'Janet Wilkie, the woman who was executed?' He nodded. 'I met her husband.'

I don't know why I said that, it just slipped out. Shocked disbelief overcame Coulter's face, then what I took to be a process of trying to assess my sanity. He didn't outright object, though, as if he didn't discount the possibility. I didn't give him time to ask about it.

'This Languoreth, if she was late sixth century, would be alive nearly two hundred years after Antonios sailed from Egypt, give or take. So would her twin, of course, whether he was Merlin or Myrddin or Lailoken. It doesn't hang together.'

'Well, of course it doesn't. Nothing about it hangs together at all, that's the fun amongst the seriousness. You'd need a time machine to go and see for yourself. Or maybe that's how you met Janet's husband? Otherwise it's all just speculation and guesses. But there is a pattern, wouldn't you say? A grain of truth in the legend?'

Mostly they're just bollocks, Venny said, and Rowan had said much the same.

'Do you know the term apophenia, Father Coulter?' I asked, considering another biscuit for the road.

But the pattern *was* suggestive, especially as Coulter named someone called Lailoken, or Lallig, and I hadn't. I searched for Languoreth on the internet on my phone and got sixteen pages of hits, only one of which, on the last page, had any merit or relevance. The rest either duplicated the same inferences tarted up as facts or were outright fantasy. For all the marvels and wonders of technology, this search required a librarian or an archivist. And time.

The whole thing was opening up like a sinkhole under a bungalow, tumbling into forgotten shafts and pits that went nowhere, dragging deeper, until every hint of a distant light made it seem we might be getting somewhere, not just groping around lost in the dark forever. But there's a rule of thumb I learned a long time ago: just because something looks orderly doesn't mean it is, and just because something looks chaotic doesn't mean it isn't rule-governed. You pays your money and you does your research and you don't jump to conclusions, even if Venny was keen for me to embrace the weird. Father Coulter and his tales of Merlin were enough weirdness for one day.

Christine was waiting when I got back to Weston House. It was unusual for her to be at the college after about four-thirty, and it was six-o'clock already.

'Is something wrong?'

'Not exactly.'

We walked along the corridor past her office and through the library to the door above the stairs to the flat.

'I came down here earlier to get some idea of what we'd have to refer to the insurance company, and I just can't explain it. I was hoping you could,' she said, leading me down.

'Explain what?'

'This.'

The flat was exactly as I'd left it when I'd left to go to Venny's. The books were neatly racked on the shelves, my HiFi was intact and my records and CDs were back in their place. The LP sleeves that had been torn were pristine, the vinyl inside shining with the rainbow lustre that warms the collector's heart in ways inexplicable to outsiders.

'But, how? This isn't …'

My clothes, previously slashed and shredded, were neatly folded in drawers or hanging in the wardrobe. In the kitchen the cupboards were as they should be. The milk in the fridge smelled fresh, the coffee was in its sealed packet. I felt a surge of pleasure when I found my old Egyptian *cezve* restored to shining glory.

'I don't understand.'

There was a knock at the door and I let Eithne in. She already knew. Christine had told her.

'We thought you'd hired someone.'

'No. I'd written it all off. I didn't expect to see any of this stuff again.'

'Well, since we're far too modern to believe in miracles, there must be an explanation. It's not as though Hairy Mag came in and tidied up.'

Christine and I looked at Eithne, puzzled.

'Something Granny used to say. Hairy Mag was a brownie.'

'What, like a Girl Guide?' asked Christine.

Eithne looked sheepish, as though letting slip an embarrassing secret.

'No, a household spirit, like a fairy. It adopts a house and tidies up at night when the owners are asleep.'

'I wish I had a fairy like Hairy Mag at home,' said Christine. 'It would save a lot of effort.'

'Well. Let's be practical about this shall we?' I said. 'I can accommodate my weekend guest here rather than in one of the spare rooms. And we should let Sydney and David know.'

'What on earth will we tell them?'

'Maybe that once the cleaners got in things weren't as bad as they looked?'

'Hmmm. We won't get *that* past the police.'

'We'll fix that when we come to it. Probably best that I go and get my stuff from upstairs and settle back in.'

'I'll help,' said Eithne. 'How was the hospital, by the way?'

Christine looked at me.

'Hospital? No one told me about any hospital. I hope it's nothing serious.'

'Just some routine tests.'

'That's what they said to my Johnny before he had his turn. He was never the same after. Routine tests indeed. You take care of yourself. And send any house fairies my way.'

I slipped out after supper to a local corner shop and found two cream buns. I set the painting of Master Dobson against the wall and laid the buns on a plate on the coffee table. I spoke to the empty room, not looking at the painting.

'That was an unlooked-for kindness. I find I have a spare cream cake here: please don't be offended if I share it with you as a small gesture of thanks.'

I ate one of the buns then went outside and walked round the college grounds a couple of times. When I got back, the plate was empty.

CHAPTER 19

I'd interrupted something. The spines of three books protruded on the shelves, as if a sergeant-major had asked for volunteers to step forward and these were left standing proud while all the rest took a step back. I pushed them back into line and went to make a mug of tea to kickstart the day.

When I returned, refreshed after a shower that was much more forceful than the pitiful trickle I'd got used to, the spines of four books now stood proud, but not the same ones as previously.

'Behave yourselves. A friend of Master Dobson is coming for the weekend.'

Apprehension rippled through the room.

Well, that was weird.

I'd held formal meetings with most of the students, but I'd been trying to find ways of getting to know them in a more relaxed setting, and meal times were the obvious occasions. I might have told Sydney that I was moving on, but the students didn't know that, and they had a right to expect me to fulfil my role as chaplain while I was in post.

Word of the flat had spread, and I could sense an odd atmosphere when I went down to the refectory for breakfast. There was a free place next to Tom Nevin, whose shoulder-length hair was, apparently, always dyed to match the liturgical season. He'd had the tips in flame red for Pentecost the last time I'd seen him, but it was now green with gold ends for Trinity. Eithne had told me he was unpopular with the other students for not flushing toilets to save water, or maybe it was because of the elaborate Yggdrasil tattoo on his right forearm. I liked him. He was deep in conversation with Ian Babbage, the regular organist in the chapel.

Helen joined us with her cereal and a bacon roll.

'All well?' I asked.

'Yes. And Zoë Lewis has been kind – have you met her yet? Glasses, shoulder-length brunette hair, takes a lot of care to look unstyled.' I shook my head. 'I hear your flat is sorted. How'd you do that?'

'It wasn't as bad as it looked, I guess.'

It sounded weak, but they didn't question it.

'How's the sermon coming on?'

'What sermon?' Tom asked.

'In the cathedral on Sunday. It's written. I checked some of my half-remembered Greek with Danny Richardson at the university and he thinks I'm on plausible ground. Now I just need to take my own advice and front it out.'

'You know Danny? I didn't realise. He was just finishing up his doctorate when I started as an undergraduate. He has a thing about the importance of understanding the sources of history, the texts, understanding their language. His tutorials are pretty good,' Helen said.

'I've only met him a couple of times. Eithne introduced us.'

Helen spread tomato ketchup on her bacon roll.

'Can I ask you a personal question?'

'Of course.'

'Will you go back to a parish or stay here?'

How to answer? Tell the truth? Obfuscate? I didn't want to lie.

'It's all up in the air at the moment. Why do you ask?'

'I wondered if you'll be here for my final year, next year. Hoping you will be, to be honest.'

'I'm flattered. Why?'

They exchanged looks, like it was something they'd spoken about between themselves already.

'Because you don't care about things other people take too seriously, and take seriously things they don't care about. We like that,' Tom answered.

'I'm not sure if everyone agrees.'

'You'd be surprised,' Ian said. 'After we stopped laughing, a lot of us found plenty to think about in what you said about Betty Boards. No one's said anything like that to us before. Does she really ... you know, in her drinks cabinet?'

'Big Jimi? Oh yes. I was thinking I ought to bring her here for a meal one night. I doubt the principal would approve though.'

'Probably not. I got the impression he was unhappy about something when he was talking to that journalist,' Helen said.

'Sorry? What's that about?'

'After that thing in the paper the other night. I was in the library and heard them in the seminar room – you know how thin the room dividers are. I didn't want to eavesdrop but I distinctly heard him mention Betty Boards and lack of respect.'

'How did you know she was a journalist?'

'I've seen her here before, a couple of days before you arrived. I answered the door and she introduced herself. I don't remember her name. She said she was freelance and here to see Father Sharpe-Thompson.'

'Martina Hartley?'

'That's her. Do you know her?'

'I'm trying my best to get her off my back. She wanted

to write a story about me and my mysterious disappearance.'

'Well it *was* the talk of the college when we heard you were coming, after the search and everything.' Tom looked worried, as if he'd overstepped the mark. I sighed.

'It would be strange if it wasn't. It was a sabbatical, a retreat, to work some things out off-grid.'

'Seeking the sanctuary of the wilderness? Sounds idyllic,' Ian said.

'Right, but not something I want to talk about with a journalist. Has she talked with anyone else?'

'I don't think so,' Helen said. 'I'll ask around. Zoë would know if she had. Zoë finds out everything sooner or later.'

'Does she? That's useful to know.'

My phone pinged: an email from Father Coulter. Another ping: a text from Fi and Beth to say they were coming round, followed quickly by one from Connie asking if she could come too.

'The day begins. And I've got a visitor coming this evening, so I need to get sorted for that.'

'Are they here for supper?'

'Maybe, depending on traffic, although I don't think she'd meet with David's approval either, or vice versa for that matter.'

'Sounds intriguing.'

Fingers, tongues, skin.

'Yes. She's definitely that.'

Maybe my face gave something away. Surprised approval whispered across their faces.

Have I just come out?

'I'd like to meet her,' Helen said.

'I'm sure you will. Sorry, got to go. That was a text saying the police are popping round for a word.'

Gretton and Connor's – they didn't seem like 'Beth and Fi' when on business – faces were a treat when I ushered them into the flat; I distinctly heard a muttered *what the f—*. Connie's eye was drawn straight away to Venny's painting.

'How did you manage this?' asked Gretton. 'We came round to follow up the lab reports and confirm you could throw things out.'

'What can I say? I have good neighbours.'

'Haha! That's what Nana used to say,' said Connie. 'She always left milk and a biscuit out at night just in case.'

'Why would you leave milk and biscuits out for your neighbours at night?' Gretton asked.

'Connie is suggesting I had supernatural help from a friendly household spirit.'

'Well I'm not putting that in a report: *the scene was disturbed by a supernatural person or persons unknown, believed by the occupant to be one or more fairies.* You might get away with folly like that in London but not round here.'

'They don't like it when you call them that, fairies I mean,' said Connie. 'Canty knows. That's why you called them good neighbours, isn't it?'

'You're serious?' asked DC Connor.

'Oh yes. You see lots of things when you're on the streets or in the parks at night, and Nana had lots of stories. Who did this painting?'

'My friend Venny.'

'You can tell her I like it.'

'You can tell her yourself. She's coming for the weekend. She'll be interested in your nana's stories.'

'She wrote a lot of them down for me when I was little. Maybe Mum's still got them.' She guessed the question forming in my mind. 'No, I'm not ready yet. Are all these books yours? They look boring.'

The spine of Paul Tillich's *Existentialism* twitched.

Stay right where you are; don't you dare show me up.

'All mine, and yes, some of them are boring. Help yourself if you see anything you fancy.'

I left her to it and went to put the kettle on, apologising for the lack of biscuits.

'So what did happen?' asked DC Connor.

'No idea. I was out, and when I got back it was like this. The cleaners say it wasn't them.'

'I really, really don't want weird shit getting back to the station, pardon my French. We'd never hear the end of it.'

'I don't especially want to be associated with weird shit either. Can't you just say I've salvaged what I could and replaced the rest? I doubt anyone will know the difference.'

They mulled it over.

'Can I borrow this?' asked Connie from the other end of the room. She held up a copy of Dostoevsky's *Crime and Punishment*.

'Sure. See what you make of it. It's quite dense, very Russian.'

'Cool.' She sat down and started reading.

Gretton and Connor's radios burst into urgent life, crackling a string of codes and jargon.

'Sorry – we need to be somewhere else sharpish.'

'No problem, we'll be here.'

I washed their mugs and went back to the living room to take a proper look at Coulter's email. After the usual pleasantries and thanks, he got down to business.

You asked who else might be taking a keen interest in the Antonios codex. I've found it difficult to find an answer in the short time since we spoke, however,

234

I think I can say with some confidence that the interest from Egypt is based on a concern for their theological and cultural heritage. At present the interest is scholarly, though political considerations may follow, both secular and ecclesiastical.

I have not found the locus of Canterbury's interest, and careful enquiries there have not drawn any response.

Although you are resistant to the idea, I have begun to wonder if there might be some esoteric interest in the matter. I remain intrigued by the confluence of names in the prophecy you found in Edinburgh. Languoreth, Nostradamus and Thomas the Rhymer would be a potent attractor for certain self-styled occultists, who rarely show themselves but leave spoors in their wake, much like the ones by which you identified me. What links Nostradamus and Thomas is a supposed gift for prophecy, which chimes with a hypothesised link between Languoreth and her brother. On reflection, I believe your insistence on the pitfalls of apophenia is justified and important, but others may not be so scrupulous.

Finally, one of the lines of the verse intrigues me:

Quhyle Iofephis gifte in gombraich keip

'Gombraich' is reminiscent of Chambrich or Chombrich, which is how Timothy Pont recorded the name of Applecross in the sixteenth century, the sanctuary area or 'garth' around Máel Rubha's monastic foundation. I understand the name still survives locally. This might explain the use of 'Sanctuary' in the Antonios codex. No doubt you will object that the dates are not congruent and warn me against seeing patterns that are not there, however I am on my way to Applecross, where I have not previously been.

If Father Coulter wanted to go off hiking around Applecross, that suited me just fine.

Connie was engrossed in Dostoevsky. I was surprised, but then there was no reason why she shouldn't be. I knew nothing about her or her background, or why she was homeless.

'Can I get you anything? Tea, coffee?'

She glanced up and shook her head, then curled her legs under her and buried her face in the book.

Esoteric interest, an interesting phrase. Venny said she'd met people she didn't like who took the occult very seriously, but I couldn't recall coming across any such people myself.

And what to make of Martina Hartley and David's tête-à-têtes? The ones that apparently started before I arrived at Weston House. He had known when I was and wasn't in the flat, including the time my external hard drive vanished. He had access to Christine's spare key, and might even have one of his own, come to think of it. But that was ridiculous: I didn't like the man, but that wasn't reason to impute malice to him. I've met clergy who are vain, capricious, spiteful and borderline sociopathic, but David wasn't like them: he was just a dickhead with bad taste in sherry.

But I didn't appreciate his gaslighting and I certainly didn't like that he'd gone out of his way to give the impression that he didn't know her when he did – or that he didn't want me to talk to her, when they were clearly working together in some way. I wondered what the pair of them were really trying to achieve.

I took a New Testament off the shelves and read the passages about Joseph of Arimathea. All four Gospels say he asked Pilate for Jesus's body for burial; none of them mention him in relation to the Last Supper, which was a Passover meal for only Jesus and his disciples. Lots of other things have found their way into the story of that meal, but Joseph isn't one of them. I did a quick search online for Joseph in the New Testament Apocrypha, but there was nothing of any particular interest there. So where did the story of the Grail come from?

My phone rang and I was surprised to see Betty Boards's name on the screen.

'Betty, how lovely to hear from you. How're things with you?'

Betty hadn't had her hearing checked after years of gigs, and shouted into the phone.

'Fine, fine, lovey. I followed your adventures in the papers, was worried for a while there. Anyway, that's not why I'm calling. I'm just tipping you off that I've had this hackette on at me, trying to dig up dirt on you. I told her ever-so-politely to *fahk orf* but thought you'd want to know. What've you been up to then?'

'This and that, but if it's who I think it is, she's been digging for a while. Did you get a name?'

'Hartley.'

'The same. I'm sorry, but it might be my fault she found you.'

'How's that, lovey?'

'I was talking to some students, said you were a good example of how not to make assumptions about parishioners. Word must've got out.'

'You didn't mention Big Jimi, did you?'

'Afraid so. The students found it fascinating.'

'I bet they did, I bet they did. Absolutely lovely man, sweet as you like. Not to worry. Did you tell them about the others?'

'Good Lord, no. Look, while you're on, I need to catch up with you sometime, maybe cadge some home baking, if you get my drift.'

'Well I'm not getting any younger, so best make it soon.'

'Will do. Here, I saw a re-release of that old Ace Inhibitor album, *Dawn Dance of the Calcium Antagonists*. Thought you'd be interested.'

'Got the original, darling, on Vertigo with the proper spiral label, pre-oil crisis vinyl, Porky Prime pressing, autographed by the boys.'

'You knew them?'

Of course she did.

'Oh yeah, I went off on a filthy fortnight with them and some really good acid in a chateau on the Riviera. Lovely lads, but I came home with four different kinds of clap. Bastards.'

'Are you being looked after properly, Betty?'

'Hah! I'm taking my carer to a gig tonight. Have you heard of Bob Weir's Shorts? A new Dead tribute band. They play *Blues for Allah* era material apparently. I want to see what they're like. You should come. The Plucked Pheasant at half-eight.'

'And your carer knows what she's letting herself in for?'

'He, darling. A strapping stud of a thing, goes to the gym every morning. Sex on a stick if you ask me, but bent as a five-bob note and more's the pity. Don't you worry yourself lovey, I'll keep my knickers on.'

She was still guffawing as she hung up.

'Who's digging dirt on you?' Connie had heard my side of the conversation, and probably most of Betty's too.

'A journalist trying to find some scandal.'

'Why would she do that?'

'I don't know, I've avoided her.'

'Maybe you should just ask her. Are you in some kind of trouble?'

'You know what? I don't know. Things are really strange,' I gestured at the tidy room, 'I mean *really* strange, and I can't figure out what to make of it all.'

'Pretty cool having the fair folk fix your flat though. How did you manage that?'

A good question. There was a lot of weirdness that Venny said I needed to embrace.

'I think it was because of Venny.'

'Your friend?'

I hesitated a moment longer than I intended and she joined the same dots as the students.

'She's more than just your friend, isn't she? She must be pretty special.'

'Yes. Yes, she is.'

'So how did she get involved with the fair folk?'

'It's a good story, but I'll let her tell it.'

'Fi said you were missing in Scotland for months and everyone thought you were dead and then you showed up again. Was that something to do with the fair folk too? Nana would have been dead interested.'

'I can't explain what happened to me in Scotland because I don't understand it, and the only person I've told is Ven because she won't think I'm crazy.'

'You can tell me. I won't think you're crazy.'

I hesitated again, unsure how to answer, how far to go.

'What's wrong, don't you trust me?'

There was an edge to her voice I hadn't heard before, hinting at hurts and betrayals she had kept hidden. She hadn't had to trust me or Fi or Beth, and couldn't have been blamed if she hadn't – but she had.

'It's not that. It's just that if I tell you everything, it puts you in an awkward spot with Fi and Beth if you know things they don't and then they end up investigating it. That wouldn't be fair to you.'

'You can't leave me hanging in suspense either, that's just as unfair.'

She was right; I either trusted her or I didn't, and if I didn't I'd be just one more White authority figure who'd let her down.

'While I was away, I met someone who asked me how long it was since something happened. We both knew the answer would hurt him but he felt the same as you, that he'd asked the question and I shouldn't leave him in suspense, and the answer did hurt him, quite badly.'

'What was the question?'

'He wanted to know how long it had been since his wife died.'

'How long was it?'

'Four hundred years.'

Connie's eyes widened then narrowed as she worked out the implications.

'You *were* in Faerie, where Nana said the dead sometimes go.'

'No, I was somewhere else. And they weren't dead, just living their lives in a different place. I thought I was only away for three days, not six months or whatever. So now you know.'

Connie went through to the kitchen and came back with two mugs of tea.

'When Nana told me her stories, I believed her. When I was a bit older, I thought she'd just told me children's stories, like Red Riding Hood or Cinderella. Then I found out no one else knew them and the teachers told Mam I was frightening the other kids and I figured out they

240

were true. Then on the streets, in the park, I saw some weird things happen. Not pervy-old-men weird – oh! I meant to say: Fi and Beth took him in for questioning yesterday, did they tell you? – anyway, I mean weird stuff like foxes and owls following me around, and seeing stags in the street where they weren't before. One night I thought I saw lights in the trees, like a parade, with fiddle and flute music and white horses, but it came from nowhere and had nowhere to go except into an old stone wall.'

'*I thocht he gait in at ane ʃchaddow in ane wall nor ony erdlie man culd haif gane throw,*' I murmured.

'What?'

'Something I read: *I thought he went into a shadow in a wall no earthly man could have gone through.*'

'Yes, just like that. That's amazing. Where's it from?'

'The trial of a woman called Janet Wilkie. She was executed in Scotland about four hundred years ago.'

'Four hundred years. Then …'

'Yes, it was her husband I met, William. Their daughters were killed too. I didn't know the details when I spoke to him. I only found out afterwards, when Venny and I did some research. But there's a lot I don't understand.'

'Did something strange happened to your friend Venny too?'

'Oh yeah, but that was *much* weirder.'

'Have you known her a long time?'

'We were best friends at school, then we had an argument and I didn't see her again until last week.'

'Wow! And you're …?'

'Yeah, pretty much. It's all been a bit sudden.'

'What's Venny short for?'

'Ravenser.'

'Cool name.'

Gretton and Connor came for Connie soon afterwards. A text from Ven said she'd been delayed getting Herbert to the dog-sitters but was on her way. I pushed some books back into place, wagging my finger at them, aware of a rising tension in the room. I looked around to find the source, but there was nothing I could see. I slipped my phone into a pocket and felt the silk of Ingrid's scarf, jammed in there and forgotten about after my walk on the moor. I pulled it out and looked at it more carefully. The repeating pattern was a series of ornate medallions, stitched in gold, each containing stylised dragon-headed longships under sail on wine-dark seas.

The room filled with the scent of mead and roasting meat, of birch sap and pine, the ozone spray of a bow wave showering the deck with blessed wet relief under a North Atlantic sun. At the prow, eyes on the land rising from the water ahead, stood Ingrid in her battle armour, hand on the hilt of her sword, surrounded by warriors under her command.

'How …?'

She turned and saw the scarf in my hand, and recognition spread across her face.

'A surprise and a delight. We may yet feast together again in a gentle land and you can tell me the story you promised. Before then you will need your courage, and wit. I'll help if I can, but the choice you must make is yours alone.'

She took her hand off the sword, kissed two fingers and touched them to my forehead. Sea spray stung my face and the deck rolled under my feet and the wind whined through the ship's rigging, and the telephone was ringing and I was trying to figure out what the hell had just happened and why Ingrid was at sea.

'Hello.'

'Ah, there you are. Tina here, Tina Hartley. Father Sharpe-Thompson put me through, such a nice man, don't you think? I couldn't reach you on your mobile.'

'This really isn't a good time, Ms Hartley.'

'Maybe we could meet again at a time that suits? It would be an awful lot easier, don't you think?'

'No, I don't think so.'

'I think it would be in your best interest to meet. Father Sharpe-Thompson thinks so too. He's worried the scandal will be bad for the students.'

'What on earth are you talking about?'

'Your old friend Miss Boards, Reverend Cant, quite the character I hear, debauchery and drugs and all that, and your secret liaison in Derby. Father Sharpe-Thompson was most concerned.'

'Ms Hartley, I don't know what games you're playing or why you keep contacting me, but I'm really not interested.'

'It would be a shame if you had all this hanging over you while you were at the hospital. It's such a worry, cancer.'

'Goodbye, Ms Hartley.'

I managed not to break the receiver as I slammed it down and sat fuming on the settee. Aside from the doctors and Venny, the only others who knew about the tests were David, Eithne, Sydney and Dorothy. And if Helen was right, David was Hartley's source.

On the other hand, I didn't think David knew the details of the burglary at the university or about the manuscript – or if he did it wasn't from me. But Hartley knew. Eithne did too, and all the other stuff, but neither of them knew I'd be in Derby before I went, and Hartley had somehow tracked me there.

Ingrid's scarf was in my hand, damp with sea spray. I was angry with Hartley about that too, for interrupting my meeting Ingrid. I lifted the scarf to my face and inhaled. Maybe it was the scarf that had triggered the connection? But nothing happened at all. Why would Ingrid be at sea on a crewed longship rather than at Yrreddell? It didn't make sense in terms of what I thought I knew about Sanctuary. And Cathal hadn't been there. But then, I didn't know anything at all about Sanctuary or how it worked, or even if that was appropriate language to use about it.

A bee buzzed against the kitchen window.

Rowan said she wasn't sure if I'd find my way back, or even if I could, but it seemed that by some … not magic, Rowan was very clear about that … but by some means and for some reason I *had* connected, even though I was hundreds of miles away from Rowan's borders, and Ingrid was at sea.

The ancient phone rang again. The light was on for David's extension. He didn't bother with preliminaries.

'Ah, you're there, good. Look here, I've had that journalist on, Hartley or whatever her name is. She was telling me lots of things I found worrying. I think we need to talk about what you've been up to.'

'Yes, she called me too. I gave her short shrift.'

'Oh? Was that wise? Her allegations are serious.'

'Ms Hartley isn't all she seems, according to the police, and they'll be interested in where she gets her information. I've already told them about her muckraking. Have DCs Gretton and Connor interviewed you yet?'

'Not what she seems? Information? What's that supposed to mean?'

'Well, it's not for me to interfere in police business by giving away details of an ongoing investigation. I'm sure you understand. Is there anything else I can help you with, David? I have a visitor arriving soon.'

'Oh? Was that cleared? We don't want anything sordid on college grounds.'

'I'm not in the habit of doing anything sordid, David, and take exception to your tone.'

'According to Hartley—'

'I really don't care about Hartley, or whatever her name is, or anything she says.'

I shouldn't have dismissed him so bluntly, but, in the end, what could he do? The worst that could happen would be I'd have to move out.

Stuff the college; the Plucked Pheasant it would be.

I hadn't used the restored HiFi yet. I put on an original UK release LP of *Blues for Allah* and let Jerry's voice wash over me, trying to relax before Venny arrived.

CHAPTER 20

Betty was in full-on Deadhead mode, arms above her head, body shimmying and shimmering, eyes closed. She wore a flowing ankle-length Indian cotton dress, tie-dyed decades before, layered over a long petticoat. She was shoeless, braless, hair down. There wasn't enough space for her to swirl but she was the closest anyone in the Plucked Pheasant would ever get to the real psychedelic deal and everyone knew it. She was the guru around whom her impromptu commune clustered, grinning, aware at some primal level they had nobility in their midst. I don't think she'd dropped acid, though it wouldn't have surprised me. It didn't matter anyway: she rode the star trails of a thousand trips. No growing old disgracefully for her, she just refused to grow old.

And the band responded, the bass player bombing out from 'He's Gone' into a primal 'The Other One'. A bit early in the evening for that, I thought. A couple of greybeards nursing their pints nodded and pronounced, 'Oakland, December 1979'.

'You like this stuff?' Venny watched Bob Weir's Shorts with bafflement. 'It's all noodling.'

'There's noodles and there's five-spice noodle soup.'

I'd reached the stage of trying to dance while seated, twitching my shoulders, shaking my head.

'This is somewhere in between, but they're new,' I said.

'How old did you say Betty is again?'

'She admits to seventyish.'

Robin, Betty's carer, was besotted with her, as was his partner Jake. They threw themselves into the idiot-dancing melee, shaken by the abdominal growl of the bass, singing along even though they didn't know the words.

The Plucked Pheasant was a traditional country pub, formerly the Victoria and Albert, to which a large function room and lounge had been added in the thirties to put on regular dances. It had a good stage and dressing room, somewhat dilapidated now, but once state of the art for travelling orchestras. A signed photo of Harry Roy hung behind the bar, with others of long-forgotten band leaders. It had been popular with airmen from the nearby airfield during World War Two, too many spending their last evenings there before flying into eternity. Inhale deeply enough there under a bomber's moon and you'll catch a whiff of Brylcreem, pipe smoke and ale; listen hard and you can hear the grumble of Merlins.

Despite the best efforts of developers desperate to buy the site for student housing, it survived while suburbia grew all around it.

At the front door, a large psychedelic-style poster advertising Bob Weir's Shorts's debut gig was pinned next to a plainer one advertising the following week's act, Dade County and the Hanging Chads, a post-punk psychobilly/ country and western outfit.

We'd got there in good time, Venny and Helen and me, just as Betty, Robin and Jake arrived. Helen had been surprised when I'd asked if she wanted to come, but hadn't hesitated, and soon fell into easy familiarity with Betty and Venny. Her eyes had widened at Ven's scarlet hair and lips, ripped jeans and Ramones T-shirt. Perhaps she'd expected someone more demure. Betty took one look and approved right away, and I just knew she'd have stories of Joey and the band if we asked her.

Bob Weir's Shorts were getting mellow with 'Ramble on Rose' when Fi and Beth and Connie walked into the pub.

'Rozzers. Can spot 'em a *fahking* mile away, lovey,' said Betty through her vodka and tonic.

'Friends,' I replied, waving to Connie, who looked stunned to be there at all. She wasn't the girl from the park of a few days ago, or even from the hospital café. In the hours since I'd last seen her, her hair had been shaved round the ears and her tight curls sculpted to a mohawk on top. She had a silver septum ring and huge dangling circular earrings that contrasted with her dark skin; paid for by Beth, I guessed. Her sparkly Converse boots were new too. The unexpected deep purple lipstick with metallic sheen popped against her skin, and, with her deep lashes and frosted eyelids, she turned the head of every man and several of the women in the room.

'Wow!' Venny said. 'She's your friend?'

I did the introductions and went to get in a round of mostly non-alcoholic drinks. I got back to the table in time to catch the end of Betty telling a captive audience how she'd once got busted coming home at seven on a Tuesday morning after a long weekend with Vivian Stanshall and Keith Moon in Soho in 'the good old days'.

'Is this what your life's always like?' Venny asked.

'Not before, but maybe it will be now.' I squeezed her hand. 'You should talk with Connie, she's smart. She was living in a tent in the park until a few days ago. She's got some interesting stories about odd things she's seen, and her grandmother's old stories about the fair folk, as she calls them.'

'How'd she end up in a tent?'

'She hasn't said, not to me anyway. Maybe to Fi or Beth. Connie's the only other one who knows anything about what happened to me in Scotland.'

'How did she manage that?'

'She asked me some direct questions, and I couldn't lie without losing her trust. So I told her about William and Janet. I had another experience again by the way, on a longship with Ingrid for a few moments.'

'I told you before: not without me, in case you don't come back. How did you trigger it?'

'Something to do with her scarf, I think, the one she wrapped the brooch in. I didn't do anything, but there I was.'

'This is fun. I had no idea,' said Helen, leaning across to us. 'Betty is everything you said she was and more.'

I hadn't spoken to her in any depth since she'd challenged me in the café.

'My pleasure, but surely life as a student isn't all work these days?'

'It is for me. And, you know, I enjoy it – in the library, in the archives.'

'First-Class Honours, wasn't it? I was never that committed. In my day the idea of university was as a time to explore and learn and do daft things in a safeish environment. We had to work too, of course, but not all the time.'

'I couldn't do that – expectations were too high.'

'Whose?' asked Venny.

'Mum and Dad, teachers, family. They didn't like my choices. Lots of people thought I'd fail, so there was pressure to prove them wrong. And I did.'

'What was your Honours subject?'

'Female sexuality and agency in the transition from World War Two to peacetime.'

'Wow.'

'It was meant to be an analysis of methodological issues with the Mass Observation survey in 1949, *Little Kinsey*. The survey is good for its time and as far as it goes, but problematic by today's standards, and shot through with class bias and assumptions. There's a discussion of prostitution that asked vicars and policemen and lorry drivers what they thought, but not the women themselves, that kind of thing. Almost entirely hetero-normative for the most part as well, though not completely. But I got to be more interested in the stories and went looking for a bigger picture. It was inconclusive in the end, but the examiners liked it.'

'What's the bigger picture?'

'Women rediscovering a lost freedom to enjoy and exploit their sexuality if they wanted, but all the time in fear of pregnancy. There was a gay subtext too, but that needed more time to research than I had. Same with interracial relationships with Black Americans over to fight in Europe and the two thousand or so mixed-race babies born.'

Connie listened in, apparently interested in the subject.

'Did you think of taking it further?' Venny asked.

'For a while, but it's difficult – academia has its expectations too if you're a Black woman; misogynoir, and all that.' She paused, as if she'd said too much. She gave me a look that told me she had more to say, but this wasn't the time or place; it struck me that Helen and Connie were the only Black people in the room. 'I decided to follow my vocation instead. And you know, most of the people I'd need to speak to as primary sources are either dead or in their nineties now, so tracking them down and getting them to talk would be difficult, if not impossible. It's not something you can explain to their grandchildren when you're trying to arrange access, and I didn't want to rely on secondary sources.'

'How did your folks react?'

'Mum still hopes I'll switch to one of the community Pentecostal churches, but I know she keeps family back in Lagos informed of everything I do. Dad wishes I'd been a lawyer or a doctor, or even an engineer like my brother. Maybe I should get rid of the relaxers and take hair and makeup tips from Connie and see how they react to that.'

It hadn't occurred to me that Helen's hair, straight and styled into a neat bob, wasn't natural – an attempt at academic neutral perhaps? A way to fit in? How had I got through life not knowing this stuff?

A rattle of snare drum and half a dozen repeated bass notes signalled that the band was about to launch into another set. Helen and Connie were in what looked like tentative conversation. Fi and Beth looked a little lost, as if they were consciously trying to ignore any surreptitious dealing: the smokers' shelter outside smelled like a hashish den in Tangiers.

Helen checked a message on her phone just before Zoë Lewis and Eithne came in with Danny Richardson and his girlfriend Caroline, the archaeologist. It was the first time I'd seen Eithne in anything other than a clerical shirt and trouser suit, and part of me was surprised she'd come as a civilian. She'd gone for smart-casual – more smart than casual – and seemed a bit self-conscious without the shield of a dog collar. The introductions were made as two of the band kicked into a good acoustic version of 'Friend of the Devil'.

'I like this one,' Venny said.

It was all very like student days. The years sloughed off my shoulders and I felt young again, when there was no pressure to do anything much except get essays in on time and pass exams. The days when I could have taken a different path. I was in our living room listening to the Dead on a cheap record player while Dad tutted and muttered that it wasn't what he called music and could I turn it down a bit. The moment felt so real I could have found a payphone and called the old number and he would answer and we'd chat about inconsequentialities before he said *I suppose you're calling for your Mam* and passed the phone over.

Maybe that was all still happening somewhere in a continuous 'now'. It felt real, and if it feels real then who's to say it isn't?

Venny elbowed me in the ribs.

'Ow!'

'Stop it.'

'What?'

'You know what.'

The full band came on stage, counted into 'Help on the Way/Slipknot!' and Betty was up, lost in memories, dancing through her years, as long as she needed them to be.

I clutched the scarf in my pocket – I'd resisted Venny's suggestion that I borrow a bag from someone – and looked round the room. The band played and Betty danced and conversation was all around but everything was off-kilter, not quite contiguous. Everyone looked strange, like creatures behind reinforced glass in a zoo, or seen from the back of a truck on safari. They were fleshy sacs of electrical impulses leaking sentience, measures in an eternal tune, falling in and out of harmony and dissonance, *legato* improvisations intersecting in ways that gave an appearance of composition, of a composer, where there was none. And Venny was the perfect counterpoint to my own stumbling song.

She took my hand, asked if I was OK, concern in her voice. I squeezed her hand back and pulled her closer as I caught glimpses of *somewhere else*, of wild lands, a forest where the Plucked Pheasant had never been. Venny caught her breath and saw it too, a glimpse of Sanctuary, a place as big as it needed to be.

It passed, but the light shining in Ven's eyes told me it was no fantasy.

'What did you do?'

'I don't know. I was musing on time and perception and holding Ingrid's scarf in my pocket. What about you?'

'Ingrid's brooch was heavy in my pocket all of a sudden.'

She took the brooch out to look at as the band's mini light show bounced spots off the ancient disco mirror ball that no one had ever managed to remove from the ceiling. The jewelled eyes of the brooch caught the light, reflecting sparkles across our table.

'Bloody hell!' Carolin the archeologist stared at the brooch. 'Where did you get that? It looks like one I saw in Denmark in a private collection of Viking-era finds. Is that gold?'

'It was a gift,' I said, before Venny could reply. 'From friend who makes replicas.'

'Bloody generous gift, and worth a fortune if it was original. You'd swear those eyes are sapphire and emerald.'

'She makes very good copies.'

'Have you got her contact details?'

'She lives off-grid. She's a bit eccentric that way.'

'Anywhere near whoever has that manuscript?' asked Danny.

'Manuscript? That was you? Danny never said where that came from.'

'Didn't you say something about Applecross, where my grandmother lived?' asked Eithne. Fi and Beth leaned closer. Eithne had taken her jacket off and her short-sleeved blouse rode up her arm a little to show a tattooed butterfly and rainbow on her right bicep. She hid it when she realised I'd seen it.

'I've been very careful not to say anything about where I was in case I …' I glanced at Venny, 'in case *we* want to go there sometime for some peace and quiet.'

Ven's arm slipped round my waist.

'Dance?'

I seized the escape route and let her pull me to the floor. She said into my ear, loud enough to be overheard, 'Yes, where *we* must go sometime.' Then, to me: 'And what was with that piglet in the forest?'

'What piglet? I didn't see any piglets.'

She flashed a smile, caught the groove as the band segued into 'The Music Never Stopped', pulled some seriously sensual moves that had everyone watching, including the band, who fell into an extended jam, irresistibly funky, tugging the feet and hips and arms of everyone on the dance floor. Betty was up, of course, Connie following Betty's every move, her earrings splashing reflections of the stage lights. Even Helen was up, tentative in her movements, as if unwilling to let herself go. Robin and Jake came back from wherever they'd been, looking for dance action, and finding it.

As the final chord rang out Venny grabbed me and kissed me with enthusiastic ferocity, to loud applause from the whole room as well as a smattering of camera flashes from mobile phones.

'Oi!' shouted the barman. 'This is a pub, save it for the bedroom.'

Which was more or less what I was thinking. The faces of everyone from our table were a treat, most smiling, some bemused, one or two shocked.

Definitely out now, then.

And over the usual pub aromas of stale beer, old deodorant and spectral Brylcreem I caught the sweet smell of burning bridges.

CHAPTER 21

I'd just buttered toast for us both when Venny's phone buzzed.

'Kirsty,' she said, and went to fetch her laptop.

'Who?'

'A genealogist in Edinburgh. I asked her to look at the court papers I ordered from National Records in Scotland and send a transcript. She's an expert in Scottish Secretary Hand. She can do in a few hours what would take us days to figure out.'

The email was an interim report with attachments. Kirsty had found Janet's trial record but nothing further about the daughters. She hadn't looked at Janet's trial yet but thought we'd be interested in something else: a court record for William Maxwell from 1607.

Mr Williame Hairt of Preſtoune, Justice-Depute
Feb. 14. Williame Maxwell of Edinburgh

The q[uhi]lk day Williame Maxwell, pryſoner being brocht furth of Ward & preſentit upon panel to heir dome pronounced ag[ains]t him as he that war convict be an Aſſyſe upone the thrid daye of Februar Inſtant of the several crymes contenit in his Dittay and convictions following thereupon The Commiſſioners therefoir by there Judicial Sentence Pronuncet be thaim this dai Be the mouthe of Henrie Wilſoune, dempſter of court decernit and Adjudget the said William Maxwell upon Fryday next the auchtent of this inſtant to be ſcurget threw the Hie Streit of the Burghs of Edinburgh & Cannongate From the Caſtlehill to the Abay [thereof] *betwix Ellevin & 12 houres in the foirnone And to be baniſhet furth fra Scotland and efter his ſcurgenge to be returned back to Ward therein to remane till ane ſhip be in reddieness for his transportation.*

'What's a Dittay?' I asked.

'It's the document setting out the accusation and evidence against the accused. An indictment.'

Unfortunately, the other case papers couldn't be found so we didn't learn what William had done, or even if it was 'our' William. It was also too early for someone to be transported to the Americas, so the banishment was one more puzzle amongst many.

The evening at the Plucked Pheasant ended at pretty much the same time as the band finished playing, but something had changed, even with Eithne, Zoë and Helen. It wasn't disapproval, more like they'd been made privy to something they'd rather not have been. Maybe it was a British thing, embarrassment at open displays of affection by late-middle-aged people. Or maybe something more intangible, as if an aspect of me had been revealed in a way they hadn't expected.

Betty had taken me aside as we left the pub.

'For you,' she'd said, handing me a large Tupperware box. 'Edibles, lovey, while those rozzers aren't looking; made with lots of TLC, not to mention THC. It's good to see you looking better, I was worried for a while there.'

'I'm not with you.'

'Before you went wherever you were, you weren't right, but you are now. And she's lovely.'

The box was next to my HiFi, tempting me.

'I didn't know you wore specs,' said Venny.

'What?'

She was looking at the twisted silver bridge that Ingrid had made.

'I used to, but haven't needed to since Sanctuary.'

'This is lovely work. Where did you buy them?'

'That's Ingrid's handiwork. They broke when I ran into the tree.'

'Does Sanctuary have healing properties then, if your eyes are fixed?'

'I don't know.'

'Could it fix whatever the tests might find?'

I shrugged again.

'Why don't you go back and find out?'

'Because I'm not sure I want to.' I spoke over her as she started to reply. 'I mean, I'd like to fix whatever is wrong with me, and, you know, it could all be another false alarm. But Sanctuary, it's ... I told Rowan that if I ever went back I might end up staying there, and I don't think that's such a great idea now. To be caught somewhere out of time, to lose touch with everything I know? I don't see the appeal.'

'We could be together.'

'We could, but with nothing else: nothing new to talk about, no one to go to the pub with, no way to catch a band, or see a film, or slob out with a carry-out Indian and a bottle of supermarket red. I think it's a cage, not an escape.' I put the glasses back in the case and placed them on the bookshelf. 'The books are on their best behaviour for you, you know.'

'Eh?'

'Ever since the place was restored, they've taken to wandering when I'm not looking. I warned them, said you're a friend of Master Dobson.'

'Seriously?' She glanced at Betty's Tupperware box.

'Yes, they shift around, mutter amongst themselves when they think I can't hear them.' I gave them a glare, but they played dead.

'Did you ever find out how this place got wrecked?'

'No. It's another mystery.'

'Did you ask the books?'

'Er ...'

'Well, they saw it all happen. Didn't you?' Venny fixed her eyes on the shelves. The room took on the sudden nervous stillness of a class of eight-year-olds when the teacher asks who wrote the rude words on the blackboard. 'Did you say you got something else from Coulter?'

'I did, and meant to ask you about it.' I opened the email and let her read it. 'It was the bit about esoteric interest that caught my eye. I remember you saying something about people you met who made you feel uncomfortable, who took things very seriously.'

She flinched.

'I'd as soon not be reminded, ducks. You think it might be to do with what happened here?'

'This was malice, not – what did you call it? – something about the Aga and Volvo crowd?'

'Edmond said that, not me. It's their style, but they'd probably keep up the pressure. They're nasty bastards.' She shivered. 'Some were middle-class types who'd read too much Dennis Wheatley and thought *The Wicker Man* was a documentary. One or two were right into the whole occult thing and got shirty if you didn't spell magic with a 'k' on the end, daft buggers. Some were downright unpleasant, especially with women, and the women were pretty odd too. There's a network of them, right across the country, and maybe in other places too.'

'What happened?'

'They warned me to keep my nose out of their business. Message received and understood.'

I waited.

'Herbert isn't my first dog.'

Venny came up behind me while I made fresh tea, slipped her arms round my waist, her cheek against my back. I put my hands over hers until she was ready to let go.

'I went over to Mablethorpe the other day, where Martina Hartley was from, to see what I could find out about her,' she said.

'And?'

'Nowt much. The paper she trained at remembered her as bright and ambitious, with dreams of breaking the story that would lead to bigger things. One of her old boyfriends said she never really gave up after she went into PR and corporate marketing. She was always working a new story, he said, trying to uncover something. And then one day she was dead.'

I took the pot of tea through to the living room.

'You know, maybe someone like Master Dobson did the damage,' she said.

'Eithne said something about a brownie, a household spirit her grandmother used to namecheck, Connie's grandmother too. But they were always helpful, and looked after houses.'

'There's plenty of tales of the fair folk acting capriciously if they're slighted.'

'It's all too vague, Ven. We don't have a clue as to what's happening, do we? Just a bucketful of guesses. Let's do something else, go for a walk or a drive or something, clear our heads.'

'I haven't had a shower yet.'

'Me neither.'

'So …'

Helen called round an hour later carrying the morning paper. She opened it to page three.

'Well, you two certainly made an impression,' she said.

Dominating the page was a full-colour photo of Venny and me in The Plucked Pheasant, eyes closed, lips locked, next to a review of the gig. I wasn't sure if I should be offended by the inevitable caption: A Touch of Grey.

'The paper tweeted it this morning and the band retweeted it. It's not quite viral yet, but getting there.'

'Well, that's any remaining dignity down the pan. I didn't embarrass you, did I?'

'No, just took me by surprise, that's all. Everyone wants to meet Venny now – well, everyone except Creeping Jesus.'

'Who?'

'Gavin Surtees. Thinks he's holier than everyone, purer somehow.'

That was news to me. I knew he was punctilious as sacristan, but he'd seemed sensible enough. Eithne described him as a gentle loner, and David had said something similar about him being over-earnest but from a close, devout family.

'What's his story?'

'Nothing really, he just rubs a lot of us up the wrong way. He's really weird sometimes. DST pushed for him to be sacristan. I mean, none of the rest of us wanted to do it anyway, but Gavin was almost too keen.'

I looked at the photo again. 'So everyone's seen this? They're OK with, um, the same-sex thing?'

'Oh golly, yes. When word got out Zoë and I were out

with you both and Betty last night there was immediate talk of having a party for everyone else. I really enjoyed myself, by the way.'

'Any time. I suppose I'll be getting a phone call from on high soon.'

'From DST? No one's seen him since yesterday evening, so you're probably safe for a while. It was a good night, and I liked Connie,' Helen said. 'We're from such different worlds – Africa and the diaspora, you know?'

'OK: you've already given me a lot to think about – the other night in the café – but you're going to have to explain that one for me. What don't I understand about Africa and the Diaspora?'

'Oh gosh, I walked into that, didn't I? It's such a big subject. Think about it this way: I grew up as a Nigerian in Nigeria; that's my identity, or part of it, not my skin colour. It was only when I came to Britain that I had to learn to be Black. Connie's never known anything else, right? She grew up in a White country. We don't see the world in the same way. She's the one you rescued from a tent, isn't she? She's very loyal to you.'

I winced. 'Really? She barely knows me.'

'She's persuaded me to give the Mission a second chance.'

'Did she? Will you be there tomorrow?'

'No. I think most of the college is coming to hear your sermon. Word is that DST isn't happy about that, by the way. He's never been asked to preach there and his nose is well out of joint. He claims he was responsible for Bishop Sydney appointing you in the first place.'

'I didn't know that.' When I first arrived, David said he and Eithne hadn't been consulted about my appointment: why would he lie?

'Apparently he said something about it at a diocesan gathering after a few too many sherries, and word reached

Zoë. I told you, she finds out everything in the end.'

Venny came through from the bedroom with a towel around her head, tying her robe.

'Oh, hello! Helen, isn't it? "Female sexuality and agency in the transition from World War Two to peacetime."'

'You remembered.'

'It's a memorable topic, and it was a good night.'

'Some people let their hair down, that's for sure. I just showed Canty this.' She gestured to the paper on the coffee table. Venny's eyes opened wide.

'Oh my word. Online too?'

'You bet.'

'Do you think they'll let me have a proof copy? Do they even do proof copies anymore? Maybe I can download a high-res copy somewhere. We can frame it. Pity you can't see our faces properly.'

'Are you serious?' said Helen.

'Absolutely I am. We might as well have our moment of notoriety.'

'Don't apologise. Don't cringe,' Helen said.

'Exactly, an excellent attitude.'

'I know, it's what Canty said to me a few days ago. Anyway, I'll leave you in peace. I just came down to show you the photo.'

'We're off for a drive somewhere. Come along if you want.'

'Can't, I've got work to do.'

We went out to the spot in the hills I'd found after I'd phoned Coulter. We took the same route up to the waterfall on the moorland. It was breezier, and there were no skylarks. A female kestrel quartered the expanse.

'What a lovely spot.'

'Isn't it? It reminds me of a place up above Rowan's cottage, where Antonios made his home.'

'Is this a favourite place of yours?'

'I only found it on Tuesday, while the flat was still a mess. You guessed something might happen, didn't you?'

'Why d'you say that?'

'Because you wanted to make sure I had your painting.'

'It was just a hunch, something I couldn't pin down.'

'Any more hunches I should know about?'

'Nothing specific, just a feeling that something is coming.'

I lay back on the dry ground, and closed my eyes against the glare of the sun, Venny next to me, one arm across me, chin at my shoulder. She took her phone from her back pocket with her other hand and angled it to get a selfie of the pair of us.

'Penny for them,' she said.

'Where to start?'

There was too much happening at once. Sydney said he'd put me in Weston House to recuperate and buy time to work something else out, and that had worked, after a fashion, just not how he'd expected. It was all about consequences: consequences of losing my vocation, consequences of loving Venny, consequences of whatever the hell happened in Sanctuary, consequences of copying Antonios's manuscript. They were all connected, and part of a bigger question.

'Helen challenged me the other day: she asked me what I'd do with myself if I wasn't a priest. We'd been talking about charity and politics and structural issues that I've never really been involved with, and it's been churning away at the back of my mind – the idea that I've been caught up in my own private world for so long that I've missed out on something much bigger. I've ignored politics, you know? I only see the outcomes of government policies when they're sitting crying in front of me and I'm trying to help. I've never even been on a protest march, and I think twice about signing petitions in case it comes back on me somehow. And she's been educating me in other ways too, about racism. Sorry: you did ask what was on my mind.'

'What will we do?' said Venny.

'Take it as it comes, I suppose.'

'No, I meant what will *we* do?'

'I don't know. I never expected this. What are you thinking?'

'I'm wondering if we live apart and see each other, or live together. If we live together, then where? My place is too small for all your stuff and mine. Things like that.'

'I want to be with you,' I said. 'I couldn't ask you to move out of your house, you've got too much invested in it. I don't have any ties here apart from Betty and now Connie. I can lose most of the books. When they were trashed it was like getting out from under a weight of learning that doesn't mean much anymore. I'd like to keep the HiFi and music though.'

'I don't know about the house; maybe it's time to move on, mix it up a bit, you know? When do you have to leave the college?'

'No idea. Sydney mentioned my staying on as a lay adviser, and Helen asked if I'd be around for her final year; that was a nice surprise.'

'Why? You've had an impact.'

'Well …'

'Helen and the other student – Zoë, is it? – and Eithne, all said the same thing last night. You've challenged a lot of their thinking in just a few days by who you are. You mean you haven't noticed?'

'I've only just got here.'

'Silly Canty. You should pay more attention to what's going on around you, and not just that political stuff you mentioned.'

'That photo'll change things.'

'Is it going to make problems for you?'

'There'll be a reaction. And assumptions. People like assumptions and narratives. But it's a blessing too, in its own way, a bit like Helen saying that she's had to learn to be Black in White society. They'll all say I've come out of a closet I was never in, because it isn't about closets, it's about you.'

'Wasn't there anyone else in all the years?'

'It was difficult, what with being in the public eye and all that, and then I sort of forgot about it.'

'You mean there was no one at all? My God, Canty. What have they done to you?'

I couldn't answer; didn't trust myself to speak coherently.

'What happens tomorrow then?' she asked.

'We go to the cathedral, I tart myself up in my uniform, say my piece and watch the last boats burn behind me. After that, who knows?'

'Will there be angry villagers in the night with pitchforks and fire?'

'No, they'll just get on with the rest of the service and write me out of things.'

I let myself drift into total relaxation, the air across my face wafting away my tension, my unspoken fear about the tests, about the future. The weight of her arm was a comfort. Maybe she was right, and the thing to do was just to disappear into a fold in the universe and be together. Goodness knows there were worse things could happen. Even with my eyes closed I knew her face was close, that I could kiss her under spring sunshine on the uncaring grass.

266

'Wish we'd brought towels. That pool looks just right for skinny-dipping.'

'There was a dipper in the pool near Rowan's house, and a standing stone with weird carvings on it that glowed in the energy of the falls. That's another thing: I keep wondering, *why me*? I mean, I have no idea what's going on. I don't have a magic sword, or a ring of power or any of that crap. I'm just me, a nearly-retired priest.'

'Maybe that's all you have to be. And you have me.'

'That must be it: you're my superpower.'

On the way down, my phone let off a series of alerts as it connected to the network. Messages came from Sydney, David, Eithne, Connie, Fi Gretton and Adrian Coulter.

'Jeez, would you look at this lot.'

Eithne wanted to warn me that David was looking for me and wasn't happy. Connie wanted to know if she could 'come over and hang for a while with you guys.' Fi Gretton said they'd had a great night, thanks. Adrian Coulter said he was just keeping in touch and had rarely seen anything as wonderful as the view over Raasay and Skye from the Bealach na Ba and was fascinated by Máel Rubha. That just left Sydney and David.

'You should ask Coulter what he meant by "esoteric interest". He might have had something specific in mind,' Venny said.

'Good idea. David and Sydney can wait, they've no idea where we are. You OK if Connie comes round?'

'Sure. You said I should talk to her?'

'She completely accepts the good neighbours, fair folk or whatever. Her gran used to tell her stories about them and Connie got told off at school for frightening the other children when she repeated them.'

'Cool!'

'Also, you might get interrogated. I told her your story was much more interesting and weird than mine.'

'What did you tell her about Sanctuary?'

'Edited highlights: William and Janet and the three days turning into six months thing.'

We made our way down to where the car was parked by the small lake. In the middle of the water, a pair of mallards bobbed. The breeze swirled in the natural bowl formed by the surrounding hills, ruffling the birds' feathers and the surface of the lake. It wasn't strong at the waterside but was noisy on the higher ground, howling, almost.

'Can you hear that noise on the wind?' I asked.

'No. What do you hear? Are you OK? You look ill.'

'Wolves. Something's about to happen. Can we go? Like, now.'

I drove off, faster than sensible on the remote road. I made a conscious effort to slow down, to ignore the fear skipping in my stomach. The sky darkened. A sudden cloudburst overwhelmed the wipers as the turns of the road became tighter. I couldn't see where I was driving or what was coming. The first chance I got, I pulled over to sit the storm out.

'Was this forecast?'

'I don't think so.'

The rain hammered the roof of the car, rattled my ears and brain and bones, and I lost it. The world beyond the car window dissolved. I looked inwards, groping for an anchor, somebody I could recognise as me, but there were only uncertain, swirling images and fragments of memories that refused to coalesce.

It was like the delirium of a viral fever and, just as I thought the viscous sludge of unreason would carry me off, I saw dancing patterns: whirls and whorls I recognised but couldn't place. The watery voices of schoolfriends called me down to lost souterrains under the watchful black eyes of deer in the pouring rain. There was a cornfield, flattened, red with gore, ravens feasting on fat and tendon. I felt the many hands on my head at my ordination, heard the keening of an unseen buzzard high in the vaulted roof of an endless cathedral. And I heard a voice, chanting words I knew: *Til ſic daye he maun dree his weird, betuixt Elfame and Middil-ʒeird* and the verse was incomplete and rain fell on my face, and I came to as Venny bundled me into the back seat, worry distorting her sweet face.

'Just you lie there.'

She rested the back of her hand on my forehead. 'No temperature. How do you feel?'

'Peculiar. Like flu – real flu, when everything gets weird and it's like you're watching yourself but can't do anything about it? Like that. And I heard that rhyme from Janet's trial.'

I struggled to sit up. Venny gave me one more look over before getting behind the steering wheel and adjusting the seat and mirrors.

'Has owt like this happened before?'

'When I first came out of Sanctuary.'

'Let's get you back. Don't fade on me, I might need directions.'

The rain lifted and beams of sunlight tracked across the hills. I wiped the steamed-up window with the back of my sleeve. In the trees by the road was a figure, standing in a halo of rain, watching from shadowed eyes in a ragged hood. He leaned on a wooden stick, bleached white by time. He gave me a mocking salute, and I heard voices again, like the call and response of a litany heard from outside a church on a winter's night:

Blameless sister
Bright the blades of the sons of Elifer
That brought your death.
Tell me again of magic
> *Noble son of Morvryn*
> *Bearer of noble Gwynddolau's gold torc*
> *Magic is gone from Ynys Pridain*
> *While Joseph's gift lies hidden.*

I opened the car door and was violently sick.

CHAPTER 22

'You're sure it was Lallig? Even though you've never seen him before?'

'Positive. He's behind everything, I'm sure of it.'

'Hartley and Sharpe-Thompson too? I don't see the link. How did the chant go?'

'The words didn't stick.'

She looked as if she was considering telling me something. 'What?'

'Nothing, or maybe it is. I don't know. After you left the other day, I had some odd dreams, and had to paint. Once I started I couldn't stop until the images were all down. There are people in the paintings, figures. Their faces are blanks, but I think that-there Lallig was one of them. It's the clothes – the rags, the hair.'

I had painful, gripping cramps in my stomach and made an unpleasant visit to the bathroom. I lay on the settee, wrapped in a duvet, shivering, gripping a mug of tea.

'You know, if he can come and go from Sanctuary, does that mean I can too?' I said.

'You'd know better than me, ducks. Just remember to take me with you when you go.'

'Do you think I should try?'

'What if that's what he's trying to provoke? If you're right and he's behind it all, we don't know what his game is. Maybe it's what you said that time about others looking for a way into Sanctuary? Maybe he thinks you can open a door for them.'

'Could be. I don't know. This is new.'

'You haven't been back long, though. Maybe he was biding his time, waiting for something to change.'

'Like what?'

'Well I don't know, do I? I'm not him. Anyway, here's what's going to happen, ducks: you'll catch forty winks right now and I'll start researching. When's Connie coming round?'

I bridled, but the next I knew it was two hours later, my head was clear and my stomach settled. Ven and Connie were across the room, focused on Ven's laptop. I struggled to push myself upright.

'It moves. Welcome back to the land of the living. How are you feeling?' Venny said, coming over to feel my forehead again.

'Fine. Really. Fine.'

'Good. I'll get you some tea. Toast?'

'Thank you. Did I miss anything?'

'We've been ordering lipstick online, trying to find more of that Poisonberry one she got from Fi Gretton last night. We almost got some for you too.'

'I don't wear it.'

'I noticed. I've added it to my list of things to work on. And Connie's been instructing me in skin and hair care – things I never even guessed. Oh, and the bishop phoned to make sure you're OK for tomorrow. I said something you ate hadn't agreed with you and you'd call him back when you'd slept it off. We were working.'

Connie's eyes were wide.

'You didn't tell me what you're involved in, Canty. I wish Nana was here, she'd love this stuff.'

I shook out the duvet. I needed a shower.

'Last night OK for you?'

'Brilliant! Betty is lovely and Robin and Jake looked out for me when Fi and Beth weren't looking.'

'And you persuaded Helen to stick with the Mission.'

'Oh yeah. I like her, but she's too serious. Everyone was nice. Old White farts' music though.'

A hoot of laughter came from the kitchen.

'Well, I'm an old White fart, so there we are.'

'You do that all the time. You shouldn't.'

'Do what?'

'Turn things round, do yourself down.'

Ven brought three teas on a tray.

'Venny told me about the painting and Master Dobson and Edmond and how she always knew how you were. That's really romantic.'

Ven kept a studiously neutral expression on her face, avoiding my look. What else had they talked about while I slept?

'Are you OK if Connie and I pop out for a bit? We'll only be an hour or so. She'll need a laptop if she's my assistant.'

'Assistant?'

'Yes. I need to sort out all my notes and articles. I'm thinking of putting together a book or two, self-published, under my old pen name. Connie'll help and we'll see what we can do about college once we've got things sorted with her mum.'

I stared at the two of them sitting looking back at me.

'I was only asleep for two hours, right?'

They'd been gone half an hour when David Sharpe-Thompson rang the doorbell and strode in without invitation. He had a copy of the newspaper with him. His breath reeked of sour sherry.

'I'll get straight to the point. I told the bishop this afternoon that this sort of filth is totally unacceptable and I can't ...'

His voice tailed off.

'What the ...? This place was a wreck, I saw it myself. How in God's name did you do this?' He pointed at the bookshelves. 'They were all over the floor, torn up.'

Several books rocked as he ran his finger along them.

'And that HiFi: it's vintage equipment, there's no way it could be replaced. Look here, I demand you tell me what the hell's going on.'

'You don't get to barge in here and make demands, David. I'd like you to leave.'

'I don't think so. I *am* the principal here. Look, to put it bluntly, I think it would be best for all concerned were you to find somewhere else. I don't like the effect you're having on the students or the kind of people you associate with. There's more than enough perversion in the Church already. You don't dress appropriately and you clearly take great pleasure in defying my wishes. So I want you gone. It's a pity, what with the medical stuff, but I'm sure some accommodation can be reached.'

'As it happens, David, I agree.'

'I beg your pardon?'

'I declined Sydney's offer of the permanent chaplain's position. Didn't he tell you?'

'That's an outright lie. He never told me any such thing and I would have to know.'

'No lie, David. He was sounding me out before making it formal. My sermon tomorrow will be my last hurrah. Will you be able to attend, or will Ms Hartley keep you up-to-date with proceedings?'

His look was guilty, shifty.

'What do you mean by that?'

'You know perfectly well. Will there be anything else? My guests will be back soon.'

He turned on his heels, I suppose to make a grand exit, but he saw Venny's painting and jumped backwards as if he'd touched a live electric cable, eyes starting, face contorted as he muttered a Latin blessing.

'In Christ's name, what is that thing? Who the hell are you?' He crossed himself with exaggerated gestures, as if trying to amplify the gesture, inscribing a sigil in the suddenly frigid air.

Master Dobson unfolded himself from behind a tree in the centre of the canvas and walked towards us. He reached forward, arm projecting out of the frame, dripping with rain, fingers clenching and unclenching as they made for David's throat.

I raised my hand.

'That won't be necessary. David was just leaving.'

For a heavy-set man, David scuttled away at speed, face blanched, his unblinking eyes fixed on me. A copy of Rudolf Bultmann's *New Testament and Mythology* launched itself from the shelf towards his head. I stepped in and caught it, holding it tight as it struggled to free itself.

'Best you leave now, David. My books have taken a dislike to you.'

'You haven't heard the last of this, Cant. We didn't know you were even an initiate, let alone an adept, so more fool us, but I'm not without friends of my own.'

'Goodnight, David.'

I replaced the book and fetched four plain chocolate digestives from the kitchen.

'I seem to have too many chocolate biscuits. I can't possibly eat them all.'

I put the plate on the coffee table and went to the bedroom to put on a cardigan. When I came back, there were only two on the plate. I wiped up the damp spots surrounding the painting.

When Venny and Connie came in an hour later they both stopped at the threshold, sensing tension.

'What happened?' they said together.

'A little contretemps with the boss. He got more than he bargained for.'

'My painting?' said Venny.

'And one of the books attacked him.' It sounded ridiculous when I said it.

'Sick. You gonna tell us?' asked Connie.

'Yes. Did you get your laptop?'

A broad grin shone from her face.

'Yeah! Do you want to see it? Venny wouldn't tell me what it cost but it looks great and it comes apart so it's a tablet too. We never had anything like this at school – it was all ancient beat-up stuff. Look: I just need to touch the screen and it does things!'

'Why don't you get it set up and sort yourself email and things, then I think we should look into the Reverend David Sharpe-Thompson.'

'What are we looking for?'

'He called me an initiate and an adept, and said he isn't without friends of his own. I'd start there.'

We passed on college supper and brought in fish and chips with extra mushy peas. I made sure I left some aside next to the painting, as did Venny.

Sydney phoned to ask if I was better. I said it was just something I ate, and I hadn't forgotten about the manuscript and relic.

'Just out of interest, who's asking about it in Canterbury?'

'One of their archivists, French-sounding name, hang on, let me check. Menvier, Mary Menvier, or maybe Marie rather than Mary. Why?'

'No particular reason, just curious how high up the ladder the interest stretches.'

'Let's talk about it tomorrow. David came to see me by the way, did he tell you?'

'He did. He came round and said some really strange things, was quite rude actually, and reeked of his vile sherry. But he made his views plain. I told him I'd declined the position of chaplain. I think your suggestion that I could be a lay adviser is a non-starter in the circumstances, more's the pity.'

'Here's another name for your search,' I said to Venny and Connie after I'd put the phone down. 'Mary, or possibly Marie, Menvier, an archivist in Canterbury.'

Later, I got a reply from Adrian Coulter.

You raise an interesting question. By their nature, esoteric societies within the Church do not advertise themselves, especially those more inclined towards cultic exotica outside the, admittedly flexible, boundaries of the mainstream.

Of course, there is no reason why such groups would be, in some loose sense, associated with Christianity; many would quite explicitly disavow any such connection or, indeed, would stand in outright opposition to it.

My thoughts on this are incomplete and I should not wish to mislead or misdirect you. With that caveat, however, I do, in the circumstances, hypothesise that, should there be esoteric involvement, it is likely to be connected to the Church. I base this on the core features of the Antonios codex and its Christian roots.

The link to the Apostle Thomas, who was almost certainly active in Mesopotamia and India at much the same time that the other apostles were active around the Mediterranean, is suggestive. Outside India, Thomas is particularly remembered in texts associated with the so-called Gnostic tradition, though that description is itself problematic.

In addition, the material you uncovered in Edinburgh resonates with a prophetic, perhaps apocalyptic, corpus.

Gnostic or Mystery sects and orders have flourished in many times and places, including in the origins of Christianity itself. Their successors are still active in Western Christianity, for example the renewed interest following recent scholarship resting on the Nag Hammadi finds. There are also the so-called Galenites who, if they exist beyond the imaginations of conspiracy theorists, have their supposed origins in an obscure fifteenth-century Italian named Galen Paleise. But now I am indulging in idle speculation, which I said I wouldn't.

I will consider this further while enjoying what has become a contemplative retreat on the beautiful Applecross peninsula. This is an area to which I should very much like to retire.

I understand you are to give the sermon in the cathedral tomorrow. I should like to attend in the spirit of ecumenism but that will not be possible. My best wishes go with you.

'Lots of words that don't actually tell us much,' said Venny.
   'How did he find out I'm giving the sermon tomorrow. I don't think I told him.'
   'He's keeping an eye on you then.'

'Why isn't anything simple?'

We put the dishes into the dishwasher and tidied up like any other couple.

'Who are these Galenites?' I asked.

'Never heard of them. He's not even sure they exist.'

'And yet he mentions them by name while protesting that he's not going to speculate. I wonder why.'

'Ooh, a suspicious mind. Another for the list then.'

'I've found her,' said Connie, her voice cracking.

'Who?'

'Mary Menvier, the archivist. Look: here's a photo.'

She turned the screen so Ven and I could see, and a familiar face stared back at me.

'Well, holy shit. That's Martina Hartley.'

CHAPTER 23

St Agatha's is mid-Victorian grand-scale Gothic fanfiction, aping the themes and tropes of the great medieval masters without any of their flair or craft. Ascending hymns and prayers are wrapped into its obsessively vertical stone and stained glass, but it's no Chartres.

Handmade banners for Pentecost and Trinity lined the side aisles, embroidered red flames in bright counterpoint to the grey-stone melody. Beyond the choir stalls and transept, a wrought-iron screen separates the aisle from the chancel and high altar, a gate allowing passage for clergy, like a sacerdotal gated community to which only authorised key holders, professional Christians, have access. The gate is always open, but the screen has stood for a century and a half, ready to keep the riff-raff out of the sanctuary, or at least those unwilling to pass between the Scylla and Charybdis of the choir stalls and approach from the front.

I left Ven with Helen and walked up the north aisle towards the sacristy, the green room for celebrants but without the gin and nibbles, where I guessed I'd find Sydney. I carried my cassock-alb and the text of my sermon in a supermarket hessian bag-for-life. In the parish I'd just write key words on index cards and wing it, but not today.

The alb had been the morning's first surprise. I thought I'd made a mistake, that I'd somehow got the wrong one in the wardrobe, but no: my initials were there on the label in blue biro. I'd chosen it for its elegant, unornamented ivory weave and wide-opening cuffs, the same cuffs now embroidered with scarlet dragonheads chased with gold highlights, their trailing bodies like longships.

My gasp had brought Ven running from the kitchen.

'Where did you get that?'

'I didn't, and it wasn't like this last week. This was the design on the sleeves of Ingrid's robe during the feast at Yrreddell.'

In the sacristy, under stained glass, the scarlet and gold dragons scampered along the weave between my wrists and elbows, a pair of Viking ouroboros exhaling Pentecostal flames.

I slipped Ingrid's scarf round my neck and tucked it under the alb's collar, only visible from close up.

We had a quick dressing-room team talk from Sydney, and then we were off. My role, apart from assisting Sydney with Communion, was solely to give the sermon. I couldn't help but see individuals in the congregation looking at me, nudging their neighbours. I found fortitude in Ingrid's dragons and the memory of her in the prow of her longship, out to wreak who-knows-what havoc on some poor souls. Was this when she thought I'd need wit and strength?

And then I was on. I climbed the steps of the octagonal pulpit where my words waited on the lectern. The choir and congregation finished the last verse of the hymn. I focused on the great rose window, a giant mandala in the west wall, avoiding eye contact with the congregation. As the organ coughed the final chords, I took a breath, feeling like the condemned on a tumbril taking a final look at the earth and sky before I was cast into the void. I remembered the golden rules for speaking into a microphone in a building that large: talk slower than normal, and ignore your own voice echoing back to you from the speakers lining the nave.

'Two thousand years ago, more or less, a man from Nazareth in Galilee was executed in Jerusalem. He died in agony, crying out to God, asking why he had been forsaken. And when he died, Mark says, the curtain of the Temple was torn in two.

'Keep that image in mind.

'Much of what we have been brought up to understand as Jesus's teaching, of what we know as the Christian message, is a gloss on the Jewish original.

'That's not a controversial statement.

'But the understanding of the Gospels we inherited is not by any means a universal understanding, either in the world as we know it now or in the history of Christian thought. From the very beginning, as the early followers of the Nazarene transformed themselves from a community meeting in houses and public spaces into an established religion with all the trappings of sacred spaces and holy texts and a priesthood, there were arguments and disagreements about what the message of Jesus really was.

'It wasn't academic squabbling. Over the centuries, rooting out heresy and heterodoxy and the intertwining of religion and politics and tyranny have brought misery, torture, death and warfare. And still do.

'If you sit down and read Mark's Gospel – and it's quite short, it won't take you long – you'll be struck by how tied up it is with late Judaism. To understand Mark you have to understand that context and the importance of the Temple and all it represented, and therefore the nature of worship and of priesthood. And that speaks to the understanding of the relationship between humans and God, and to the ways that relationship is mediated by the institutions of organised religion, rather than our personal experience of the sublime.

'Mark writes of Jesus doing and saying things that can only be explained as a direct assault, by an insider, on the temple practices and doctrines of late Judaism. It isn't caprice; it isn't the iconoclasm of a hothead.

'Mark tells us at the very beginning that he's writing about Jesus's message, not about Jesus the man. This isn't a superhero franchise. There is no complex origin story. We don't get the tale of Mary and her Magic Baby. There are no wise men or shepherds or censuses or stables or lengthy genealogies or massacre of the innocents or flight to Egypt, because Mark isn't bothered by that stuff. He doesn't even tell us where Jesus got his detailed understanding of the Hebrew Bible and the Law, though he clearly has a very good understanding of them.

'For Mark, the story of Jesus's teaching starts with the baptism of Jesus the man by John the Baptist, a baptism, says Mark, of repentance, for the forgiveness of sins, and the Greek words Mark uses are *metanoia, aphesis* and *hamartia*.

'Sometimes it seems we understand repentance to mean not a great deal more than expressing sincere regret and resolving to behave differently. Forgiveness, well that's what God does, isn't it, or what a parent does with a naughty child? Forgives us for sins, which are things we've done wrong or, following St Augustine, for a condition we find ourselves in through no fault of our own as a result of the cosmic order.

'But the Greek is more nuanced than that. *Metanoia* means changing or opening your mind, or coming to your senses, and the Aramaic means returning to God. *Aphesis* means forgiving in the same sense that you might forgive a debt, making it as though it had never existed. It could also mean releasing, letting go, sending away. And *hamartia*, in Classical Greek at least, didn't refer to some cosmic bad thing, or to things that you have done wrong, but to an error of understanding, an error in the way you see things.

'So Mark says baptism is a way of opening the mind to a new way of looking at things, of wiping away the old understanding as though it never existed. It is a completely new start, a new way of seeing and perceiving, a liberation. And Jesus of Nazareth undergoes this initiation and puts his new understanding into action: he gathers followers and begins healing, and firmly rejects all attempts to put religious titles on him.

'And so we come to today's Gospel reading, Jesus and the disciples picking ears of grain on the Sabbath and immediately being attacked because such a thing is not lawful. It is not *proper*.

'The force of Jesus's response is lost on us because we are not the audience for whom the passage was intended and so we miss the point.

'Jesus says: *Did you never read what David did, when he was in need and hungry, he, and those who were with him? How he entered into the house of God when Abiathar was high priest, and ate the shewbread, which is not lawful to eat except for the priests, and also gave it to those who were with him? And he said to them, the Sabbath was made by humans, and not humans by the Sabbath: so a human is master of the Sabbath.*

'This was shocking, revolutionary stuff. And here's why.

'Shewbread was the twelve loaves of bread, replaced every Sabbath, left in the Temple in Jerusalem on a special table as an offering. The loaves were so significant that only

Temple priests could eat them, and only so long as they ate them in a holy place.

'For David and his companions to eat the shewbread was roughly the equivalent of starving men or women coming into this cathedral and asking for food and eating the reserved sacrament. Many people, perhaps many of you, would view that with horror, as an act that defiles a sacred thing, that defiles a holy place. But Jesus says no, it's fine. And he doesn't just defend the picking and eating of grain on the Sabbath if you're starving. The story is itself a metaphor in which Jesus attacks the deepest notions of ritual sanctity in the Temple and the priesthood.

'He says, you've got it all wrong: it's not about holy places and ritual food and sacred things. That is not where you encounter God. He says that the idea that our actions and behaviour are subordinate to religious and ecclesiastical norms of temples, priests and tradition has to be wiped away.

'He says that you don't find God in consecrated spaces or in liturgies or texts: these things are made by people. By healing the sick and feeding the poor he showed that opening your mind to a new understanding of self and of the transcendent must flow into your personal ethics and how you conduct yourself.

'It means you don't refuse shelter to the homeless, even in a cathedral. It means you don't condemn the poor and homeless as wasters and inadequates, or those who provide them with food as do-gooders. It means you don't turn away the hungry or rely on governments to deal with the hungry person standing right in front of you.

'And it isn't a change you can effect from within an institution, it isn't a matter of make do and mend. Jesus says, *you don't patch up an old coat with new cloth, because it will shrink and tear the stiches. You can't put new wine into old wine skins because the skins will burst and you'll lose everything. New wine needs new wine skins.*

'It's for you to consider what this means for your own personal faith and your own observance. But when thinking about it, recall that the experience of the sublime is not to be mediated by institutions or by priests in holy places, because the curtain of the Temple has been split in two.

'The experience of the sublime is mediated through you as an individual and the community of those who share the same experience.

'You must decide for yourself if the Church as we know it is truly that community, or if it is an old wineskin.'

And then came the second surprise of the day, when my mouth kept talking beyond my brain – the final ad-libbed line I wouldn't have dared to say had I thought about it beforehand. I looked at Venny.

'Of course, these are things I must apply to myself as well, as I start a new life outside the Church with my partner.

'Amen.'

I stuffed the alb into the supermarket bag, rolled the scarf into my pocket and left the sacristy in cargo trousers and an old shirt. Stragglers from the congregation, chatting in the nave, cast disapproving glances at my scruffy clothes but didn't recognise me. Only Sydney's partner Geoffrey gave me a smile and a nod and mimed applause. Ven and Eithne and most of the students waited outside the front door.

'Mary and the Magic Baby?' said Venny, eyes pink and puffy.

'I stole that one.'

'It had some bums shuffling, ducks, I can tell you.'

'They were listening? I can never tell.'

'That's what you meant about the fig tree, isn't it?' Eithne said. 'I didn't quite get it before.'

'Fig tree?' asked Venny.

'An earlier sermon, a bit of a dress rehearsal,' said Eithne. 'I think the students have a lot of questions.'

'Well look, why don't I get the car and pop round the supermarket for wine and orange juice and nibbles and we can all meet up in my flat in an hour or so,' I said.

Eithne motioned me aside.

'David wasn't happy at all. He left as soon as you'd finished attacking everything he stands for. He was in a really foul mood last night, wobbly on his feet, and he stank of that dreadful sherry.'

I looked up at the sky beyond the broad-leafed canopy lining the avenue, wondering how much to say.

'It's a shame you're leaving,' Eithne went on. 'I've had two years of that man and can't abide him. I got an offer from a university in Toronto that I've been putting off making a decision about. I'd be more likely to stick it out here, at least until the current ordinands are on their way, if you were around. Any idea what you'll do?'

I glanced at Venny, who was chatting with Helen, Zoë and other students.

'Vague ideas, nothing concrete. I'm not sure where I'll be based either, but I'd like to do something practical and focused. Something will come up, assuming the medical stuff gets sorted.'

'How's that going?'

'Still waiting for test results. I try not to think about it too much. D'you think you'll go for the job in Canada?'

'It's tenured, which is good, but it's a long way from home. And it means breaking up the networks I have here.

The students will be disappointed that you're leaving.'

'I only came here two and a half weeks ago; it's not as though I'm deeply involved with their lives. I've barely met some of them.'

'Don't underestimate the connection you've already made. You're not what anyone expected, and I mean that in a good way. You challenge their thinking just by who you are, how you dress, who you choose for your friends – and partner.'

I thought of her butterfly and rainbow tattoo.

'Ven said that too. She picked it up from Helen and Zoë.'

'She's right, and that sermon will hit home as well. If they take time to think about it they'll find you've challenged their vocation, once they've got over questioning your every premise, that is. And I wouldn't be surprised if a couple of them decide to come out.'

Wine was opened and pizzas sliced. I put *Explorations* by the Bill Evans Trio on repeat with the volume turned down and no one noticed for three hours, until they drifted off, leaving only Ven, Eithne and me to tidy up and put out the six empty reds and six empty whites.

I'd hoped Eithne would open up a little. I knew nothing of her personal life, but she didn't stick around once the tidying was done. I'd never been inside her bungalow, and she hadn't invited me.

'Well, that's that,' I said to Ven.

'Interesting lot, your students. They tried lots of ways to find out more about me.'

'What did you tell them?'

'The truth: that I write about oddities for obscure magazines and websites.'

'How did they react?'

'Bemusement, curiosity, but no hostility. It was nice to talk to them, actually. I should do it more often. It's something I picked up back in the day. If you mention the weird and paranormal in any random group of people, something always comes back at you unsolicited. People have these experiences and they keep quiet because they don't want to be laughed at, so none of their stories ever get told. We've lost touch with something.'

'What did you get this afternoon?'

'Stories of when they were spooked, of encounters they couldn't explain, general weirdness. I'll bet you I'd get more if I gave them my email address and a promise of anonymity.'

'You should.' I put my arm around her shoulder and pulled her closer. 'I was thinking about yesterday, about what we'll do now.'

'And?'

'I want to be with you. Everything else is up for grabs. Although we'll need to accommodate your assistant too.'

'Are you OK with that?'

'More than, it's just ...'

'What?'

'Just that there are so many more like her on the streets.'

My phone rang.

'Speak of the devil.'

Connie sounded excited, and I put the phone on speaker so Ven could hear.

'I've found something!'

'Yes?'

'Yes! I was practising some of those searches that Venny taught me, looking for more information about that Mary Menvier. And I found all this stuff about her brothers, Christopher and Gordon.'

Ven and I looked at each other, wondering where this was going.

'And it's them!'

'Them who? What?'

'Christopher and Gordon Menvier own a company called St Leonard's Development and Construction Ltd. According to the Companies House website they're the only directors.'

'OK, and where does that get us?'

'Well according to another site I found, St Leonard's Development and Construction Ltd is the company that wants to buy the Mission.'

I got the reference: when David had suggested to Sydney that the diocese should sell the Mission, to recoup the losses of a charitable trust that David managed, he had recommended a company run by the brothers of an acquaintance who had been pestering me, with his connivance.

'That's really good work, Connie, really good.'

I remembered that I hadn't asked about her friend Tracy for a few days.

'She should be getting out soon.'

'Has she anywhere to go?'

'Fi and Beth found her family. Her mum wants nothing to do with her, but an aunty says she'll take her in until she's better. She hasn't really got her head together, and she likes to be out of it, you know? She's not as lucky as me, thanks to you.'

'Well, not all of it.'

'Yes, it is. You helped me, talked to me, asked Fi and Beth for help. That's where it started. I could be just another dead Black kid, like Joe, or out of it, like Tracy, or inside, like Tom, but I'm not.'

'You know, you've just given me an idea. I have some big decisions coming up and I need your advice.'

'Mine?'

'No one better. Remind me to tell you about it when I've thought it through a bit more.'

'Will do. I've got more about the Menviers, by the way. I was looking up my family tree on an ancestry website to see what I could find out about Nana Margaret, and put Mary Menvier's name in the searchbox out of curiosity – that's how I found her brothers. Anyway, I only went back a couple of generations – it was really easy – and her grandmother was called Lilian Horsfall, who had a sister called Miriam. Lilian married a Gabriel Menvier, who was French, and Miriam married a man called Edward Sharpe-Thomson. So Mary and your David Sharpe-Thompson are cousins twice removed.'

Another email arrived from Adrian Coulter.

I hear you preached revolution this morning, empty-the-pews style. I should have liked to be there to hear it. My congratulations on your personal happiness. You must send me a copy of your text. No further thoughts on the esoteric interests, I'm afraid.

I replied:

News travels fast. Impressive. Regarding interest from Canterbury: does the name Mary Menvier mean anything to you?

'I wonder who his informant is,' I said. 'He obviously has a hotline to someone.'

'It could be anyone in the cathedral this morning. I'm more interested in why he's keeping tabs when he is also so affable. He's not hiding that he has a contact.'

'There's so much crap flying around, I'm losing track. There's something I want to ask you, but I'm not sure how to in case it comes over wrong.'

'Oh, that doesn't sound good. What is it?'

'The painting, with Master Dobson. How did you do that?'

'I didn't. I made the painting like any other and I think Master Dobson did the rest. Why?'

'Because it gave David a hell of a fright and he obviously thinks something else is going on, something esoteric. And there's that painting of you dancing in the circle – that's suggestive of rituals and stuff.'

'I get you. I think Master Dobson involved himself because you're important to me.'

'If he's here, wherever he is, is your house protected?'

'As far as I know. What's worrying you?'

'David calling me an adept and what you said yesterday about the people who scared you off. Maybe I'm overthinking it, but if someone comes after me again because they think I'm something I'm not, you could be in their sights too.'

Ven thought for a while.

'I don't think it's them. What happened to you was disgusting and nasty, but if the other lot were after you they'd be even more more relentless, I think. I'll ask someone to go by the house tonight and tomorrow and check everything's fine, though. I have to go and get Herbert from the sitters on Tuesday anyway.'

She picked up a mug and examined it.

'I had a fling with a witch some years ago and got caught up with her coven. I took part in some circles like the one I painted. I eased myself out in the end. It was all very nice and focused on the light, but it didn't do anything for me and I had no reason to hang around once the fling was flung. I'm not keeping anything back, Canty. I'm not involved in anything. There's more than enough weirdness to keep me occupied without any magical shit.'

Neither of us wanted a big supper so I sorted out cheese on toast. We were settling down to hit the internet for more clues when Sydney phoned.

'Sorry I didn't get time to speak with you this morning, but you caught me off guard with that sermon. It's causing quite a stir, on top of all the other problems.'

'Really? No one said anything while I was there, I just got the third degree from the students.'

'Well, there are one or two people absolutely fizzing, I can tell you, and I need to indulge them a little. On the other hand, I've had quite a few wanting to know more about what you said.'

'What did you think, Sydney?'

'Me? Oh, you were unorthodox, but unorthodox in an interesting way and very challenging, though you left a lot to inference. Wise of you. It wasn't what I expected, but it ties in to that stuff about the fig tree, so I should have twigged where you might go with it. Anyway, could you send me a copy? I noticed you were reading rather than speaking from notes. I thought I'd circulate it around the diocese, see what comes of it. The audio is on the website but you know how some people prefer to pick over a text.'

Audio?

'I'll tidy it up and email it tomorrow morning, if that works for you.'

'Splendid, splendid. Look here, there's something else. I had David in here earlier. Between you and me, he was in his cups, but he made all sorts of disobliging comments about you again. I'm not sure quite how I'll handle it, but you ought to know in case any of it comes back to you.'

'Thank you, I appreciate it. That reminds me, the

developer David proposed for the Mission, was it St Leonard's Development and Construction Ltd?'

'The very chaps! Why?'

'Funny thing, but quite by chance I found out the company is run by the brothers of that archivist from Canterbury who keeps pestering you.'

'Good Lord, small world, eh?'

'It is. It might be worth asking David how he came to be in touch with them. It's an odd coincidence.'

Ven gave me two thumbs up from the other end of the settee.

'Just out of interest, was it David who suggested me as temporary chaplain?'

'Not as such. He certainly mentioned it, when I was trying to sort things out when you reappeared. I suppose that could have put the idea in my head. Why?'

'Nothing, really, just gossip. What were the other problems you mentioned? Not something else I've done, I hope?'

'No, nothing to do with you. It's just that one of our more prominent laymen, leading light of the Diocesan Board of Education, was questioned by police the other day about inappropriate behaviour in the park. It's all very unfortunate. One last thing: Geoffrey and I would like it if you both came to supper one night. He was quite taken by your forthrightness and told me off because I'm not the same. Anyway, we'd be delighted if you said yes. I promise there won't be sherry.'

'That Galen Paleise is a tricky one,' said Venny four hours later, pointing to scribbled notes. I'm not sure if the research was helped or hindered by our sampling of Betty's home baking.

'What have you got?'

'It looks like he entered a monastery near Genoa around 1424. There's nothing about him completing his novitiate, but he wanted to be called Brother, or, later, Father, for the rest of his life. It's said he was a gifted linguist who hunted down ancient hierophantic texts, Gnostic, mystic, that sort of stuff, and used them to found an Order, saying they were the true inheritors of the secret teachings of Jesus.'

'Oh, one of those. I wonder if Eithne's heard of them – her speciality is sects and cults.'

'And rock'n'roll? Anyway, the only other thing everyone agrees on is that the Order required strict celibacy because of the insistence on the evils of sexuality in early texts. And that's it. Whether or not any of it is actually true, your guess is as good as mine.'

'And that's who Coulter nudged us towards? I don't get it. Gnostics and mystics, secret teachings, words of power and meaning, rituals and stuff, OK, but I thought he meant something else.'

'There's darknet gossip that some Galenites incline to the Chaos Magical school of thinking, and there's older whispers of dark magic, but that's just internet stuff, unsourced, unverifiable.'

'Anything to do with ritual and symbolism is pretty much indistinguishable from High Church Christianity. The focus on ceremonial and words of knowledge and power sometimes brings it very close to magical thinking. There's this whole thing about using ritual, gestures, words and will to frame intercession with God through the saints, just like ancient Romans trying to make a plea to the emperor through imperial flunkies.'

Ven was giving me a look.

'What?'

'You're going off on one, aren't you? One sermon's enough for today, thank you. Will it be like this all the time, when we're living together?'

'You got the munchies? There's some of Betty's baking left.'

'Nah. Could do with some water, though.'

I picked up the scattered mugs and plates and took them through to the kitchen to leave in the sink until morning. It felt good to have no more worries about the Church. There was still all the stuff I didn't understand – Lallig, the mysterious Gnostics and all the other crap that was happening with David and Mary – but I had a chance to put that behind me. I just had to get the test results and live my best life with Ven for as long as I had left. For the first time in nearly forty years, I felt I might actually be in control of things.

But when I got back to the living room with her water, Venny wasn't there. She wasn't in the loo or the bedroom. Her laptop was on the table, her phone next to it, her bag was in the bedroom and her car in the car park, but of her, there was nothing at all.

CHAPTER 24

The flat overflowed with her absence, her scent. Breathing was difficult, laboured. I couldn't focus. I looked everywhere again.

Whatever had happened was so fast, she hadn't even struggled or shouted.

Please, no. We've only just found each other again.

I wanted to call someone, but it was late and I didn't want to make a fuss in case it turned out to be nothing. Minutes ticked by. I sat next to the laptop and phone she wasn't there to use. I came down from the edibles quickly but the cotton mouth was intense. I kept drinking water and refilling the glass.

Focus!

She would have told me if she'd been popping out for a moment. The flat was compact and I was just in the next room.

I looked over to ask the painting – and how bizarre does that sound? It wasn't there. The frame hung on the wall surrounding the stretched board, primed with white gesso. The pigments were in the piled nap of the carpet, a cracked kaleidoscope of acrylic fragments.

Should I call Fi or Beth? What would I say? And if I called them, Connie would want to know why. I didn't know the students well enough, except Helen, but I wasn't too sure about the ethics of calling her. That left Eithne or David.

David, who'd threatened me, who'd got drunk and gone to Sydney to complain about me. I glared at the ancient internal phone: his extension light was on. I locked the outside door and went up the stairs that hadn't squeaked any telltales. The door at the top was locked from the inside. I stalked through the library, not sure what I would say, but not about to take any shit. David's voice was loud behind the closed door of his office. I walked in without knocking.

David was sitting on the floor in the far corner of the room, wearing his usual black double-breasted cassock and his cloak, an open bottle of sweet sherry on the floor near his right hand, an empty on his desk. There was no glass. The phone was off its cradle. He rocked backwards and forwards, talking to himself, the back of his head hitting the plaster of the wall over and over again.

He glowered for a second, then diminished, his face an old walnut collapsing into itself. His eyes darted around the room, looking anywhere except at me.

'What have you done with her?'

He tugged his cloak tighter about him, knocking over the sherry bottle. A sickly-sweet-smelling trickle ran across the old wood floor, dribbling into the stale air.

'What did you do?'

He shook his head; wouldn't look at me.

I tapped the cradle on the phone to reset the line, and called Eithne.

'Sorry, I know it's late, but can you come over to David's office? We have a problem.'

He looked at me again then, eyes wide, horror in his stare. He pointed at me and shouted twice, nonsense syllables, incoherent guttural consonants, then sobbed. He was like that when Eithne arrived in *Star Wars* pyjamas and a tartan dressing gown, the tired annoyance on her face turning to concern.

'Oh, hell. What's happened?'

'I don't know, I found him like this.'

'Why were you here?'

'I'll tell you in a minute, but we need to get him sorted.'

I picked up the nearly empty bottle and put it with the other on the desk. I grabbed a handful of tissues from a box and mopped up the spillage. I couldn't do anything about the smell.

'How much of that stuff has he had?'

'Sydney said he was round there earlier and was already drunk then.'

Eithne scowled and shook her head.

'Can we pick him up?'

I looked at the way he sat, his body rocking, mumbling to himself.

'Where would we put him? He'd slide out of a chair. He might be better off where he is but in the recovery position.'

We manoeuvred him until he was lying on his front, head on cushions we'd taken from the two armchairs David used for interviewing students. We arranged his cloak as a kind of blanket.

'What's got him into this state? He's a pain in the arse but I've never known him get this way before,' Eithne said.

I shook my head, but had a shiver of memory, an old physics-student lover talking about stable systems suddenly flipping to what she called new equilibrium states when chronic tensions and stresses snapped.

David's desk was strewn with books. On the top of the pile was the 1955 impression of *A Directory of Ceremonial*, open, upside-down on a copy of *The Church Times*.

I leafed through the short volume. Its earnest solemnity as odd and alien to me as any esoteric rite. It represented the opposite of everything I'd said in the cathedral. There were pencilled annotations in the margins: numbers and diagrams, single words in Greek or Latin. I didn't know if they were in David's hand, though they looked old – made by a previous owner perhaps. About two-thirds of the way through a slip of paper was lodged, torn from an old account book, with scrawled writing and symbols, written in ink by a very fine nib.

'What's that?' said Eithne.

'An old Directory of Ceremonial. Very High Anglican.'

'Not your thing?'

'It's ritual as performance art.'

There was something about the scrawled writing and symbols that didn't look right to me. I'd need time and a good dictionary to translate the writing, though I recognised γνῶσις – gnosis. The doodles were familiar.

There was nothing personal in the office: no photographs of relatives, no obvious keepsakes or curios on the shelves. Everything was strictly functional, nothing frivolous. I looked around the desk itself. The bottom right-hand drawer was deep, made for vertically hung files. Inside were six more unopened bottles of sherry.

'My God, he's got a cache of that stuff here.'

Behind the sherry was my missing hard drive, covered in foul-smelling slime, glistening in the lamplight. I took it out using a tissue to avoid making even the least contact with my fingers. Someone had prised the case open, exposing the innards to the gunk.

'Is that …?'

'It's one mystery solved at any rate. Hello, what's this?'

Something glinted underneath where the hard drive had been.

I took out a crucifix on a leather cord, polished pewter perhaps. It was free of slime.

'What an odd design,' said Eithne.

A Chi Rho wheel surmounted the cross-piece, making it reminiscent of an ankh, exactly like the one I'd seen worn by Mary Menvier, otherwise Martina Hartley. The wheel was made from strands of metal twisted together, similar to the knotwork on Celtic crosses. Where the wheel met the crosspiece it joined in the form of a classic reef knot, in the centre of which was set a small interwoven pentagram. *Oh David, what on earth have you got yourself into?*

'Isn't it? Anyway, these are his personal things, we shouldn't snoop.'

I put the cross and leather cord back where I'd found it and closed the drawer.

'You didn't say why you're here.'

I considered how much to tell her, whether to tell her about Ven, whether to involve her.

'David and I had a bit of a row before he went to see Sydney. I came along to see if we could sort it out.'

Eithne looked at her watch.

'How did you know he was still up?'

'The extension light on the phone was on. It was off the hook when I got here. I found him in the corner, just as you saw him.'

'What was the row about?'

'He came to tell me exactly what he thought of me. Filth and perversion apparently.'

'Oh hell, no. What will you do?'

'Go back up to Derby with Venny as soon as I can. Anyway, there's no need for you to stay up. I can tidy here and make sure he's comfortable for the night.'

'Do you think we should leave him?'

'He'll be fine in the recovery position. He'll have a horrible hangover in the morning, though. I'll stay until I'm sure he's settled.'

'That's more than he deserves after what he said. Say goodnight to Venny for me. I have to sleep, I've a lecture to give first thing.'

'Will do. Oh, I meant to ask: was Barbara ever disciplined for that assault on Helen?'

'Assault? Mmmm, that might be a bit strong. David had a quiet word, I think. We're lucky Helen didn't make a fuss.'

I opened the desk drawer again once she'd gone, and took out the amulet, weighing it in my palm. I sent a couple of photos to Adrian Coulter, asking if he recognised it.

I had a quick rummage through the rest of the drawers when I put the amulet back, to see what else might be there, but there was nothing of interest. David's mobile phone was on the leather desktop under the pile of books. He hadn't set a passcode, so I scrolled through his contacts out of nosiness. Christopher, Gordon and Mary Menvier were all there.

His photo gallery held very few pictures. The most recent were six shots of my flat after it was trashed. There were messages from Mary Menvier/Martina Hartley but they had no words, only photos, all of me or me and Venny. Later ones were taken outside Venny's house, including a shot of us at the chip shop, another in the pub, several of us in the distance by the canal.

His other messages and recent emails all looked routine, including one or two from Gavin Surtees about rituals, presumably in the chapel. There was a lengthy phone call, twenty minutes or so, with Mary Menvier that afternoon, and a much longer one the previous evening, after he'd come to see me. He'd called her both times.

I deleted everything relating to me or Venny and put the phone back under the books. I had another look at his shelves, but there was nothing I wouldn't expect from a High Anglican: standard theological texts and concordances, devotional books and ecclesiastical histories. There was an impressive collection of books on liturgy and ritual, though nothing modern. Several had slips of paper used as bookmarks, but there was nothing written on them.

I picked up the *Directory of Ceremonial* and leafed through it again. I didn't want to leave David alone just yet, but all the water I'd drunk earlier meant I had to go to the loo. I checked he was breathing properly and went to the toilets along the corridor. He hadn't moved when I got back to his office, and was snoring fit to wake the dead.

I sat at the desk, trying to work out what to do next about Venny, and noticed the bottom drawer was open a crack, although I was sure I'd closed it. The amulet was gone.

As I took this in, a reply came in from Adrian Coulter.

I'm in two minds about that. On the one hand it looks just like the sort of faux esoteric rubbish that's everywhere on the internet these days, bought by the gullible or the naïve. On the other hand, if it is authentic, it ties to some of the rumours about the Galenites I previously mentioned. One of the stories is that some on the fringes have taken their interest in ritual to extremes. The Order venerates Jesus as something more than the Saviour of mainstream Christian tradition. The magical stories of the New Testament Apocrypha and the more 'out-there' teachings of the Eastern and Egyptian Gnostic traditions, as well as elements of Roman Paganism, supposedly infuse their beliefs. It's said, though it is only conjecture and rumour, they believe Jesus is Saviour, Son of God and Man, Holder of the Keys to Heaven and Hell, Shaman and Wizard, all rolled into one, and this leads to an overlap with the interests of practitioners of magicks, real or imagined.

I'll see if I can find out more. In the meantime, you must take care. If such a group has gone against all of its traditions and broken cover, they must have what they think is good cause.

Nothing on your Mary Menvier yet I'm afraid – although there is an old family of French occultists by that name. I'll keep looking.

When I got back to the flat, it was as I'd left it, with no signs of entry. It was one in the morning and I had no idea what to do.

I tried to think it through, who might be involved, what the hell was happening with David, but my mind wouldn't cooperate. Eithne was the obvious culprit for the disappearance of the amulet, but I couldn't believe it: nothing about her suggested anything out of the ordinary, and she hadn't reacted to my fib about going to Derby with Ven. In fact, she'd asked me to say good night, as if she didn't know Ven was gone.

All the same, I wasn't convinced I could trust Eithne to help, and Fi and Beth wouldn't appreciate me dropping major weirdness on them at one in the morning.

I'd come full circle: I needed someone to talk to but didn't want to get anyone else involved in case they disappeared too.

'Oh no, no one else to talk to. All alone in the world.'

I leapt to my feet, but there was no one there. A shuffling noise came from the ceiling and walls, and the stench of someone who hadn't bathed in who-knows-how-long, foetid, layered with the scent of rotting mushrooms and leaf mould.

'Is that you, Lallig? Are you going to show yourself?'

A rough sphere of mist condensed in the expectant room, equidistant from the corners of the floor and ceiling. Something physical was trying to get through the vapour from some other place but its way was blocked by barriers I couldn't see. An angry, frustrated voice gasped and panted and cursed. I gripped Ingrid's scarf, my silk talisman.

'Say your piece. What do you want?'

The ball of mist rotated about its vertical axis, gathering speed, whirring widdershins, dripping beads of moisture to the carpet, more and more oblate as it spun. The room was warm now, tense as a hot afternoon before a thunderstorm. My books shook, spines vibrating, rattling, chattering, readying themselves to launch. The overhead light dimmed as energy was sucked from it.

'What have you done with her?'

The mist came to an abrupt stop and cleared sufficiently for me to see the cracked and haggard features of a very old man glaring at me.

'Lanweth's twin shall take no sleep while Joseph's gift in gombraich keep.'

'Oh for Christ's sake, not that doggerel again? Do better.'

He cursed and howled over the song of wolves until, with a soft pop, the ball of moisture imploded.

'No! Come back! Where's Venny?'

But only the smell and dampness remained.

Did Lallig take Venny? I couldn't see how, if he couldn't get through himself. I picked up the *Directory of Ceremonial* again. All of the slips of paper in it fell out onto the settee.

I flicked through them, feeling useless in the face of the Latin and Greek scrawls, until I came to the one with the doodles. This time I recognised them – the same incised markings that were on the stone above the waterfall by Rowan's cottage.

I did sleep eventually, but not much. My mind was stuck in a loop of endlessly repeated thoughts of Ven: where she was, what could happen, who had her. With every repeat, things got worse and worse for her as my imagination ran untrammelled. I finally dropped off around five and woke up with a sore neck and cotton mouth at seven, disoriented, grubby in yesterday's clothes.

I showered and dressed and went to see how David was, but his office was locked.

In the flat I put my laptop and my phone on their chargers and did the same for Venny's. Daylight didn't make my options any clearer and my brain was hardly at peak efficiency. I texted Eithne to see if she'd had any contact with David, but she hadn't and was rushing off to take her class.

I hoped Monday wouldn't throw anything else at me, but, right on cue, the doctor's surgery called at eight-fifteen. They said the cystoscopy had caused the consultant some concern and could I please contact Urology at the hospital. I didn't like the emphasis on *as soon as possible*. But I couldn't make any appointments until I knew what had happened to Venny. Everything crowded into my tired brain again, whirling, leaving me helpless to do much more than flick through photos on my phone, following a futile hope that there might be a clue or detail there, however small, that I'd overlooked.

I would have agreed with Coulter that David's amulet, with its odd mish-mash of elements, looked like the sort of stuff you find on the internet, had Martina or Mary or whoever she was not worn one just the same. And Zoë had said David and Mary, cousins or whatever they were, had talked before I even arrived at Weston House. And if Coulter's suggestion was right, Mary was descended from French occultists. Was that why David called me an adept? That might explain the amulet and his obsession with ritual.

The only reason for their interest in me had to be my disappearance and, as I hadn't mentioned Sanctuary to anyone at that point, they must already have had an interest in that bit of Sutherland, just as Ven suggested. I'd been convinced after the incident with Lallig out in the hills that he was behind it all, and maybe he was, but I couldn't see the thread that tied him, Mary and David together, except Antonios. In the end, everything came back to Antonios – his codex, the relic, and maybe even the man himself – and my breach of Rowan's trust.

Some other force is at work, Cathal had said. *You are here for a reason.* But I refused to go down the path of mysterious forces. Despite all the weirdness that had overtaken my life, I wanted to find some rational explanation for it all. *Not everything is so neat*, Rowan had said, but I wanted it to be neat: if it was neat I might be able to see a way out of it.

I let my head fall back on the settee and pressed my fingers against my shut eyes.

I jumped when Venny's phone pinged. It was an email from Kirsty the genealogist to say she'd put a copy and full transcript of all the documents relating to Janet Wilkie's trial in the post, first class, on Friday.

I found the details of the dog-sitter in her contacts and sent a message that Venny wasn't well and couldn't come for Herbert as planned.

Her laptop was password-protected but I had a quick check on her phone for anything that might be a message or threat from whoever had taken her. There was nothing.

She'd taken a selfie of us together on Saturday and I sent a copy to my email. I had a look to see if there were any more but there weren't, just snaps of her recent paintings, five of them. I sent them to my email too. The dog-sitter replied, apologising she wouldn't be able to keep Herbert beyond Tuesday and could I arrange for pick-up please. I jotted down the address and number.

It was only then that I spotted a message from Connie the previous evening, saying Beth would drop her off here about nine o'clock to talk about her role as Ven's assistant. I checked my watch just as the doorbell rang.

Connie bounced into the flat with the energy of a woman who's got her life back and can't wait to live it, just like I'd been yesterday. She had a new messenger bag on her shoulder for her laptop, and no doubt a notebook and pens and my copy of *Crime and Punishment* too. It only took a moment for her to catch my mood.

'What's up?'

I rubbed the heels of my palms against my eyes, not sure what to say, where to begin.

'Are you OK? Where's Venny?'

'I don't know.'

She saw Ven's phone and computer on the coffee table. 'Is she out?'

'I don't know where she is, Connie. She's disappeared.'

'How could she just disappear?'

'She just did. Last night. We were talking, I went to the kitchen, and when I came back she was gone.'

'How is that even possible? Is it a joke? Why are you saying this? I'm calling Beth and Fi.'

I put up my hand.

'No. Think about it. Whoever took her did it right here without making a sound. They didn't go out the front door because I'd have seen and heard them. And they didn't go out the other door because it was locked from the inside and I'd have heard the squeaky stairs. And there's all the other bizarre shit I haven't told you about.'

Maybe I would have done things differently had I slept properly, if Venny hadn't been missing, if the hospital hadn't wanted to see me immediately, if I'd been thinking straight. Instead, I did what I'd told myself I wouldn't do, couldn't do, with this girl I barely knew: I told her everything.

'You're going to get her back, right?'

'Look at me. Do I look like an action hero?'

'Nobody looks like an action hero: you use what you've got. You helped me, now we need to help Ven. We just need to work out how.'

'I don't know where she is, or who has her. I don't know where to start. And I've got this hospital stuff to sort out.'

'I'm her assistant, right? So I'll assist.'

'Connie ...'

'Don't you dare. Don't you dare push me away. We need to draw up a to-do list.'

Well, that was unexpected.

'You think?'

'Yes. I read about it last night. I was reading about how to make an impact as an assistant and it was right there: make a list, prioritise it and get cracking. You go and put the kettle on.'

By the time I got back she had a list written in her notebook, neatly laid out in large letters with swirls and loops and emphatic bullet points.

- Allies. Who?!!
- Enemies. Who?!!
- Go back to Sanctuary?
- Find the relic
- Save Venny
- Collect Herbert

Not a bad list, all things considered.

'So, where do you propose we begin?' I asked.

'Well, that's hard because we don't really know any of these, except fetching Herbert. After that, I'm stuck.'

'Me too. OK. I'm not sure about *enemies*, but people I can't trust are David, Mary Menvier and Lallig. I don't know about the rest. Friends and allies would be you, maybe Beth and Fi ... let me finish. Beth and Fi are "maybe" because this could cause a problem for them – you remember they don't like weird shit? And then there's Ingrid and Cathal I think, and probably Rowan and William.'

'What about this Father Coulter?'

'He's an unknown. So is Eithne. I don't know about the bishop and I don't really want to get Betty or the students involved.'

'So it's just me and you then?'

'It is, but I'm worried about you.'

'Why? It's like before. Don't you trust me?'

'No, it's just that ...' I sighed and rubbed my eyes again. 'I got Ven involved, and look what's happened to her. I can't do the same to you. I can't put you in danger.'

'I'm nineteen years old and quite capable of deciding that for myself, thank you very much.'

'I thought like that once too. Venny disagreed, and that's why we fell out.'

'Well that settles that then. *We're* not going to make the same mistake, are we? I'm already involved and we're not about to fall out. I'm choosing to be involved of my own free will. Now, is there anything you have to do today?'

'Send copies of my sermon to Sydney, that's the bishop, and to Adrian Coulter. The hospital can wait a bit longer. That's all I know about.'

'Right, well you get on with that and drink your tea.'

And I did. Despite my misgivings, despite knowing better, I did as I was told, grateful for a moment when someone else was making decisions and telling me what to do, nineteen or not.

I edited the sermon, changed the font size, reset the line spacing, checked for obvious typos and formatting issues, then opened my email. My heart did somersaults when I saw two messages from Venny until I remembered I'd just sent them myself from her phone. I opened the picture of the two of us, both of us relaxed, her face happy, and blinked back tears, wiping strays away with my cuff.

I looked more carefully at the pictures of her new art – more detail was visible when I expanded the images – and what I saw injected cold emptiness into my guts. The strokes were imprecise, impressions of form and colour only, as if executed quickly, but the scene was clear enough. A group of figures gathered at the top of a waterfall, like the one above Rowan's cottage. Just as Ven had said, none of the figures had faces, just featureless blurs of paint, but the two in the centre of the picture held all my attention, one a wild thing in rags with unkempt hair and beard, the second, in his grip, an elfin form with a shock of cropped red hair.

I closed my eyes to hold back fresh sobbing.

'What? What is it?' Connie was by me in an instant, looking at the picture.

'I know where she is, who has her. I have to go back to Sanctuary.'

'*We*. We have to go.'

'I don't know if I can take you there.'

'Of course you can.'

'How? How can you possibly know that?'

'Look.' She pointed at a figure with dangling, looped earrings that glinted against skin roughly rendered in black and umber pigments. 'That's me.'

CHAPTER 25

I sent the sermon to Sydney with a note to say Ven had been taken ill and I was driving her home, adding that I might be away for a few days. I phoned Beth with the same message, saying Connie was with me and I'd bring her up to speed when I could. I left messages for Eithne and David to say Ven's car would be in my parking space for the duration, and told the books they had the bridge until I got back. I left Betty's box of edibles where it was.

I put my hill-walking gear in the car with Venny's things, and we stopped at an outdoor store to kit Connie out, then a mall for other clothes and toiletries for the journey north – her messenger bag had her 'emergency stash' of cosmetics, more than I'd owned in my whole life.

I planned to pick up Herbert, stay at Ven's overnight in the hope that Kirsty's package would be delivered the next morning, then aim for Scotland. I still wasn't convinced of the wisdom of taking Connie, but I was glad of the company. She kept me awake with chatter about her family while I drove.

She was surprised when I said one of my great-grandfathers was Kenyan. I never knew the whole story: I'd asked but was firmly told that in those days children were seen and not heard and certainly never told anything interesting like that. Gran said it was OK because 'we passed'. I was an adult before I understood what that meant. I heard Venny in my mind chiding me for not investigating further.

'That's like us then,' Connie said. 'Except in reverse – all my family that I know of were Black except Nana, and Jody, I suppose.'

Her great-grandmother Jody was what they used to call a 'brown baby', her dad was a Black GI killed in 1944 without ever knowing he would be a father.

'What happened to Jody?'

'She married my great-grandad, Cliff Walcott. He came here from Trinidad. They had lots of kids too. Then my gran – that's Annie, her husband Edwin was Trini too – was killed by the police, resisting arrest they said. He fell down stairs in a police station.'

'Did you tell Fi or Beth?'

'What do you think?'

'Your accent isn't Caribbean.'

'Nah. Issa Trini ent? But Nana brought me up. And it helps to fit in, you know?'

Connie 'went haywire', she said, when her great-great-grandmother, Margaret, whom she called Nana, died in 2014 aged ninety. She was close to Nana and Annie, because of their shared experience of the good neighbours, although I had a strong sense that there was more to that than she was ready to tell me.

I did the sums in my head as I drove, and realised that all of Connie's recent maternal line had given birth when very young.

'Is that why you were in the tent?'

'Yeah, that and Mum's boyfriends being dicks. It was easier to get out. I was in a few places before the tent.'

Herbert was pleased to see me, but fell in love with Connie, refusing to leave her side, his adoring eyes watching her every movement. We took him for a walk round the park near Ven's house and fed him bits of the fish suppers we bought afterwards.

I didn't want to go through Ven's things when she wasn't there, but I did want to look through her paintings.

Her studio was her spare room. Paintings were stacked ten or twelve deep against every wall. I flipped through them like they were records in a rack.

Ven's range of subjects was broad and the execution varied, though none of them were the kind of decorative scene you'd want in a vicarage living room. She favoured muted colours and the tones of twilight. There were more scenes of women and men dancing sky-clad, several that looked like events from my life, celebrating Eucharist, leading funerals. Some made no sense to me at all. I could tell there was meaning there, but they were too abstract to understand without a guide. One was of my flat, trashed, exactly as I remembered it when I first found it. A dozen or so were good portraits of unnamed nude sitters, mainly women.

There were three paintings of Dun Dornaigil, all similar in composition and viewpoint, but only two were of the present ruin. The third was of Yrreddell as I remembered it on the night of Ingrid's party. It looked like a broch, not the hall it had turned into inside, but its photo-realist accuracy almost had me falling in. Not like Narnia, Rowan said, but the sense was strong that I could reach through the pigment and canvas and be there, transported like Lucy, Edmund and Eustace in *The Voyage of the Dawn Treader*. Two blobs of ochre and white near the door confused me until I recognised them as the lanterns Rowan and I had carried. Whose eyes had Ven seen this scene through?

On an easel in the centre of the room, angled to get natural light from the only window, was the most recent painting, the one that had convinced me to bring Connie on my search. It was large, a piece of hardboard about three feet by four. It didn't have the same realist quality but had just as much impact. It was like a photograph taken too quickly, the scene blurred by the moving lens, but not so unfocused that forms could not be made out. Aside from Connie, Venny and Lallig I couldn't identify anyone else, as if the others were peripheral to the action. If I had the orientation right, the person through whose eyes the view was seen had their back to the cliffs above the pool into which the waterfall tumbled.

Connie pointed to a brown blob on the edge of the scene, white ruff and black-tipped ears roughly sketched in, but unmistakeable.

'That's Herbert!'

She was right. We were looking at something that hadn't happened yet. I shivered when I noticed something else: one slashing brush stroke indicated Venny was bound, another that Lallig had a long knife in his hand, poised to slice her throat.

I phoned Beth to say everything was fine and Connie and I were off on a road trip for a couple of days. I felt bad about the implicit lie, but told myself I was protecting them. I slept in Venny's bed. Connie chose the settee. When I drew the curtains, I scanned the cars parked across the road. I thought there was movement in one, but it had gone when I woke up.

We left Derby at ten-thirty after the postman had, as I'd hoped, delivered genealogist Kirsty's package. The journey was uneventful and the roads mostly clear. I took the M6 and A74 and turned off at Abington to take the old Roman Road up through Biggar to Edinburgh. We'd had lunch at Tebay and let Herbert have a run-around there. Connie was quiet, watching the scenery go by, dozing off from time to time with Herbert on her lap.

I took the Biggar road partly for a change of pace and scenery but also so that I could more easily see who was behind me. I watched for the grey Astra, but the only two cars I kept seeing were a scruffy-looking old Toyota and a more modern but nondescript Ford. Both stayed well back; neither tried to catch me and overtake. I lost sight of them both as I took the bypass round Edinburgh and over the Queensferry Crossing.

We made good time on the A9. The schools hadn't broken up, and the roving packs of motorhomes and caravans hadn't left their lairs yet. Connie was transfixed by the scenery through Perthshire. I pressed on to Bruar, where we stopped for a toilet break and to stock up on overpriced snacks. I wanted to reach Inverness around supper time and find a B&B or cheap hotel that would take Herbert. In the end we crossed the Kessock Bridge and drove on until we found a place near Dingwall that had a couple of rooms and owners who were happy to feed Herbert bits of rabbit.

I was knackered. My head ached and my back and shoulders were seized tight.

Connie phoned Beth and gave her a huge, excited story of mountains and lochs and bridges and how it was the best holiday she'd ever had. I sat in a deep armchair in the B&B's lounge and opened the package from Kirsty. It contained the full transcription of Janet Wilkie's trial. All was familiar until the prophetic verse. Venny was right: there were four more lines:

Bot magikis ʒetts ſal marryt ſtay
Quhen quha wis funde wyl find þe way
Þane preſt fra preſtis yrnys aſtart
And Hrafn's Eyr ſchall ſnair a hart

317

I hadn't the first idea what it meant, although I didn't like the look of the snaring a hart bit – something to do with trapping a deer? Ingrid had said something about a hart too.

I was ready for bed and could think of only one thing to do: I sent the extra lines to Father Coulter.

I didn't sleep well in the strange bed with all that was on my mind. I'd received a couple of texts during the drive, one from my doctor, one from the hospital, and hadn't replied to either, pushing them to the back of my mind, only for them to re-emerge in the early hours, swirling around my imagination in the half-state between waking and oblivion, when nothing is certain and everything is menacing.

I clutched the silk scarf, hoping Ven knew we were coming for her. God only knew how we'd do it, and She wasn't letting any spoilers slip. In the darkest hours I listened for distant wolves, but there was only the air in the trees, the creaks of the house and the whispers of other people's restless dreams.

Rain rattled the windows of the guest house as we tucked into a full Scottish breakfast and answered the curiosity of our hosts. I told them the truth, more or less: we were heading north via Lairg and Altnaharra. They told us at length about the idiot southerner who'd got lost up there in winter without telling anyone where they were going and turned up months later fine and dandy as if nothing had happened. Disgraceful, we concurred, we would certainly do no such foolish thing, we said as we accepted their offer of a packed lunch for the road.

We were on our way by nine, and my phone buzzed several times as we went in and out of pockets of reception. I pulled over to see what the messages were. Sydney wanted me to get in touch as a matter of urgency, the hospital was chasing me again and Eithne asked if I could call when I got the chance. There was an email from Adrian Coulter thanking me for the new lines but not hazarding a guess as to their meaning. He added that he would be leaving Applecross that day after extending his break to take account of the good weather.

'What do you think?' I asked Connie. 'Should I tell him where we are?'

'Have you decided he's an ally?'

'I used to think he was an enemy, but now I'm not so sure.'

'Could he help?'

'He knows more about some of this than I do. He's researched it for a long time.'

'What does your gut say?'

'My gut says we need all the help we can get.'

'That's your answer then.'

I reckoned it would take him three to four hours to get from Applecross to Altnaharra. We'd be there in an hour and a half with luck. I couldn't be sure of reception for a text so I called him and said if he wanted to know everything we'd see him at the Altnaharra Hotel around one.

'What will we do to do to kill the time?' said Connie.

'We'll take the scenic route.'

I took the top road over to Bonar Bridge, stopping a couple of times to let Herbert bounce around in the scrubby heather and for Connie to take in the view, impressive even in changeable weather. When we next got a signal she sent photos to Fi and Beth. Beth texted me to ask where we were.

At the Falls of Shin I took Connie and Herbert to see the salmon leap, before popping into the gift shop for a bottle of malt whisky. We stopped at the Crask Inn for a pot of tea and a toilet break. As I locked the car, a scruffy old Toyota went past.

We got to Altnaharra about twenty minutes before Adrian Coulter. He joined us in the hotel and received Herbert's seal of approval which, I decided, was good enough for me. As seemed to be his constant habit, Coulter wore a clerical shirt and collar, albeit with moleskin walking trousers and sensible brogues.

'And what's your plan now?' he asked after I'd told him my story which, I have to say, he received with a pleasing lack of scepticism.

'I plan to go up over the back road to Dun Dornaigil and see if I can find a way into Sanctuary.'

'Alone?'

'No. With you and Connie and Herbert if you're up for it.'

'Why me?'

'Because I need all the help I can get, and maybe something will strike a chord with you and give us an edge.'

'And your friend is definitely there?'

'I believe so.' I told him about the paintings.

'And then what?'

'I haven't the foggiest idea.'

He didn't quite roll his eyes, but did cock a single eyebrow.

'Do you think you can get in?'

'Yes, but I'm not sure how. All I have is this.' I took the silk scarf from around my neck. 'It was a gift from Ingrid.'

'When will you go?'

'No point hanging around.'

The way was mercifully free of tourist traffic as we climbed away from the main road and up past Mudale. I'd scribed a line with a compass on the Ordnance Survey chart to mark the rough position of Rowan's boundary, and the map lay open on Connie's lap. I felt a shiver just before Loch Meadie, though whether that was when we crossed the boundary or just my anticipation, I don't know.

I parked on the verge by Dun Dornaigil broch and Coulter drew in behind me. The quiet was near absolute. High above us, a pair of golden eagles wheeled on the high thermals, drifting south and west. Below us the river was swollen by the last of the spring run-off from the hills.

'What now?' asked Connie, eyes wide at the landscape.

The scruffy Toyota came up the road behind us. It parked behind Coulter and two people got out. The hackles on Herbert's neck rose and he growled at them: his instincts were definitely sound.

'Mary Menvier, I thought you might find us. And Gavin, I didn't expect to see you here.'

CHAPTER 26

Gavin Surtees aimed for a defiant look but missed and settled for shamefaced. Creeping Jesus, Helen had called him. He and Mary both wore the familiar amulet.

'David not with you?' I asked.

'He was called to see the bishop,' said Mary.

'Ah! Explaining how he came to recommend your brothers' company for the Mission site, or something else? I hope his hangover wasn't too bad.'

'I don't know what you're talking about. Are we waiting for Miss Odd? I assume she's joining you here.'

'Why do you say that?'

'You have her dog with you.'

Herbert growled again.

'Why on earth have you followed us all this way?' I wanted to stay on the front foot if I could, not give anything away, let her do the talking.

'Aren't you going to introduce us to your friends?' Mary asked.

'No, I'm not. Well, I hope the rest of your trip is pleasant, there's plenty to see and do up here. Come on, Herbert.'

I took my daysack from the back seat and settled it on my back, then made my way down the rough grass embankment, looking for an easy route to the riverside, picking up pebbles for Herbert to chase. He bounded ahead, ears cocked, tail wagging, scattering rabbits. Connie and Coulter followed.

'You can't just leave them there,' said Coulter.

'Sure I can. They weren't invited.'

'Aren't you curious what they're up to?'

'I want to get Venny back. That's it, that's all I've got. Besides, Mary was on my case before I even got to Weston House. She'll follow us and blurt something out sooner or later, or Gavin will.'

I hunkered down and scratched Herbert's ears.

'What do you say? Do you know where Ven is?'

He cocked his head to one side and barked. In my mind's eye I saw the raised wooden causeway that led from Rowan's cottage to Yrreddell. I tried to overlay the route onto what was in front of me, but it looked an awful lot further than when Rowan and I had walked it, and this landscape was mostly unforested and bare, where Sanctuary was native forest.

I felt the pressure of Connie's and Coulter's eyes on my back, waiting for me to do something. It was as if I were back in the parish, dancing the old transubstantiation tango with everyone watching and waiting for me to make the magic happen. But there was no magic, just me in the middle of nowhere, wanting to get Venny back.

I sat on a rock and watched the water flow over the stony riverbed. I thought of the broch as I remembered it when Rowan and I first approached it. I conjured the smell of smoke, the sound of bees. I closed my eyes as the sun broke through the clouds and I was caught in a shaft of light and warmth, comfortable in the light breeze that stirred the grasses and bracken. My ears tuned in to the rhythm of the valley and far away, from another time and place, I heard a rumour of wolves in the chitter-chatter of the river's gossip. I knew then that I could do it.

I grasped Ingrid's scarf, gestured Connie and Coulter to come close and hold on to me, and took a firm grip of Herbert's collar. An uncertainty gathered around us. A bee landed on my sleeve, another on my knee. Shouting and footsteps came from far away as Mary and Gavin tumbled and scrambled down to us.

This time there was no fear, no sense that I was hunted, no tree to run into. This time I opened my eyes to find Cathal staring at us, an arrow nocked and ready, and Ingrid in fighting stance, great sword raised.

Everyone was with me, frightened, unsettled, unprepared, except Connie, who looked all around with wide eyes and joy on her face.

'Fuck me, Canty. You did it.'

Ingrid grinned her broadest grin and swept me into a powerful hug that squeezed the breath from my chest.

'These are your friends?'

'This is Father Adrian Coulter of the Church of Rome, and this is Constance Williams, who is a very good friend. The other two weren't invited but came anyway.'

Ingrid surveyed Connie with the practised eye of a leader.

'Welcome, Constance Williams, you have strength in you, I can see. You are from Nakūr?'

Connie looked confused.

'North Africa. I think it's an old name for Morocco. Irish and Islamic annals recount Norse raids in the ninth century,' said Coulter, attracting an appraising look from both Ingrid and Cathal.

'Nah, mate. Swindon. I've heard a lot about you.' I was surprised to see Connie attempt a curtsy. Cathal gazed on her as the Magi gaze on the Madonna in a Renaissance painting. Herbert had a rival.

'And them?' Ingrid cocked her head at Mary and Gavin, dishevelled and shaken from tumbling down the slope, staring all around them, at each other, bewilderment on their faces.

'We'll find out what they want when they recover their senses. It's good to see you both again. Were you warned I was coming?'

'Warned?'

'The weapons.'

'These are strange times, with unsettling presentiments on the wind and in the earth. The heavens are ambiguous. The bees still tell me nonsense stories of ravens and harts and a lynx and a fox. When the mist swirled, I feared some evil had found us.'

'And Rowan?'

Ingrid and Cathal exchanged glances.

'Rowan isn't herself. She hasn't visited.'

'Then I'm in the right place. You warned me a time was coming when I would need all of my courage and wit. I think it's now.'

Ingrid looked puzzled.

'I did?'

'I held the silk scarf you gave me and we met on a ship, perhaps *Skarfr*, tacking against the wind. The deck shook as the prow cut the waves. You were in fighting gear, surrounded by warriors, a sunlit shore ahead.'

She gave me a look of wonder and confusion.

'That was a dream I once had, so long ago I can't remember when.'

I took the bottle of malt I'd bought at the Falls of Shin out of my pack and presented it with a flourish.

'This time I remembered my manners and brought you a gift. It's humble compared to your excellent mead, but it will free stories loose from stuck tongues on long nights.'

'Excuse me.' Mary Menvier had recovered herself. 'Where exactly are we? This isn't on the map and wasn't here five minutes ago. Where did all those trees come from? Why has the course of the river changed? And who are these people?'

'These are my friends Ingrid and Cathal, and this is their home,' I swept my hand to take in Dun Dornaigil, now resplendent as Yrreddell. 'When I was lost they showed me hospitality. If you're lucky, you might have it too.'

I turned to Ingrid. 'I need your help to rescue a friend. I believe Lallig has her.'

Ingrid and Cathal winced.

'There's mead in the Hall. Let's talk there.'

'I asked you where we are,' said Mary.

'You can drop the attitude, Mary – I think you already know where we are.'

'Should I gag her?' asked Cathal.

'Tempting, but she's just mislaid her manners somewhere.' I looked at her. 'Mary, perhaps you should just tell me why you're both here.'

'This is ridiculous,' said Mary taking out her phone. 'Oh for f— no signal. Bloody Highlands! Right, come on Gavin, we'll walk until we find a network.'

'You'll have a long walk, but it's your choice. And watch out for the wolves, they usually keep to the high ground, but you never know,' I said.

'Don't be ridiculous. There aren't any wolves in Scotland.'

A long howl echoed around the valley; answering cries rose from the hills about us.

'Of course there aren't. Well, have a nice walk. Are you with us, Gavin, or will you take your chances with Mary?'

It was my fourth time telling my story, or as much of it as was necessary for Ingrid and Cathal. I left out anything I thought they wouldn't understand about the modern world, but had no choice but to show them the photos of Antonios's manuscript on my phone. They looked with stunned awe.

Mary and Gavin, who'd decided to stick with us, sat in sullen silence by the fire, pretending not to listen. I wished they weren't there – I could do without my story circulating further – but maybe it was already too late for that. On the other hand, I thought about the crap I'd had to wade through on the internet. Chances were that if my story got out it would fade into the background until it was indistinguishable from noise, just another internet fantasy that no one with any sense would believe.

'You missed out the cancer,' said Mary. I hadn't mentioned that to Gavin or Coulter or Connie.

'What cancer?' asked Connie.

'The tests I've been having.'

'Shit! Have you got it? Where?'

'I don't know. I haven't had the results. Venny comes first.'

'What do we know about this holy treasure?' said Ingrid. 'Why do people want it?'

'We don't know what it is. All we have is a brief reference that tells us it's a "most holy relic". Not knowing what it is gives it more power over people's minds; it lets them fit it into their own stories and fantasies. And that power was enough to set everything in motion. Father Coulter and his brothers are keen to understand it. Mary and Gavin followed us all the way here, presumably to try and get it, though they haven't said why, and I assume Venny was taken because of it, though I don't understand that either.'

I told the story of Joseph of Arimathea, that he purportedly visited England in the years after Christ's death, bringing with him the cup from the Last Supper.

'I hadn't heard that story before,' said Cathal. 'It sounds unlikely.'

'Correct,' said Coulter. 'It was an invention some time after you made your home here, if I understand the chronology.'

'Then what does it have to do with Lallig and your friend?' Cathal asked.

'Antonios wrote that he was instructed to hide a treasure blessed by Jesus himself, and he brought it here,' Coulter said. 'Lallig – or Lulach, as it's written there – shows up in the record of the trial of William's wife, prophesying about "Joseph's gift". We surmise that Joseph is Joseph of Arimathea, who passed the treasure to the Apostle Thomas, who left it for safekeeping with the monks in Egypt.'

Mary and Gavin crossed themselves at the mention of Jesus.

'And Lallig has taken your friend?' Ingrid said.

'I believe so. But she is more than my friend. She carries your brooch.'

Understanding flared in her eyes.

'So these two didn't take her?' She jerked her thumb at Mary and Gavin.

'Look at them. They couldn't spirit Venny out of my house and bring her here if they wanted to. They didn't know she'd gone.'

'A curious name, *Venny*,' Ingrid said.

I smiled. 'It's a diminutive, her name is Ravenser.'

Ingrid stood, gesturing to Cathal. 'I've neglected my duties as host. You'll want to visit Rowan and find answers, but first you must eat.'

She led us through a doorway into a hall. Not the great hall I'd eaten in before, but a hall nonetheless. Down its centre ran a long table, with bread and cold meats, cheese and fish, and ale or water for those who wanted it. A huge bowl of scraps was provided for an ecstatic Herbert.

I hoped the food and drink might take the edge off Mary and Gavin's earlier confusion. I needed to know more about why they'd followed me, and what the story was with David. Mary had done all the talking so far, so I turned to her first.

'Nice necklace.' I kept my tone conversational. 'David had one like it. You didn't tell me how his hangover was.'

'Cut the chat, I'm not playing. Where are we?'

'Funny that, after you were so keen for me to talk with you. And like I said, I think you know where we are already. What do you think, Gavin?'

'Don't talk to her!' Mary spat the words out just as Cathal led William into the room. William froze and stared.

I waved to William but kept my attention on Mary. 'You were on my case with Mrs Mackay, contacted me as soon as I got to Weston House and talked with your cousin David about me before I even got there. No, don't deny it – you were overheard in the college.' Her eyes narrowed. 'The more I think about it, the only thing that makes sense is that you know something about this part of Scotland. There's another funny thing – why would David have suggested me to Sydney as a potential chaplain at Weston House? He had no reason at all to do that and then act as if my arrival was a surprise. It was silly of him to lie, really, unless he was doing what he'd been asked, or told. Was that you as well?'

She snorted but said nothing. I was disappointed. Not because I'd expected her to monologue like a Bond villain and confess, but because I'd hoped for better from her.

I shook my head and left her. I clasped William's hand.

'It's good to see you again. I'm afraid my Greek hasn't improved. These are my friends Constance Williams and Father Adrian Coulter.'

'Mistress Williams, the pleasure is mine. And Father Coulter: I had not expected to be visited today by a papist, but my friend's friend is my friend.'

'I hope you'll still be my friend when I ask something of you. There is a rhyme, perhaps a prophecy, you might help me understand.'

'You can only ask and I can only answer, but why do you think I can assist?'

'It comes from Janet's trial records in Edinburgh.'

He slumped onto a bench. Cathal gave him a cup of water.

'Then you know something I've never shared with anyone here, save Rowan who took me in. How may I help?'

'Your tale is yours, not mine, but the papers record two names, Roan and Lulach, whom I take to be Rowan and Lallig.' William closed his eyes and nodded. 'This Lulach made a prophecy, but I don't understand the words because language has changed.'

'Four hundred years, you said.'

'More or less.'

'One would think four hundred years would be enough for the pain to fade, but it's not. They were so beautiful, so kind. So innocent. And they were strangled one by one, my bairn Marioun first. I've often wished I were dead too, that we might rest together in His merciful arms. And yet I linger. Let me see this rhyme. It is past time I faced this.'

I took a folder from my backpack and selected a printout.

Quhan Iefuis twin in Ynde gangand
And hailly gofpel proclamand
He Iofephis gyfte giftit awa
Til Egipt þyns til Scottis fchoir
Quhair Lanwethis twynne fchall tak na fleip

Quhyle Ioſephis gifte in gombraich keip
Fals Noſtradam and Hercyldoun
Fra hie renoun be nacht caſte doun
Til ſic daye he maun dree his weird
Betuixt Elfame and Middil-ʒeird
Bot magikis ʒetts ſal marryt ſtay
Quhen quha wis funde wyl find þe way
Þane preſt fra preſtis yrnys aſtart
And Hrafn's Eyr ſchall ſnair a hart

'I don't recognise this. You say it was in the trial papers?'
I took another sheet from the folder. 'It was a reply to a question. This is the relevant part: *Interrogat, gif Lulach, at his awin hand, had ſend to ony perſoun, to ſchaw thame thingis to cum? Declarit, that he ſend hir to na creatour in middilyerd, bot ſpaik and propheſiet thingis to cum to her in versis, videlicet.*'

'So from the dittay itself, from my darling Janet's confession. Oh, my dearest dear, what did they do to you that you would say such things?'

He read it through again. 'I won't honour it with verse, and the missing punctuation makes it difficult, but roughly it reads: *When Jesus's twin proclaimed the Holy Gospel in India, he gave Joseph's gift away to Egypt, thence to the Scottish shore, where Lanweth's twin shall not sleep while Joseph's gift is kept in Sanctuary. False Nostradame and Hercildoun will not be cast down from their high renown; until such day he must thole his fate between Elfame and Middle-Earth. But magic's road will remain blocked. When the one who was found finds the way, then priest from priest's shackles escapes, and Hrafn's Eyr shall snare a hart.*'

'Hrafn's Eyr, Raven's tongue. That I recognise,' said Ingrid.

Coulter sat up.

'Yes. And anglicised as Ravenser.'

'What? Where was it anglicised?' I asked.

'There's a lost sea port at the mouth of the Humber, drowned under the North Sea. It was on the end of a spit of sand that Ingrid's fellows called Hrafn's Eyr, the Raven's Tongue, because of its shape. So that's the last line of the prophecy: and Ravenser will snare a hart.'

'But what does it mean? How can Venny snare a hart?' I said.

'Don't you see, silly? She already did,' said Connie, touching the back of my hand. 'Yours.'

I spiralled, wafted through refractions and reflections of light and dark, unanchored, until I looked into my heart, and Venny looked back at me.

'You have the soul of a poet, Constance,' said Ingrid. 'When this is done we will compose the tale, you and I, and tell it at the great feast I will hold to celebrate the triumphs and sorrows to come. And we can discuss your jewellery. And your hair.'

'Sorrows?' I asked.

'Of course. No triumph is without sacrifice; there is always a toll demanded by the All-Father. All warriors who live to taste victory leave behind them crows gorging on the blood-soaked fields where friends and foes alike lie, equal in death. Perhaps it will be the blood of those two shitting themselves over there.' She gave me a broad wink as she indicated Mary and Gavin.

'But what does this mean?' asked William. 'Are you saying these words have prophetic meaning? Who is Jesus's twin?'

'The Apostle Thomas. Thomas Didymus: both parts of his name mean twin in Syriac and Greek respectively. He travelled to India on the monsoon winds with traders and the legend is he founded churches there far beyond the influence of Peter and Paul in Rome. He left something in Egypt that passed into the keeping of monks in the desert, but when trouble came it was given to the safekeeping of a monk called Antonios, who brought it here. To Sanctuary.'

'And how do you know this?'

'Because Antonios wrote it down and left his words with Rowan before he set off to sea again, never to be heard of since.'

'And what was this gift?' asked Cathal.

'The Grail. It must be,' said Gavin, speaking up for the first time.

'And so we are in Avalon, last home of Arthur,' said Mary. 'We were right.'

Surely she wasn't serious? Would she really harass and follow me, would David want me at the college and then want me gone, just for the sake of a piece of medieval fiction?

'Weren't you listening? That's a story dreamed up in the twelfth century. There is no Holy Grail. Haven't you read your Bible? There was just a Passover feast in a borrowed room.'

'That's a lie. You want its power for yourself. David was right about you.'

'What on earth are you on about?' I said. But before I'd finished speaking, before Mary could answer, Ingrid took a carving knife from the table, congealed fat from the meat smearing the length of its leather-stropped blade. She nicked the end of her thumb and smeared a bloody sigil on Mary's forehead.

'You are in my hall as my guest. You eat my food at my table and drink my drink. I follow the old ways and you are safe under this roof as long as I live. But you are marked with my own red blood now. Speak that way to my friend again and there will be feud between us. Your life will end the moment you step beyond my door. Do you understand me?' Her tone was amiable.

The fear on Mary's face was all the answer Ingrid needed.

'You.' Ingrid pointed at Gavin with the knife. 'Attend us. You will tell us all you know. Your mistress won't object.'

Gavin didn't find it easy to stand, despite, or more likely because of Ingrid looming over him, her blood running down the greasy knife blade. He looked at Mary for guidance, but Ingrid was having none of it. She put a hand on his shoulder and propelled him towards me. I had no idea what circumstances had brought him here with Mary, but he was a student in my care and I had a duty to look after him. I gestured to him to sit with his back to Mary, so he couldn't see her, and couldn't take cues from her.

'The lad's terrified, Ingrid. Have you a cup of mead to steady his nerves?'

I sat forward and put my hand on his, pressing firmly down as he tried to pull it away. 'Gavin, I know this isn't what you expected, that it all feels like something has gone awfully wrong and you don't know why. That's OK. I've been there, done that, and it's shitty and horrible and feels like the end of the world. But it isn't the end, it just feels that way. So. Tell me about what Mary just said: what power?'

I kept my voice low enough that Mary couldn't hear me.

Gavin looked confused, conflicted. I felt sorry for him, and put the cup of mead in his hands. William came and sat next to me. He put a finger under Gavin's chin and raised his face so that he had no choice but to look at us.

'Laddie, they took my wife and daughters and examined them and tried them as witches. They took them away and fastened them to posts and killed them one by one, my Janet, Beatrix, Christiane, Annabel and wee Marioun. Then they tossed their bodies onto pyres like so much rubbish onto a midden, and the people of the Good Town came out to warm their arses on the flames. I tell you this because I want you to know that the world goes on, however difficult it is for you at the moment, and your way through this is to talk.'

Gavin took another gulp of mead, draining the cup. Ingrid, behind his shoulder, looked at me but I gave the slightest shake of my head.

'The Grail, of course,' said Gavin. 'We're looking for the Grail.'

'But why here? Why follow me?'

'Because of the stories about this area and you getting lost here. This is where the signs all pointed – this is where ancient knowledge and power reside. When you left so quickly after what you did to Father Sharpe-Thompson, Miss Menvier said that this was where you were most likely to come. Please, I'm only a novice, I had no choice. I'm sorry. Miss Menvier and Father Sharpe-Thompson told me what to do and I couldn't refuse.'

'What do you mean by what I did to David?'

'With your painting and when your books attacked him – even the strongest in the Families can't do that. No one expected it and he took it badly. Miss Menvier won't tell me any more than that.'

'Who are the Families?'

He didn't answer, and had a look on his face as if he'd already said too much. Connie had found out that Mary and David were related – was Gavin somehow related to them too?

I glanced at Ingrid, who put a little more mead in Gavin's cup. I caught the scent as it poured and looked at her, my nose twitching. Her face was a mask of bland innocence.

'What are you sorry for, Gavin?'

'Your flat. They ordered me to wreck it. I'm so sorry. I didn't want to. I like you, we all do, and everyone says you're kind and I know what you did for Helen after the egg thing, and there were those times I found you in the chapel alone.' He had another sip. His tears flowed down his cheeks and into the cup.

'So that was you.'

'Yes, but Miss Menvier and Father Sharpe-Thompson helped.'

'How?'

'They said they would perform a ritual, a summoning, something to help me. I was the one in your flat, but some things happened by themselves. I just did the books and music and the kitchen. I'm sorry. I didn't have any choice. You don't know what they're like. I don't know what happened in your bedroom.'

So there it was: the quiet loner, the earnest boy from the devout family who, it turns out, did the most disgusting and personal damage to my stuff. What had happened to him to make him do that? I didn't have time for it: I had Ven to find, and a terrified student sitting in front of me.

'Gavin, listen to me now.' I waited for him to settle. 'Listen to me very carefully. I understand, and I want you to know that I forgive you. No: listen to me. I forgive you as if it never happened. I won't ever mention it again. Tell me about the Grail. What will you do with it?'

'Say the Holy Eucharist of course, what else?'

'Is that all?'

Finally, that drew a sharper reaction.

'What do you mean, is that *all*? It's the cup our Lord raised to His own lips. By the words and actions of the Holy Eucharist it will contain His own blood. Can't you see the power in that? Just think of all the wonders we could do, the glory we could reveal on earth, the healing and peace that would follow. We could bring the Kingdom itself and ascend with Him to our true home as spiritual beings. It's what you said in the chapel about there being no spiritual nourishment: we could change that overnight.'

I rested my face on my palms, elbows on the table, and rubbed my fingertips against my closed eyes.

'You're talking about transubstantiation.'

'Why yes! What else?'

'Papist idolatry,' said William.

'Metaphor,' said Adrian Coulter with a sigh, shaking his head.

Magic. Why can they only think about magic and not discipleship?

Only Mary could tell me more, and she wasn't in any mood to be helpful.

'Thank you, Gavin. Would you like to stay there or go back to Miss Menvier?'

But he was already teetering on the edge of sleep, thanks to whatever Ingrid had put in his drink. He rested his head on his forearms, crossed in front of him on the table like a tired puppy.

'That didn't get us very far, did it?' said Connie.

'No, not really.'

But I was disturbed by Gavin's casual mention of Menvier and Sharpe-Thompson performing a ritual – a summoning he called it. Adept, David had said. What had ruined my bedroom? Who were the Families? And what did they think I'd done to David?

'I think it's time to go and see Rowan. That's where this started, that's where I'll find the end.'

'Alone?' Ingrid asked.

I didn't want to go mob-handed, like villagers advancing on the monster's lair, but now it came to it I didn't want to go by myself.

'I'm coming,' said Connie.

'Yes. Yes, you are. All right: I'll go with Connie. Father Coulter, William, could you give more thought to this prophetic verse and see if any further meaning can be squeezed out of it? As William said, the lack of punctuation is unhelpful. Ingrid, Cathal, this is your hall, your choices are your own, but it would be helpful if Gavin here were looked after and Ms Menvier kept out of trouble.'

Connie slipped her arm through the crook of mine. I looked at the others around the table but had no more to say. Herbert gave a single bark.

'Yes, you too then, Herbert. Let's go find out what's happened to Ven.'

CHAPTER 27

'You OK?' I asked Connie as we walked along the causeway.
'I don't know how this will pan out.'

'I wouldn't be anywhere else. This is some some shit by
the way, *way* weirder than lights in the park and that Master
Dobson stuff of Venny's. Do you think whatshisname
Coulter will find something in that prophecy?'

'I'm sure he will.'

'Why?'

'Because he wants to. It's how he thinks. He'll find a
way to make it relevant to me whether it is or not.'

'What did Gavin mean about you and Helen and the
egg thing?'

I told her the story.

'Her hair? That's awful. I mean, did that Barbara even
know what she was doing when she did that? You don't
mess with a Black girl's hair, man. You just don't.'

Herbert ran ahead, leaping off the walkway into the
undergrowth, bounding back in triumph with a stick in his
mouth, making sure we were following.

'These people, Rowan and Ingrid and Cathal and
William, they're all really old, right? They don't die.'

'Rowan said everything dies, including her. But time is
screwy here.'

'What I mean is, if you have cancer and you came here,

you wouldn't have to die. Not yet, anyway.'

'I don't know how it works.'

'But it's a chance, right? You and Venny could have a proper life together and I could see you sometimes, somehow?'

The sun was lower in the sky, not yet behind the hills, but it wouldn't be long. The river rippled across its bed in the warm air, following gravity's insistent call to the sea. Birch trees lined the riverbanks. There were no sheep, and the deer kept to the higher ground. This was how it was before we 'improved' it, and improvement always seems to mean ruining. It was a kind of Eden, and that was the lure, and the hook.

'I can't promise that, Connie. I don't want to die, but living out endless days with nothing to do doesn't appeal to me either.'

'But I don't want you to die. You can't.'

I couldn't look at her. 'We all do, some day. Look, we're almost here.'

Connie didn't like my attempt to close things down, but I had other things on my mind. The walkway was now an earth track. Rowan's house stood in the clearing on the side of the hill ahead of us, the chickens strutted around at the gable end, pecking and clucking, ten hens plus cockerel; the rowan trees heavy with bright red berries.

'But how ...? We've only just left Ingrid's? And there's a hill in the way?'

'The paths here are as long or as short as they need to be, like time. We're here because it's the right time to be here. Herbert, to me.'

Remarkably, Herbert obeyed and walked at heel past the nervous fowl.

'When you told me your story, it was like Rowan and Ingrid were next door to each other, then when we parked the car it all looked bigger and everything, but now it's like it's next door again.'

'I can't explain it, Connie. You just have to go with it.'

I tapped the door and it opened almost immediately. Rowan was exactly as I remembered her, in the same white linen gown, an apron tied around her waist.

'So, you found your way back. I hoped you might. I'm glad, very glad. And you have friends with you.'

'This is Constance Williams, Connie to her friends. And this is Herbert. They've come to help me find another friend who I think was brought here against her will.'

Rowan pursed her lips, then sighed and opened the door wide.

'Yes, that makes sense. Welcome to my home, Constance Williams. Shall we have something hot to drink? It's getting to be that time of the evening. And you, Herbert, shall have some scraps.'

The map and guidebook lay on the counter of the ancient dresser. The kitchen was unchanged. I wanted to know how much subjective time had passed for her since I'd left, but let it go unasked. Now I was with her again I didn't know where to start, how soon to admit my duplicity in taking the copy of Antonios's document, whether to put my hand up to it straight away or slip it into conversation and hope she didn't notice.

Connie looked round the room with an intensity that made me sure she was memorising it all. Rowan noticed too.

'My house interests you, Constance Williams?'

'It reminds me of my nana's house, or what she told me about how it was when she was a girl – the furniture, the iron range. I expected it to be different here.'

'What did you expect?'

'When Nana told me stories of Faerie and her childhood,

341

she made it sound stranger, weirder. This is normal. Sorry, I don't mean to be rude.'

'You're not rude in the slightest, I'm pleased you think I'm normal. What did your nana say?'

'She told me about the fair folk living under mounds in tiny palaces surrounded by music and dancing. How did you get that big metal cooker up here and working?'

I'd never thought to ask that, and Rowan didn't answer.

'That's how it appeared, once, before things changed. And maybe it still is in some places. But not here. I would like to meet your nana.'

'She died four and a bit years ago, and anyway I saw it myself in the park.'

'What did you see?'

'I told Canty about it: lights in the trees, like a procession, with fiddle and flute music and white horses, but there was nowhere it could be coming from and nowhere for it to go except into a hole in an old wall.'

Rowan's face transformed into a picture of joy, her eyes wide. She looked hard at Connie, but said nothing more about what had pleased her: was it news of the fair folk or Connie's ability to see them? From the other side of the kitchen came the enthusiastic sound of Herbert attacking his bowl of meat scraps, his second of the day. He would be unbearable when he had to go back onto supermarket pet food if we made it home.

Rowan turned back to me. 'You said your friend was brought here against her will. You'd better tell me about it, although I think I can guess some of it.'

'Her name is Ravenser and I think she was brought here by Lallig, or Lulach, or whatever his true name is. It's something to do with the relic Antonios carried here from Egypt. I think he wants to exchange her for it. He seems to think I can do that.'

342

'And can you?'

'I would do anything and give everything I have to get her back.'

She gave me the same penetrating, unsettling look she once gave when I denied I was running from anything, the same look she had just given Connie.

'How did you know about the relic? I thought only three people knew about it, one of whom was Antonios.'

'Ah. Well. That's embarrassing. I did something you asked me not to do.'

I retold the basics. I expected Rowan would react badly to my deceit, would show anger or disappointment. She did neither.

'I suspected something would happen from the first time I found you unconscious by the tree.'

'How can that possibly be?'

'Because of how you said you got here, chased by wolves, and the voices you heard. There was only one answer, and I didn't want to admit it.'

'Lallig?'

'His name is Lallawg. His story is complicated, but everything you said about him and his madness is familiar. He saw something about you that makes him think you will fulfil the prophecy that's obsessed him for centuries.'

'How? How can what I do now fulfil a so-called prophecy that's centuries old?'

'That's not how prophecy works. Things don't happen now because of the prophecy, the prophecy could only be made because you'll do them now. If they don't happen then the prophecy couldn't be made in the first place. Do you see?'

'Like Venny's paintings,' said Connie.

'I don't even know how it applies to me anyway.'

'You've heard it?'

'Yes, but it's so vague it could mean anything; it could justify any outcome.'

'Oh very clever, you noticed that. Then there is hope after all.'

'Now you've lost me. What hope?'

'Hope that this ends well. Tea?'

I let what Rowan had said run through my head while she prepared an infusion.

'So you guessed when I was first here?'

'I suspected. I let things run their course.'

'Is that why you showed me Antonios's book?'

'I thought you'd be interested anyway, but also I wanted to see what happened. I don't understand how you managed to get a copy though. I thought you might do something, but that's not what I expected.'

I showed her my mobile phone, noticing it was low on battery.

'I captured an image of each page on one of these.'

'It's like magic!'

'No, just technology, remember?'

'Do you understand how it works?'

'Well, no, but ...'

Rowan smiled. She touched Connie's hand.

'I'm not sure how you fit into this, Constance Williams.'

'Canty saved me.'

'We've already gone through this ...' I said, but Connie talked over me, assertive.

'I was in trouble. I can't live at home and was living rough with friends, or I thought they were friends. Canty talked to me when I was alone, fed me when I was hungry, and helped get me somewhere to live. No one else cared, and she didn't even know me.'

For the second time in five minutes, Rowan's long scrutiny made me uncomfortable, as though the accumulated experience of all of her centuries was focused only and entirely on me.

'I owe you an apology. We once talked about priesthood and ministry. I misjudged you. I'm sorry.'

'You were right – I *was* running away from all that. My problem is to work out what I'm running towards.'

'And yet in running from it, you've found its heart, discarded the irrelevant, become truer to your calling.'

'*Then priest from priest's shackles escapes* – that could be you again, couldn't it?' said Connie.

Rowan lifted the lid of the pot and peered inside. Satisfied, she brought out three mugs.

'So, who is Lallawg?' I asked.

Rowan's hand wobbled and hot liquid spilled onto the table. She put the teapot on a trivet and fetched a rag to wipe up the spill.

'He is my grandson.'

'Canty didn't say you had family,' Connie said, before I could react.

'I didn't tell her. The last person I told about them was Antonios.'

'Them?' I asked.

Sometimes I've sat with parishioners who've held their tongues about something for so long I thought they had nothing left to say. Then something breaks inside and words spill like spaghetti from a spoon.

'It was so long ago the world has forgotten. I had twins, a boy and a girl: Fearghus and Meadhbh. But my babies weren't safe, because men wanted me dead. They would have killed the children and me and their father to erase us from the face of creation. A man who chose me as consort couldn't be suffered to live though he were the King, because it was contrary to what they thought of as

Nature's laws. So I crossed the narrow sea in secret and made my *termonn* here, gathering my borders around me, safe from the eyes and ears of men, beyond the confines of history, and beyond the reach of my kin.

'But time did as time does and my bairns grew up. They wanted to be who they thought they were meant to be and to make their own way. And they each said things they shouldn't have said, like every child who ever struggled towards adulthood. They left Sanctuary with my unwanted blessing, refusing my protection.'

Connie lifted her mug and drank, but didn't take her attention off Rowan.

'Fearghus was his father's son: strong, with a warrior's blood and the temper of a callant. He sailed away to find his father, but Crimhthann was dust in the ground at Tara, utterly forgotten except in winter stories. Fearghus came back once to rage at me, then left forever, renouncing the name I gave him. I watched from a distance as he rose in authority and power and had children by many women. And those children had their own families and so his blood and mine flowed through the veins of history, some of it through lords and kings, most through ordinary men and women.

'Fearghus lived a long life until one autumn morning he died on the end of a sharp spear, as men thought was honourable then. His beautiful head was cut from his body and mounted on the spear that killed him. He turned to dust in the soil, and so joined his father in the end. None of his children in all their generations ever knew me, though some had the Sight and glimpsed me in visions. Some still do.

'Meadhbh and I reconciled, and she lived here with me all the years of Fearghus's life and more, until she left and made her life with Morvryn, a well-regarded warrior in the south. She too bore twins, but died giving birth. Morvryn and his new wife only knew me as Meadhbh's mother and made me welcome. I saw my grandchildren often and brought them here sometimes through secret ways. Morvryn named them Lallawg and Languoreth. They were very close, closer even than twins often are, though at first I didn't know just how close.

'It was Antonios who realised their secret: although they seemed to be two children, boy and girl, they shared one another's thoughts as if they were one person. They loved Antonios, who was gentle and kind and told them stories of Egypt and India and storms at sea and sand in the desert, and of the Nazarene whom he worshipped as his Saviour. Both became Christians in the way of the time, praying for God's aid to grow the crops and His strength to slaughter their enemies.

'Lallawg wore the gold torc of his king, Gwynddolau, and was a trusted and subtle counsellor. His sister was a powerful seer who also guided Gwynddolau, and helped anyone else who asked her advice. She knew the uses of plants and trees and the songs of the wind and loved to sing and dance. People who saw her called her the Lark because of the sweetness of her voice on the hillside.

'One day Languoreth said she was pregnant but wouldn't say who the father was, even to me. She had strong and jealous suitors, Gwynddolau himself and Roderc of Ystrad Clud, although both already had wives. Like her mother, she had twins, a boy and a girl, whom she named Constantine and Angharad, names which had significance for her, though she never told me what.'

Connie, rapt, poured herself more tea. Herbert curled up in the warmth of the range, tail-tip twitching.

'Then there was some kind of misunderstanding involving Lallawg, and a great battle was fought near Languoreth's home at Arfderydd.

'The few witnesses I found said the wind was up and the air was chill and no one in the heart of the fierce fighting could tell who they killed because blood and gore covered everything and everyone. But they kept on killing, friend and enemy alike, thinking only of their own survival. They said dead men's hair flew through red air and caught on the tips of spears, and clogged the slicing of hard metal through soft flesh.

'Lallawg sent men to save his sister, but it was too late – she had already slaughtered the geese and read their blood and so knew her fate. Languoreth saw Constantine and Angharad butchered before her eyes before she too met death on the blood-bright blade of a bone-blunted sword.

'And because they shared their thoughts, Lallawg saw it too and died with her, even as she lived in his head.

'He became insane, and fled Arfderydd into the wilderness, far from the old tracks and the roads the Romans left behind. I found him at last, wild, his ragged clothes still red, and brought him here, hoping he might find peace and healing. And his madness did seem to settle for a long time, until one of his great schemes failed and broke his mind again.'

She paused, searching for words and memories, but didn't find them.

'And that's my story. He is obsessed with two things: the relic, which Antonios must have told him about, and Languoreth's prophecy that a time would come when the relic would be found and it would free him from his pain and restore magic to the world.'

I looked around the kitchen with its ancient comforts, its homeliness, the place Rowan had created to protect her children from the violence of the outside world. Her jars of ingredients lined the shelves of the dresser, kept against what contingencies, I couldn't guess. Herbs and heathers hung in bunches from the beams on the ceiling, drying. The bonsai pine Antonios had given her sat alone on a rough side table where it caught the light most of the day, close enough to the range to be kept moist by condensing steam and moisture, not so close as to be scorched.

'And you guessed he'd brought me here the first time?'

'I suspected, but suspicion isn't knowledge.'

'And the rhyme that I heard?'

She looked away. I'd seen that face on other people, a pain she wasn't ready to share yet. I hadn't known what to expect coming back, but this vulnerable woman wasn't part of it.

'I thought that if the time of the prophecy was approaching you might want to come back, so I helped things along a little.'

'What did you do?'

'I left a little bit of here in the wound on your head under your hair, some dirt from my land, so a piece of Sanctuary would become part of you.'

All along I'd thought it was Ingrid's gifts that had done it. I wanted to be angry, was angry, at the manipulation, but I was thankful too: without it I might never have been able to come back for Venny. And, after all, I'd copied the manuscript, so perhaps it evened out.

'What does Lallawg want?'

'He wants things how they were before, before everyone was slaughtered. He wants to be able to live in the world again, and he, or Languoreth, there's no difference between them now, wants the magic back – their foresight. It was their great failing – their certainty of their own of superiority over other magicians and seers, whom they scorned as mountebanks and charlatans.'

False Nostradame and Hercildoun.

'And how does the relic help?'

'I don't know. I don't think Antonios ever even looked to see what it was, and he never told me what he'd done with it. For all I know, he took it with him when he sailed off to the end of the world, despite what he wrote.'

I looked back at the bonsai pine.

'No, he left it here. And I think I know where.'

'How will you let Lallawg know we're here?' said Connie.

I thought of the long wail of wolves around the glen when we arrived.

'He already knows.'

CHAPTER 28

The stream was below us and to our left as we trudged up past the narrows to where the water spilled from the bottom of the bowl. The path got steeper there as the day grew silky and a light, persistent drizzle came on. Connie was panting more than me when we got to the top. We rested by the top of the waterfall while she caught her breath.

'Is this safe?' asked Connie, peering over the edge to the churning pool below. 'I don't do well with heights.'

'So long as it's still light and relatively dry, I guess, but best stay back from the edge. There aren't any emergency services up here to haul you out if you go over. Let's get on. It might be rough going, even in boots,' I said. Herbert ran ahead as usual, yapping, scattering mountain hares.

'Where now?' she asked.

I pointed out the line of the track as it passed through scattered and stunted pines that thinned out as we reached higher ground.

'That way. There's a dead pine along there near the far treeline – that's where I'm heading for.'

'Why do you think this Antonios guy left something there?'

'Did you notice the miniature tree in Rowan's kitchen?'

'By the range?'

'That's the one. It was a gift from Antonios. I think it was his way of leaving a pointer.'

'What if it isn't?'

'Then I'll have to think again. He lived up here, so we could go out to his house, though Lallawg probably ransacked it long ago.'

'Rowan didn't answer my question, the one about that iron cooker.'

'Ask her again some time. I doubt the answer will make sense.'

'There's loads I don't understand about all this, like there's something bigger going on,' Connie said.

'Yeah, I know what you mean, but one thing at a time.'

'Why is this happening *now*? Why not do something when you were here before, at the mercy of wolves? That would make a lot more sense.'

It was a good question, and I couldn't answer it without thinking about that ridiculous prophecy – that somehow the time wasn't right before, but was now. We walked between the trees, hoods up against the penetrating drizzle, until we reached the dead pine, its petrified branches piercing the uncertain sky.

'What are we looking for?'

'I think he put the relic in this tree, in a hole.'

'But there aren't any holes. Are you just making this up as you go along?'

'I've never done anything like this before, so yes, I'm improvising.'

The white bones of the tree had long ago been stripped of bark by time and the wind. It hadn't occurred to me that there'd been plenty of time for the tree to grow before it died, even here.

I took a couple of steps back and walked round the trunk, looking for anything that looked like a hole. I could see only one, a good three feet above my head, just below a branch.

'How will we get to that?'

'We'll use what's lying around to try and get high enough to reach in.'

'You're kidding. Won't it be slippery in the wet?'

Rocks and stones and old branches were scattered around the tree, but the rocks were heavy and the branches *were* slippery and prone to snapping if weight was put on them. And we couldn't just heap them up, we had to try and put together something robust enough for me to stand on.

'What about me? I'm lighter and taller,' said Connie. But I was stubborn, or stupid, or something like that. I might even have started to believe in that damned prophecy, and convinced myself it had to be me.

We made a scrappy-looking platform of sorts, maybe a foot and a half high, and I tested my weight on it. When I was sure it was solid enough to risk, I clambered on and reached up to the hole. I tossed a couple of pebbles in first, just in case something with sharp teeth or a beak was inside.

Satisfied, I reached up and put my hand in. My wrist rested on the rim of the hole but no matter how I twisted my hand I couldn't feel the bottom.

'We need to make this higher.'

Connie gave me an exasperated look from beneath her dripping hood that said *I'm lighter and taller; I'm younger.* But I persisted in my pig-headedness.

More grunting and heaving of stones followed, harder work because we had to look further about us for suitable material. The drizzle didn't let up. If anything, the clouds grew darker as the light faded. When the makeshift platform was another foot or so higher, I was impatient to try again.

It felt much less secure, but I climbed up anyway, willing the whole thing not to collapse under me.

I was able to get my arm in as far as my elbow. I felt around in the cavity but still couldn't feel the bottom. I was about to give up and fetch more rocks when my fingers brushed something that didn't feel like tree.

I was right!

I adjusted my position to stand on tiptoes and raised my other arm high to grasp the branch above the hole and pull myself up, make myself taller. My waterproof hindered free movement so I unzipped it and shrugged it off and tried again.

This time I took hold of the branch above me with my left hand as my right-hand fingers managed to get purchase on whatever was in the hole. It felt like a leather pouch, and I managed to manipulate it with my fingertips until I had enough grip to lift it out.

I looked in triumph at what was in my hand, only to see a barely recognisable, long-dead thing.

Yuck!

'What is it?'

'A dead squirrel, I think.'

I tossed it away. Herbert leaped up and caught it mid-air then trotted back to drop it at my feet.

'You're soaked, let me have a go.'

'One last time, then you can try.'

I raised myself up again on tiptoes, ignoring the complaining tendons in my calves. I thought I might get a better angle if I grabbed the branch with my right hand and used my left to explore the hole. I rummaged around and found something else in the bottom of the cavity. Wary of another mummified squirrel, I took my time getting a grip, trying to sense through touch the contours and textures of what I had. It felt like old leather, but so had the squirrel.

Whatever this was, it was heavier. I heard it clink as it moved.

I took a tight grip and pulled it out of the hole at the same moment that the platform collapsed beneath me.

The branch in my right hand couldn't take my sudden weight. The old wood snapped and I felt a tear in my shoulder. My left foot and ankle rolled under me as I hit the loose rocks below. I tumbled to the wet ground, cracking my left knee on a stone.

'Shit, Canty! I said you should have let me do it.'

Connie was at my side, wrapping my wet coat around me. I winced at the touch of her hand on my shoulder. Herbert sat in front of us, head cocked.

'I've hurt myself.'

Of course I had, and she knew it.

'Is it just your shoulder?'

'No. Give me a moment.' I could barely get the words out. I knew I had a nasty sprain in my ankle if I was lucky, a break if I wasn't.

I made my right leg do the work of getting me part-way up, but standing brought profound pain in my left knee and agony in my left foot. I wanted to vomit.

'I need to get to the stream.'

'Why?'

'Because the water is cold and I need to put this ankle into it as soon as I can. My knee too, if I can. I think I need one of those sticks as a crutch.'

My left hand gripped tight on whatever it was I'd taken from the hole. I could see it was a leather bag tied round the top with leather cord. It looked intact, with no sign of fraying or wear or animal damage, despite its centuries in the tree. Whatever was in there could wait a little longer. I put the pouch in a large pocket in my hillwalking trousers and concentrated on getting to the water.

It was slow and painful. The stick got slick very quickly, and that was when I discovered the deep gashes in my right palm. The back of my left hand bled freely too.

'Fuck's sake, Canty. I told you, but would you listen? You should have let me do it. Do you think I should go and get help?'

'In a minute. Let's get to the stream.'

I took my left boot and sock off. It wasn't the most sensible thing to do, but dipping my ankle in the cold water brought relief, once the aching cold turned to numbness. There wasn't enough light left to see the ankle properly, and we had no torch. I could move it, so it probably wasn't broken, but there was ligament damage. I rinsed my cut hands in the water, ignoring the stinging, and submerged my leg in the cold stream to the height of my knee.

Rest, ice, compression, elevation. One out of four is a start.

Connie took off her anorak, then her T-shirt. Her mohawk, already flattened by the hood of her anorak, was quickly soaked through, flopping over her forehead. She tore the shirt into strips for a makeshift bandage for my hands, then rolled the rest into padding to rest in the fork of the long branch I was using to support me.

I had to get my boot back on to get down the hill. If nothing else, Rowan would make me comfortable. I tried not to think about what I'd done to my shoulder and hand.

The twenty-minute walk from the waterfall to the tree took an hour and a half in reverse, lit by moonlight refracted through fog. Connie got more frantic every time I had to rest. A functioning part of me knew I was in shock and borderline hypothermic, which was very bad news. I desperately wanted to go to sleep but knew that I mustn't.

'I'll stop at the waterfall and you can go and fetch Rowan, OK?' I said.

We crested a slight ridge and dropped out of the mist that enveloped the trees. Burning torches glowed below us.

Oh God, it's the villagers with pitchforks.

I laughed, and couldn't stop.

CHAPTER 29

Lallawg's stench announced him, well before I saw him waiting near the standing stone at the head of the waterfall. He was holding a sword – nothing fancy, just brutally functional. Kneeling in front of him, hands bound behind their backs, mouths gagged, were Venny and Father Coulter. Behind him stood almost everyone else, Menvier and Gavin included, held at bay by five wolves. I couldn't see Rowan or William.

Two crude cages of roughly twisted wood, bound with twine, were on the wet grass beside Lallawg. An albino fawn was in one, something black and angry in the other.

Lallawg tickled Venny's back with the blade and muttered something as he watched Connie and me descend out of the mist. Ven struggled to her feet, unaided. Her eyes took in my crutch and painful movements then locked onto mine. I managed to smile at her and nod. She wore the same clothes as the night she'd disappeared, jeans and sweatshirt and DMs. No coat. Her hair flared red in the flames of the torches, just as it had in her paintings.

'Stay behind me, Connie.'

'Stop being heroic, moron.'

I giggled. I was happy to have her here at the endgame, this brave, random girl I'd helped in the park, who wanted to return the favour if only I'd let her.

The path was muddy and treacherous after the drizzle, now falling as steady rain. The echoing roar was a constant reminder of the height of the cliffs, the depth of the scoured stone bowl below.

I stopped at the standing stone and let my weight fall against it, relieved it didn't wobble, happy not to aggravate my shoulder any more with my makeshift crutch. I couldn't walk any further anyway. Even if my ankle would take it, my knee wouldn't. And my hands hurt like hell; the strips of ragged cloth binding them dripped but I didn't know whether it was rain or blood.

'What now?' asked Connie. 'You need an ambulance. You look awful.'

'His move, and he's got the sword and the wolves.'

And I can barely move at all.

Lallawg was nothing much to look at in person, his emaciated body draped in rags. His long hair was thinning, but what was left was tangled and matted; his beard was knife-hacked. His only adornment was a thick gold band round his upper right arm, held in place by twigs and mosses stuffed into the gaps where muscles used to swell.

A jab with the sword and Venny shuffled forward, Lallawg behind her. They came closer, but only by a couple steps, and he stayed within a swift sword's reach of Adrian Coulter. He talked to himself all the time. His teeth, formed before any idea of refined sugar, were surprisingly sturdy, but filthy, protruding from receding gums.

I ask my sister
Twin tongue of time's telling
Flesh of shared womb
Tell me what will be.
> *I will answer, long-lived Lallawg*
> *As you ask so skillfully.*

> *The White Spectre will take the treasure*
> *And Christ's blood will set us free.*

Alas for fair Languoreth
Bones picked bare
By blood-beaked ravens.
Who is the White Spectre?

There was movement behind the wolves, but nothing that might provoke him to sudden violence. Rowan and William were definitely not there. What had happened while I was at the tree?

> *Long may my songs linger*
> *Though the lark lies laide in lame.*
> *The White Spectre walks between the worlds*
> *For Hrafn's Eyr.*

Uh-oh! I tried to tell myself not to get caught up in the ravings, but I was very, very tired and all my pains came together as an all-consuming throbbing. Why were they calling me the White Spectre? It had to mean me, bizarre as it was.

Loving Languoreth, lithe of limb
You are dust at Arfderydd.
Tell true your tongue
What sacrifice sets free the magic?
> *Long the lonely years that lie*
> *Since my bonny bairns' blood bled.*
> *Here cry of raven's tongue be heared*
> *And priest of priestly fetters freed.*

The dark thing in the cage must be a raven, and Coulter the priest, marked for death, I guessed. Through the pulsing darkness of my pain, a clear white light burned through my seized-up brain and I perceived what they did not: *they don't understand their own prophecy.* Lallawg and Languoreth had interpreted everything literally, though I had no idea why they'd picked me as the vehicle for their scheme.

Emissary of Eve
Eater of apples, wearer of wisdom
Tell me at last your secret
Tell me of the treasure.
> *Four the thorns that pierced His body*
> *Four the thorns that shed His blood*
> *Four the thorns that free the magic*
> *Four the thorns of Holy Rood.*

And there it was, plain at last, though I had to be losing it completely to find meaning in a dialogue between a mad brother and his dead sister.

The old stories were wrong: why would Joseph of Arimathea, who was not at the last Passover meal, have a cup? He wouldn't. He was only ever described as the man who took Jesus from the cross and prepared him for burial. What else would he have taken and kept but the nails driven through Jesus's wrists and feet?

Was that it? Were the nails the relic that passed from Joseph to Thomas to Antonios? That had been left in a hole in an old pine in a pocket reality? Were they in the leather pouch in my trouser pocket?

I had to keep them out of Lallawg's hands, without letting any harm come to Venny or Coulter. I took the pouch out, ignoring the pain as the torn skin of my hand snagged the edge of the sodden cloth.

'I believe you're looking for this, Lallawg.' My voice was weakened, but firm enough to carry.

I untied the cord that bound the leather and took one of the nails out. In the flickering torchlight I saw the black, dried blood encrusted on it. No transubstantiation necessary, this was the real thing.

Coulter's eyes widened as he realised what I held. Beyond him, Mary Menvier and Gavin Surtees fell to their knees in the mud, genuflecting, muttering prayers or incantations, if there's a difference.

Lallawg froze, fixated on the old metal in my hand, on the blood of the poor sod from Galilee who dared eat wheat on the Sabbath.

And there, on a wet hillside in a place that shouldn't exist, even I believed for a moment that I had in my hand a way to heal my wounds and banish the treacherous cells within me. All the ways I could use the magic frolicked through my exhausted mind, like childish fantasies of flying or invisibility.

But my body didn't stop hurting, and my torn hands bleeding.

Lallawg reached into a cage and seized the albino fawn.

'The White Spectre, the raven, the hart and the priest!' cried Lallawg. 'Magic will come again to Ynys Pridain.'

He spread his arms wide and howled to the rain-drenched sky, ready to draw the sword across his victims' throats, just as Herbert bounded down the path behind me, a squirming rabbit clenched between his triumphant jaws. At his first sight of Venny, he dropped the rabbit and barked.

For a fraction of a second Lallawg was distracted, and that was all Ven needed. The heel of her DM scraped down Lallawg's shin as she threw her head back, catching him square on the nose, smashing it with the force of her anger. She jumped aside as he dropped his sword, turned and slammed her right foot into his shrivelled balls with all the force she had.

'Ingrid!' I called, as she and Cathal drew long knives and despatched the wolves with five swift slices of sharp steel.

I emptied all the nails from the pouch into my bloody right hand and leaned out to hold them over the deep water below, a weak smile on my face.

'And the curtain of the temple was rent in two.'

'No!' bellowed Lallawg and Mary Menvier in unison, leaping towards me. Gavin Surtees flailed in the mud; Mary left him sprawled there as she scrambled after Lallawg.

Menvier slipped in the mud and fell into Lallawg's back, and he tumbled towards me. I had nowhere to go. My ankle and knee wouldn't even take my weight, let alone carry me out of their way. All three of us went over the cliff into the black tumult below.

The fall took two seconds, three at most, but it felt longer, long enough to hear Ven and Connie scream, long enough for Lallawg or Menvier, I don't know which, to hit the cliff wall and cannon into me, pushing me further out. I hit the water on my right shoulder and blacked out from the impact and overwhelming pain.

I came to on the surface, bumping against a rock, but what was left of my conscious mind knew that, with the shock I was already in and the hypothermia, I wouldn't survive. And I was OK with that now I knew Ven was safe.

I let go of the nails, still clutched tight in my wounded hand, my fresh blood colouring the surface, the blood from the metal dissolving into it. As the nails sank to the bottom of the pool, irrecoverable, a Sunday-school jingle wormed its way into my head. *I am washed in the blood, washed in the blood of the Lamb,* I sang, and felt the deep peace of knowing it was time to let everything go.

CHAPTER 30

Dim light. Old-fashioned bedlinen. Smells of heather and polish and cooking. I felt my arms: no saline drips, no machines monitoring and bleeping, no bustle of nurses, no smell of hospital antiseptic. I raised my head, looking around. The movement of my head brought pain to my shoulder. My hands stung, my knee and ankle ached.

The furniture was old wood, handcrafted by a master. By the window was a table on which a vase holding fresh-cut wild flowers stood on a lace doily. The walls were whitewashed stone and above them were old wooden beams. No ceiling as such, just a cavity and thatch above, as if I were in a folk-life museum.

I heard other voices, women's voices, and I knew where I was.

'Hello!' I called, and running feet pattered over stone flags. The door burst open and Ven and Connie ran in with Rowan following behind.

'You came for me,' said Venny.

'Always.'

I gathered Ven and Connie in a hug as best I could and smiled at Rowan, her eyes shadowed by sadness.

'How long?'

'Two days,' said Ven. 'Rowan looked after you.'

'How bad?'

'Two nasty cuts, a bad sprain, a torn muscle in your shoulder and a very swollen knee, but you're getting there. No infection that we can see.'

'Lallawg?'

Rowan shook her head.

'I'm truly sorry. I never meant for that. What about everyone else?'

'Menvier's dead too. Gavin Surtees is in a bad way, in the care of Ingrid and Cathal. Coulter is staying with William,' said Connie.

'And Herbert?'

'The hero of the hour is sleeping off another meal of rabbit scraps in the kitchen and enjoying getting fussed over by everyone.'

I let my head sink into the feather pillow, then asked if they could help me sit up.

'When will I be able to get out of bed?'

'Soon as you like, me duck. You'll probably only get to the kitchen and back for a while, mind.'

I took Connie's hand.

'Thank you. I wouldn't be here if you hadn't helped me down the path.'

'Too right you wouldn't. Idiot.'

Later, Ven and Connie, for whom rooms had somehow been created, took Herbert for a walk, and I was left with Rowan. However you look at it, I'd triggered the chain of events that had killed her grandson, her only remaining link to her deep past. I couldn't find any words to say.

'You don't need to say anything,' she said. 'Whatever you think now, it wasn't your fault. The Lallawg I knew died long ago.'

'I'd like to see him if I can, to say farewell.' And sorry.

'Not until you can walk. Your leg isn't ready yet.'

She made one of her infusions, her response to any situation.

'They told me what you said, at the end, about the curtain of the temple. What did you mean?'

I sipped the hot drink and gathered my thoughts.

'It's what Jesus talked about but it all got distorted when his followers made a religion out of it. They all wanted magic in their own ways – Lallawg and Menvier, and even Coulter. At the end I was tempted too, but it was never about magic at all. It's about understanding who you are, how you relate to the unknown, how you behave. We don't need temples and holy relics and magic to meet the transcendent. We meet Her in our hearts and in our heads and how we choose to live. The nails were a distraction, a distortion, even. They had to go.'

She was quiet for a long time. Through the kitchen window, beyond the tumbling stream, the hills stood as they had for millennia, always the same, always changing.

'Are you staying this time?'

'No. If I stayed, if *we* stayed, we'd be running neither from nor to anything.'

She gave me one of her looks.

'What will you do when you go home?'

'I don't know. It was awkward enough last time when nearly six months had passed, not three days. And this time it isn't just me, there're others to think of. And I have the hospital stuff to sort out.'

'Hospital?'

'They think I might be ill, that I have cancer.'

'What is cancer?'

'Something growing inside that will eventually take all my strength and then my life.'

'Do you have it?'

'I don't know. The doctors want to see me soon, so it

doesn't sound good. But if they've found it in time I can be treated. That was my temptation with the nails: the chance of magical healing. And what about you, Rowan, what will you do now?'

'What I always do: wait until it's time for me to move on. I meant to say, Ingrid wants to hold a feast for you, to celebrate.'

'How can I celebrate with Lallawg and Mary dead? Where is Mary's body? How awful of me not to think to ask.'

'She is with Lallawg. We can celebrate what Lallawg once was, if that makes you feel better. And I have this to help remember him.' She took the gold torc that had been on Lallawg's arm from the folds of her apron.

Ingrid's words came back to me: *no triumph is without sacrifice; there is always a toll demanded by the All-Father.* Lallawg and Mary had sacrificed everything they had. What had I given?

I limped to the waterfall alone, leaning on the same hazel staff I'd used before, forced to rest more often than I'd like. I stopped at the standing stone and its enigmatic inscriptions. Wind hissed through the leaves and water flowed under the endless sky for all the world as if nothing had happened there.

In the pool where I almost died, where Lallawg and Mary did die, a pair of dippers flittered in and out of the water, washed in the blood of the Lamb and none the wiser for it. Beyond the standing stone sat a mountain hare, maybe the same one as on my first visit, frozen, hoping I couldn't see it. It was in its summer colours now, its nose twitching.

When it had come to the crunch, I'd been at peace with death, ready to let everything go once Ven was safe. All the things that I'd abandoned could stay at the bottom of the pool.

> Bot magikis ʒetts ſal marryt ſtay
> Quhen quha wis funde wyl find þe way
> Þane preſt fra preſtis yrnys aſtart
> And Hrafn's Eyr ſchall ſnair a hart

> But magic's roads shall stay blocked
> When who was found will find the way
> Then priest from priest's shackles departs
> And Hrafn's Eyr shall snare a heart.

What I'd told Rowan was as wrong as it was right. Lallawg thought that if he gathered all the ingredients together then the prophecy would fulfil itself, like following a recipe. He mistook a rhyme for a prophecy and a prophecy for a spell. He ignored any difficulties, like the bits of the rhyme that made no sense, because he really wanted it to be about him. He'd assumed that the meaning would be clear in retrospect, once the spell was cast.

But magic's road was always open – magic of the sort that wrapped me in its spell. My heart was snared, and I was ready to surrender to the consequences.

Don't apologise, don't cringe, keep on being you.

I walked down the path. I did not look back.

Ven waited in my bed. The bed was as big as it needed to be and we had all the time in two worlds. Time enough for love.

There was mead and ale and meat and laughter. There were toasts to the memory of Lallawg and Mary Menvier. Cathal made spaniel-puppy eyes at Connie. William and Adrian

Coulter were deep in earnest conversation, and Gavin Surtees, withdrawn, unwell, sat with Rowan. Herbert ate scraps. Ingrid, who had spent a long time huddled with Connie and a mirror, wore smoky-brown eye makeup and a deep crimson lipstick, with coral-red and gold threads woven through her hair.

In sombre mood, Rowan said she was pleased Connie had seen the fair folk, but was sad the last of her own line had passed.

'Oh no,' said Venny. 'That's not right at all.'

'This is a riddle I would like to hear you explain, Ravenser Odd.'

'You said you had two children, Meadhbh and Fearghus, and Fearghus had many children, who also had children who survived to have children of their own.'

'Yes …'

'Each of us has two parents, four grandparents, eight great-grandparents, doubling every generation until the number of our possible ancestors is very soon greater than the number of all the people who ever lived.

'But that's impossible, so it means that all of our ancestries are intermingled. Looked at it from the other side of history: if your Fearghus went into the world somewhere before the year 500, then, in the fifteen hundred-plus years since, there have been maybe sixty generations or more. During that time, his descendants have multiplied. It's certain that anyone from his time with any descendants alive in our time is an ancestor of all of us, and so, you see, we're all your children.'

Rowan's smile shone like a summer sunrise.

My leg and shoulder ached but were improving. Ingrid examined the furious scars on my hands with a fighter's eye and declared them honourable wounds and cause for another toast. She insisted I had a sip of what she called her special mead, barely a thimbleful. The drink was so refined it was almost non-existent in the mouth, so rarefied as to be inhaled rather than swallowed. Ven and Connie had some too. Connie was transfigured by the sensation, savouring every moment the mead lingered in her mouth, eyes wide, as if for a moment she were somewhere else entirely.

Ingrid wouldn't say what made the mead 'special', but she noticed its effect on Connie too, and looked thoughtful.

I sat next to Gavin. I hadn't spoken with him much; he'd been distraught after the waterfall and Mary's death, and had avoided me. In fairness, and to my shame, I hadn't gone out of my way to talk to him either, telling myself it was better to give him space. Like it or not, and I didn't, he shared my secrets; he knew about Sanctuary. His fellow cultists, or whatever they were, would want to know about that and, as a novice, he'd feel compelled to tell them.

'How're you doing?'

He flinched, and withdrew further into his shell.

'I want you to know I'm here for you and will be with you when we go back. Going back can be difficult. I know, I've done it before.'

He'd barely touched his food and sipped only water. He didn't look well enough to make the transition back to the world, especially if it made him feel as I had. But I couldn't leave him in Sanctuary against his will, for time to pass at an unpredictable rate, and he was in no fit state to decide that for himself.

'Is there someone I should contact when we get out of here? Your parents, maybe?'

He flinched again. Obviously not such a great suggestion.

'Gavin, I want to help, but you need to throw me some hints.'

He shook his head and turned away.

'He's been like that since his friend died,' Rowan said. 'Even I can't get through to him, and I've tried.'

'He's badly traumatised. I have to get him somewhere he feels safe. He's in my care, and he wasn't like this when we got here. He should never have been here in the first place. And I still don't know the full extent of what he and Mary were involved in. I don't want it to lead people back to you.'

'My borders are secure.'

'Are they? I have a terrible feeling that my coming here set something in motion. First it was just me, now it's me and my friends and Gavin. Mary died here. Lallawg died here.'

She touched my hand, my cheek.

'Perhaps it's time for things to change. You do your best for Gavin, and trust me to take care of myself. I've had a lot of practice, and there's more to Sanctuary than you've seen.'

When no more food could be eaten, even by Herbert, who waddled rather than walked to a rug by the open fire, I had the pleasure of witnessing Ingrid's first taste of single malt whisky, seeing the smile of an angel spread across her face.

'Truly this gift, this Ledaig, honours me. I have nothing its equal to offer in return, except ...' She looked at Venny and me sitting side by side, inseparable since my strength had returned enough to be up and about. Venny wore the gold brooch at her lapel, I wore the Byzantine silk scarf around my neck.

'Cathal, my good sword.'

Ingrid went to a workbench at the back of the hall and picked something from a shelf while Cathal took the great ceremonial war-sword from the wall. Etched runes darted up and down the length of the blade, invoking the old gods of Ingrid's home.

'Stand,' she said, as much a command as a request.

'There is no doubt of your love for each other, a love for which you,' she looked at me, 'were willing to die. Nor is there any doubt that an alliance between your houses would be formidable indeed, and mighty in the face of your foes.'

'Is she planning to marry us?' asked Venny.

'Is that what you want? Will you?'

'More than anything, if you do too?'

'Now and always.'

Ingrid took our hands and drew us towards her.

'Do you choose each other, before everyone here in the Hall, to be partners in life, forswearing all others, trusting your voyages to the same timbers and sail, until death alone casts you ashore?'

'Yes,' we said together.

Cathal wrapped a cloth around our wrists with a loose knot, and put a silver ring on each of our ring fingers. Ingrid touched the flat of the blade on the knotted scarf.

'May your love bring you long life and the blessings of friends, of family and of true companionship. And may all know that from this time forth you are united as one.'

She gave the sword to Cathal to return to its mount and bowed towards us.

Connie squealed and everyone except Gavin stood and applauded while Ingrid insisted that Ven and I down mugs of ale, then hugged us and gave us each a bronze amulet.

'The gift of Freyja,' she said. 'Her blessings on you both.'

'And mine too,' said Rowan, taking our hands. 'For as long as I have life you will be in my heart.'

'Now then,' said Ingrid. 'You made me a promise last time you were here. It's time to honour it. Here is a cup of this *uisge beatha* to unstick the words from your tongue.'

Oh Hell, no.

'Promise?' asked Venny.

I gathered my wits and tried to sort out the story in my fuddled mind, what parts would appeal to Ingrid, what parts to the others. I thought of the bright stars under the black skies of Sanctuary, of the Plough and the Little Bear, Orion and Taurus and the Pleiades.

'I am no skald, and I will not attempt verse, but it is my honour to recount the saga.'

'Saga?' asked Connie.

Outside the broch walls, wind rolled around the tower, and from far away came the reassuring howl of wolves, mourning their lost companions under the shimmering Milky Way. I sipped the whisky and wrapped a sheepskin around my aching shoulders. I leaned forward on my new walking stick, carved from blackthorn by Cathal, with a silver collar and silver-tipped horn pommel crafted by Ingrid. I smiled at my wife.

'Come closer, friends. This is the story of Leia Anakinnsdotir the Wise, and her hot-headed brother Lúkr, at the dark hall of their father.'

CHAPTER 31

We scattered Mary and Lallawg's ashes at dawn on the high top of Bheinn Shith. Coulter and I performed the rite; Rowan and Ingrid built the pyres.

Coulter accepted Rowan's invitation to remain in Sanctuary with his new friend William, ostensibly to keep vigil over the pool, but more likely to argue about the interpretation of Greek texts. With the mystery of Joseph of Arimathea's gift solved to his satisfaction, Coulter found he yearned for an extended retreat, fully aware that it would be permanent. I carried a letter from him to one of his brothers.

Rowan told us that we'd re-enter 'our' world only a couple of hours after we left. She said no time travel was involved, just the *careful alignment of continuous nows*. I have no idea what she meant, nor, it occurred to me much later, why she hadn't done it the first time I'd left.

Gavin's condition was my first concern. He had the same memory loss I'd had when I first left Sanctuary and didn't know where he was or why. I didn't need the Sight to know that meant trouble, but it was trouble for another day.

Connie and Ven didn't seem to be affected by the transition and nor, this time, did I. Ven and I talked about driving south straightaway, but there was no way we could explain how we'd just happened to bump into Gavin so far away from the college on a remote road in the north of Scotland. And he needed medical attention.

I plugged my phone into a power block in the car, and a couple of messages came through, one from Sydney saying I was needed as soon as possible because David had taken a turn and was in hospital, and Eithne and a student were missing. I called DI Buchan at Police Scotland, asking him to come and meet me at Dun Dornaigil if he could, and to bring a doctor.

Ven and Connie took Coulter's car to Edinburgh to drop off with the rental company. I waited by Mary's car, Gavin asleep in the back of mine. I phoned Sydney to let him know Gavin was with me and I'd be back as soon as I could, and then called Christine to get contact details for Gavin's parents.

Buchan and MacKenzie arrived an hour later in a Police Scotland SUV. I told them I'd come back to find some sort of closure. I'd gone on a long walk up Glen Golly and got back to find Gavin unwell by Martina Hartley's Toyota. I had no idea why they'd followed me, or why he was with her, though I assumed she was still looking for a story. Gavin obviously needed medical attention. I was happy to call his parents as I had a duty of care as college chaplain.

The police would search for Mary, but she wouldn't ever be found and would become one more cautionary tale.

The next day I drove south with Gavin asleep on the back seat of my car, and met Ven and Connie in Edinburgh. They'd left flowers on the Castle Esplanade in memory of Janet, Beatrix, Christiane, Annabel and Marioun. Ven had bought a bottle of mead – Ingrid insisted we had to drink a glass a day for a month. We had a sip each, then set off to drive home through the night.

'Were they really the nails from the crucifixion?' Venny asked.

'I don't know. And it really doesn't matter in the end, so long as people thought they were.'

We were south of Biggar, with Gavin wrapped up and still asleep, when Connie said, 'I quite liked being called Constance.'

'What did Cathal call you?' I asked. She blushed, the first time I'd seen her do that, and fingered his gift to her, a beautifully worked piece of Ash in the form of Yggdrasil, hanging on a thin gold chain around her neck.

'None of your business. Anyway, I think I'd like to be Constance again.'

'You got it.'

She paused in the way that meant a question was coming.

'What was it you wanted to ask me about? Before all this happened.'

'I want to help the homeless, but do it properly, and I don't know where to start. I don't know what the real problems are. I need your help.'

'You got it,' she said, and turned her head to watch the view go past.

I played with the ring on my finger, feeling its weight, its presence. Ven noticed and smiled.

'I've been thinking,' she said. 'Why would Lallawg sacrifice Coulter? Was it because he was the one in the clerical collar? And how could he have known Coulter would be there at all?'

'Lallawg was born before anyone thought of clerical collars. His mistake was more fundamental: he assumed a priest could only be a man. And Adrian was never necessary, really – Lallawg would have found a way to interpret whatever happened as fulfilment of the prophecy. Coulter's presence just reinforced Lallawg's view of his own correctness.'

I kept looking at the way the light reflected from her ring, inscribed, like mine, by Rowan in a script we didn't understand. Ingrid's amulet hung on a cord around my neck.

'Why did he call you the White Spectre?' Ven asked.

'I haven't the foggiest.'

'Do you think that's the end of it?'

I thought of all the unanswered questions I had, of Constance's suspicion that something else was going on and Gavin's mention of 'the Families'. And there were the questions we'd have to face and couldn't answer, not least about Martina/Mary's disappearance.

'No. We haven't heard the last of it.'

We crossed the border into England. Constance said, 'Can I ask you a personal question, Canty?'

'Sure.'

'What did your mum call you?'

'Jennifer.'

'Can I call you that? Would you mind?'

'Of course you can. It's my name.'

'Jennifer Cant. I like that.'

And yet, now I had my name back, it didn't feel right anymore.

'Thank you, but do you know, I think I prefer the sound of Jennifer Odd. Yes, I like that a lot.'

NOTES AND ACKNOWLEDGEMENTS

The text I created for Janet Wilkie's trial is based on real cases transcribed in Pitcairn's *Ancient Criminal Trials in Scotland*. The PhD thesis that puts most it into modern English is an invention. I've left some of the trial material in the original spelling and orthography including yoghs and thorns. Elizabeth (Bessie) Dunlop, Aliesoun Pierson, Agnes Sampsoun RIP.

The sentence of scourging and deportation passed on William is based my reading of the original text of the trial of David Andro (unpublished).

The prophetic rhyme, Lallawg's dialogue, and Cathal's impromptu tumble into Scaldic verse are all my own invention. I know Cathal's verse doesn't conform to classic rules of alliteration, but it was too hard in modern English. The kennings in Cathal's verse are based on Norse originals taken from Penguin Classics editions of the Sagas.

Placing Lallawg and Languoreth at the battle of Arfderydd (ca 573CE), and the link to Myrdin/Merlin are invented to suit my purposes from historical sources and academic materials. Tim Clarkson's *Scotland's Merlin* was suggestive of some of the background to my invention.

The verse/dialogue between Lallawg and Languoreth that crops up throughout the story is based on the form of *The Dialogue Between Myrddin and His Sister Gwenddydd* in the Red Book of Hergest, which is of uncertain date.

The route of Antonios's voyage to India and the cargo carried is taken from a surviving first century CE text (*The Periplus of the Erythraean Sea*). I have assumed that accounts of the apostle Thomas Didymus in India in the latter part of the first century CE are correct.

Master Dobson's name and description come from Suffolk folklore. JK Rowling went to a similar source for Dobbie the House Elf, I assume, but they are different characters.

The lectionary readings for Jennifer's two sermons are accurate for the Church of England calendar in 2018.

Ace Inhibitor's classic, mellotron-drenched prog concept album *The Dawn Dance of the Calcium Antagonists* is entirely an invention of my own. Ace inhibitors and calcium antagonists are classes of blood pressure medication.

To the best of my knowledge, at the time of writing there is no Grateful Dead tribute band called *Bob Weir's Shorts*, although there ought to be. Nor is there a post-punk psychobilly/country and western outfit called *Dade County and the Hanging Chads*.

*

Constance will return in *The Magpie Rhyme*.

ACKNOWLEDGEMENTS

I've had the benefit of comment and encouragement while writing this book. Special thanks to first readers Rachel, Rosie, Mara and to Rev Neil Campbell for his early enthusiasm.

Rt Rev George Connor looked over a draft of Canty's sermon and gently chided me for unconscious use of gendered language.

Lorna King provided invaluable comment, thoughts and encouragement about Helen and Connie.

Thanks to Richard Bradburn for comments on a draft of the first part of chapter 1 (http://theopeninglines.com/page/9/) and to Jonathan Oliver (https://www.jonolivereditor.co.uk/) for comments on an early draft of the first three chapters.

My editor is Helen Bleck (editingforwriters.com).

Book design and layout is by Heather Macpherson at Raspberry Creative Type in Edinburgh (https://www.raspberrycreativetype.com).

Author photograph by Tom Migot (https://tommigotphotography.com).

Thanks always to Kirstin, for many reasons including reading the final draft of this book and gently pointing out errors in the text.

Ian Burdon lives in Scotland, north of the Pentlands, south of the Forth, where his stories have their roots and inspiration. He likes to play with the weird and mythological, while keeping the stories grounded. His first published story was in 2017.

Find him at https://linktr.ee/IanBurdon

Printed in Great Britain
by Amazon